YA
SHINN

DISCARD

DARK MOON DEFENDER

Dark Moon Defender

SHARON SHINN

ACE BOOKS, NEW YORK

THE BERKLEY PUBLISHING GROUP
Published by the Penguin Group
Penguin Group (USA) Inc.
375 Hudson Street, New York, New York 10014, USA
Penguin Group (Canada), 90 Eglinton Avenue East, Suite 700, Toronto, Ontario M4P 2Y3, Canada
(a division of Pearson Penguin Canada Inc.)
Penguin Books Ltd., 80 Strand, London WC2R 0RL, England
Penguin Group Ireland, 25 St. Stephen's Green, Dublin 2, Ireland (a division of Penguin Books Ltd.)
Penguin Group (Australia), 250 Camberwell Road, Camberwell, Victoria 3124, Australia
(a division of Pearson Australia Group Pty. Ltd.)
Penguin Books India Pvt. Ltd., 11 Community Centre, Panchsheel Park, New Delhi—110 017, India
Penguin Group (NZ), Cnr. Airborne and Rosedale Roads, Albany, Auckland 1310, New Zealand
(a division of Pearson New Zealand Ltd.)
Penguin Books (South Africa) (Pty.) Ltd., 24 Sturdee Avenue, Rosebank, Johannesburg 2196,
South Africa

Penguin Books Ltd., Registered Offices: 80 Strand, London WC2R 0RL, England

This is an original publication of The Berkley Publishing Group.

This is a work of fiction. Names, characters, places, and incidents either are the product of the author's imagination or are used fictitiously, and any resemblance to actual persons, living or dead, business establishments, events, or locales is entirely coincidental. The publisher does not have any control over and does not assume any responsibility for author or third-party websites or their content.

First edition: October 2006

Library of Congress Cataloging-in-Publication Data

Shinn, Sharon.
    Dark moon defender / Sharon Shinn.
        p. cm.
    ISBN 0-441-01430-5
    1. Magic—Fiction.   2. Moon worship—Fiction.   3. Cults—Fiction.   4. Convents—Fiction.
    I. Title.

PS3569.H499D37   2006
813'.54—dc22

2006013756

PRINTED IN THE UNITED STATES OF AMERICA

10   9   8   7   6   5   4   3   2   1

For Joe
Because you, too, have had to fight so hard,
and because you love the books

~GILLENGARIA~

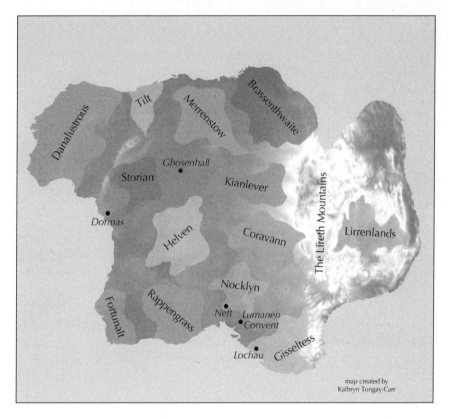

Danalustrous
Tilt
Merrenstow
Brassenthwaite
Ghosenhall
Storian
Kianlever
Dormas
The Lireth Mountains
Helven
Coravann
Lirrenlands
Nocklyn
Fortunalt
Rappengrass
Neft
Lumanen
Convent
Lochau
Gisseltess

map created by
Kathryn Tongay-Carr

DARK MOON DEFENDER

CHAPTER

I

THE woman lay facedown on the floor of the hut, her long brown hair spread in bloody tangles across the dirt. She had stopped moving, so it was possible she was dead. She had never cried out, never begged for mercy—never said a single word, not for the entire two hours they had had her. Kelti had found that almost as unnerving as the torture, the fact that she did not answer, did not speak.

This was his first time to go hunting mystics, and he was afraid he would disgrace himself by being sick.

Rostiff toed the lifeless woman with one hard boot. "Is she still breathing? Someone feel for a pulse." None of the other three men moved, so Rostiff jerked his head in Kelti's direction. "You do it."

Kelti knelt beside the battered body and gingerly pushed through the dark hair to find the back of her neck, then slid his fingers around the bruised column of her throat. There—a steady, sluggish rhythm that seemed more obstinate than anything. *I am harder to kill than you think.* Kelti shivered a little. For her sake, he wished the woman had chosen to be a little less stubborn. The sooner she died, the sooner she would be out of her misery. There was no chance she would be spared.

"She's alive, Captain," he said, and pushed himself to his feet.

"Then let's wake her up again," Rostiff said.

From over in the corner came the sound of a strangled sob. Everyone else ignored it, but Kelti glanced over. Huddled on the ground, wrapped in a tight a ball of misery, was the woman who had led them to the mystic. Poor woman living on a small plot of land, didn't appear to have a husband or son or any kinfolk to help her manage, and it was clear she was barely able to scrape together enough food to sustain her body. Always a reward for turning a mystic over to the Lestra's men, so she'd eagerly made arrangements with them yesterday morning when she spotted them in the village. But, like Kelti, she had probably had very little experience with inquisitions. She had not expected the interrogation to be so brutal or last so long.

One of the other men came forward with a bucket of water and dumped it on the mystic's head. She stirred and coughed, then lay still again. But Kelti, watching closely, could see the movement of her ribs. Still breathing.

The stupid fool.

Rostiff sank to a crouch beside her and rolled her over. Even by candle-light, it was easy to see that her face was a mesh of cuts and bruises and that blood stained the entire front of her plain gown. Her hands were tied before her with a thin silver chain set with moonstones. It wasn't a bind-ing that would hold an ordinary person—the chain was so delicate that even a woman could snap it in two—but the moonstones burned the skin of mystics and muted their power. Made them helpless. Stole their magic.

Stole their lives.

"Let's try this again," Rostiff said, putting his face down next to the young woman's. He was a big man and hard in every way. His face was severe and bony, his bunched muscles were tough, and his personality was absolutely unyielding. Until this evening, Kelti had viewed him with an awe so great it bordered on worship. Had wanted to earn his respect. Now he was ashamed of himself for being so horrified at Rostiff's actions. Wasn't this the job of the men who served the Pale Mother? Hadn't they been chosen by the Lestra to seek out and destroy mystics wherever they might be found? Was this not a holy calling, blessed by the moon goddess herself?

Then why did it feel so terrible to watch this young woman being slowly murdered?

"All I want from you is two names," Rostiff said in a reasonable voice. He had pulled his dagger out again and held it just under the mystic's left eye. With no effort at all, he could open the flesh on her cheek—or blind her on one side. *Tell him what he wants to know,* Kelti thought miserably. "Two names of two of your sorcerous friends, and where they might be found. That's it. Two names, two locations. Then I'll let you go."

The mystic had had her eyes closed, but now she opened them. They were a muddy green, unremarkable in color, and pain had dulled what-ever brilliance they might normally possess. At the moment, she didn't even seem to be able to focus, for she did not look at Rostiff, looming over her so menacingly. Instead, her gaze wandered to the others in the room—to the two veteran soldiers standing behind Rostiff, looking impassive and even bored with the whole evening. To a younger soldier standing to the right of Kelti, his face eager, his body tense, a man excited by his first taste of blood. To Kelti. He held his breath as she held his gaze. Almost he thought she might say something—whisper a message to him, beg him to intercede on her behalf. He came a step closer. She blinked and looked away.

Rostiff leaned closer. "One name," he said in an intense whisper. "One name, one location, and your death will be quick."

At that exact moment, the door to the hut blew open and a rush of darkness swirled in. Astonished, Kelti fell back. He sensed the other men in his party drawing their blades and dropping into fighting stances.

Two men had burst inside and now crouched just inside the doorway, armed for battle.

"I'm Cammon, and I'm right here," said one, shaking back his ragged hair. "That's one mystic's name. Good enough?"

With a shout, Rostiff lunged across the room, driving his sword straight for the intruder's heart. Kelti was frozen in place, but the other three soldiers launched themselves right behind Rostiff, blades winking in the insufficient candlelight. *Two more bodies to lie on the floor this night,* Kelti thought, and watched to see how quickly the mystic was cut down.

But the man who called himself Cammon danced away from Rostiff's sword. And danced away again as Rostiff sliced and hewed the air. Kelti stared, amazed. No one could outlast Rostiff for more than a few rounds, even the fiercest soldiers in the Lestra's brigade. But this young man— almost a boy, Kelti's age, perhaps, and slim as a girl—parried and ducked away and evaded every single blow Rostiff tried to land.

His companion, meanwhile, had made short work of the eager young soldier so entranced at the sight of mystic blood, and was now engaged in a furious duel with the two veteran fighters of the Lestra's staff. Kelti took a step forward, certain he should go to his companions' aid, far from certain where he could enter the battle. Blades were flying so swiftly, so mercilessly! One of the older men took a sword to the heart and dropped to the dirt with a choked cry. The other one loosed an oath and redoubled his attack, striking so hard and so often that Kelti was dazzled at the swordplay. But the stranger was simply too good. More thrusts and grunts and oaths, then a single fluid dart of silver, and the third soldier fell.

The swordsman pivoted quickly, taking in the scene with a single glance. He was burlier than his companion, maybe five or six years older, fair-haired, clean-shaven, and alight with righteousness. His gaze came to rest on Kelti—assessed him as being of no immediate threat—and then went on to take in the motionless mystic on the floor, the weeping woman in the corner, and the heated but inconclusive battle still under way between Cammon and Rostiff. He charged forward, bloody sword upraised, and entered the fray at Cammon's side. Kelti held his breath, afraid to watch, afraid to hope for one outcome or another. Rostiff snarled out a string of taunts and curses, but the fair-haired swordsman did not answer. Cammon fell back as the other men wove their swords together in a complicated pattern of threat and rescue, keeping his own weapon ready but not as if he thought he'd need it.

Indeed, he did not. A rush—a clash—a great cry of anguish—and Rostiff crumpled to the ground on top of one of the other corpses.

Kelti could not move or speak. *Four bodies on the floor. And the mystic still lives.*

The ferocious young soldier spun around one more time, as if looking for new adversaries, but his companion shook his head. "That's all of them," Cammon said. "There aren't any reserve soldiers on the road, either."

The other man pointed the red tip of his sword in Kelti's direction. "What about him? Will he be a problem?"

Cammon gave him one long, considering gaze, and Kelti found himself shivering, waiting for a terrible judgment. He had failed everyone tonight. Failed Rostiff, whom he should have been defending; failed the Pale Mother, whom he had sworn to serve; failed the Lestra, who had believed in him.

Failed this wretched mystic girl, who had not deserved such a dreadful fate at anybody's hands.

"He's harmless," Cammon said.

His friend snorted. "Not wearing the Pale Mother's colors, he's not."

A strange, flickering sort of smile came to Cammon's face. He was still watching Kelti. "I don't believe he understood until this night exactly what it meant to be a soldier in the service of the moon goddess. I don't think he has the stomach for too many nights like this one."

Another grunt from the swordsman, and he dropped to his knees next to the mystic on the floor. "What about the woman? Can you tell? Is she alive? Will she survive?"

Cammon knelt beside him. "She's alive, but she—Justin, untie her hands. I can't touch the moonstones."

Kelti shivered again. A mystic, of course, this peculiar boy. Possibly the kind they referred to as a reader—the kind who could pick up the thoughts in a man's head, tell what he was thinking, what he was feeling. How had these two happened upon this hut, in the back of an untraveled wood, in the middle of the night? What had led them in this direction at such a critical moment? Could this young man have felt the woman's pain—even through its silence and over an appreciable distance? Was such a thing remotely possible?

If so, wasn't the Lestra right to fear mystics and their friends?

Justin had snapped the slight chains with two quick twists of his hands. Cammon bent over the still form, touching his hand to the worst of the cuts, murmuring indistinguishable words in the woman's ear. She must have closed her eyes sometime during the fight, and she did not open them now, but Kelti saw the regular movement of her chest. Still alive. Still breathing.

"Surprised she's not dead," Justin said. "Pretty bad wounds."

"She's a strong one," Cammon replied. "And she's—amazing. She has some kind of healing power that she can bring to bear even on herself."

"The others can't do that," Justin said.

"I know."

"So how quickly will she be well? Will she be able to sit up in a few minutes?"

"Not that fast."

"Then how long? We can't spare much time to care for her."

A tentative unfolding from the corner, and then the weeping woman came to her feet. "I'll watch her," she said in a quavering voice.

"You!" Kelti burst out, taking a step forward. Everyone looked at him, but he was too agitated to subside. "You're the one who betrayed her to the Lestra's men!"

"I know, I know." The woman sobbed. "I didn't think—there was the money—I didn't think they'd try to kill her! I thought they'd scare her—and make her tell them things they wanted to know—and let her go. I swear I did, I swear by the Pale Lady's silver eye!"

"Not an oath that will get you very far in this company," Justin said dryly.

The woman was back on the floor, kneeling beside the others. "Please let me help her," she begged. "Please—I have to atone—I have to—"

Justin looked at his friend. "Well? Can she be trusted?"

Cammon didn't lift his gaze from the hurt woman's form. "She's sincere at the moment," he said. "But I don't know how long the conversion will last."

Justin sighed. "Then we stay awhile."

"Possibly no more than a day," Cammon said. "It's miraculous, the way the power is moving through her body. Healing her."

"Who is she? Do you know? What's her magic?"

Cammon shook his head. "I don't have any idea. I've never seen anything quite like this. I'd have to ask her. I wish I knew her name."

The other woman looked up eagerly, as if glad to have something of use to offer. "It's Lara," she said.

"And what do you know about her?" Cammon asked.

She shook her head. "Not very much. She helped one of my neighbors with his vegetable garden this summer. Made plants grow like you've never seen before. Big and delicious. Other folk, they were amazed, but I was afraid. I knew she had to be a mystic."

Cammon looked at her, his boyish face severe. "And when had she ever hurt you or anyone you loved, that you had to turn her over to the Lestra's men?"

"She's a *mystic*," the woman repeated, starting to cry. "Everybody's afraid of them. They're evil."

"I've met a damn sight more mystics than I ever thought to, or wanted to, and I haven't yet come across one of them that particularly struck me as *evil*," Justin growled. "Not the way these men are, hunting down and killing people who never offered them any pain or trouble. If you want to start looking for people loosing harm into the world, look to the Daughters of the Pale Mother and the soldiers who fight for them."

The woman was still crying. "What am I going to do now?" She wept. "Dead men in my house and an injured woman on my floor—and him! Him!" She was pointing straight at Kelti, and her voice had risen to a hysterical pitch. "He'll go back to the convent to tell the Lestra what I did, and next she'll send her soldiers after *me!*"

Now the mystic and his friend, reminded of Kelti's presence, were staring in his direction. "Yes, just what do we do about him?" Justin demanded in a menacing voice. "Let him go running back to the convent to describe this night's activities? I'm not opposed to having the Lestra discover that four of her men were killed as they were off on her witch hunts—let her know that she can't send her men rampaging through the countryside at will! But I am not so eager to have her learn that I am in the vicinity. Which he will certainly tell her if we let him go."

Kelti fell to his knees, his hands raised in an attitude of supplication. Now they were all on the hard dirt floor—the dead men, the hurt mystic, the weeping woman, the avengers, and Kelti. "Please don't kill me," he begged. "I will do whatever you say. Please let me live."

"You don't deserve to live," Justin said in a stern voice. "Look at what you and your fellows were about tonight! Torturing a helpless woman— almost murdering her! What made you think you could *do* such things? Why would you want to?"

"The goddess—" Kelti stammered, meaning to tell him the whole philosophy, but the words stuck in his throat. *The goddess abhors mystics. The goddess demands of her faithful followers that they eradicate magic from the land.* It had seemed to make so much sense back at the convent.

It had seemed so brutally senseless tonight.

Justin leaned toward him over Lara's body, his face fierce. "Any goddess who demands wicked behavior is wicked herself," he said flatly. "Why would you choose to serve a deity like that?"

From Cammon, a choking sound. Disbelieving, Kelti saw that the younger man was trying to hold back a laugh. "Oh, and from *you*. A lecture about the gods from *you*. No one will believe the story when I tell it."

Justin settled back on his heels, a suggestion of a grin on his face. "Then don't tell it."

"Ah," Cammon said, "I think she's reviving." He leaned down and spoke deliberately at Lara's ear. "Can you hear me? What can I do to make you more comfortable?"

Lara opened her green-brown eyes and looked up at him. No surprise she didn't answer; she had not said a word all night, no matter what Rostiff did to her. But she must have communicated something to Cammon, for he nodded and looked over at the others. "She needs time. A day, two at most, and she will be able to travel on her own."

"So we can leave her? With this one?" Justin made a sweep of his hand to indicate the traitor woman, and disgust colored his voice. "Will she be safe?"

Cammon shook his head. "I'm not convinced."

"I'll care for her," Kelti said.

Everyone in the room was surprised to hear him say the words, Kelti included. The others stared at him, even Lara watching him with her dull eyes. "I will," he repeated.

Justin studied him with elaborate skepticism. "So that you can then return to the Lumanen Convent and tell your mistress where she can find a mystic in greatly weakened condition?"

Kelti shook his head. "I won't ever return to the Lumanen Convent. I'm done with that way of life."

Justin still sneered, but Cammon shook his head. "He means it," the mystic said. "He can be trusted."

Kelti waited for Justin's ridicule or disbelief, but apparently this rather fearsome swordsman was willing to believe whatever the slim young mystic said. "Then we're done here?" he said. "We can be on our way?"

"Well," said Cammon, "I think we first ought to take the bodies out."

A snort from Justin. "Woman who betrays someone to the Lestra's men deserves to have corpses rotting in her house."

"But the mystic who will be recovering here does not," Cammon said gently.

Justin nodded and came easily to his feet. "Then let's get started digging."

"I want to stay with her a little while longer," Cammon said.

Justin turned his bright gaze on Kelti. His eyes were light brown and full of a restless intelligence. "Then I guess *you'll* have to help me," he said, an edge of malicious laughter in his voice.

Kelti stood rather unsteadily. "I—I will," he said. He turned to the woman who was now nominally their hostess. "Is there a shovel anywhere?"

Sniveling, she rose and led them out the front door. The night air felt cool and velvety against Kelti's skin, for all that it was still the tail end of summer and the day had been overwarm. But the air in the hut had turned rank with sweat and terror and blood. Any fresh breeze would have been a relief after that.

They collected the woman's tools—a dull shovel with a splintered handle and a couple of rusty hand trowels—and picked their spot. "I'll just go in and put on a kettle," the woman said in a hopeful voice.

"You just go and do that," Justin said indifferently. He had already begun to dig.

Kelti was not surprised to see that Justin attacked this task with the same energy and intensity he had brought to the swordfight. He seemed like the sort of man who did nothing by half measures. Quickly enough, they fell into a sort of rhythm, as Justin shoveled out big scoops of dirt and Kelti darted in after him to clear away loose clumps. He only faltered once, when he allowed himself to realize what he was actually doing. *Digging a grave for four companions.*

Never had he expected his day to end like this.

"How long have you been with the Lestra's men?" Justin asked after a period of silence. His voice sounded normal, not even winded. Kelti thought the muscles under his dark clothes must be extraordinary.

"About four months," Kelti said, trying to keep his own voice level, unalarmed.

"This your first trip out hunting mystics?"

"Yes. I didn't know—I—" He couldn't figure out how to explain himself. Maybe there was no explanation. He just stopped talking.

"Harder than you think it's going to be to take someone's life," Justin said. "Even when you think he deserves it."

"You did it," Kelti said in a low tone. "Killed Rostiff and the others."

Justin grunted, more a conversational element than a response to the effort of digging, Kelti thought. "Easier to do when someone's trying to kill *you*."

"How did you get to be so good?" Kelti burst out. "No one's ever been able to take Rostiff! He wins every contest! And you kil—you *killed* him after you'd already taken down three others."

Justin paused a moment and peered at him in the dark. "It's my life," he said quietly. "Combat. It's what I'm built to do. I only know three or four men who are better than I am. And I've beaten even them a time or two."

"No one's that good," Kelti whispered. "Unless you—are you a mystic, too? A warrior mystic?"

Now Justin's grunt sounded more like a laugh. He returned to the digging. "No. Though if I was going to ask for magic, that's what I'd ask for. A cool head and a strong sword arm. The ability to fight anyone and win."

"Seems like you've already got that," Kelti muttered.

Justin laughed outright. "So what do you do next?" he asked. "Once this mystic—Lara?—once she's well enough to travel and you move on. If you're not going back to the convent—"

"I'm not," Kelti said quickly.

"Can you go back home? Or will you be shamed to have deserted the Lestra?"

Kelti thought a moment. He was the seventh of eight children, most of them boys, living in a house too small for half that number. He had been so pleased to find a place for himself at the convent, where even the crowded barracks seemed roomy, where everyone welcomed him because every new convert to the Lestra's cause was another sword arm trained to serve the Silver Lady. He could not return to Lumanen, but there was no place for him in his father's house.

"I won't go home," he said at last. "I'll find someplace—I don't know. Work somewhere."

"You any good with a sword? You didn't fight tonight, so I couldn't judge."

"Not really," Kelti admitted. "I'm getting better though. Was, anyway."

"The king's raising an army," Justin said in a casual voice. "If you wanted someplace to go."

Kelti almost dropped his trowel. "An army . . ." he said, his voice trailing off.

Justin shrugged and kept shoveling. "Lot of people think there's a war coming. King Baryn is one of them. He needs recruits. Some of them are training up by the palace in Ghosenhall and some are on the regent's lands in Merrenstow. Steady work, good pay, something you can be proud of doing. Defending your king."

It would never have occurred to Kelti to think of such a career, but now, the instant the words were out of Justin's mouth, it was something he passionately wanted to do. But. "He wouldn't have me—the king wouldn't," Kelti said bitterly. "He hates the Lestra and she hates him. He'd never take me after he learned I was in the guard for the Daughters."

A sort of hooting laugh from Justin. "Well, it's not the king you'd be answering to, not if you join the soldier ranks, but I think any captain would be happy to hear you knew the layout of the Lumanen Convent and were willing to share the information. As for whether or not they'd take you—" Justin shrugged. "Many a man has started out on one side and found it wasn't as just as he'd thought. Mind you, you'd have to be loyal. You can't keep switching sides, or no one will ever trust you. You have to find the cause you believe in, or the man, and stick to it, no matter what comes. If you can't be faithful, you'll never be any kind of man."

Rostiff had said similar words when he'd come recruiting Kelti and other boys in the village, and they had sounded good then, too. "How do you know?" Kelti said, almost stammering. "How do you know it's the right cause or the right person? I've never met the king. Why is it any better to be killing for *him* than killing for the Lestra?"

Justin nodded, as if that was a question worth asking. "It's hard to know. And killing should always make you sick. But it should make you sicker to stand by and watch it being done than to stand up and hit back. You should always feel like you're fighting on the side of someone who only fights when he has to."

Kelti dropped one trowel and rubbed his muddy hand across his eyes. He was suddenly so tired. What a night of tragedy and radically shifting emotions, of hard labor and even harder thought. And not done yet, for the injured woman would need care all through the night. "I don't want to fight for the Lestra anymore," he said in a small voice.

Justin nodded. "Then go to Ghosenhall and sign up with the king."

"Is that what you are?" Kelti asked a little nervously. Justin's reluctance to have the Lestra know he was in the area had made him think the other man was here in some kind of disguise and might not appreciate questions. "A king's man?"

Justin laughed aloud. "Yes," he said, "that's exactly what I am."

And so swiftly that Kelti might almost have imagined the motion, Justin put up a hand to his black coat and pulled it briefly open. Within seconds, he had covered himself again, but in that instant Kelti had seen the golden insignia proudly rearing across a black field, the royal lions parading across a dark sash. He sat back on his heels, staring, his hands lax on his tools, his mouth agape. No wonder Justin was such a skilled swordsman—no wonder he spoke so eloquently about loyalty and grand causes. He was a member of a handpicked cadre, one of fifty elite fighters, chosen to guard the royal house and do anything his monarch bid him.

He was a King's Rider.

CHAPTER

2

J USTIN and Cammon rode into Neft shortly before noon, having camped beside the road and slept in late. Justin was usually a light and restless sleeper, particularly when he was traveling and no guard had been posted. But he trusted Cammon's extraordinary senses to wake them both if trouble came prowling, and so he had allowed himself to relax enough to fall into a deep and dreamless slumber. They were both exhausted after the events of the night before—rescuing a mystic from the Lestra's men, engaging in desperate swordfights, digging graves until well past midnight, then traveling on by moonlight. Still, Justin had been annoyed to see how late in the morning it was by the time he finally rolled over and sat up.

He was annoyed about this whole trip. *Annoyed* wasn't the right word, not strong enough. *Angry* was too strong. He had objected strenuously when Tayse suggested him for this assignment: setting himself up as a footloose laborer in the city of Neft, so close to the Lumanen Convent. He was to watch the comings and goings of the convent guard and see if he could discern any pattern. Was Coralinda Gisseltess raising an army? Making alliances with noble marlords from the Twelve Houses? Was she, as some reports had whispered, sending her men off in the middle of the night to burn down the estates of individuals who were sympathetic to mystics? In fact, was Coralinda Gisseltess—the noblewoman who had given herself the fancy title of *Lestra* as she took over the religious order known as the Daughters of the Pale Mother—plotting against the king?

Important work, Justin agreed, to be spying on her. But he didn't want to be the one doing it. He wanted to be in Ghosenhall, where armies were being trained and decisions were being made and all the action of planning for a war was centered.

He did not say that he disliked the assignment because he would be alone, dependent on his own wits, far from his friends and fellow Riders. Tayse suspected it, but Justin would not admit it aloud.

"It must be you," Tayse told him. "You know the city, you have some familiarity with the convent, and you have a healthy respect for Coralinda Gisseltess, so you will not be careless enough to fall into her hands."

"No Rider would be so careless," Justin grumbled—then remembered that Tayse had been just that careless about six months ago. He hesitated, saw Tayse's ironic smile, and grinned. "No *other* Rider," he amended.

"I also think you have the ability to pull off a disgruntled air that some of the other Riders cannot manage," Tayse added. "Yes, that one. That very expression. Anyone would believe you're a malcontent who left some rich man's employ because you could not get along with your captain. No one will think to question you too closely."

"Moxer and Brindle can be just as loutish as I can," Justin said. "Send one of them."

"I trust you more," Tayse said, and that was the end of it. Since Tayse had recruited Justin a little more than twelve years ago, there had been nothing Justin wanted more than to earn Tayse's respect. Though he was sworn to protect the king and to put the king's interests and well-being above any other consideration, Justin knew that it was Tayse for whom he would die, Tayse whose opinions and judgments drove his own efforts. If he ever had to choose between saving the king's life and saving Tayse's, he would save the king's, but only because that would be what Tayse would expect of him.

"You won't be alone the whole time," Tayse told him next. "I'll send messengers now and then so that you can safely courier information back. And you can take someone with you for the journey down."

"I don't mind being there alone," Justin said.

Tayse grinned and didn't answer that. "And Senneth thinks you should learn something within a couple of months. You won't be gone that long."

"I don't mind," Justin insisted. He had not been on his own, of course, for practically more years than he could remember. Even when he was running with packs of thieves on the streets of Ghosenhall, he'd had friends at his back. Once he'd joined the ranks of Riders, five years after Tayse found him, he had not spent a day or a night by himself.

"None of the Riders likes being on his own," Tayse said seriously. "I don't, either. You get used to having a comrade you can count on. You get used to someone validating your plan. But I think you have to be solitary on this mission. We have drawn too much attention in the past. We need stealth. Someone who will not excite any interest."

Justin snorted. "You couldn't send Senneth then," he said, making a joke of it. "She'd set the place on fire."

"And Coralinda Gisseltess would recognize her," Tayse said, smiling faintly. "And she would recognize me. And you are the one I want to send to Neft to spy on the Lestra."

And so Justin had gone.

He could have taken any of the other Riders with him, all of them his friends and all of them willing to make the journey. But he had asked Cammon instead. It was strange. Since the trip last winter with Tayse, Senneth, Cammon, Kirra, and Donnal, no other friendship quite measured up. If he could be with one of the other five—even Kirra, who was the most infuriating woman he'd ever met—Justin would always make that choice before looking for other companions. He did not bother to analyze that too closely. He tended not to think too much about his own emotions. He was just glad Cammon had been happy to come along.

Cammon was riding beside him now, glancing around Neft with interest. It was a crowded, bustling place, bigger than the average market town, though by no means the size of Ghosenhall. "Doesn't seem to have changed much since we were here last," the young mystic commented. "See that? There's the shrine to the Pale Mother we saw last time. And I still see moonstones hanging in the windows. Look, there's even some novices from the convent stopping travelers on the road."

Justin glanced up the slight hill to see four young girls, clad in white robes, standing on the side of the main road and calling out greetings to passersby. Some travelers stopped, clasped the girls' hands and accepted the benediction of the Pale Mother. Others nodded curtly or hurried on by, not interested in the goddess's attention. Last time they'd been here, Justin remembered, convent soldiers had massed behind the novices, paying strict attention to who received the Pale Mother's blessing and who did not. The four mystics in their group had excited quite some attention when they refused to give their hands to the novices. But all of the Daughters of the Pale Mother wore bracelets and rings made of moonstones, and mystics could not bear the touch of those gems.

"Better stay back," Justin said abruptly. "You don't want them burning *you* with their stupid jewels."

Cammon grinned. "I think I can stay clear of them," he said. "It's pretty hard for anyone to take me by surprise."

"Someday someone will surprise you," Justin said, grinning back. "I hope I'm around to see it."

They picked their way through the crowded streets, getting a feel for the city. Most of the commerce was clustered around the crossroads of major thoroughfares, and here the corners were packed with shops and taverns and inns. North and west of the commercial district were residential streets lined with one- and two-story houses, and even farther out were smaller houses, mostly unadorned and in need of repair.

"What kind of work do you want to take up? Where do you want to live?" Cammon asked, as they circled back toward the crossroads after investigating the outlying neighborhoods.

"Not sure," Justin said. "At first I thought I'd try signing on as a guard if there were any nobles living here, but that would restrict me too much. And, well, the first time I worked out, someone would start asking questions."

"You could try to fight badly," Cammon said.

Justin laughed. "I don't think I could pull it off. No, I'd probably have better luck working in the stables. Or maybe hiring on as a laborer if there's some kind of industry. Looked like a shipping yard back there. I could haul barrels and load wagons. I'm strong enough."

"Moonstones in all the windows at the freighting office," Cammon observed.

"Maybe, but they won't burn *me*."

"Still, do you want to work for someone who's that devout? You might get into trouble quicker."

"'Quicker,'" Justin repeated. "Like you think it's going to happen sooner or later anyway."

Cammon gave his quick, boyish smile. He'd worn relatively new clothes for this trip, had his hair cut, and shaved every day on the road, but he still looked like a gutter urchin without a copper to his name. "It always seems to," he said, "with the six of us."

"Anyway, I might get a moonstone of my own," Justin said. "So I blend in a little. I don't know where I go to get one, though—I mean, do they sell them at shops? Do you have to get one from the Daughters?"

"You could have borrowed Senneth's," Cammon said. Senneth was the only mystic Justin knew who could wear moonstones. She claimed the gems didn't burn her skin and in fact worked to keep some of her power in check. Since, even fettered, her power was frighteningly strong, Justin often wondered what kind of ability she would display if she took the bracelet off.

"Too late now," Justin said. "But I'll figure it out."

They circled the town again so Justin could fix its layout in his mind, would know where the alleys lay and where the main roads emptied out. He would spend the next few days exploring, of course, but it was automatic with a Rider to want to familiarize himself quickly with his terrain.

You never knew where the next attack might come from. When you might have to fight, when you might have to run.

"I wonder how she is today," Justin said, thinking of their adventures the day before.

Cammon did not need any explanation to know Justin was speaking of the wounded mystic called Lara. Cammon always knew what you meant. "I was wondering that, too," he said. "I told Kelti to take her with him to Ghosenhall, if he goes there, because she'll be safe in the royal city, but that doesn't mean she'll want to go. She didn't seem like the kind of person who let other people tell her what to do."

Justin wondered how he could know that when the woman had barely been conscious before they left and had only said a few words, none of them about her personality. Then again, if Cammon made an observation about somebody, Justin always assumed he was right. The mystic had an uncanny ability to gauge emotion and judge character. It had been Cammon, of course, who insisted they detour from their planned route when he somehow picked up the echoes of Lara's suffering and knew that a mystic was being brutally interrogated. Justin had hesitated only a moment—not because he doubted Cammon was right, but because he was not sure he wanted to start his residency in Neft with such a display of bravado. He was supposed to be in this region incognito, after all. But if Senneth had been here, she would unquestionably have ridden to Lara's rescue, and Tayse always supported Senneth's decisions. So Justin pulled his horse off the road and followed Cammon three miles through untracked woodland to find the isolated hut where torture was under way.

Three miles. How was it possible Cammon could feel the pain of a total stranger over such a distance? Justin wished one of the others was here so he could share his sense of eerie marvel.

"What kind of power did she have?" he asked Cammon now. "Could you tell?"

Cammon shook his head. "Nothing I've ever come across before. It seemed like she was full of—dirt—and gardens—and—and—*green.* I can't explain it."

"Huh. So if Senneth's right and the mystics all draw their power from one of the gods, what kind of god would be watching over that woman?"

Cammon laughed. "That might be easier to answer if we knew anything about the other gods! But I thought, maybe, a goddess of plants and trees? A goddess of growing things?" He reflected a moment. "Or a goddess of spring, if such a thing could be."

"Doesn't seem too useful," Justin commented.

Cammon stared at him. "Doesn't seem *useful*? Well, of *course* it would be useful! You could have—fields that always yielded crops and trees that always bore fruit, and you could compensate for famine and drought, and you could—"

Justin was laughing. "Useful on a battlefield," he explained. "I mean, Senneth can call fire, and I can see how you can use that skill in a war. And Kirra and Donnal can change shapes, and *that* comes in pretty handy when you're facing enemies. But growing a field of wheat? In the middle of a war? Well, who cares?"

Cammon was shaking his head. "You're so single-minded."

"Every Rider is."

After their second pass through town, Justin settled on the area that would best serve his purpose. It was on the east edge of the city, not far from the main road. If he was living there, he could casually slip out of town and go exploring along the route that led toward the convent. There were a couple of rather run-down taverns in this quadrant as well as some fairly extensive stables, and he thought he had a good chance of finding both work and lodging.

"Let's try here," Justin said, and led the way to the stable's main entrance.

They dismounted and went inside, finding themselves in a fairly large open space that seemed to serve as reception area, granary, and all-around storage facility. Wide double doors opened off to one side, most likely leading to the stalls. The whole building was fragrant with the smells of hay, horse, leather, and dirt.

They called out their arrival and waited a few moments before the double doors swayed open and a short, thin, middle-aged man hurried through. He looked a little harried, as if he'd abandoned another task to respond to them. "Leaving your horses?" he inquired in a friendly enough voice. "How long?"

"Just overnight," Cammon said.

Justin scowled and let his face turn sulky. "*You'll* be going back tomorrow, but *I* won't," he said. "You work for a man five years—five years!—you expect he'll treat you with fairness. But, oh no! One slip, and you're out the door, and no one cares what becomes of you."

"It was more than one slip," Cammon said in a reasonable voice. "And she was his daughter."

That hadn't been scripted, but Justin assumed Cammon had his reasons for introducing the topic. "Well, I didn't insult her," he said, still sullen. "So I'm just a common soldier! I can't talk to a noblewoman? So what if he's a marlord, living on his great property? I'm still good enough to talk to his daughter."

"She wanted to say good-bye to you," Cammon said. "If you let me tell her where you went, maybe she'll send a note."

Justin shook his head. "I'm done with that life," he said. "Don't tell her anything. Besides—who knows? I might only stay here a day or two. I don't even know if there's work here in Neft."

The stableman stepped forward at that. He'd stood by quietly while they argued, but it was clear he'd been listening to every word. Sympathetic to Justin's situation, too, by the warm look in his eyes. Justin wondered if this man had romanced a serramarra at some point in his life and Cammon had that quickly been able to pick up on it.

"There's work here, if you were looking," he said. "My nephew ran off to sea and the other boy who worked here went and joined the Daughters last week. Too much for one man to do, but if you're good with horses, I could use the help."

He didn't want to appear too eager. Justin let his face assume a somewhat scornful expression and looked around. "I know horses," he said. "How many do you usually board? What kind of hours? What do you pay?"

"I can't afford to pay much, but you'll pick up tips," the stableman said. "Lot of fancy folks riding through Neft, hoping to meet up with one of the Daughters, or even the Lestra. Lot of merchants and traders coming through, too. They're not stingy people."

"I need a place to stay, too," Justin said.

The man gestured back toward the recesses of the building. "If you can't find anything better, there's the hayloft. You can bed down for a few nights. Longer, if you like."

It wouldn't do to be restricted to one location like that. Justin had to be free to move from point to point, with no one having a strict accounting of his hours. He kept his expression just shy of a sneer and said, "I have some coins in my pocket. I think I can pay for a bed."

"Well, sleep on it if you want, but I could use the help," the stableman said. "I'm Delz."

"Justin. Let me go find dinner and look for a room. I'll be back in the morning, one way or the other."

"Golden Boar, just up the street, has a good dinner pretty cheap," Delz said.

Justin nodded. "Appreciate it. We'll try there. Come on, Cam."

A few minutes later they were seated in the Golden Boar, which was dark, crowded, and not particularly clean. The place had an appetizing smell to it, though, so someone knew how to cook, Justin decided. Their waitress was young, yellow-haired, and smiling, but Cammon started laughing as soon as she took their orders and departed.

"What?"

"She thought you were handsome. Would have liked you to flirt with her. But you didn't even notice her."

Justin was surprised. He never overlooked anybody. He couldn't—a Rider always had to assess every stranger for threat and ability. "She was about five feet two inches, probably weighed less than a hundred pounds, light hair up in some kind of bun. Moonstone necklace. No visible weapons. Didn't look very smart. I noticed her."

Cammon was laughing even harder. "Right. She wanted you to think she's pretty. She wanted you to smile at her, talk to her a little bit. Be interested in her."

Justin grunted. "Too much work."

"That woman or all women?"

"All women." He thought that over. "Well, not Senneth. She doesn't need anyone taking care of her and making a fuss over her."

"Kirra?"

"She wants people to make a fuss over her all the time!" But he had to think that over, too. "Although she doesn't need anyone to take care of her. But she's more trouble than anybody."

"Well, that might be a way to disguise your reason for coming to Neft, and staying," Cammon suggested. "Find a girl you like. Or pretend to find a girl."

"Right. Then I'll have even less time to be looking around." He grinned. "Anyway, I just left some woman behind, didn't I? How faithless do you want me to be?"

Cammon smiled. "I think it was a good story. It'll get around."

"What was up with Delz? He fall in love with a marlord's daughter?"

"I didn't pick up the whole tale. Just some thought that there was a woman he cared about, and no one believed he was good enough for her. Seemed like he'd respond if that was your own situation."

"Though I'm glad it's not."

Cammon laughed. They talked idly till the waitress brought their food and a couple of glasses of ale. Mindful of Cammon's gaze, Justin gave her a smile, but was annoyed to see her dissolve into giggles and blushes. So then he looked away, concentrating on his food till she left again, slowly as her feet would take her.

Women. The first ten years of his life had been filled with them when he had lived with his mother and three sisters in the hovel that someone called a boardinghouse and was more properly a brothel. But there had been no women in the fighting gangs he roved with once his mother died. Hardly any girls on the streets at all—most of them gone to true whorehouses, or dead before they were fifteen. Too fragile for the kind of life Justin had led. Once he signed on with the Riders, he'd been astonished to find there were women among them, women as tough and skilled and fearless as he was, but they weren't *female* the way this waitress was. They were just people, companions, friends to be absolutely trusted, because they were Riders and because they were good.

Then there were Senneth and Kirra—different from all other women in his experience.

"I think you're right. You shouldn't try to find yourself a girl," Cammon said. He was laughing again. "Just stay with your original story. Left a noble's service and came here to look for work."

"I think the stables will do, don't you? Any reason I shouldn't work with Delz?"

Cammon shook his head. "He seemed honest. Try not to intimidate him too much."

Justin laughed. "Did I? All right, I'll be friendlier." He looked around the tavern, which was filling up even more as they sat there. A group of seven men settled at the last empty table, situated just inches away from theirs. "Not too friendly, though. I'm supposed to be surly."

"I think you can pull it off," Cammon said.

Justin laughed again, but a few minutes later they were arguing, loud enough for anyone nearby to hear. "I'm just telling you that if you would offer him an apology—" Cammon was trying to say, as Justin talked over him.

"I won't say I'm sorry! I didn't do anything to be ashamed of! A man has a right to stand up to another man even if he *is* a marlord from one of the Twelve Houses! Times are changing, my friend."

"And what's *that* supposed to mean?"

Justin nodded darkly. "You'll see. The marlords think they own the world, think things are always going to go on like they have. But there are people who don't want to be living on the sufferance of the Twelve Houses. They're going to take what should have been theirs all along."

Cammon slapped a hand on the table. "I am so tired of all your vague talk of war."

"Well, it won't be vague for long. You'll see."

"So—what? You're just going to keep riding around Gillengaria, looking for other malcontents? Come home, Justin. This can all be worked out."

"No, I *won't* come home! You've been a good friend to me, but you don't understand. I've left that life. You go on in the morning, but I'm staying here. Or I'll find some other place. Someplace they're not in fear of the Twelve Houses," he added with a snarl.

Their quarrel had drawn the attention of the men at the adjoining tables, and from across the room, Justin could see the blond waitress watching them with a worried look. She didn't seem to like loud, outspoken men. Good.

A patron sitting with the group of seven now leaned over to give Justin a nod and a serious look. "Plenty of men in Neft who aren't afraid of the marlords," he said. "This'd be a good place to settle down."

"Well, if I can find work," Justin said crossly.

"Always looking for men over at the convent," one of his tablemates said. "Any good with a sword?"

"I can fight some," Justin said. "But I just left one civil guard. Don't feel like shackling myself to a captain again anytime soon."

"Other work to be had in Neft," the first man said. "Good place to be—if war really does come."

Justin lifted his glass in a toast. "Oh, it'll come," he said. "About time, too."

The other men raised their glasses and drank in agreement, then turned back to their own conversation. Justin caught Cammon's eye and nodded infinitesimally. That had been just enough. Any more ranting would draw too much attention. He just wanted to have a story in place, a persona that had been shaped from the very first moment he rode into town, in case anyone seemed interested in him later and started investigating. He stood, tossing coins to the table, and turned to go, Cammon right behind him. Then he paused and turned back to the table of seven men.

"So, if I'm going to stay a few days," he said, with studied disinterest, pretending he didn't care. "Where would be a good place to put up? Honest place, not too expensive, but clean."

"Harry's got rooms by the week at his place," said one of the men at the table, and his companions all murmured agreement.

"Left as you walk out the door, then not but a quarter mile from here," someone else directed. "Two-and-a-half stories. Easy to find."

"Appreciate it," Justin said, nodding again, and walked out the door.

They found Harry's with no trouble, and Justin haggled just loud enough and long enough to convince anyone who might be listening that he didn't have much money but did intend to stay awhile. Eventually, they agreed on the attic bedroom, Justin to take care of all his own needs, and a weekly bath thrown in. When they climbed to the third floor, they found two narrow, lumpy beds, a window that wouldn't open, and severely slanted rooflines that allowed Justin to stand only in the very center of the room.

"Well, you *definitely* don't want to be courting a woman if this is the place you'd be bringing her back to," Cammon said.

"Slept in worse," Justin said, slinging his travel pack onto one of the beds. He'd left the bulk of his possessions with his horse at Delz's stables. "So have you."

"And will again," Cammon agreed, stretching out on the other bed. "So what will you do tomorrow?"

"Go back to Delz. Take his job. Spend a couple of days in the city looking around, trying to see if there's any activity. I want to be in place a few days before I go off roving toward the convent. I don't want to make people suspicious."

"How long are you going to be here?"

Justin shrugged, irritable again. "Senneth thinks a couple of months. I don't know. I suppose till they call me home."

"Maybe I can come back and visit in a few weeks."

"That'd be good. Tayse said he'd send messengers now and then so I can give him news. Maybe he meant he'd send you."

Cammon sat up, swinging his legs over the side of the bed. His odd eyes were alight with excitement. "I know. You can try to send me information. See if I can pick up on it all the way in Ghosenhall."

Justin laughed in disbelief. "And do you think you can?"

"I don't know. Maybe. I knew something was wrong with Senneth the other day, and I was worried, but she'd only turned her ankle."

"*And* you were both in Ghosenhall," Justin reminded him. "Not hundreds of miles apart. Besides, what kind of information do you think I could send you? Details about troop movements? Names of nobles who've come to visit Coralinda Gisseltess? You can't pick up on anything so specific, can you?"

"I don't think so," Cammon said regretfully. "But you could *try*."

Justin rolled his eyes. "All right. I'll try. If I remember. We'll see how good you really are."

They talked awhile longer, but they were both tired, and these were the first real beds—however uncomfortable—that they'd had for more than a week. So it wasn't long before they both started yawning, then dropped off to sleep.

In the morning, they shared a quick breakfast and headed to the stables. Cammon was gone with a cheerful wave, and Justin was left moody and alone.

Well, alone except for Delz. "So did you give any thought to taking a job here?" the stableman asked.

Justin nodded and said, "Sign me up."

He was here, and he would do his best, because that was what Tayse expected of him, but he couldn't bring himself to be happy about his circumstances. What was a Rider without Riders at his back? There was nothing for him in Neft. He would endure his sentence of separation, but he would find it an entirely joyless time.

CHAPTER

3

Ellynor stood in the courtyard with all the other girls and turned her face up toward the quarter moon. Cool, finally, now that the sun was down, now that a breeze had bothered to meander in from the west. The stone walls of the convent, white to reflect the light, still managed to hold enough of the summer's heat to make some of the smaller rooms unbearable, but it was almost autumn now. Soon, thank the Mother, to be winter again, cold, still, crystalline.

Shavell led the prayers tonight, facing the rest of them, her eyes closed and her thin hands moving with birdlike motions through the phases. In the darkness, Shavell's violet robes looked almost as black as the Lestra's, though you would never mistake one woman for the other. The Lestra was shorter, more powerful-looking, with a commanding presence you felt instantly any time she entered a room. Shavell was skinny, tall, pale—intense in her own way, but without nearly the force of the Lestra's personality. All the novices were afraid of Shavell, of course, because she could be sharp-tongued and unforgiving, but what they felt for the Lestra was awe bordering on terror. They respected her, of course, but from a distance; they were all afraid she would look at them, speak to them, call them up for some momentous and valiant task. Ellynor herself had never had a conversation with the Lestra and frankly hoped she never did.

"Mother, we praise you," Shavell was intoning, and all the novices murmured after her again. "Mother, we bend before you. Mother, we draw from you all grace and offer to you all our own strength. Grow full with the riches of our bodies . . ."

Around her, Ellynor heard the voices of the other novices, rising and falling with the same melodic cadences of Shavell's. Beside her, Ellynor's cousin Rosurie had her eyes closed, her hands clenched; her whole body appeared tense with rapture. Rosurie had embraced the Pale Mother with all her heart, flung at the Silver Lady's feet all her considerable ability to love. Ellynor marveled at the transformation sometimes, for Rosurie had always been the most passionate and willful of girls, the one most likely to inspire the anger of her father or the sorrow of her mother. The one all the kinfolk had shaken their heads over. "She'll be one who comes to ruin," the uncles and brothers had predicted. "She's the one who'll bring disgrace to the family."

And she had, or almost. Falling in love where it was most disastrous, causing great consternation and negotiation among the clans, the *sebahta*. Almost causing a clan war, to hear Ellynor's father talk about it. And yet here she was, at Lumanen Convent, speaking the Pale Mother's name with the sort of reverence she had once reserved for her wholly unsuitable lover. The truth was, Rosurie had inexhaustible passion. If her father or her brothers had been able to convince her to marry within the clan network, the *sebahta-ris*, she would have been the most devoted wife imaginable. She would have borne many children and loved them all so deeply their hearts would never have been lost or cold. She would have been an icon among the *sebahta*, a beacon, a lesson held up to all the young girls. *See, this is how a Lirren woman lives. Make her actions your ideal.*

Shavell lifted both arms above her head, the elbows pointed out, the fingertips just touching. The complete circle, the full moon. The novices giggled and twittered as they made their matching pattern on the ground, grouping themselves into one large, round shape made up of many girls in white robes. From the sky, Ellynor supposed, they did resemble a full moon, albeit one made up of restless, moving components that could not stand entirely still no matter how much they were admonished. Shavell led the singing, and they all raised their voices in the sweet ritual of the evening song. There was always some jostling for position, some girls preferring the outer edges of the circle, some the core, all of them trying to guess where Shavell would make her first divisions. Some wanting to stay, some tired and wanting to go.

Shavell, still singing, walked the perimeter once, then began tapping on the arms of the novices bunched on the east side of the circle. Slowly, gradually, they drifted away, still singing, their voices growing fainter. Slowly, it was as if the moon-shape on the ground went through its phases—full, almost full, gibbous, half—till finally what was left in the courtyard was a quarter moon that mimicked the waning crescent that would rise later tonight. The novices who had been dismissed entered the convent and disappeared. Those who had been chosen remained outside to sing until midnight.

Ellynor was content to be one of those left behind. Shavell was uncannily good at making sure no one sang too many late-night rituals in a row—though, of course, during the earliest phases of the full moon, they were all out almost every night, reflecting back a whole, round shape to the brilliant Silver Lady. Late in the month, though, fewer and fewer voices were needed until, on the evening of the new moon, no one stayed and no one sang. The next night, Shavell would single out fifteen or twenty novices to create a bare sliver of a curve; the next night, a larger group would stay. And so it went every night after that, until the moon was full again and all five hundred and some novices stood beneath the Pale Mother, reciting her praises and her glories.

Ellynor did not mind the grand choruses, the full-throated choir of five hundred offering exultation to the goddess, but she preferred the smaller groups, the quieter ensembles, the rituals under a night sky that held almost no moon at all. She always tried to be on the proper side of the circle the night before the new moon so that she would be among the women Shavell selected to sing. On those nights, it was as if the moon had disappeared completely and only the stars looked down.

Cold, still, crystalline.

It was only on nights like those that she did not miss the Lirrens.

They had not asked her to accompany Rosurie to Lumanen Convent, her father and her uncles. They had not discussed with her whether or not she wanted to go. They had merely told Ellynor to pack her clothes, she would be leaving with her cousin in the morning. She would be off to take vows at Lumanen Convent, where she would live with the Daughters of the Pale Mother and dedicate her life to the moon goddess.

It is just temporary, her mother had whispered to her as she helped Ellynor pack. Her mother was weeping, holding up first one simple dress, then another, and burying her face in the familiar folds. *This exile is temporary. Only until the men decide what's to be done with Rosurie. A year perhaps, two at most. You will be back among us soon.* But now, a year into her life at the convent, Ellynor knew two things that her mother did not. Novices rarely left Lumanen; so far, in fact, Ellynor had not seen one of them go. And Rosurie had developed a fanatic's blissful attachment to the moon goddess. She would not want to leave—indeed, she would throw all her considerable force of will into a show of intractability if they tried to take her. And if the formidable Lestra decided she wanted Rosurie to stay at the convent, Ellynor thought it very likely

Rosurie would never leave. The men of their family might finally have met their match.

It was something that gave Ellynor an intense satisfaction.

Shavell moved among them, poking and prodding to make sure they all kept in their proper scythe formation, tilting her head to listen critically to their singing. Ellynor required no realigning; her feet had barely moved. She was not a restless girl who could not stand quietly for a paltry hour or two. Ellynor had as much will and resolve as her cousin Rosurie, but she exercised them in a much different fashion. She could focus; she could narrow down. Shavell nodded in approval and continued her way around the outer curve of their pattern.

Ellynor had been glad to learn she was leaving with Rosurie. Glad of a chance to get free of her father's constant attention, her brothers' imperious, impatient criticism. She loved them but, Great Mother, she could not breathe when they were around! That was her life; that was the life of every Lirren girl, to be guarded and guided by the fierce men of the *sebahta*, and a girl never rebelled against them and won. Since she had been a child, Ellynor had dreamed of slipping away in stealth, of climbing out her window some starless night and running from her father's house. She had studied maps in secret, tracing her best route, noting which roads ran too closely to other clanholds and must be avoided. She had listened to tales of the country over the Lireth Mountains, trying to divine what life was like for women who lived in Gillengaria and wondering if she would find it any more to her taste. She even listened to stories brought back from the true adventurers, the ones who had sailed to foreign lands with names like Arberharst and Sovenfeld. What kind of life did women lead in those places? Could Ellynor travel so far and be happy? Was there a way to escape?

She never ran. Never packed her bundles and tried. In truth, Ellynor was afraid she would miss them all too desperately to enjoy her freedom, if she was able to attain it. What she wanted, she realized, was to live among the *sebahta*, close to the many that she loved, but free of their incessant surveillance and interference.

To quit the influence of her father and brothers—and uncles and male cousins—she would have to marry. And then she would be subject to her husband's dictates, and answerable to *his* relatives, who would feel perfectly free to scold and correct her.

To be free of them all, she would have to leave.

So she had been thrilled at the prospect of crossing the mountains into Gillengaria and going to live at this convent she knew nothing about, to serve a goddess she had never heard of, in order to provide company for a cousin she had never been particularly close to.

She had quickly learned that, in its own way, life at the Lumanen Convent was just as restrictive as life in a Lirren household. Every novice had a rotating set of household duties—cooking, cleaning, working in the laundry room, chopping wood, gardening—and every novice was expected to participate in at least two of the six devotional rituals held every day. Decorum was strictly enforced, and, except for singing, raised voices were not allowed. There was no running, no dancing, and very little laughing, though novices were encouraged to keep pleasant smiles upon their faces. It almost went without saying that absolute chastity was required—even though several hundred soldiers lived inside the Lumanen compound, many of them young and handsome enough to stir any girl's heart.

No, the convent was not the right place for Ellynor, either. But she was not unhappy here. The quiet, contemplative life suited her, and she enjoyed the quick friendships she had formed with the other girls. She found it easy to avoid Shavell's ire because she was not high-spirited and dramatic, and she rather liked doing her part of the domestic chores every day. Now and then she rather wistfully watched the soldiers stride from their barracks, through the courtyard and out the great gate. What would it be like to get to know one or two of them, form a friendship with a man who had not been approved by her father? But more trouble lay down that road than she was willing to risk, so she would watch them a moment or two, and then look away.

She found herself fascinated by the religious ceremonies, by all the rituals designed to honor the Pale Mother. She loved the circles the novices formed every night, the slowly slimming and burgeoning shapes designed to reflect the changing phases of the moon. She loved her moonstone bracelet, glittering with a private fire that she could always feel as a definite heat against her wrist. She was curious about this goddess who seemed so powerful, so pervasive, and yet so elusive, shyly hiding her face one week, brazenly staring down from the heavens the next. Capricious and beautiful—*like Rosurie,* she thought wryly—the Pale Mother was a bewitching mistress who held everyone at the convent in thrall.

Ellynor herself loved a different goddess, but they were sisters; surely they did not mind sharing worshippers.

In the Lirrens, there was only one deity—the Black Mother, the Dark Watcher—the great goddess of the night, whose attention was just as close and protective as that of anyone in the *sebahta*. It was said she knew the name of every child, every crone, in every clan, and spent each night counting them over again before she fled the oncoming day. Concerned that something might have happened to her people during the hours she was gone, as soon as the sun went down, the Black Mother hurriedly spread her shadow back over the Lirrenlands and began her counting all over again. To help her in her task, the Lirrenfolk often turned to face the eastern horizon right at sunset and softly offered up their names. *Ellynor. Rosurie. Wynlo and Torrin. I am here where you left me last night.*

Ellynor had worried, just a little, that the Black Mother might not be able to follow her over the Lireth Mountains, that when she left her family, her *sebahta*, and her country behind, she might leave her goddess as well. But the Dark Watcher was here in Gillengaria as she was in the Lirrens, comforting and omniscient, wearing as always her scattered jewels of starlight. Whenever Ellynor looked up to sing her praises to the Silver Lady, the Black Mother was always there as well. In fact, most of Ellynor's hymns and obeisances were offered up to the Dark Watcher, not the Pale Mother, but no one had to know that but Ellynor herself.

A$_T$ midnight, the quarter moon dissolved—at least the one on the ground, shaped by novices—and the girls moved slowly through the courtyard, up the stone steps, and into the convent. The massive doors opened onto a huge hall, echoing and not particularly welcoming. The high ceiling, ribbed with supporting stone arches, was lit by wheeled chandeliers; the stone floor was cold underfoot even in the middle of summer. Ellynor always moved as quickly as she could through this space and into one of the labyrinthine corridors that honeycombed the five-story building. For the first two weeks she had lived here, she had been lost every day. Now she took the twists and turns without thinking.

Rosurie was in the room they shared, but not asleep. There was a single candle burning in the window, similar to candles set in every window of the convent, and faithfully lit as soon as the sun went down. In addition, the room was illuminated by a branch of candles pulled over by Rosurie's narrow bed. Rosurie was braiding her long chestnut hair for the night.

"Shavell will be furious if she sees you're burning candles this late," Ellynor commented as she stepped inside.

Rosurie shrugged and blew them out. The room instantly filled with shadows, only the flame in the window giving any light to see by. Ellynor waited by the door until her eyes adjusted, then carefully crossed the room to her own bed. Rosurie said, "I just wanted to wait up for you. And it's so gloomy sitting in the dark."

Ellynor rather liked the dark. More than once, back at home, she had stayed up all night, just to watch the changing constellations across the night's obsidian face. Of course, back home she'd been able to sleep the next day through, which wasn't an option at the convent. Here, everyone was up and working shortly after dawn. "Did you get a letter from home?" she asked, because she'd seen the unfolded sheets spread out on Rosurie's bed.

"Yes," the other girl said happily, and instantly launched into a recitation of who had gone courting, who had been sick and recovered, who had argued with his father but quickly come to his senses. Ellynor listened while she cleaned her face and put on her night clothes. There were blood ties between their families, so they were related to many of the same people, but they would have called each other cousin in any case. Ellynor's Alowa family and Rosurie's Plesa family were both part of the Domen *sebahta*, and everyone in the *sebahta* considered everyone else kin. More tenuous were the relations between clans within the *sebahta-ris*—those alliances were based on friendship and necessity as opposed to blood, though a man might call another man cousin just because they both belonged to one of those nine great networks of interconnected families. Those of the Domen *sebahta* belonged to the Lahja *sebahta-ris*; any man of the Lahja alliance might call on any other to defend him if he fell afoul of an enemy. These days there was much less clan warfare than there had been in the past, of course, but there was still great hostility between some *sebahta*, some alliances that would never be made.

Rosurie, for instance, had fallen in love with a boy from the Bramlis *sebahta*, bitter enemies to the Domen. It was for this transgression that she had been exiled to the Lumanen Convent. She had announced her intention of running off with him, crossing the Lireth Mountains and disappearing somewhere in Gillengaria, where they would live as husband and wife, with no fathers or brothers to interfere. Ellynor had actually rather been hoping Rosurie made the escape, just to see if it was possible, but, of course, Rosurie had not been successful in her bid for freedom. The Bramlis boy's father had been just as eager as Rosurie's to make sure the match did not occur. Only the Great Mother knew how his family had dealt with *him*. Rosurie had been shipped off to the Lestra.

"Oh, and our uncles are back in Coravann." Rosurie was continuing with her recitation. "My mother thought they might come by to see us here, but I don't think that would be allowed, do you?"

"I'm certain it wouldn't be!" Ellynor said with a laugh. "Do you want to ask Shavell for permission? Or, no, would you like to go straight to the Lestra?"

Rosurie giggled. "That's what I told her last time she asked, but she doesn't seem to understand that *sebahta* means nothing in the convent. I don't know how to explain it to her."

No, for anyone raised in the Lirrens would have a hard time comprehending that the Lestra—a woman—could be absolute law within her own defined circle. Ellynor and Rosurie, used to submitting to authority, had recognized it immediately in the persons of the Lestra and her dedicants, but the men of their families would never find it so easy.

Ellynor lay back on the narrow mattress and half listened to Rosurie's continuing story. Strange as it still seemed to her, Ellynor had kin in Gillengaria—so did Rosurie. One of the Lahja women had eloped more than thirty years ago with a man named Heffel Coravann, marlord of one of the Twelve Houses. Naturally, the men of her family went after him, for that was the Lirren way: If an outsider tried to ravish or romance a Lirren woman, one of the men of her family would face that outsider in a duel to the death. Usually, the *sebahta* men won—or, more often, the threat itself was enough to keep Lirren women safe from the attention of interlopers. Not this time. Heffel Coravann had killed his bride's father and carried the woman off to his estates at Coravann Keep.

Normally, that would be the end of it—the woman would have been lost forever to the *sebahta-ris*. But somehow Heffel had managed to earn the respect of his wife's relatives and had forged a durable relationship with them. There was visiting and some commerce between them, across the Lireth Mountains. Ellynor was not sure exactly how it had all unfolded, but she knew that Heffel was the one who had suggested the Lumanen Convent as a place to send the wayward Rosurie. He was a devout man, a follower of the moon goddess, and he had described the convent as both safe and holy.

And so here they were.

"I would like to go to Coravann someday," Ellynor murmured as Rosurie's voice drifted to a stop. "Wouldn't you?"

"No. Why?" her cousin demanded.

"To meet the man who stole a Lirren woman from the clans."

Rosurie sniffed. "He did not steal her. They let him take her."

"He killed her father!" Ellynor reflected a moment. "Although her father wasn't very well-liked and maybe wasn't such a loss."

"That's what I mean. The *sebahta* allowed it."

"I'd still like to meet him. I'd like to meet his daughter—you realize we have a cousin who is only half Lirren?"

"Two," Rosurie corrected. "She's got a brother."

Ellynor nodded in the dark. "So I'd like to meet him, too. And I'd like to see Coravann. Oh, I'd like to see any part of Gillengaria! Ghosenhall or one of the Twelve Houses! I'd like to be free to roam anywhere I wanted to. Wouldn't you?"

"No," said Rosurie, turning over on her bed and twitching her blankets up to her chin. "I'm happy where I am. Except I miss the Lirrens. I miss the *sebahta*. If I could, I would spend half my life on this side of the Lireth Mountains, and half on the other side."

Ellynor sighed. "I miss the *sebahta*, too," she said. "If we were home right now, we'd be planning the baking for the high harvest—"

Rosurie chimed right in, describing the recipes they would be selecting, the spices they would be mixing into the pies and soups. It was a game they played often. *If we were home right now* . . . Ellynor could not decide if the exercise made her more homesick or less, but she did know that she could remember every detail, every scent, every color, every name. She did not think she would ever forget any of them, if she lived at the convent until she was a hundred.

Her whole life, she had wanted to run away from the clans. But she had always wanted to be able to go back home. Once she left the convent, she would be able to return to the Lirrens. But if she left on her own? Slipped away in the night, or chose a rash lover and eloped? She would never be able to return. She would forfeit the Lirrens forever.

In the morning, after they had attended the first set of devotions, Rosurie asked Ellynor to dye her hair. "I'm baking today," Ellynor said. "I'll be free in the afternoon, and I can do it then. And you can do mine."

So shortly after lunch, they returned to their room and set about the time-consuming but pleasurable task of marking their hair with *sebahta* patterns. A few of the other girls who lived on their floor had always been fascinated by this particular ritual, so Rosurie had invited them in to watch. When Ellynor arrived in the room, buckets of water in hand, she found Rosurie sitting on a stool in the middle of the room, hair unbound and touching the floor. Five other novices had crammed onto the two beds and were giggling and gossiping. They were all boy crazy, always discussing the charms and characteristics of the young men in the Lestra's guard. Never mind that they were forbidden to speak to the soldiers or interact with them in any way. Talk about the soldiers formed their primary topic of conversation.

"Did you *see* him? I think he's from Tilt. *So* handsome. I never saw eyes so blue."

"Shavell will murder you if she thinks you're flirting with one of the new guards."

"I wasn't flirting! Well, I would have, but he wouldn't flirt back. I think he's shy."

"I like that other boy. The one with the fair hair and the scar on his left cheek. He has the sweetest smile."

Ellynor pulled up a second stool right behind Rosurie's and ran her palm down the thick, straight hair. It was a reddish chestnut, many shades lighter than Ellynor's own night-black hair. It was marked all down the back with the sickle-rose-and-star design of the Plesa family, done in a blond dye. Every few weeks, as new hair grew in, Ellynor added another row to the pattern near the top of Rosurie's head; every few months, she trimmed off the ragged ends at the bottom, and some of the old designs with them. Every Lirren woman wore her hair this way—long and marked with her family heraldry. Of course, in most situations, certainly in public, a Lirren woman kept her hair rolled up in some manner on her head—in braids or in a knot—so the patterns were not visible. But everyone knew they were there.

"I talked to Daken the other day," one of the other girls said in a dreamy voice.

"You didn't! And Shavell didn't see you?"

"Just a few words. He was so serious."

Rosurie sat very still while Ellynor dampened her hair with a sponge, then separated the thick locks into five sections. She opened the small container of dry dye and rubbed the top with a damp sponge, then transferred the color in deliberate strokes to Rosurie's hair. The sickle was easy, the star a little more complicated, the rose the hardest symbol of all to translate. Ellynor worked carefully with the skill of much practice, knowing how important it was that the final result be perfect. If anyone were to come across Rosurie, lost or ill or dead—unable to speak—he could unpin her hair and know exactly to which family she belonged. Even if she was found by one of the warring *sebahta*, one who hated the Plesa family, she would be returned to them, safe from further harm.

If a Lirren girl were ever to chop off all her hair, she would be lost forever. No one would recognize her, no one would know how to send her home.

"You know who I haven't seen for a few days?" said one of the novices. "That young man from Fortunalt. Kelti. I liked him."

There was a gasp and then an ominous silence that lasted long enough to make Ellynor look away from her task. Even Rosurie turned her head, carefully, to keep the dye from running.

"You haven't heard?" That was Astira speaking. The tall blonde from Merrenstow was the one Ellynor liked best of all the novices. At twenty-two, Astira was Ellynor's own age, and both of them were older than most of the other girls. "Kelti's disappeared. They found Rostiff and three others, but Kelti—just vanished."

"Found them? What does that mean?" Ellynor demanded.

Astira gave her a wide-eyed look. She had patrician features and a well-bred air, and Ellynor had always assumed she was part of the Gillengaria nobility. "Found them dead," Astira said solemnly. "Murdered."

All the girls were exclaiming now with dismay and fascination. Their words tumbled over each other. *Murdered? How? Who killed them? And why?*

"What happened?" Ellynor asked.

Astira shook her head. "I don't know all the details," she said, which meant that she only had this much information because she'd been eavesdropping on conversations she was not meant to hear. "They were about a day's ride away from here, maybe two. Someone said they were looking for mystics—someone else said, no, they were merely carrying messages for the Lestra. At any rate, their bodies were found outside some little hut miles off the main road, buried in a common grave. Blood all over the floor inside the house. No one else around. None of the people who lived anywhere nearby knew what had happened to the soldiers—or the woman who used to live there."

The novices all listened, rapt with horror. Ellynor and Rosurie, who had grown up with violent men and knew a bit more about combat than the rest of the girls, were even more shocked and impressed than the others. They knew what kind of skill and manpower it took to overcome five soldiers fighting for their lives.

"But then—what happened to Kelti?" one of the girls asked. "If his body wasn't found—"

"Maybe he was abducted," another novice replied. "Whoever killed the others took him. To torture him. To make him—tell them things."

The first girl, the one who was sweet on Kelti, started crying. "They took him," she said with a sob. "They took him, and they'll hurt him, and then they'll kill him after all."

She didn't specify who she meant by *they*, but all of them knew. Everyone else in the room was nodding.

"May the Pale Mother strike them all down," Astira said. "Mystics."

"Are they really so terrible?" one of the younger girls asked. She hadn't been at the convent very long, so she could get away with asking the question that Ellynor knew better than to raise. Though she had wondered it silently many times.

"Yes," Astira replied with emphasis, while Ellynor returned her attention to Rosurie's hair. "They're evil. They contravene the laws of nature and the laws of the goddess. They—well. Here's a story I just heard. There's an island off of Danalustrous, on the western coast. That's where they send people who are dying with a fever that has no cure. But now mystics who have the power to change themselves and *other people* into animal shapes—these mystics are going to the island and turning sick people into dogs and horses and who knows what? Changing them! From humans into beasts!"

"Why?" breathed the youngest novice.

"I heard about that," Rosurie said. "Animals get that same fever, don't they, except there's a cure for it in dogs and horses. Isn't that right?"

Ellynor looked up from the pattern forming between her fingers. "You mean mystics change people into animals so they can be cured? Do they change the animals back into humans when the fever's gone?"

"I don't know! But it's still an abomination!" Astira exclaimed. "The goddess made each of us into the shape she most desired. We can't just decide to be something else—something she did not sanctify! You should have heard the Lestra when somebody brought her this news. I'm surprised the whole convent didn't come tumbling down, she was so angry."

Ellynor concentrated on her task again, holding the dye-soaked sponge to Rosurie's hair. But she was thinking about this extreme form of healing. Ellynor herself was very good in a sickroom; only a few times in her life had she encountered a fever that she could not defeat. She rather liked the inventiveness that had caused a mystic to take such drastic action, simply to save a few lives.

She knew better than to say so, of course. Here in Lumanen Convent, no one would ever defend a mystic.

WORD of the soldiers' deaths had spread through the whole convent by dinnertime, but there was never any official announcement about the incident. The girls sat in their usual orderly fashion at the long tables in the dining hall, completing the meal in three shifts as they rotated through the stages of cooking, eating, and cleaning. Shavell passed among the tables for all three dining shifts, more tense and critical than ever, so no one wanted to speak too much or ask for additional helpings.

Ellynor and Astira were among the final group of diners, trying to eat as quickly as they could so they could leave the oppressive atmosphere, when there was a stir and a murmur from the girls closest to the door. Soon, in one graceful ripple, the whole crowd had come to its feet, and the Lestra walked down the aisle between the two center tables.

As always, Ellynor found herself both hoping she didn't draw the Lestra's attention and incapable of looking away. There was such a heavy, insistent glamour to the woman—her very body seemed to absorb whatever light was available, whatever air was in the room. While she was nearby, it was impossible to look anywhere else or think about anything except pleasing her.

The Lestra paced slowly between the tables, nodding coolly as each novice dipped her head in a submissive bow. She wore her usual black robes, heavily embroidered in silver. Her hair, long as a Lirren girl's, fell in a loose braid of gray and black all the way to her knees. Her face was set, her dark eyes unreadable.

She stopped right in front of Astira and stared for a moment at the tall blond girl. Astira had lowered her head and did not look up as the Lestra studied her. Astira was a good five inches taller than the older woman, but she did not seem to have the advantage; there was something about the Lestra that was magnificent despite her short stature.

"You. You shall come with me tomorrow," the Lestra said. "We shall leave at noon."

"Yes, my lady. As it pleases the goddess."

"Pick someone else to come with us as well. We shall be gone two days, possibly three. You ride a horse, don't you?"

"Yes, my lady."

"Make sure your friend does also."

That was it. The Lestra abruptly turned and retraced her steps, leaving as swiftly and deliberately as she had entered. Not until the door had closed behind her and there was no chance she was still near enough to hear did the room erupt into an excited chattering of awe and speculation. The Lestra had moved among them! Spoken to one of the novices!

"Where will you be going? What does she need you for?" Rosurie demanded.

Astira shook her head. "I don't know! Not just to offer benedictions to travelers, because she would send us out with Shavell or one of the other dedicants. A two- or three-day trip! Surely we will be going to Neft, at least? I have not been outside of the convent for two months!"

"Neither have I," several girls replied in wistful voices. The Lestra had said Astira should pick one of her friends to go on this journey with them, and it was clear everyone at the table was hoping she'd be the one Astira favored.

But the Merrenstow girl was already smiling at Ellynor. "You'll come, won't you? I know you can ride."

Ellynor actually shivered with excitement. To be out of the convent for two days at least! Whether they went to Neft or merely camped out on the side of the road, the prospect of a change of scenery was giddily alluring. "I will. I do. Let's go pack right now! I can't wait till morning."

CHAPTER

4

THEY set out the next day shortly after noon, a cavalcade of eight. In addition to the Lestra, the novices and four guards, their group included Darris, another one of the dedicants. Despite the violet robes, she was nothing like Shavell, being plump and short and altogether more kind. She was also one of the oldest Daughters at the convent, for she had to be more than sixty, Ellynor thought. She was the one all the novices turned to if they had a problem, and if they could find her. She was most often closeted with the Lestra or working in the infirmary or bustling about on convent business and hard to track down. Shavell, on the other hand, was always available, especially when you least wanted her.

They traveled in near silence except for the noise the horses made. Astira and Ellynor, of course, were too overwhelmed to speak, though they exchanged wide-eyed glances now and then. Two guards rode before the women, two behind, and made no conversation that Ellynor could overhear. Now and then Darris and the Lestra murmured together, but never for long. Ellynor imagined that, in years of living at the convent together, the two women had already discussed every topic that might come up.

At first they traveled through woodland, for the convent was located deep in the forest, but gradually they won their way to a main road cutting through more open terrain. The day was warm and a little humid, so Ellynor was a little sorry to leave the shade of the trees, but at least now she could gauge the position of the sun and guess their direction. She nearly clapped her hands together as she realized they were heading northwest. *Neft!* she mouthed to Astira, who smiled in delight.

Sure enough, by the time the sun began to set, they were pulling up on the outskirts of the city. Ellynor felt her head practically swivel on her neck as she tried to take in all the sights at once. There was no such thing as a city in the Lirrens—just the occasional clusters of *sebahta* families living in a more tight-knit community than others. Astira had said Neft was small by the standards of Ghosenhall, but Ellynor found it hard to imagine anything more grand than this place, with its crisscross of streets, its clutter of buildings, its press of people, its sounds, its smell, its energy.

The guards did not pause as they crossed into the city proper, though they had to make their way more slowly through the crowded streets. Even Ellynor could tell that some parts of town were more respectable than others, for they moved past buildings that had a slovenly look, dirty and ill-kept, and into districts where the storefronts were neat, the window boxes weeded, the doors covered in fresh paint.

Eventually they climbed a rather steep hill and came to a halt. They were outside an elegant three-story building located on about an acre of land enclosed by a wrought-iron fence. One of the guards helped the Lestra from the saddle. The other women dismounted without assistance, then the guards gathered up the horses. "Come for us tomorrow around noon," the Lestra directed. "We will know then if we want to leave or stay another day."

"Yes, my lady."

Darris pulled back the iron gate and the Lestra strode in, the others trailing behind her. The wide front door had already been opened, and servants were bowing low, some of them touching their fists to their right shoulders. The Lestra swept by them as if they were invisible. Feeling just as invisible themselves, Astira and Ellynor followed Darris inside, then craned their necks to take in the opulence of the furnishings. Lush carpets, gold statuettes, high ceilings, stained glass. Certainly richer than Ellynor was used to, either at the convent or back home.

They were quickly ushered into a large parlor that was littered with chairs and sofas and small tables. An elegant, middle-aged, dark-haired woman rose to meet them, holding her hands out to take the Lestra's in a warm clasp.

"Coralinda! So good of you to come. You're looking well."

"Thank you, Jenetta. The goddess watches over me."

"Are you tired? Are you hungry? Would you like to eat or rest awhile?"

"We can do that later. Take me to your mother first, since her situation is so grave."

The woman swept a doubtful look over the rest of the entourage. "All of you?"

"Yes. We shall take the night watch in shifts, so they should all meet her now."

"Follow me."

Another parade through the lovely house, this time up a curving staircase whose walls were hung with formal portraits of rather grim men and women. Down a hall, past a few closed doors, and then into a chamber that was obviously a sickroom. There was the odor, for one thing, of bitter herbs and fevered flesh. There was the low light. There was the sticklike woman on the wide bed, a smothering of covers concealing everything except her head. Her nose was prominent and sharp, her hair loose and gray; everything else about her was vague and indeterminate. Her eyes were closed and her breathing was so shallow it did not disturb the blankets over her chest.

"We shall pray for her," the Lestra announced. "And then we shall stay with her, one of us, from now until she dies."

Their hostess flinched at the uncompromising word. "The doctor said it could be as early as tonight, but he did not think it would be more than another three days."

The Lestra nodded. "We shall stay that long, if that is the case."

She made a motion with her hand, and the Daughters arranged themselves around the bed. Darris and the Lestra stood on either side of the woman, near her head, the novices at her feet. Together they chanted the prayers that asked the Pale Mother's mercy upon this woman, that begged the Silver Lady to gather this soul into her own bright radiance and add its light to hers. *Take her gently. Turn her sacrifice to glory. May her face shine beside yours from the wide circle of the moon.*

Ellynor itched to come close enough to lay her fingers on the old woman's forehead, to stroke her hands, now buried under the covers. Back in the Lirrens, everyone wanted Ellynor nearby if there was illness in the house. But she had to be able to touch her patients to gauge what was wrong and if she could help them. This old woman was so frail and so ancient that it might be merely age that was shutting her body down, in which case there was nothing Ellynor would be able to do. But if there was a disease, a fever, a rebellion in the blood—well, it was possible Ellynor would be able to make her well, or at least ease her transition from this life to the next.

But there was no chance to touch the old woman, even to lean forward and lay a hand across the covered feet. The Lestra concluded the prayers and turned to look at her hostess. "Very well," she said. "Darris will stay with your mother for a few hours, then I will, and then my novices will take the night hours at her side. Feed us, let us get some rest, and we will do what we can."

*   *   *

WITHIN half an hour, Astira and Ellynor were curled up in a small bedroom on the third story, having eaten a quick meal in the dining hall. They were supposed to be sleeping, of course, but they were both too excited by the strangeness of their circumstances to be able to settle down. First they discussed the journey itself, then the sights that had caught their eyes as they moved through Neft, before turning their attention to their current situation.

"So why are we here?" Ellynor wanted to know. "I didn't think the Lestra went to private houses to perform sacred rituals—or sent her novices in to watch over the dying."

Astira was sitting up in the bed they shared, her arms locked around her updrawn knees. The room was dark except for the light of a single candle set in the window. "Usually not," she agreed. "But Jenetta Gisseltess is a cousin of the Lestra—and she married into money. She is constantly donating funds to the convent, so there is every reason for the Lestra to show her special attention."

"She looks noble."

"Jenetta? Yes, but only Thirteenth House. Like me."

"I don't understand what that means," Ellynor said.

"There are twelve great Houses in Gillengaria," Astira said patiently. She had explained this more than once before. "The owners—the marlords—possess most of the property that's worth having, and when they die, they pass it on to their sons and daughters. The serramar and the serramarra. But they own so much land that they can't really control or cultivate it all, so they each have vassals—highborn lords and ladies who hold properties in trust for the marlords. Many of them are second cousins of the marlords, or seventh sons of sixth sons—nobles, with noble blood, just not the highest connections. They're referred to as the Thirteenth House, no matter which of the Twelve Houses they hold allegiance to. It doesn't tell you where they're from, it just tells you their status." She shrugged. "They're good, but not good enough. Or I guess I should say *we're* not good enough."

"And Gisseltess? That's the name of one of these Twelve Houses?"

Astira giggled. "Yes, silly! One of the most powerful."

"And the Lestra? She's from Gisseltess?"

"Yes. If she was not the Lestra, you would properly call her serra Coralinda. Her brother is ser Halchon." Astira gave an exaggerated shiver. "Have you ever met him? He's a little frightening. Very intense. The way the Lestra is, only—only—with him you think it could turn to

violence. I don't like him much. Fortunately, he doesn't come to the convent often."

"It's all very confusing. We don't have titles and nobles among the
Lirrens."

"No, you just have these complex arrangements of kin! No one could
keep track of such things!"

Ellynor was surprised. "It's very easy. There are individual families,
and they band together to make up a *sebahta,* or a clan, and a number of
clans make up the *sebahta-ris*—"

Astira flung up a hand. "No, please, I won't be able to keep it straight.
Everyone was so astonished when you and Rosurie came to live at the
convent. I don't believe any of us had ever met a Lirren girl before."

"I never thought to travel across the Lireth Mountains," Ellynor said.

Astira unwound her hands and stretched out on the bed, yawning a
little. "And why did you? Because Rosurie fell in love with some boy, is
that it?"

Ellynor laughed and lay down beside her, though she wasn't at all
sleepy. "A boy from the Bramlis *sebahta,* yes."

"Is it true that Rosurie's father would have killed him if he'd caught
them together?"

"No, but it might have started a clan war."

"What's that?"

It was difficult to explain. "It's when—when all the families of the
sebahta-ris declare hostility on the families of another *sebahta-ris,* and if
members of one family see members of another somewhere, they'll start
fighting. Brutal fights, bloody—a lot of people die. You never want to be
the clan that's overmatched, so if anyone in your family needs to travel,
he takes five or ten brothers or cousins with him to defend him on the
road. It's stupid and it's pointless and it can go on for years," Ellynor
added bitterly. "All the young men dying, all their friends swearing re-
venge. Rosurie's father wanted to do anything to prevent another clan
war. That's why he agreed to send her away."

Astira had lifted her head and was now supporting it with her hand,
clearly fascinated. "But that's so—so exotic!" she exclaimed. "People taking up arms against each other and, what, dueling in the streets if they
happen to encounter each other in the town square?"

"There are no town squares. There are no towns. But there is a great
deal of travel on a few essential roads, and the battles are most likely to
occur on one of these journeys." Ellynor stretched her arms over her
head. "Oh, you're right, it *is* complicated! There are some *sebahta* that al-

most always stay neutral, and they try to mediate disputes. There are some families that live close to the roads, and they want to avoid having their own young men get swept up in other people's battles, and so they will post watchers on the road and try to make sure warring *sebahta* don't accidentally meet. But there are some men who are always ready to fight. Who are always looking for the stranger's insult or the dangerous pathway. The Lirren men are proud of their ability with knives and swords—and bare hands. Even when times are peaceful, they fight each other, just to keep their skills sharp."

"Even the men in your family?"

Ellynor laughed. "Especially the men in my family! Not my father so much now, though my mother says he was always quarrelsome when they were younger. But my brothers—Hayden and Torrin—oh, they would fight anybody with hardly an excuse. Torrin especially. He is two years older than I am and just stuffed with pride. No one has ever beaten him, either friend or enemy. He is too good."

"I can't imagine having brothers like that. They sound dreadful."

Ellynor laughed, though the sound was half a sigh. "Oh, in their way, they are wonderful. They both love me very much, though their love is smothering sometimes. I don't think I've ever talked to a boy without Hayden and Torrin watching, ready to strangle the poor man if he said something too familiar or tried to take my hand. And if he tried to kiss me—! Some man from the Cohfen *sebahta* did kiss me one feast night, and I thought Torrin would tear the head from his body. Hayden stopped him, but only because he was Cohfen, and not someone we wanted to fight with."

"I heard something once about the Lirrenfolk," Astira said. "That the women aren't allowed to marry anyone except Lirren men. Is that true?"

Ellynor nodded, ruffling her hair against the pillow. She had unbound it and combed it out after their ride. She'd need to braid it or put it in its customary knot before taking her turn at the old woman's bedside. "It's true," she said, lowering her voice even more. "If a girl tries to marry outside the Lirrens, her lover will be challenged to a duel to the death. Anyone in the *sebahta-ris*—her father, her brothers, her cousins—whoever is the best fighter can do battle on her behalf, but the lover must fight for himself. And they fight until one of them is dead."

"That's terrible!" Astira exclaimed.

Ellynor nodded again. "I know. You can guess that not too many Lirren girls are willing to risk it. For which one of them would you want to see bleeding his life away? You understand, the families are very close.

The ties of affection are so strong, and not just between blood relatives, but between everyone in the *sebahta*. What kind of girl would put her father or her brother at risk? And yet, how could she stand to see her lover cut down? Wouldn't she just rather give him up? Wouldn't she just tell him, the very first time he showed her any affection, 'Go away. I'm not interested in you'? Better that than to someday fall in love with him, and have to choose between giving him up or seeing him dead."

"That's even more terrible," Astira said. "I would despise anyone who put me in a position like that. I would hate my father to think he would force me to make such a dreadful decision."

Ellynor shrugged in the dark. "Well, there are not so many strangers who come traveling through the Lirrens," she said. "A few merchants—now and then some of the king's soldiers—and every once in a while, sailors from Arberharst and Sovenfeld. But mostly the men we see are the men of our families and of the *sebahta-ris*. We don't have many chances to ruin our lives by falling in love with forbidden men."

Astira leaned closer. "There are the men of the Lestra's guard," she whispered. "You might fall in love with one of them."

Ellynor laughed. "And they're forbidden, too, but by the Lestra herself! No, thank you, I'm not looking to fall in love with anyone just now. I just want to be a good Daughter, serve the goddess, watch over my cousin, and make my family proud."

Astira yawned again. "I just want to sleep for an hour or two before it is my turn to watch the old woman," she said.

"Then close your eyes. I'm sure we're both so tired that we'll fall asleep right away."

Indeed, Astira slept almost immediately, but Ellynor was wide awake. The moon had been an even thinner crescent tonight, only a few days away from dark, and the Black Mother had almost complete dominion over the night sky. Ellynor's very favorite time. She crept from the bed and went to lean out the window, resting her arms on the sill next to the candle. A deep inhalation brought her the mixed scents of ripe gourds in the gardens and turning leaves on the nearest trees. Almost autumn. Soon to be winter. The best time of year.

She was still awake when a servant knocked and quietly entered. "One of you is wanted in the sickroom," the girl informed Ellynor.

She glanced at the bed, but Astira's eyes were closed and her breathing was soft and regular. "I'll go," Ellynor said, catching up her hair in one quick twist. "Give me a moment to put on my robe."

* * *

A few minutes later, Ellynor was ushered into the sickroom. The Lestra stood there still, a dark shape bowed over the broad bed. She looked up when Ellynor entered.

"She is breathing still, but her lungs draw poorly," the Lestra said in her deep, musical voice. "I don't think it will be much longer now. Are you afraid to be alone if death comes into the room?"

"No," Ellynor said. "I've been present for such visits before. But who should I call if it happens?"

"Jenetta told me there will be a servant just down the hall. Make use of her. And send her to fetch your sister novice after you have watched a few hours."

"I will. Thank you, my lady." Ellynor inclined her head as the Lestra passed her and left the room. She waited till the door clicked shut behind her.

Alone with the dying woman.

Ellynor pulled a chair up next to the bed but did not immediately sit, just leaned over and examined the patient's face. So thin, so pale, with breath so slow and labored that indeed it seemed each one might be her last. Again, Ellynor wondered: Was it age or illness that had brought her down?

She placed her hands carefully, lightly, along the woman's sunken cheekbones, stroked her palms down the flat covers across the woman's slight bosom. Fever in the noblewoman's skin, a rattling congestion in her chest. The stomach and bowels were functioning, as far as Ellynor could tell.

She passed her hands over the upper torso again. Yes, this was the trouble, clustered around the heart and the lungs. Infection and pressure, and not enough strength to resist. "I wish I had been here a day or two sooner," Ellynor murmured.

Dropping to the chair and making herself comfortable, she pulled back the blankets and spread her fingers over the woman's thin nightshirt. She could feel the slight fall and rise of the patient's ribs, catch the faint gurgle as her breath came haltingly in. The fabric of the nightgown felt warm to the touch, as if it had been set close to a fire. Fever, Ellynor knew, seeping upward from the flesh.

"Great Mother, lay your hands over mine," she whispered, as she had whispered at so many sickbeds of the *sebahta*. "Pour your strength into me. Heal this woman through the medium of my body."

She closed her eyes and opened her heart. Above her, through the layers of wood and stone, she could sense the arched bowl of the Dark Watcher's hands, cupped over the world to keep it safe. She could almost hear the goddess's rhythmic chanting as she counted each of the souls under her protection. *Here's one . . . and another . . . and another . . . and one more. . . .*

She could tell the exact moment the goddess recognized her, heard Ellynor's call for help, and kindly responded. She felt the power blossom through her, like heat, like excitement, prickling along her veins. Her hands grew warm, her head felt dizzy, and the moonstone on her bracelet flared with fire. Behind her eyelids she had the impression the room itself grew darker, as the Black Mother flowed in, past the closed shutters, down the banked chimney, and pooled around the patient and the supplicant.

The old woman coughed and stirred under Ellynor's hands. Her breathing grew easier, if only a little. She moved her head on the pillow, shifted her lax arms, then gave a sigh of relief. Ellynor guessed that some squeeze of pain had been lifted from her chest—a small blessing, even if that was to be the only one.

"Thank you, Great Mother," Ellynor whispered. "You never fail me."

She opened her eyes, taking a moment to clear her head and let the sense of light seep back into the room. The goddess had done her part; now it was Ellynor's turn. She stood and moved rather briskly around the bed, checking to see what medicines had been gathered to ease the old woman's way. Ah—here were some curative herbs, here was water, and something that smelled like a healing concoction. She would guess none of these had been administered within the last day or two, since the patient's case had seemed hopeless. Now, she thought, the old woman would swallow whatever she was offered.

And so she did. In the next two hours, Ellynor induced her to take a glass of water as well as some powdered herbs, and she had the satisfaction of seeing a little color return to the wan cheeks. The old woman did not speak and barely woke, but she turned on her side and moved her hands as if to check for something that was not there. Ellynor caught the restless fingers and held them in hers.

"Take a little more strength from my body—I have plenty," she said in a low voice. Almost as if she heard and understood, the woman's grip tightened. Then with another sigh, she released Ellynor's hand and seemed to fall into an even deeper slumber.

The woman was still sleeping three hours later when Ellynor sent the servant to wake Astira so she could seek her own bed. She didn't tell Astira what she had done, merely said, "You might try giving her some water every half hour or so. She took some when I offered it, and it seemed to make her easier."

"I pray she doesn't die while I'm alone with her!"

"I don't think she will. I'm off to get some sleep."

"I hope they let both of us sleep in tomorrow morning."

Ellynor laughed softly and left. Once in her own room, she was so tired that for a moment she could not remember which side of the bed was hers and which was Astira's. It was always that way, when the Black Mother used her to heal someone else. It was as if all the energy was stripped from her body, washed into someone else's veins. Too tired to even scrub her face or change out of her clothes, Ellynor climbed into bed and fell instantly asleep.

WHEN Ellynor went down to the dining hall the next morning—so late it could hardly be called morning any longer—she found a half dozen strangers in the room, along with Astira, the Lestra, and Jenetta Gisseltess. Everyone seemed excited, though they spoke in low voices and continually looked toward the door as if they were expecting fresh news to walk across the threshold. Ellynor gathered food from the sideboard and sat next to Astira.

"Did something happen?" she whispered.

Astira nodded. "The old woman is much better this morning! Jenetta is trying not to be too hopeful, because the Lestra told her people often seem to get stronger just before they die. But Jenetta called her sisters and her nieces over because she thought her mother might be well enough to wake up and maybe recognize everyone enough to say good-bye."

"Doesn't anyone think she might live, after all?" Ellynor asked, spooning up a mouthful of fruit. She was so hungry she could eat everything on her plate and go back for more.

"Oh, I thought she was too sick to pull through, didn't you?"

"It depends on the will of the goddess," Ellynor said. Not specifying which goddess. No one ever asked.

"Of course," Astira said, instantly pious. "The Pale Mother will choose what is best."

Ellynor ate most of a piece of bread in three bites. "Does this mean we won't be leaving today after all?"

"I don't think so." Astira tried not to smile, but she couldn't quite help it. "The Lestra is a little vexed, I think. She had said she would stay through the end, but now it appears the end will not be coming quite so soon. She does not want to offend Jenetta, of course, but—anyway, I don't know what she will decide! I think we are here another day, at least."

"I wonder if we'll be allowed to leave the house. Perhaps get to see a little of Neft," Ellynor said hopefully.

Astira yawned. "You can ask, if you want. I'd just like to sleep a few more hours. Particularly if we're going to be up again tonight, saying prayers over a sick woman. Darris is back in bed already."

Ellynor felt guilty a moment, remembering that she had not, in fact, chanted prayers all night. Well, she had prayed to the Dark Watcher, of course; surely that was good enough?

"You're right," she said. "We should sleep while we can."

But a few minutes later, when the chance came to leave the house, she took it without hesitation.

She was just finishing her breakfast (seconds of the eggs and fruit, *thirds* of the bread), when the Lestra rose and approached the novices. Astira and Ellynor hastily stood up, Ellynor brushing crumbs from her robes. "I have a commission for one of you, if you would be so good as to carry it out," the Lestra said.

They both nodded so deeply they might be bowing. "Yes, my lady," they replied in unison.

"I need a gift delivered to a visitor in town. I do not wish to send it by one of Jenetta's servants, for it is a moonstone, and holy to the Pale Mother. It needs to rest in hands that will treat it with extreme care."

Ellynor gave a quick sideways glance at Astira, who nodded slightly. "I will be happy to carry it for you, my lady," she said respectfully. "Someone must tell me the streets to take and how quickly I must be back before we leave."

"We shall not leave today," the Lestra said, and, indeed, Ellynor thought she caught a tone of annoyance in that lovely voice. "We are now considering tomorrow. That does not mean you should dawdle in the streets."

"No, my lady. Of course not, my lady."

A slight relenting; she could hear the faintest trace of a smile in the Lestra's voice. "That does not mean, if a stranger stops and asks you for a benediction, that you should turn away. Give the Pale Mother's blessing to anyone who inquires."

"I will, my lady."

"Come with me."

Ellynor followed the Lestra to a much finer bedroom than the one she shared with Astira, and received a silken pouch drawn shut with a gold cord. For a moment, the moonstones on her bracelet burned with a sympathetic heat, but as soon as she stored the pouch in a voluminous pocket, the extra warmth died away. The Lestra handed her a formal card written with a woman's name and address, and a footman at the front door described the streets she would have to traverse to find her destination.

"I could come with you, at that," the footman said. He was maybe a year or two younger than Ellynor and had a friendly grin. "Neft can be a confusing place if you're not used to it. I was lost twenty times my first week here!"

If she was accompanied, even by someone so casual, Ellynor was sure part of her glorious sense of freedom would be destroyed. "Thank you, but the Lestra does not like us to associate with attractive young men," she said, adding the adjective and a half smile to take any sting from her words. "I'm sure I'll be just fine."

He was smiling even more broadly. "If you get lost, just ask anyone where Jenetta Gisseltess's house can be found. Everybody knows us."

"I will. Thank you. I will be back as soon as I can."

And she stepped off the porch, across the yard, out through the wrought-iron gate, and onto the street.

She was alone in Neft! Alone for the first time in her life!

CHAPTER

5

Ellynor did fairly well on her walk *to* her destination, for the footman's directions were fresh in her head and she was concentrating closely. Down the hill, turn to the left, down another street, cross a major road, go three-quarters of the way around a town circle, turn right, turn left at another corner . . . Still, there was so much to see that she couldn't help getting a little distracted. The streets were full of conveyances of every description, from farmer's carts to noblemen's carriages, and pedestrians dodged through horse traffic somewhat to their peril. Some corners were quiet, lined with small buildings or what looked like private homes, but the farther she got from the Gisseltess house, the noisier and busier the streets became. Look, these appeared to be shops, selling—everything! Lace and fabric and shoes and wine and tools and even clothing. Even *food*, already prepared for people who must be too lazy to make it themselves. It smelled wonderful, though. If she'd had any coppers to her name, Ellynor might have been tempted to sample some. Though she could not even guess what such a luxury might cost.

Past the shops and over another small hill, the terrain changed again, became a little more inhospitable. Ellynor thought the women she came across looked dispirited, even degraded, while the men she passed frequently smelled of ale. The streets were none too clean, either, in this part of town, muddy and smelling of hastily emptied chamber pots. Ellynor picked up her skirts and stepped delicately around the more unidentifiable substances in her way. She was glad she'd brought a fresh robe to Neft with her; she wasn't sure she'd want to wear this one again till after it had been cleaned.

It was hard to imagine who from this part of the city might claim a friendship with the Lestra.

Her destination, when she reached it, proved to be a small building set among a row of other such buildings that looked like they each might contain several living spaces inside. The girl who answered the door seemed to be about fourteen and underfed, but her face and dress were clean.

"I'm looking for someone named Bertha," Ellynor said.

The girl nodded. "That's my mother. I'll get her."

A few moments later, Bertha appeared, a tired-looking but respectable enough woman who could have been the age of Ellynor's mother. "Are you from the Lestra?" she asked hopefully.

"I am," said Ellynor. "This is for you." And she pulled out the moonstone (that rush of heat again) and handed it over.

Bertha pressed her lips to the thin bag, closing her eyes as if in ecstasy or gratitude. "Thank you," she murmured.

"Praise the goddess and her goodness," Ellynor said piously.

"Praise the Silver Lady."

Opening her eyes, Bertha gave Ellynor a bright smile. "Did you walk here from the Gisseltess house? Would you like to come in? I could give you something to drink."

"Thank you, no. I'm not supposed to linger."

"And you can find your way back?"

"I'm sure I can. May the goddess watch over you."

"Oh, and over you, too!"

Smiling a little, Ellynor started out on her return journey. But somewhere she made a wrong turn, since she found herself on a street she had never seen before. She retraced her steps, but could not find the corner where she had gone awry. Nothing looked familiar no matter which direction she turned. That was a hill, true, but it didn't seem to be lined with any of the shops she'd noticed on her way here.

She was lost.

A pulse of panic caused her heart to race and her cheeks to flush, but she told herself sternly not to be ridiculous. It had taken her less than an hour to get from Jenetta's house to her destination; even with a few missteps, it should not take her much longer than that to find her way home. *Everyone knows where the Gisseltess house is*, she reminded herself. *Just find someone and ask.*

She had happened upon a block where there were not many vehicles in the street, and not many pedestrians, either. By the scents she could pick up, there were many horses nearby—stables, maybe—and a wide variety of alcoholic beverages. Could these buildings be taverns, which she had heard about but never actually seen? Didn't people behave very badly when they were in such places? She hesitated to knock on one of the closed doors. She would walk a little farther and see if she passed someone on the street.

Indeed, she hadn't gone another hundred yards before she spotted a man standing on a corner, one hand on his hip, one hand raised to his eyes as if gauging the hour by the angle of the sun. From behind, he appeared to be impeccably dressed, and his boots were well polished. A man of some means, apparently. She would ask him how to find her destination.

Still, it took some courage to approach a stranger, a man, without a friend or brother at her side.

"Excuse me," she addressed the back of his coat, which appeared to be made of fine wool. "Could I ask you for directions?"

He spun around at the sound of her voice, and she instantly knew she had made a bad choice. He couldn't have been much older than Torrin, but his face looked lined and hardened, and she could smell stale wine on his breath. She did not like the expression his face showed when he realized he had been accosted by a lone woman. In simple white robes. Who looked terrified.

"Well," he said softly. "Who might you be, little lost girl?"

Ellynor took a step backward, trying not to be obvious about it. It had never occurred to her before, but a man was so much bigger than a woman, with such powerful hands and arms. If he wanted to, this one could strangle her before she had time to draw breath. She had no idea how to fend off a violent attacker—she had never needed to know.

"I am a novice in the Lumanen Convent, one of the Daughters of the Pale Mother," she said with as much dignity as she could muster. Most folks in this region were in awe of the Daughters; this credential might earn her some respect. "I am looking for the house of Jenetta Gisseltess."

He smiled and shook his head. He had copied her action, stepping forward as she stepped back, almost as if they executed the motions of a dance. "Never heard of it," he said. "Don't know where it is. Plenty of other houses I could take you to, though."

She stood firm, refusing to back away again, and made her voice icy. "Thank you, no. I'll continue on my way without your help."

His hand flashed out and caught her by the shoulder. The grip was tight enough to leave a mark. "Not so fast," he said. "Stay and talk to me awhile."

She tried to shake free, but his hand only tightened. "I am here to do the work of the Pale Mother," she said, her voice even colder. "Stand aside."

"I need a little attention from the Silver Lady," he murmured. "Why don't you share a little of her light with me?"

He pulled her roughly into his arms and kissed her hard on the mouth. She tried to struggle and she tried to scream, but the contest was too unequal. She had nowhere near the strength she needed to resist him. Her lips were bruising under his, her ribs were cracking in his hold, and she felt herself grow faint and dizzy. Still holding her, still practically devouring her, he forced her backward so that her spine was against the nearest building and the whole weight of his body lay upon her. She felt one of his arms uncoil from around her waist and his hand go groping at his belt, and she experienced a surge of panic so violent that she thought her bones might shatter.

Suddenly he flung himself off of her and went spinning to the ground. He had released her so abruptly that she nearly lost her balance and fell.

But no—he had not let her go. Someone had ripped him away.

Choking and breathless, she rested a hand against the wall and gaped at the scene before her. Her attacker leapt to his feet, fury in his eyes and a dagger in his hand, but he faced an opponent who looked every inch a fighter. The newcomer was sandy-haired and burly, not particularly well-dressed but holding a sword that gleamed with loving polish. He had the very tip of it pressed under the other man's chin, and he looked absolutely prepared to drive the point home.

"I don't think you're wanted here," her rescuer said in a steely voice. "Go now, unless you truly want a fight."

"I'm not afraid of a gutter boy like you," the first man snarled. Indeed, if she was going by their clothing, Ellynor would guess her attacker was a merchant or a low-ranking noble, while the man who had come to her aid was a peasant or laborer. She was not sure how things worked in Gillengaria, but she couldn't think an aristocrat would allow himself to be intimidated by a serf. "Stay out of a matter that does not concern you, or I'll cut your throat right here on the street."

Ellynor gasped, but her rescuer was unfazed. "You have no idea how quickly I can kill you," he said in a calm voice.

"With a blade already at my throat? I suppose you could."

The sandy-haired man stepped back, lowering his weapon. "Draw your sword."

Instead, the noble flung himself at the other man, his dagger leveled to pierce the heart. Ellynor shrieked, looking around wildly for assistance.

But there was no assistance needed, or even time for help to come. A whirl of fists, a flash of metal, and the nobleman was on the ground groaning, his hand pressed to his shoulder and blood streaming down his shirt.

Ellynor knew enough about duels to realize he had not sustained a fatal wound. Still, she was a little shocked when the other man put a hand gently on her arm and said, "We should leave now. Before he gets up to try again—and before anyone comes to investigate."

She gazed at him numbly. "But can we—should we—can we just leave him here like this?"

The man turned a contemptuous look on the nobleman, still moaning and cursing, trying to roll to a seated position. "He'll be fine. Disabled, not really hurt."

"Then we—"

A door opened down the street, and someone stuck his head out, looking curious. The fair-haired man pushed at Ellynor's arm with a little more urgency. "Come on. We'll talk someplace else."

And because she was really too disoriented to think what she ought to do instead, she allowed him to whisk her around the corner, up the street, and into a large, low building that she belatedly realized was a stable. Just as, with a spurt of fear, she wondered if she might now be in an even worse situation, he turned and grinned at her.

"Now," he said, dropping his hand. "What was that all about? I hope I didn't come between you and a suitor you cared about. That's not what it looked like, but sometimes—" He shook his head.

"No! I was lost and I stopped to ask him for directions and then he—he—well, you saw what he did. I thought he was going to—I was really afraid." She paused to take a deep breath and try to quell some of her shaking. She was not usually so helpless and so easily overset. But she had never, ever, felt at such risk before.

This was why Torrin and Hayden would never let her out of their sight.

"Thank you so much for saving me," she added in a calmer voice. "I don't know what I would have done if you hadn't come along."

She expected him to respond with a gracious *You're welcome* or *I'm glad I could be of assistance*. But his voice was almost as stern as Torrin's would have been. "What were you doing out by yourself in this part of town, anyway?" he demanded. "Especially if you don't know how to take care of yourself?"

Her own temper rose. "I can take care of myself if people behave with some decency!" she shot back. "What kind of city is this, where men accost young women on the streets? Women who serve the *goddess*? He should be struck down by the Pale Mother!"

"Well, it didn't look like she was about to intervene anytime soon," her companion said dryly. "If you can't defend yourself, and if you don't have the sense to stay where it's safe—"

"I shouldn't have to stay where it's safe! People like him should be the ones who are kept off the streets, not me!"

Unexpectedly, he grinned at her, the expression so boyish that all her anger melted away. "I'd say you're right about that," he replied. "But since that's not the way the world works, you'd better either get yourself an escort or figure out how to fight back."

Reluctantly, she smiled in return. "I don't expect to be walking unaccompanied around Neft too often," she said. "In fact, probably never again. So I guess I don't need to learn how to defend myself."

He shrugged. "Never a bad skill to learn, anyway. Never know when trouble might come."

"*You* certainly seem to know how to fight."

That grin again. It made him look a little raffish. "Always did."

"You probably enjoy it, too. Just like my brothers. They're never happier than when they've got swords in their hands or their fists up to hit somebody."

"Fighting's a skill, and I'm good at it. Don't *you* enjoy whatever skills you have? Don't you work at getting better?"

Nonplussed, she stared at him a moment. She couldn't remember anybody ever asking her that before. As a Lirren girl, she had domestic abilities that all women were expected to cultivate, and she had been praised from time to time for her cooking or her sewing. But no one had ever said, *Ellynor, you set a stitch so beautifully! Practice your embroidery and you will be a fine seamstress someday.* No one had expected her to have aspirations. Everyone appreciated her talent for nursing, of course, but it wasn't something she had considered building her life around.

She had never really thought about having a calling, and dedicating her life to it.

Though now that she was a novice at the Lumanen Convent, theoretically she had found her calling. Theoretically her life would be devoted to the Pale Mother.

She shook her head, shaking the thought away. "I—I suppose I do," she said. "And you're right. Your ability to fight was a very useful one today."

He held his hand out in a friendly gesture. "I'm Justin, by the way," he said. "Am I allowed to ask your name?"

Not something they'd covered in convent etiquette, though Torrin most certainly would not approve. "Ellynor," she said, and put her hand in his. His palm was warm and callused; she could feel the power in his grip, though he closed his hand very gently over hers. "I serve at the Lumanen Convent."

Another grin. "I recognized the robes. Why do you think I'm being so polite?"

"You think you've been polite?"

A laugh for that, as if he was surprised. "Well, a lot of people think it's something I've never really mastered. Can I get you some water to drink? To wipe off your face? You might not want to go back to the convent looking like you've been mauled in the street."

Suddenly self-conscious, she put her hands to her cheeks, to her hair. Oh yes, she could feel the disorder in her coiffure, and her face probably bore all manner of scratches and bruises.

And she was dying for a chance to wash away the taste of that other man's mouth.

"Yes, please," she said in a rather small voice. "Thank you. I wouldn't want anyone to see me looking mussed up."

He nodded, then called out what must have been someone's name. "Delz?" He waited, but there was no answer. "I think we're alone for the moment," he said. "Let me get you some water and a clean cloth. Here— you can sit on that while you wait."

She perched on the rough, unpainted bench he indicated and looked around. She was definitely in the town stables, though the room she was in at the moment held no horses. It was a big work and storage area, with bags of grain piled on the floor, pitchforks leaning against the wall, tack and bridles hanging from hooks. Justin had disappeared through two wide, half-opened doors that must lead to the stalls where the horses were kept. Ellynor could smell the distinctive odor of hair and manure and hay, and catch the occasional whinny and snort. One of the horses must have stuck his nose over his stall door, asking to be fed, because she heard Justin's voice, low and soothing. "Not now, boy. Your turn comes later."

Hard on the heels of his voice came his person, striding through those same doors. He had a white cloth in one hand and a bucket in the other.

"I just pumped it, so it's clean enough to drink," he assured her, seeming to read the expression on her face. "But I couldn't find a mug. Can you use your hands?"

She looked down at her palms with some doubt. The fingertips were bleeding from where she'd tried to claw at her attacker's skin, and she had dirt on both hands from catching herself on the building so she wouldn't fall. "If I scrub them first," she said.

He set the bucket down next to her and settled on the other side of it. "Here," he said, dipping his own hands in the water and bringing them up in a rough cup. "I just washed mine."

She bent her head down and sipped, unconsciously bringing her own hands up to hold his steady. Water seeped through his fingers and onto hers, then dripped down to make small dots on her robe. She thought she could taste soap from his hasty cleaning, and, under that, maybe even the flavor of his skin.

She drank till the water was gone and she was almost licking Justin's wet palm. She could still taste her attacker's brutal kiss.

"More?" Justin said.

She nodded. He scooped up more water, held his hands out for her. Again she fancied she caught the residue of soap and skin. Her chin was dripping when she finally looked up and smiled at him, dragging her sleeve across her mouth.

"Thank you."

He smiled back. "You still look like an urchin."

She laughed. "Well, let me clean myself up." She glanced around. "Is there a mirror in here?"

"In the stables?" He snorted. "No. I can wipe your face for you."

"I think I'd rather do it myself, thank you very much!" But she was laughing again. "Just give me that cloth and I'll do it blind."

He handed her the white rag, and watched her as she dipped it in the bucket and passed it over her face. It came away soiled with traces of grime and a thin smear of blood. Where had that come from? She dabbed at her lips again, and again the cloth came away stained with red. She envisioned her mouth, puffy and torn, and her hair, no doubt an utter disaster.

"I must look awful," she said, sighing. "Anyone who sees me is going to know something happened."

"Were you going to try to keep it a secret?"

"I don't know," she said honestly. "I think I just wanted to tell the story so that I didn't seem quite so helpless and stupid."

"Well, you might not be stupid, but a lone woman on the streets can be pretty helpless," he said. "I don't think the Lestra should be sending her novices out alone."

For a moment it occurred to her to wonder how he knew the Lestra's title, and then she supposed that everyone did. From what she could tell, most people in Gillengaria worshipped the Pale Mother; surely they would all know the details of convent life.

"Usually we don't go out by ourselves," she said, wiping her cheek again. "I was running an errand, and I got lost. Normally we're in groups, and the guards are with us." She glanced up and gave him a rueful smile. "I was glad to be out alone," she admitted. "My brothers would never have let me walk through the city by myself! They're so cautious and protective. I thought, 'Finally! A chance to be free of everyone's attention!'" She grimaced. "And then this happened."

"Seems like your brothers might be right. Somebody *should* be watching after you."

The tone was provocative. She flashed him a quick look to find him grinning again. "Do *you* have sisters?" she asked pointedly. "And is that how you treat *them*?"

Another laugh, but this one a little bitter. "I have sisters," he said in a curiously flat voice. "And, no, I don't watch out for them."

"Are they older or younger? How many?"

"Three. Older."

"Are you close?"

He shook his head and did not answer. Ellynor decided it might be a touchy subject and she probably shouldn't pry. After a final swipe at her face, she turned her attention to her hair, putting her hands up to the back of her head. She'd hoped she could just poke the pins in place, but the knot was too loose. With a sigh, she pulled the pins free, and the whole long mass came tumbling down. She swept it around over her right shoulder and combed her fingers through it to straighten the tangles.

Justin's eyes were fixed on the *sebahta* pattern dyed into her hair. Similar to Rosurie's except that hers featured a sickle, rose, and bird design to mark her as being of the Alowa family. The dye was a rusty blond against the jet-black of her hair.

She felt a sudden unreasonable pang. Now he would know she was a Lirren girl; now he would know his life could be forfeit if he so much as talked with her for twenty minutes. All the novices at the convent knew her heritage, of course, but Ellynor had not thought to mention it to this young man. This Justin. Not that she would ever see him again, not that it mattered whether or not he knew who she was, not that she had expected him to come courting until he found out she was off-limits for any suitor except those sanctioned by her family. It was just that—despite the real terrors of the day—she had rather enjoyed sitting here talking to him, bridling at his scolds, laughing at his observations. She had rather liked him, and now he would recoil and walk away.

But he didn't. "Your hair—that's so beautiful," he said. "What have you done to it? *Why* did you do that?"

So he didn't recognize a *sebahta* pattern when he saw one. Beginning the braid with swift, sure fingers, Ellynor remembered that Astira hadn't recognized it, either. No, nor had any of the other girls from the convent. It seemed Lirren customs were not so well-known here across the mountains. Justin still had no idea who she was.

Her spirits rose. Ridiculous though that was.

"It's just—a kind of decoration," she said, stumbling over the false words. To deny the *sebahta* like this! And to feel so delighted as she did so! "Do you like it?"

"Yes. It's striking. But you should wear your hair down all the time, so more people can see it."

"Oh—it would be in my way. I wear it down on social occasions sometimes." Weddings. Feast days. When she was safe among her family members.

Maybe it was her imagination, but it seemed like Justin was visibly restraining himself from reaching out to touch the patterned black silk of her hair. "It's so beautiful," he said again.

She laughed. "Hard to take care of, though! When I travel, it's almost impossible to keep it clean."

"Do you travel much? How often do novices leave the convent?"

Not often enough, she thought. "Actually, I think this is only the fifth or sixth time I've left the convent since I've been there. The girls who've been there longer leave more often—come in to Neft, sometimes, or go to some of the other nearby towns to proselytize."

"How long have you been at the convent?"

"A little over a year."

His eyebrows rose, and she wondered what he was thinking. But what he said was, "And why did you want to join the Daughters?"

It was hard to know how to answer that, so for the moment she concentrated on her hair. Finishing the braid, she looped it in a knot on the back of her head and fixed the pins in place. She gave him a quick sideways glance and saw him watching her. Waiting with some patience for her answer.

Oh, what did it matter? She would never see him again, so she might as well be truthful. To a point. "My cousin wanted to join, but she didn't want to come by herself," she answered. "And I liked the idea of leaving home, at least for a little while."

"Getting away from those protective brothers," he said.

"You have no idea how protective! So I thought it might be—an adventure of a sort. Something different. Exciting, maybe."

"I don't know that much about it," he said, "but it would seem to me that if you were going to live at the Lumanen Convent, you'd have a bad time of it if you weren't completely devoted to the Pale Mother."

She gave him a swift, unhappy smile. "Yes. You're right. For some reason, I hadn't thought it through like that."

He raised his eyebrows again. "And you're finding that you don't love the Silver Lady quite as much as you should?"

"Oh, I rather like her," Ellynor said, which made him laugh. "I do! She's so beautiful and mysterious. And I like the rituals that honor her. But I find some of the—there's a kind of—I'm not quite as devout as some of the other girls."

"They're fanatics," he said bluntly.

"Yes. And while there are a lot of novices who are—oh, they're silly girls who joined up on a lark, or to please their families, and who aren't so passionate about the goddess—the Lestra and the senior Daughters are all very stern and dedicated. They're a little—sometimes they frighten me a little."

"Do you have to stay?" he asked.

She had never allowed herself to really face that question and it made her uneasy to contemplate it now. "I don't know," she said slowly. "I wouldn't want to leave my cousin there all alone, of course, and *she* has become one of the fanatics."

"Would your family let you come home?"

"Oh yes. I think they expect that I will be here another year or two at most and then return to them."

"So you think it's the Lestra who might not allow you to leave."

How quickly he had put his finger on it, saying aloud the thing she did not like to think. "Since I have been there, I have not seen any girls go home," Ellynor said carefully. "Perhaps none of them wanted to, but—" She shrugged. "It's strange. I would have thought, in a group that large, *someone* would have gotten homesick, or been called to her family to nurse her ailing mother, or decided the convent life was not for her. But none of that has happened since I've been there."

"In a year."

"Right."

His face wore a look of heavy skepticism, but he did not make any of the comments that were obviously circling in his mind. Ellynor gave her head a little shake and practiced a smile.

"But I don't mean to sound so sinister! It would probably be a simple thing to leave if I decided I wanted to."

"Very simple," he agreed. "You're out now. No one knows where you are. Just don't go back. I'd help you hide if anyone started a search."

She laughed uneasily. Just imagining what would happen if the Lestra came looking for her—if *Torrin* came looking for her and discovered she had disappeared with the aid of an unknown man—made her feel physically ill. "Thank you," she said as lightly as she could. "I'll keep that in mind if the need ever arises."

He nodded, as if he'd been serious. "I'm usually to be found right here in the stables. Or at least, I will be for a few more weeks."

Yes, indeed, let us talk about you *for a while,* Ellynor thought. "So tell me your story, Justin," she invited. "Why are you in Neft?"

She saw an odd expression cross his face—odd, because she was sure she had worn a similar look when she was trying to decide how much of the truth to tell him. *Justin has secrets of his own,* she thought, though the idea did not particularly displease her. Rather, it made her more curious. "More or less just drifted here by chance," he said. "Had a job working for a noble—we got into a disagreement—and I left. Not sure what I want to do next, but I came to rest in Neft for the moment and took a job at the stable because it happened to be open. And I'm good with horses."

"You're good with a sword, too," she observed. "Couldn't you sign on as a soldier somewhere?"

Something amused him, though he tried to hide his smile. "I could, I suppose. That's not what I want at the moment, though."

She spoke with some excitement, as if she'd just thought of a grand plan. "The Lestra's always hiring men. You could come be a guard at the convent."

He gave her a sharp look as if to be sure she was joking, and then his smile widened. "I think I'd find the life a little too confining," he drawled. "Though I suppose there would be some advantages. You and I could become better friends, for instance."

"Probably not," she said regretfully. "The Lestra doesn't like the novices to spend much time with the soldiers. We have to speak to them sometimes, of course, but we're closely watched. We'd never have a real conversation."

Justin looked cynical. "I'd lay money that somewhere at the convent, right this minute, there's a guard and a girl meeting in secret," he said. "That's just the way of men and women. *Particularly* when they've been forbidden to see each other."

She laughed. "Well, you may be right! The women, at least, are always watching the men, trying to judge who might be nice and who might be—exciting."

"And I'll wager they like the exciting ones more than the nice ones."

"Oh, I don't know," she said seriously. "I've spent a lifetime around men who were—who are—hotheaded and sometimes dangerous. Arrogant and strong and quick to fight. Those are the kind of men most of the girls at the convent seem to be drawn to. But I say, let me meet a kind man instead. Let me meet someone who knows how to be softer. I am so tired of violence and bluster. I'd like to meet a thoughtful man."

The cynical expression was back on Justin's face, or maybe he was thinking that she had just described him when she had meant to be describing her brothers. Justin, too, looked to be dangerous, hotheaded, and capable of violence. Well, as for the last part, she'd witnessed that for herself. "I have a friend you might like, then, if you're looking for a different sort of man," he said. "Not a bit of brutality in him."

She smiled. "I didn't say I was looking. Not right now," she said.

"And I'll keep my eyes open, but I don't know that you'll find too many men like that in Neft," he added. "More of them seem to be like the fellow you encountered earlier."

"The one you knocked down for me," she said. "Was that why you had to leave the last place you worked? Because you got in a brawl with someone?"

"Not exactly."

"What was the disagreement about?"

He hesitated, and again she knew he was considering how much of a lie to tell. She was more and more intrigued. "The story you'll hear is that I was a little forward with a nobleman's daughter," he said. "It's just the tale I told because it's the sort of thing people believe and I didn't want them to ask more questions. But I wouldn't want you to hear it and think it was true."

"Well, I would believe it," she said with a smile. "I can see why a nobleman's daughter might like to flirt with you."

He laughed, as if that was genuinely funny. "I've only ever met one serramarra to talk to, and she'd rather claw my eyes out than have a conversation," he said. He clearly remembered something and said, "Well, two serramarra. But I wasn't flirting with her, either. Not much of one for flirting in general."

"So why did you have to leave?" she asked.

She didn't care about what he'd done so much as how he would answer—whether he would tell another falsehood or whether he would give her the truth. He considered his answer for a full minute, and then he offered a twisted smile. "I guess I was looking for a reason to walk out," he said. "I guess I wanted to be somewhere else."

She was oddly relieved. He hadn't told her anything, but he hadn't lied, either. He didn't want to lie to her, that was what mattered. "I guess you have a reason for being in Neft that you don't want to talk about," she said softly. "And maybe this time it *is* because of a girl."

"No," he said swiftly—and then he grinned. "Well, it wasn't *before* I met you."

That made her laugh out loud, Justin joining in, both of them giggling and shaking their heads like schoolchildren telling stupid jokes. "See, you *can* flirt if you try," she said. "Though maybe you were just trying to change the subject."

"Maybe I was," he said, still smiling.

She stood up, shaking out her skirts. Great Mother's glory, her robe was filthy! Not only street scum clinging to the hem, but streaks of mud and dirt in strategic spots, and a drop or two of blood. She looked down in dismay. "I don't know that I'll be able to get this clean. I may just have to burn it. I have no idea what Darris and Astira will say when they see me."

He had come fluidly to his feet, rising when she did. They had been sitting for so long that she had almost forgotten how big he was. Well, she was slender and not very tall—it was his muscle mass as much as his height that made him seem so large, she thought. "Didn't you say you planned to tell what happened?"

"Most of it," she replied. "I might change your part a little."

He lifted his eyebrows. "How so?"

"I think I'll make you a sweet old woman who invited me into her house and helped me clean up. I think that's a tale my listeners will find more to their liking."

He looked amused. "They might not believe it if they've noticed me walking you home."

"Oh, but you don't have to do that!"

"Maybe not, but I'm going to."

"Truly. Just give me directions—do you know where the Gisseltess place is?"

"No."

"And then you can—what? You don't know where it is? The footman told me everyone knew it."

"I haven't been in Neft all that long. Describe it to me. Maybe I just don't know it by name."

"It's a three-story house in a very pretty part of town. No ruffians on the street smelling of wine. There's a wrought-iron fence all around the property. Oh, and a flag on the roof. It's got a clan device, I think—a black bird holding a red flower."

Now the expression on his face was sardonic. "Oh, *that* house," he said. "Flying the Gisseltess colors. Yes, I know it."

"Excellent! So can you tell me how to get there?"

He held a hand out, as if ushering her toward the door. "I told you, I'll walk with you."

Uncertainly, she stepped outside, Justin right behind her. "But I told you, the Lestra doesn't like us to socialize with men."

"I thought it was your brothers who didn't like it."

They had started strolling together down the street at a rather leisurely pace. Ellynor had no idea where she was, so she had to assume Justin was, in fact, leading her in the proper direction. "Well, the Lestra is the one who's more likely to see me today," she replied tartly.

He grinned. "I'll only walk beside you till we're close. Then I'll let you go ahead, and I'll come a few paces behind you. No one will know we're together."

"If you'd just tell me the way to go—"

"When I held my last position," he said, interrupting her, "I rode with the noble's house guard. It was my job to see that he was safe. If I rode with his daughter, it was my job to keep *her* safe. Anyone who was assigned to me, that's what I did. I guarded them till they were at their destination." He glanced down at her, his brown eyes cool. "That's the only way I know how to go on. Finishing the task that's given to me. Taking care of whoever falls under my protection. Today that's you."

She was silent a moment. She had the sense that this was the truest thing he'd said to her all afternoon, and the confidence she would most have to honor. She understood what it meant to be compelled to do something, because it was integral to the soul. She understood people who could not compromise.

"Then I appreciate it," she said quietly. "I was lucky today that you were the one who found me."

"Luckier maybe if I'd found you first," he commented.

Now she smiled again. "Oh no! Because then you would have just pointed me in the proper direction and I would have been on my way. We would have exchanged maybe twenty words. We wouldn't have gotten to know each other at all."

He was the one to be quiet for a few paces. "So I suppose there's no chance we'll ever have a chance to talk like this again," he said.

"*See?*" she said merrily. "Flirting again! You're so much better at it than you pretend to be."

"I was only asking."

She stifled a sigh. "I don't think so. I don't even know if I'll be in Neft again for months. And you'd be gone by then."

"I might not be. You never know. I might settle in."

That was a lie, though she wasn't sure how she knew. "Anyway, if I did come back, I'd probably be with a whole cadre of novices, all here to hand out moonstones and give blessings to travelers. I wouldn't even have a chance to talk to you."

"But if you did," he said stubbornly. "If you were here and you were alone for some reason—"

"Then I'd come by the stables and look you up," she finished softly. "Yes, Justin, I believe I would."

More quickly than she'd expected, they were in a respectable part of town and she started to recognize landmarks. "I think I know where I am now," she told him.

"Left here and then up the hill."

"That's what I thought."

"I'll let you walk on ahead then," he said. "Don't worry, though. I'm right behind you. If anyone stops you, I'll be at your side in a matter of seconds."

"Thank you," she said, but he had already dropped back, and within a few paces they were entirely separated. Ellynor moved more quickly now, realizing just how much time had elapsed since she'd left, wondering if her companions were worried about her or furious, thinking she had idled away the day. One look at her robes would tell them most of the story; she did not think she would be in trouble for long.

Up the hill and there it was, the imposing home of Jenetta Gisseltess. Ellynor could not keep herself from glancing behind her once, right as she reached the front door. She was just in time to see Justin strolling past the high gate, eyes forward, mouth pursed in a whistle, hands carelessly in his back pockets. He did not look at her. He did not seem to be aware of her at all.

Her heart made a little plunge of disappointment just as the door opened and Astira started shrieking.

CHAPTER

6

I⊤ took about an hour to tell the whole household what had transpired on the streets, since not only Astira, but Darris and the Lestra had to hear the tale, and then the Lestra thought their hostess should know the details as well. "There is a civil guard in the city, and a magistrate who manages them, but I don't know any nobles who put much faith in any protection but their own soldiers," Jenetta said regretfully. "I will certainly send Faeber a message, but I don't know that he will be able to find this young woman's assailant."

Everyone had seemed to accept without question her tale of a teenage boy who had rescued her and a good-natured old woman who had taken her in. No one had bothered to ask how Ellynor had found her way home through streets that had baffled her once. The Lestra seemed most offended that the robes of a Daughter had not been enough to protect Ellynor from assault, and less worried about Ellynor herself. Jenetta continued to decry the dangers of the city streets, a sad commentary on the way the old king had allowed the realm to deteriorate.

Only Astira really seemed concerned with Ellynor, and she demanded the whole story in greater detail when the two girls were alone in their room. By this time it was late afternoon, and Ellynor found she was both exhausted and hungry.

"Do you realize what could have happened to you?" Astira demanded, helping Ellynor strip off her robe and investigate any bruises underneath. There were quite a few, mostly on her arms and ribs.

"I have a pretty clear idea."

"It can be painful enough if it's something you want, but to have a man take you against your will—" Astira shuddered. "Awful."

Ellynor opened her eyes wide. "So you've been with a man?" Unmarried Lirren girls found it hard to lose their virginity, since they could rarely evade their families' scrutiny, and Ellynor had not ever been in the position to try.

Astira busied herself checking the rips and tears in Ellynor's garment. "Once or twice."

"A man that you wanted to be with?" Ellynor pressed. Astira nodded. "And what was it like?"

Astira sighed. "Oh, it was wonderful and it was frightening and it was not at all what I expected. There was a lot more grunting and a lot more soreness," she said. "Still, I thought the world would end when he said he didn't love me."

"And your family didn't hunt him down when he dishonored you?"

Astira's woeful look dissolved with a laugh. "Is that what happens when a man abandons a Lirren girl? I rather like the idea of a father or a brother going out to thrash my unfaithful lover."

"Thrashing would be the least of it," Ellynor said.

"But no, they didn't. I didn't tell them all the details, though I know my mother suspected. It was humiliating. I just wanted to get as far away as I could."

"The Lumanen Convent?" Ellynor guessed.

Astira nodded. "That's why I joined."

"And are you glad or sorry that you did?"

"Oh, I'm very happy at the convent!" A pause. "Most days." Another pause. "Sometimes I wish we had a little more freedom. But I love the Silver Lady. I would not have you think I'm complaining."

Ellynor had never been sure how much she could confide in Astira, and she still wasn't sure. So she said lightly, "Oh, I think we all love the Silver Lady—and we all have days when we chafe somewhat. Even the Lestra must wish for a little more contact with the outside world from time to time."

Astira smiled and shook out Ellynor's robe. "I don't think you can put this back on," she said. "I'll give it to the servants, but I'm not sure they'll be able to get it clean. Did you bring another?"

"Yes, but only one. I hope it doesn't get soiled."

"I brought three. You can wear one of mine if you have to. Though it will be too long on you."

"How much longer will we be here, do you know?"

"Impossible to guess! Jenetta's mother is so much better today. Everyone is amazed. There is some talk that she might actually recover."

"So are we to keep watches again tonight?"

"Yes. The Lestra promised."

"Then I've got to get some sleep now. And some food! I think I must have missed a meal somewhere along the way."

Within the hour, Ellynor had eaten a simple meal and curled up on the mattress, Astira napping beside her. She had expected to fall directly to sleep, but instead she reviewed the events of the day. The lovely walk through Neft, with all its unfamiliar and fabulous sights. The few terrifying moments in her attacker's power.

The long talk with Justin. She could not decide why he appealed to her so much. Well, he had saved her virtue and possibly her life—she would have been grateful to anyone for such a service. But it was the conversation in the stables that had made her like him. She was comfortable around him, she thought, because he reminded her of men she knew—fiery men ready to skirmish at the slightest excuse, easily ruffled, quickly engaged, deadly with a sword. And his insistence on escorting her back had put her strongly in mind of her brothers' own unceasing watchfulness. But there was something about Justin's attitude that was different from her brothers'. He had accompanied her back to the Gisseltess house because he wanted her to be safe, not because he thought she was incapable of caring for herself. Because he valued her, not because he distrusted her.

And he had talked to her as equal to equal, seeming to be unaware of any gulfs that might be caused by gender, social status, or intellect. He had said he was not much of one for dalliance, but she guessed he knew a few women even so. Whoever they were, they had taught him to treat women with easy acceptance and practical friendship. He did not seem ready to offer them either worship or disdain.

She touched her lips, remembering how patiently he had held fresh water to her mouth. She thought he would be surprised to learn she considered him a kind man—she thought he probably did not think of himself that way. She thought perhaps he was not always kind. But he had been gentle with her. She had fallen in his path and he had taken her on as a responsibility, and he was clearly a man who discharged his responsibilities with utter thoroughness.

And with an absolutely disarming smile.

Remembering it, she smiled herself, and then smothered a sigh. Unlikely she would see that expression again, unlikely she would ever encounter Justin a second time. Better this way, both as devout Daughter and as obedient Lirren girl. No use courting trouble. Especially when it was so attractive.

* * *

By the evening of the following day, the Daughters were on their way back to the convent.

The old woman had improved so markedly by morning—partly, Elly-nor knew, due to her own secret ministrations—that it was clear to every-one she would not die after all. The Lestra had wanted to set out at noon, but some message arrived at the house, detaining them all, and so it was late afternoon before the cavalcade began its trip home. Ellynor thought the guards did not like the idea of traveling by night, but the Lestra had some reason for wanting to be at Lumanen early the following day. And so they were on their way, knowing nightfall would come before they were halfway home.

Ellynor herself loved to travel at night, so she was not at all discom-posed. It was the night of the new moon, so it was particularly dark out, and the icy stars seemed even more remote and unhelpful than usual. But she had no trouble seeing the path before them, following the shapes of the guards who rode in the lead, even discerning the shadowy silhouette of the Lestra in her black robes, almost invisible on her black horse.

Astira was in some distress. "I feel like something is going to leap out from the trees and jump on me," she whispered to Ellynor as they rode into the outer fringes of the forest. "And I can't *see* anything. What if I trip over a fallen log? What if there's a snake or a—a bat hanging in the tree, and I brush up against it as we ride by?"

"Don't worry. There's nothing in the path ahead of us that will harm you," Ellynor said in a soothing voice. "Here. I'll describe it to you as we go. To your left is an oak tree—there's a possum sleeping in the lower branches. It doesn't want to hurt you. Birds are resting in the trees on the other side of the road—a whole flock of them—and there's an owl cir-cling overhead. It's the only thing awake on this stretch of road except us. Now up ahead a little bit, there's a low branch hanging over the road—you might want to duck when we get close, but I'll give you warning—"

She continued with her ongoing descriptions, painting the way ahead in such an unalarming light that Astira relaxed beside her. Both of them were surprised when the small party came to a halt and one of the lead soldiers reined back to warn the Lestra of possible trouble before them.

"There's a shape on the road—we can't tell from here what it is—Daken's going to check and make sure it's not a body. Beast or man," he added grimly.

"I would hope it's not a man," the Lestra said sharply.

The guard shrugged. "Well, since we lost Rostiff and them—"

"It's not a body," Ellynor said, speaking before she'd paused to think.

"It's just a branch that's fallen and broken on the road. And there's a dark patch a little farther up, but that's just a mudslick. I think there must have been a storm that moved through here and pulled down trees and left a lot of water behind."

The guard looked at her, probably not realizing how clearly she could see his slight sneer. "Don't know how you can tell from here what's ahead and what isn't," he said, his tone more polite than his expression.

Ellynor shrugged, already sorry she'd opened her mouth, but feeling the need to defend herself. "I don't have much trouble seeing at night," she said.

That comment earned her the full, complete attention of the Lestra, who turned in her saddle and motioned Ellynor closer. By starlight, the square face seemed even more broad and set, the dark eyes even more intent. Silver sparkled along the Lestra's black robes, and moonstones cast a baleful glow around her throat and wrists.

"You can see clearly in full dark?" the Lestra demanded.

Ellynor nodded. "Pretty much so. Almost as clearly as in daylight. My brothers used to take me night hunting, sometimes, because I could always recognize game."

"So you have had this skill for how long?"

"I can't remember when I didn't."

The Lestra was regarding her with a narrowed attention that was completely unnerving. Ellynor thought Coralinda Gisseltess didn't have much trouble seeing in the dark, either. "It was you who watched with Jenetta's mother in the blackest hours of the night, was it not?" the Lestra asked now.

"Yes, my lady. Both nights."

"And she recovered some of her strength after you sat with her."

Alarm sparkled through Ellynor. She had never claimed any particular healing skill while she'd been at the convent and she did not want to take any credit now. She did not want to draw attention to herself. "We all sat with her the past two days, my lady," she said in a subdued voice. "And we all prayed to the Pale Mother for mercy."

The Lestra nodded. "You know, do you not, that the Silver Lady marks some of her servants for greater honor, greater strength?" the older woman said now. "And that each of her Daughters feels a special relationship to her at a particular point in the Mother's cycle? I, of course, am at my strongest—my mind is at its sharpest—when the moon is full and I can bathe in all her glory. I am the Lestra, the Whole Moon Daughter. Shavell and Darris are Split Moon Daughters, Shavell at her peak when the moon is halfway through its waning cycle, Darris when the moon is halfway to full. There are many who thrive under the three-quarter moon, who feel the Pale Mother's power run silver through their veins when she takes a crescent shape. But I think you might be that rarest creature of all—one who is most closely bonded to the Pale Mother when she is at her most secretive and unknowable. I think you must be a Dark Moon Daughter."

Ellynor bowed her head. She wondered if the Black Mother was witnessing this scene, and if so, whether she was laughing. "I would be honored if that were true, my lady," she said.

"We cannot yet be sure," the Lestra said. "But I will watch you, and I will judge. For tonight, can you make yourself useful? Can you ride ahead with the lead men, and help them determine where hazards lie?"

"Gladly, my lady."

"Then lead us, my Daughter."

Ellynor spurred her horse forward to ride next to the surly guard, nodding her head civilly and hoping he would not blame her for how this hour had unfolded. "Just tell me what you see as you see it," he said in a neutral voice. "I'll decide if we need to stop or slow."

"All right," she said, and began to recite for him all the sights of the night woods, much as she had for Astira. "There. See it? That shape in the woods? It's a wolf, but it's not watching us. And ahead, about twenty yards, there's a dip in the road, pretty abrupt. We might have everyone be a little careful there. Don't worry about that shadow hanging down—it looks like a snake, but it's just a vine. Nothing that bites."

As she kept up her running commentary, which she was sure the soldiers did not appreciate, she reflected that she had one thing to be thankful for. She had caught the Lestra's fierce and unrelenting attention, something she had hoped never to do; she had made herself visible to those unwinking black eyes. But the Lestra still did not know her name. Ellynor still might skate through her days at the convent anonymous as any other novice.

As long as she kept herself out of trouble.

CHAPTER
7

I<small>T</small> had been a calculated move to rescue the novice as she fought against an unwanted embrace. Justin had taken only a split second to react, but in that space of time he had weighed what he might stand to gain from such an intervention, what he could potentially lose. There was no chance that he might be jeopardizing his own life by deciding to battle this clumsy stranger. However, he might win an ally at the Lumanen Convent. That was worth taking a risk for, he thought.

Senneth would have wanted him to save the novice, whether or not he could turn such an action to his advantage. Cammon, too. But Tayse would have understood Justin's overriding motive, and approved.

It had been an unexpected bonus to be charmed by the girl who had so recently been a victim. She was small-boned and delicate (what was she *thinking*? traipsing about a city like Neft entirely undefended), but with a force of will that quickly made him stop viewing her as helpless. Not a beauty, not the way Kirra was, but with a pretty, dainty face and a creamy complexion. Her eyes were a blue so dark that at first he had thought they were black. And she had that incredible hair. He had never seen anything like it.

The minute he left her behind at the Gisseltess mansion, Justin was sorry she had stepped out of his life.

But he had so much more to do than think about a slim and smiling young woman, whether or not she was a Daughter of the Pale Mother. He had a job at the stables, for one thing, which took up a little more of his time than he would have liked.

And he had a second job, which had yielded precious few results during the week he had been in Neft. Justin did not like a waiting game. He did not thrive on enforced inactivity. He liked to have a target, an enemy, a goal.

This assignment in Neft was likely to drive him mad.

After leaving Ellynor at the Gisseltess place, Justin circled the neighborhood once, just to make sure she hadn't been cast out of the house when the others failed to believe her story. But, somewhat to his disappointment, Ellynor did not reemerge. He returned to the stables to find Delz there and irate that Justin had left the place unattended.

"Anyone could have come in and walked out with half the horses!" the older man fumed. "And the Silver Lady only knows how many came by, wanting to leave their mounts behind, but there was no one to take their reins—or their money!"

"I was only gone twenty minutes," Justin said, which was a lie, but he was guessing Delz hadn't been back much longer than that. "Nobleman asked me to lead his horse while he hauled a package halfway across town. Didn't want to offend him, did I? He might be back needing more favors."

Delz looked both mollified and skeptical. "Marlord?" he asked.

Justin shrugged. "I don't know. I can't tell one from another."

"He pay you?"

Justin pulled out a silver coin and flicked it to Delz. "Here. Keep it. Didn't mean to make you worry."

Delz pocketed it but still looked disgruntled. "You're not as steady as I'd like," he grumbled. "Gone a lot when a man expects you to be in place."

"I get restless." A pause. "I can look for work elsewhere if I don't suit."

"No, no. I still need the extra hands. It's just that—you're gone a lot."

Justin shrugged again. "Well, I'm back now. What's left to be done?"

They worked together the next couple of hours, cleaning stalls, forking out hay, and pumping fresh water, and by then Delz was back in charity with Justin. He hadn't seemed to notice that his new employee wasn't particularly talkative, or maybe he didn't mind carrying the bulk of the conversation, for he frequently engaged in long, rather dull monologues about episodes in his life. Just from boredom, Justin had put together a fairly coherent picture from the tales Delz told out of sequence. Farmer's son, once married, wife ran off, almost married a second time but the girl's family had decided Delz wasn't good enough for her and made her a better match. Odd jobs in Fortunalt and along the southern coast before he ended up here. Now that he was a business owner, he hoped to find a third woman who might be persuaded to take him, and to stay.

Justin thought he'd rather still be living on the streets of Ghosenhall than endure such a life.

A half dozen riders came in as they were doing the evening chores, dropping off horses for a night or two. This hour of the day, and early morning when travelers headed out again, were their busiest times. Delz mostly handled the money while Justin got the animals settled in. The tired and placid ones were the easiest to put away, but Justin liked the spirited ones better, nervous and edgy around strangers. "Come on, girl," he said, coaxing a particularly wary mare into a stall. "I'll take care of you. No need to be afraid at all."

Once it was true night, they were less likely to do any business, so Delz took off for his dinner and Justin finished sweeping. Delz owned a tiny house not ten yards from the stable. He had rigged up a cord that customers could pull at the stable door to ring a bell in his house, so he could be on hand in minutes if someone needed him.

This meant no one had to stay overnight with the horses.

Once Delz returned from dinner, Justin was free for the day. By this time he was ravenous, so he usually took his meals at one of the local taverns, most often the Golden Boar. Tonight he sat alone at a small table in the corner; other nights he might take a seat at the bar counter. He always ate in silence, keeping a look of indifference on his face but listening as hard as he could for any information someone might drop. So far, nothing of interest had been inadvertently revealed to him over his meals. He'd heard plenty about the road conditions, the king's misguided foreign policies, the excellence of Helven beer, a certain woman named Dorina, and what kind of opportunities there might be for employment in Forten City, if a man wasn't afraid of the sea. But nothing about Coralinda Gisseltess or her activities.

No mention of troops leaving the convent in secret and carrying out illicit raids for the Lestra. No reports of houses burned down in the night, of fights between the Lestra's men and the civil guards paid to keep a minor nobleman protected. Such things had been whispered back in Ghosenhall. There had been dreadful tales of mysterious fires started in the night on the property of aristocrats who had done something to offend the Lestra. Tales of whole families gone missing after an unmarked cadre of soldiers passed through.

But Justin hadn't seen any large body of convent men march down the streets of Neft. The biggest contingent of soldiers he'd seen had been the group torturing the mystic Lara.

And the ones who'd come to town yesterday escorting Coralinda Gisseltess and a smattering of her novices. That particular group of soldiers had holed up in a small inn on the other side of town and hadn't been seen all day. If they were doing damage to nonbelievers, they were doing it in a high state of secrecy.

Justin needed to get to the convent itself. He needed to be able to watch the various roads that led to and from the compound in order to judge what kind of activity the Lestra's guards were engaged in. He wouldn't learn much loitering here in Neft.

He had just laid his fork down and pushed his plate aside when a man dropped into the seat across from him. Keeping an impassive expression on his face, Justin inspected the newcomer. Older man, possibly in his late fifties, with disorderly gray hair and a lived-in face, wearing clothes that he might have had on his back for the last four days. Everything about him looked rumpled. His expression was mild, but his eyes were extraordinarily keen. A smart man who didn't mind being taken for a fool, Justin decided.

"You look like the gambling sort to me," the older man said and laid down a pack of cards.

Justin relaxed a little, smiling slightly. "I can play most games," he said. "Don't like high stakes, though. I have a lot of other uses for my money."

His companion shuffled the deck with enough competence to show he wasn't going to pretend he didn't know what he was doing. This was not an attempt to con; this was an attempt to combat boredom. "Still, you have to put money down, or what does it matter who wins?" the other man said. "Care for a few hands?"

"Sure," Justin said. "Name your preference. I'm Justin, by the way."

"Faeber. How about two-point cross-cradle?"

Justin nodded. "I'm in."

They played a few rounds, talking sporadically, watching each other over the cards. Their luck was pretty even, although, within an hour, Faeber pulled ahead by a few coppers. Justin was interested to note that most of the other men who came and went through the tavern doors glanced in their direction, and nodded if Faeber noticed them, but no one else came to join them.

Justin took the next hand, winning back the coins he'd lost and a few of Faeber's. "That was neatly done," the older man approved. "You play a patient game."

Justin grinned broadly and shuffled the cards. "Only sometimes," he said. "I can be reckless in a certain mood."

Faeber leaned back in his chair. "Feeling reckless this afternoon?" he asked in a genial voice.

Justin kept his gaze on the cards, but all his senses sharpened. He had wondered if anyone had witnessed his brawl in the street, and if so, whether someone would come to investigate. "I saw a young woman who looked like she needed help," he replied quietly. "I could have walked on by. That wasn't the mood I was in this afternoon."

"Perhaps you didn't notice that the man you took issue with considers himself a nobleman."

Interesting phrasing. "Perhaps you hadn't heard that the lady he accosted was a Daughter of the Pale Mother," Justin countered.

"Oh, I'm absolutely certain you did the right thing by protecting one of the Silver Lady's own. Wish I'd been there myself to earn a little credit with the goddess. I'm just telling you that your overeager suitor came to me to complain about bad behavior from strangers on the street. I told him I'd look into it."

"And why would you be the one he complained to?"

Faeber resettled his weight. "I'm magistrate of the town. We have a small civil guard in Neft, and they answer to me. But there always seems to be something else that folks think I should be responsible for. So now I collect taxes for the king. I mediate disputes between merchants. I officiate at weddings. I say a few words at funerals. Kind of have my fingers in a whole lot of different pies."

"So some idiot who's probably not even Thirteenth House thinks he can behave like a ruffian and then complains to you when somebody stops him," Justin said.

"That's right. I told him I'd find you and take care of everything."

Justin lifted his eyes to give Faeber one unfriendly stare. "And how do you intend to take care of me?" he asked in a level voice.

Faeber's face split in a grin. "Why, buy you a drink, of course! I've wanted to punch that boy in the face many times these past three years. Assaulting women in the streets. My streets. And then whining when a good man steps in to stop him!"

Justin laughed. "You hardly know I'm a good man. Can't judge by just one thing."

"You don't cheat at cards," Faeber observed. "So that's two things."

"Well, I'd appreciate the drink, in any case."

Faeber called over the waitress, an older woman who was plain and efficient, and they sipped a couple of glasses of ale, idly talking. Well, the conversation appeared to be idle. Justin was well aware that Faeber was still trying to gauge what kind of man he was, while Justin was engaged in his own complicated game, trying to appear honest and harmless, if a little malcontented.

"So how long do you plan to stay in Neft?" Faeber asked as they finished their drinks.

Justin shrugged. "Till I figure out something different to do."

"Heard you had a little trouble up Storian way. Or was it Danalus-trous?"

Justin didn't know the Twelve Houses well enough to know whether Storian boasted daughters of the age to be forming disastrous liaisons with soldiers, but he was ready to bet Faeber did. Just his luck, Justin knew plenty about the serramarra of that other House. And Kirra would be only too happy to pretend she'd had a relationship with him, if he was ever required to produce proof.

"Danalustrous," he said shortly.

"I hear marlord Malcolm has two daughters, both of them beautiful. One's a dark-haired thing, one's fair."

"That's right."

Faeber took the last sip of his beer. "That yellow-haired girl, they say she's a mystic. A shiftling."

Justin's hands stilled on his glass. "She is."

Faeber shook his head. "People around these parts, they don't care much for mystics. Well, let me put it more plainly, son. If that girl were ever to think of coming to visit you here? Anybody who knew about it would want to stone her in the street."

Justin refrained from retorting that anyone who tried to harm Kirra would find himself slashed to ribbons by a great golden cat—or whatever shape Kirra chose to take at that moment—and would undoubtedly be further mauled by Donnal, who was never far from her side. He also had to discard the idea of saying she was unlikely to come visiting him here, because it was *exactly* the sort of thing Kirra might do—show up unannounced and start looking for entertainment. Instead he leaned back in his chair and coolly inspected the other man. "I'd think the magistrate of a town would have something to say about that," he said softly.

Faeber's mouth twisted. "You would think that," he said. "It was truer before the Lestra's men started running tame in Neft. I've broken up a mob or two in my time, but I've found it's easier to warn people off. The Lestra's made it plain that she abhors mystics, and what the Lestra does, people around here are like to take up. So I'd just as soon turn mystics back at the city limits. Let 'em find someplace else to go, and not bring their magic here."

Justin pushed his empty glass back and forth on the table. "So you don't despise mystics yourself?" he said.

Faeber's keen eyes grew keener. "Didn't exactly say that."

Justin shrugged. "You don't know me. You don't know where I stand.

But I can tell you now that I'm not wearing a moonstone, and I wouldn't lift a rock to throw at any man just because he was different than me."

"Might draw your sword to defend someone, maybe, if you saw anybody else throwing those rocks?"

Justin shrugged. "Maybe."

"You might not be saying that out loud to too many folks here."

"Well, I haven't bothered to have that many conversations," Justin drawled.

Faeber let loose a crack of laughter. "You're a tough one, aren't you?" he said, but his tone was somewhat admiring. "I don't quite have you figured out."

"In an hour? I wouldn't think so."

Faeber placed his hands on the table, as if getting ready to push himself out of the chair. "You'd be surprised how many men you can read in five minutes," he said. "But I know enough about you now, I believe."

Justin looked inquiring. "What do you think you know?"

Faeber hauled himself up, but stood there a moment gazing down at Justin. The look on the magistrate's face was considering. "You're a dangerous young man," he said abruptly. "But you're not looking for trouble. At the moment. I imagine that when you do, you can be fairly destructive."

Justin gave him one long, sober look. "All I did was take on one bully in the street. I'm not trying to make a name. I just want to settle in and lead a quiet life."

Faeber nodded. "See that you behave yourself then."

"I'll do my best."

So there had been at least one unfortunate consequence of coming to Ellynor's aid: Justin had drawn the attention of the local magistrate, who was likely to keep watching him. But even that might not be so problematic, if Justin had read Faeber as correctly as Faeber had read him. The older man wasn't pleased by having his town overrun with convent soldiers, though he probably didn't waste his energy trying to control them. And he didn't hate mystics. He hadn't said so outright, but he hadn't burst out with the virulent rhetoric Justin would have expected if Faeber was a true believer. So that was something to keep in mind. If he ever had need of an ally, Faeber might be one. Particularly if Justin asked for help as a King's Rider. He thought he was likely to get a great deal of assistance then.

And even if he'd guessed wrong—even if Faeber was at this very moment telling his own men to pay special attention to this sullen new arrival, to watch him night and day—he couldn't be sorry he'd interfered this afternoon. Not if it meant he'd saved Ellynor's life.

There was still the matter of how to get enough free time to take a closer look at the convent, which Justin judged to be about a four-hour ride away. He wasn't sure Delz would be moved to give him a couple days off merely because Justin announced he had "business" to attend to. He was in luck, though. Three days later, Delz's nephew arrived for a brief stay, and Delz himself came sidling over to Justin.

"It's my sister's boy, and I've promised him some work," the stable-master said. "Now, I'm not saying there's not enough here for three sets of hands to do, and I'll certainly pay you your share while he's here, but if you were wanting to take off a couple days, well, this would be the time to do it."

Justin scowled. "You said you had work for me. You didn't mention that it would dry up every other week."

"No, no, the boy's only been here one other time in the past six months! Feel free to stay! I'll set him to mending tack and fixing the back stall where it's been kicked out. I just thought if you were looking for an opportunity—"

Justin hunched a shoulder. "I've got things to attend to, as it happens," he said ungraciously. "I'll take a day or two and go about my own matters. And maybe sometime when it's convenient for *me* to take time off, you'll remember how obliging I was now."

"Yes, excellent, we'll work this out," Delz promised, looking relieved. "I'll tell my nephew he'll earn full wages tomorrow."

That afternoon, Justin loaded up provisions and headed out, taking the northern road in case anyone happened to be watching him. Once well outside the city limits, he cut sharply southeast, following back roads and overgrown trails till he entered the forest surrounding the convent.

By this time, it was dark, and he proceeded with caution, staying well off the main trails that wound through the woods. He wished he had Donnal with him to take animal shape and sift the night air for any signs of danger.

He wished Kirra was here, to turn Justin himself into a wild beast. Such an act was forbidden, but she had done it anyway, twice, and each time Justin had found himself exhilarated by the experience. Now he often found himself wondering what it would be like to be a bird, a fox, a snake. Next time he saw Kirra, he would ask.

Nonetheless, his human stealth was good enough to bring him unobserved to the edge of the clearing holding the great convent. Still behind a scrim of trees, Justin observed the huge building, white and imposing even by starlight. It lay at the heart of a fenced compound so big that it also contained guards' barracks, stables, small gardens—what was in essence a self-contained community.

At every window, in all five stories, a single candle burned, giving the place a look of appealing warmth and welcome. Justin was close enough to see shapes patrolling the top edge of the thick walls—close enough to catch what sounded like women's voices raised in song. What kind of people would be outside at midnight, singing? Justin supposed they were novices engaged in some convent ritual. The voices were sweet, ethereal, impossible to understand from this distance. Still, they had a sort of mesmerizing effect, making Justin want to push through the tree limbs, run up to the wall, and vault to the top, so he could look into the upturned faces of the girls who must be gathered in the courtyard.

He wondered if Ellynor was one of the singers. The thought made him even more desirous of getting a closer look.

He stayed where he was.

In about twenty minutes, the singing stopped. Now the night air carried fainter sounds back to him, light laughter, muted voices, the echo of a door pulling shut. The guards walking the high perimeter conferred as they passed each other, but there was no other movement, no other noise, from within the walls.

Soon, he thought, everyone would be asleep for the night.

Justin scouted the terrain a little more closely, decided he was better off above the sight line. He retreated a dozen yards to secure his horse even farther back—close enough to retrieve quickly, not close enough to be seen from the road—and returned to his first vantage point to climb a sturdy tree. Tayse had been pretty certain the convent boasted only one entrance big enough to allow a contingent of men and horses through. If Coralinda Gisseltess was planning to send her men out on a raid, they would leave through that exit.

Justin made himself as comfortable as possible on a broad shelf of tree, and settled in to wait.

CHAPTER

8

VERY little happened during the next twenty hours. Justin dozed in his tree, less comfortable all the time, and half listened to what he could overhear of convent life. In mid-morning, there were the distinctive sounds of metal against metal—soldiers training for combat, he guessed—and now and then pieces of conversation would float to him when guards on the wall stopped to exchange comments. A couple of times during the day, there was a surge of girlish voices as a wave of novices broke through the front door into the courtyard. At those times, Justin sat up straighter and tried to pick Ellynor out of the crowd. But they were too far away, and her most distinctive feature, her hair, was not on display. None of the women left the compound, though from time to time a solitary soldier would exit and take the road south. Just as infrequently, groups of two or three men would return. No way to know what business they were on, but they did not look large enough to be raiding parties.

A few hours after sunset, however, he caught the sense of purposeful movement from behind the walls, and the sound of many hooves in motion at once. He craned his neck and saw massed shadows inside the courtyard, and then the ringing voice of some kind of sergeant at arms calling out commands. "Move out. Follow me." A small detachment of soldiers was about to go on a ride.

Justin hurriedly shimmied down the tree, collected his own horse, and waited in silence till the column of men made an orderly exit through the gate. Justin counted about twenty men, all wearing the black-and-silver of the Lestra's livery. When it was clear there were no more stragglers, Justin followed a fair distance back. They would be easy to track, he thought—though, to tell the truth, they were moving with a practiced quietness that would be the envy of the Riders.

Justin couldn't think that any group of soldiers setting off in full dark and enforced silence could be on anything except covert business.

They rode straight west until the trail out of the forest connected them to a wider and more well-used road, and then swung north. Nocklyn territory, Justin realized. He was not conversant with all the alliances and political leanings of the Twelve Houses—where was Kirra when you actually needed her?—but he remembered that Kirra and Senneth had considered Nocklyn likely to ally with the rebels if there was ever an uprising against the king.

But some of the Nocklyn nobles might not side with the marlord. There might be a few pockets of gentry that considered themselves loyal to the crown.

Or noble estates where mystics were welcome—who might even claim sons and daughters who had magic in their veins. The Lestra might very well have a quarrel with such individuals.

The convent soldiers moved a little more quickly once they hit the main road, and Justin increased his own pace to keep up. Still, they maintained a fairly steady gait, designed to cover a considerable distance, and Justin was yawning in the saddle by the time they'd been on the move more than three hours. Around midnight, he guessed. How long did they plan to ride?

Not much longer, as it turned out. A few miles later, there was a short, sharp order, and Justin sped up in time to see the whole contingent turn toward the right down a much smaller road. They were in flatlands, with trees only in unhelpful and widely spaced configurations, so Justin hung back as far as he dared, not wanting anyone to glance back and catch his shadow on their trail. He almost missed the next turn the group made, onto a well-kept lane that looked like a private drive, but thereafter, it was easy to guess their destination.

Two turns later, they had entered the grounds of what appeared to be a small estate. Details were hard to see in the dark, but there was a pretty sweep of ground down to a house that was small by the notions of the nobility, but spacious by anyone else's standards. Behind the house at some distance Justin thought he could spot outbuildings—a barn, a dairy house, possibly a small barracks for the house guard, if there was one—and then an undulation of land into what might be gardens or farmland. Fortunately for him, the eastern edge of the property was delineated by a curve of decorative woods, planted as a windbreak or landscaping element. Justin made his way there while the soldiers rode straight up the carriageway that led to the house.

Someone was on guard just inside the ornamental gate. Justin had barely found his position inside the tree line when he heard a shout and a challenge, then the quick clash and ring of battle. Two house guards, he judged—both silenced within seconds. He saw the convent guards still in motion, slowing only as they came right up against the house and fanned out.

A bright golden flare as someone lit a torch. Then the globe of light danced, reproduced, moved down the line of soldiers, so that each individual raised his own flaming brand aloft. Justin found himself suspending his breath, his hands taut on the reins, as the soldiers all leaned forward at the same moment to hold their torches to the timbers of the house.

Bright Mother of the blue morning, they were going to burn this house, and everyone sleeping inside it.

Justin's horse danced under him, unnerved by his sudden tension or the hard pressure of his hands and knees. What should he do? Shout a warning? Charge in for a rescue? He could not possibly defeat twenty men, not by himself. But to sit by and do nothing while who knew how many people were incinerated in their beds—he did not have to hear Senneth's strictures to know that was wrong.

Then—a shout—the sound of shattering glass—voices raised and a sudden commotion. Someone in the house had roused at the smell of smoke or—no! Bodies were pouring from one of the outbuildings. A civil guard was at hand after all. Justin relaxed a little; at least now it was not his obligation to raise the alarm. He saw faces at the top-story windows, heard more muffled screaming, caught the frenzied music of blades playing against blades.

It was quickly obvious that the house guard was too sparse and too poorly trained to offer the Lestra's soldiers any real challenge. One by one, the lesser fighters were cut down, furiously though they battled. The leaping orange flames threw a garish illumination over the field of combat, and Justin could clearly see each unequal battle, each violent death.

There were not enough house guards to engage all of the Lestra's men, and so some of the convent soldiers were watching at the doors as the residents came streaming out. One by one, the soldiers cut them down.

Justin watched with his stomach clenched, his throat aching with the shouts he swallowed. Many who raced through the front door, intent on escaping fire, appeared to be servants, dressed in plain sleeping garments or very little clothing at all. They were shown no mercy. The few that Justin picked out as the property owners—an older man and a woman who could be his wife, a middle-aged man who might be a brother, a boy and a girl who looked to be fourteen or fifteen—all of them came running out into the flame-streaked night.

All of them ended up with a sword through the heart.

Justin felt his own heart grow small as a lump of coal, felt it contract in his chest and catch fire.

There was a shout and a great rush of motion from the back of the house—apparently there had been an exit there that was not as well-guarded as the main one. Three figures broke free of the melee of flame, shadow and sword, racing up the slight incline toward the line of trees where Justin waited. Two soldiers gave chase. More shapes came around from the back of the house and were instantly engaged in battle. The mounted soldiers quickly caught up with the men on foot. But the nobles offered a spirited defense and did not go quietly, shouting out hoarse insults as they lifted their fine, expensive dress swords and tried to bring their tormentors down to death with them.

Overlooked in the frenzy was a small, lone shape, fleeing on short legs straight to the woods where Justin was hiding.

A child. A boy. Maybe five or six years old. Seconds away from escaping the slaughter.

Justin swung himself down from the saddle and crouched, gauging the child's trajectory. Not a single look back—someone must have told the boy to start running and never once stop. He was three steps from the woods—two—and still no one had seen him. All of the soldiers were preoccupied with larger game. The child came tearing through the trees, head down and fists pumping. Justin snatched him up in one easy motion, his hand across the boy's mouth, his arms crushing the small body to his chest.

Not surprisingly, the boy fought, pummeling Justin's face and shoulders with ineffectual hands, landing a few kicks with surprising force, trying to bite, trying to scream. Justin squeezed him tighter, attempting to hold the boy still enough to understand his words. "I won't hurt you. I want to save you. I'm not with those men. I can help you. Be quiet. I can help you."

Abruptly the boy stopped fighting and looked up at Justin, his eyes huge and liquid in the impossible light. For a reflexive moment, Justin was reminded of Cammon, whose own eyes were so limitless, whose own expression was so fey. Maybe this was the magic child, the one the soldiers had slaughtered the house in order to destroy.

Maybe Justin had had to sit there, helplessly witnessing all this horror, merely to make this simple find.

Save this single life.

"Trust me," he whispered now. The boy didn't nod, didn't move at all, didn't stop staring up at Justin. "Don't scream. The soldiers will hear you if you scream, and then we'll both be dead. I'm going to put us on my horse and ride out of here. We'll be safe."

Cautiously Justin lifted his hand, but the boy did not scream—didn't make a sound at all. His little body, at first so full of rage and terror, was now alarmingly limp, though he was still conscious, still aware. By the Bright Mother's red eye, what was Justin going to do with this child? Take him to safety, yes, but where was safety? Could Faeber be trusted? Would someone in Neft recognize this boy, know which household he belonged to? And once word got out that the mansion had burned down, wouldn't someone wonder how Justin had happened to be on the scene to effect a rescue?

And if the soldiers truly had been hoping to kill this child, wouldn't they quickly realize who had come to safety in Neft—and try again?

Well, Justin would deal with those questions after he'd accomplished his first task, which was to get the child away from this scene of carnage to someplace that was even marginally more secure. Mounting quickly, moving quietly, and frequently looking over his shoulder to make sure no one saw him, he turned his horse back up the private drive and down the quiet avenues that led toward the wide thoroughfare.

And then—oh, thieves' luck, which had graced him so often in his miscreant days!—a carriage turned from the main road and began a lumbering descent toward the private property below. Friends or family members gone on a long journey, chancing the night travel because they were so eager to make it home.

Justin didn't even hesitate. He charged forward, one hand upraised, one arm holding the lost boy tightly to his chest. "Hold there! No farther! There's trouble below!" he called out.

There was a confusion of shouts and horses as the coachman hauled the carriage to a stop and two guards jumped off the back, swords already drawn. A man stuck his head out of one window, demanding to know what was happening, and Justin could hear a woman's voice, anxious and frightened, sounding inside the carriage. The coachman fumbled for a torch, and there was a sudden brief, inadequate light. Justin rode forward, the boy balanced between his knees, both hands now lifted to show he offered no threat.

"Go no farther," he warned. "The house below is on fire. The—"

"On fire!" the man in the carriage cried. "We must go! Maybe we can help! I see it! Look, Jassie, through the trees—the sky is all lit up! Hurry!"

"No," Justin said sharply. "Soldiers are there ready to kill anyone who might arrive. They set the blaze."

"Soldiers!" the man repeated, and peered hard through the darkness. "Who are you? What are you doing here? What is—why are—"

But the woman in the carriage was smarter than her companion. She thrust her head out the window beside him, pale and pretty by torchlight. "Soldiers—from the convent?" she asked in a breathless voice.

Justin nodded. "Yes. Looking for mystics, I'm guessing—or those who sympathize with them."

"Mystics!" the man exclaimed, rearing back as if slapped. The woman stilled him with a touch on the arm.

"And they've—they've burned the place down? Everyone in it—dead? Are you sure? Everyone?"

Justin kicked his horse a few paces closer. "Except this one. I saw him running and I snatched him up—"

But he didn't have to explain the rest. With a muffled shriek, the woman flung herself out of the carriage and stumbled the few paces to Justin's side. The boy stirred in his arms and cried, "Jassie! Jassie! Jassie!" Clearly Justin had found the one safe haven the boy might have in this world—assuming Jassie and her escort had the sense to get away fast. He lowered the boy into Jassie's arms, and they collapsed into a small heap on the ground.

Jassie's companion had climbed more slowly out of the carriage, and now he stood staring down at the two on the ground. In a moment, he looked back up at Justin, his face grim. "Hunting mystics, are they?" he said in a quiet voice. "Coralinda Gisseltess is going to have to spread a wider net than that if she wants to catch them all."

"And I think she is prepared to do so," Justin said. "You must leave. Now. There is nothing you can do for the folks below. Save yourselves—take this child. Keep going."

The man nodded and put his hands on Jassie's shoulders, pulling her and the boy up and bundling them, still embraced, into the carriage. One foot on the step to climb back in, the man turned around to give Justin a final somber inspection.

"Who are *you*?" he asked. "You didn't come here by chance."

Justin shook his head. "I saw the soldiers going by with such stealth, and I was curious. I followed. I never thought to see—to stand by and do nothing—" He shook his head. "It has been a terrible night," he ended quietly.

"More terrible than you know," the man said. "But your part in it at least has brought some brightness. His life saved—and certainly ours."

"Not if you linger any longer," Justin said. "Go."

"Tell me your name, at least?"

"I am in service to the king," he said, and the man gave a jerky nod and ducked inside the carriage. The coachman and the guards, who all this time had hovered uneasily, resumed their places. In moments the carriage was turned around and back on the road. Justin stood guard at the intersection until the coach was well and truly out of sight—far enough away that the Lestra's men would not even realize it had come this way.

He took one last look over his shoulder, where indeed the sky was a hazy yellow from the fire, and then he nudged his horse forward. One turn and he was back on the main road, heading south toward Neft.

More tired and more wretched than he had ever been in his life.

He had thought he had a fair grasp on cruelty, understood the passions that could drive a man to violence. There had been times in his life he had been none too picky about the methods he employed to get what he wanted, and he was capable of extreme action if he was fighting to stay alive. But he had never engaged in cold-blooded murder. Could not understand what drove a man to try it—especially when there was no immediate gain. No riches to be had, no feud to settle, no insult to avenge. Just—a desire to eradicate an enemy.

An enemy who possessed magic. Or tolerated magic. Or loved someone who did.

Someone who was different. Not a threat, except to a way of life. Offering no harm except a point of view.

Those people were dangerous in the Lestra's eyes.

Justin rode slowly home, wearier by the mile.

The only solution was to grow even more dangerous to the Lestra than she thought the mystics were. To draw her attention.

To fight back.

CHAPTER
9

SENNETH was sweating and out of breath when Coeval called a halt to their workout. The Rider—a tall, lean man whose black hair had given way only partly to silver—sheathed his sword and gave her an approving nod.

"Better," he said. "You've been practicing."

"Lifting weights," she said, wiping a sleeve across her face. It was early autumn and cool enough outside that most people were shivering, not sweating. But most people hadn't just spent an hour in the training yard of the palace trying to prevent Coeval from killing them. "I'm getting stronger, but I'm still not as fast as you are."

He gave her a spare smile. "You'll never be as fast as I am."

She laughed. He wasn't bragging, he was merely telling the truth. She would never be as fast as any of the Riders, although she had nearly defeated one of the younger men a couple of days ago. Her finest moment in the weeks since she had begun regular workouts with the king's elite. "My goal is to defeat Tayse someday," she said, a challenge in her voice. "Will I ever achieve it?"

"No," he said simply. "There are days that I can, or Hammond, or even Tir, but not two days in succession. You'll never be that strong."

They began walking slowly toward the big building where all their practice gear was housed and where they trained in truly inclement weather. Though Senneth had found herself training outdoors in rain, in sleet, and in biting wind, and the Riders hadn't seemed to find any of *those* conditions inclement. "What about Justin?" she asked.

Coeval nodded. "Justin's not as good as Tayse, but he will be. When he's Tayse's age, no one will be able to touch him."

If he lives that long, Senneth wanted to say. A soldier's life was chancy at best, and if they really did find themselves in a war, the Riders would all be in the heart of it, battling to defend their king. It was a gloomy thought. "Well, I hope he hasn't realized that," she said lightly instead. "He's already too sure of himself."

Coeval laughed. A rider named Janni came jogging up, inviting Coeval to a match, and the older man turned away to spar with her. Senneth continued trudging toward the open door of the great shed.

Tir was leaning against the outside wall, one foot against the building, arms crossed on his chest. He resembled his son so much that Senneth always had to look again to make sure it wasn't Tayse standing there, mysteriously aged by twenty years but still powerful, still watchful, still wrapped in an aura of brooding menace.

Tir had not been interested in the slightest when Tayse told him he had found the woman he loved. But he had paid Senneth some attention when she started working out with the Riders, and from time to time he had offered her a critique of her stance or her swing. His comments always proved to be both accurate and helpful. She knew he didn't care if she broke his son's heart. But if she was going to be in any way involved in protecting the king, he wanted her to be invincible.

"How'd I do?" she asked him now, slowing to a stop.

He gave his head a quick, negative shake. "You fight like someone with a knife up her sleeve," he said.

That made no sense. Every soldier carried a variety of blades; who knew when one might be lost or batted away? "I don't know what that means," she said.

"You don't care if you lose the first bout. You know you have another weapon. But that's a dangerous way to fight. It almost always means you *will* forfeit the first round."

He wasn't talking about weaponry. He was talking about magic. Senneth knew that if her opponent outfenced her, she could drop her sword and call up fire. "You're right," she said slowly. "I'll try to change my attitude."

"But your swing is improving," he said, almost grudgingly. "You're gaining power."

"More to work on."

"There always is."

She left him in the training yard, dropped her practice sword in its allotted slot, and walked slowly from the training yard to the palace. She had already requested the maids to bring a tub and a few buckets of water to her room, ready to be used whenever she returned from her workout. She didn't care if the water was cold—she'd bathed in her share of freezing mountain streams during her travels, and, anyway, she could warm it with a touch—but she *had* to be clean. She had two appointments today, equally important in her eyes. One with the king. One with Tayse's mother.

She bathed quickly and changed into more conventional clothes than she usually wore—a simple blue dress that accented her gray eyes and her short, pale, flyaway hair. Sturdy walking shoes, a cloak to ward off the chill, and she was ready to stroll the length of Ghosenhall.

There was a knock on the door, followed immediately by Tayse's entrance. It amused her still that he never just walked in, though this suite of rooms could be as truly called his as hers since he slept here almost every night. They had not exactly gotten around to discussing what their long-term living arrangements should be. Senneth was perfectly willing to take up residence in one of the tiny cottages that dotted the grounds behind the Riders' barracks, cottages set aside specifically for the few Riders who bothered to marry. But Tayse seemed to feel that a serramarra of the Twelve Houses should be living in a palace and was unwilling to install her in such humble quarters.

And, of course, they were not married.

"You look pretty," he told her.

She laughed. "I'm trying to look demure."

"My mother likes you. You don't have to try to create an impression."

Your mother has no idea what to think of me, Senneth wanted to say. "I think it makes her more comfortable to see me in women's clothing," she said. "Instead of my boots and my trousers, with my sword on my hip."

He shrugged. "You are what you are."

And she is glad that someone loves you, because you never allowed her *to love you,* Senneth thought. She was still amazed, most days, that he allowed Senneth to do so. "I need to be back within a couple of hours," she said. "Baryn has asked for a meeting."

Tayse opened the door and they stepped into the hall and headed in a leisurely fashion for the stairs. Senneth loved the sensation of walking beside him. She was a tall woman, but he was so big he made her feel almost dainty. Yet he moved with such grace that she always tried to match him, taking smooth, gliding paces and minimizing the noise of her passage.

"What was my father saying to you as you left the training yard?" he asked.

She laughed. "He said I fight like a mystic, not a soldier."

Tayse thought that over for a minute, reconstructing the probable conversation. "If he'd ever seen how a mystic fights, that would be a compliment," he said at last.

"Someday I'll set him on fire," she said. "That will make him respect me."

He was grinning as they stepped onto the broad porch and down the marble stairs to the courtyard of the palace. "*Then* he'll regret any unkind observations he's made in the past."

They talked idly as they crossed the courtyard, saluted the guards at the gate, and set out for Tayse's mother's house. Both of them were familiar with the districts of Ghosenhall that were edgy and dangerous, but their route didn't take them there this day. Instead, they traveled wide avenues lined with pretty stone houses and crossed through small common squares decorated with trees and fountains. The day was cool but fine. Ghosenhall, always a charming city, seemed to preen and glitter in the light.

Tayse's mother lived in a modest but well-kept house shoulder to shoulder with almost identical buildings, distinguished mostly by a riotous garden now filled with fading flowers. She was waiting for them at the door, as Senneth imagined she had been waiting since dawn. Nothing made her happier than Tayse's appearance on her walk.

"Come in! Come in! Oh, it's such a beautiful day. Don't you hate to think it'll get cold so soon?" she greeted them, throwing her arms around her son. He towered over her and he returned the hug carefully. She was small-boned and short, rather plump now, but Senneth guessed she had been a tiny wisp of a thing when Tir first caught sight of her forty-some years ago. She was still attractive in a very ordinary way, with hair of an indeterminate shade of light brown, and eyes as dark as Tayse's.

"Hello, Carryl," Senneth said when the woman reluctantly let go of her son and turned to her other visitor. She was taken in a rather less enthusiastic embrace, but Carryl smiled at her, too. "Have you been well?"

"Little aches. I have a cough in the morning. But otherwise I'm very healthy! Come in, sit down. I made a pie, will you eat something?"

"I love your pie," Senneth said.

"We can't stay very long," Tayse said, and Senneth wanted to kick him. Carryl's face fell immediately.

"Long enough for *pie*, certainly," Senneth said, and Carryl brightened again. "We have about an hour, I think."

"Oh, good. Then I'll make some tea as well."

She left them in the parlor and bustled off to the kitchen, casting one hopeful glance at Tayse over her shoulder. "Go help her with the tea," Senneth hissed.

He looked surprised. "Surely she doesn't need my help."

"It's your company she wants, not your assistance. You. Five minutes alone with *you*. Go talk to her."

He shrugged and obeyed. Senneth took a seat on one of the over-stuffed chairs, leaned her head against the back, and sighed. She was hardly qualified to tutor anyone else in family relations, she thought. Her own parents were dead, bitterly hated by her for years before they went to their graves; she had only the most tenuous relationship with her brothers now. But it was so obvious that Carryl wanted nothing so much as a strong bond with her son, equally obvious that nothing in her life, in her personality, could claim his attention for long. He tried to be kind to her, because Tayse was never deliberately cruel, but nothing about her softness or her longing made an impression on him. He was so completely his father's child.

Tir must have loved her once, Senneth thought. *He married her. He had several children with her. Did he just grow tired of her? Did the novelty wear off, did the affection grow inconvenient?* Tayse had told her that Carryl was the one who moved out of the shared cottage by the barracks, taking her daughters with her, but Senneth was entirely certain that Carryl was the one whose heart was broken. She had fallen in love with this handsome, powerful, dangerous man—she thought she had domesticated him, she thought he would lay that glittering sword at her feet—but she was the one who had been made over. She was the one who had given up all her illusions.

"You won't change him," Carryl had said to Senneth the first time they met. Tayse had left the room with one of his sisters to go inspect some improvement in the back garden. Her voice had not been hostile, but a little wistful. "He's too much like his father. He will only love you for so long."

"I don't want to change him," Senneth had replied softly. Which was both the truth and a lie. He had already changed for her. She wanted him to stay exactly the way he was now; she certainly did not want him to change back. "And I will take his love for however long he wants to give it."

"Don't make him your whole world," Carryl had said, leaning forward and almost whispering in her intensity.

Too late, Senneth had wanted to say. But she had only smiled and changed the subject.

Every time she returned to this small, somewhat sad house, the same conversation replayed through her head, the same questions demanded to be answered. *Will he only love me for a short time and then grow weary?*

Will I one day be like Carryl, lonely and grieving, missing one man for the rest of my life? For, once having loved Tayse, I will never be able to love anyone else. My heart has been reshaped to the size of his, and no amount of tugging and stomping will ever force it back to the size it was.

A small clatter in the hall and then Carryl and Tayse returned, she carrying a tray of desserts and he with the platter of tea things in his hands. Carryl was glowing; that rare few minutes of privacy with her son had been the best gift Senneth could ever have given her. Tayse carefully set the platter down on a fussy ornate table by his mother and then took a seat across from Senneth.

"You pour out the cups, Senneth, while I cut the pie," Carryl said. "I like lots of sugar in mine."

Senneth poured Tayse's first, though he didn't care much for tea and looked ridiculous with the fragile porcelain in his big hands. But he took it from her with a smile and watched her as she prepared another cup for his mother. It didn't really matter if Senneth was serving tea or practicing her swordplay or lashing out with her hands to conjure up fire, Tayse was always watching her, interested in seeing what she would do next. Since the day she had met him, he had studied her with an unvaried fascination. She paused a moment to return his smile.

I think you will love me till I die, she thought. *And even if you don't, that's exactly how long I will love you.*

I‌t was a relief to escape the small house, though the price was a promise to return in a couple of weeks.

"Unless we're gone from Ghosenhall, which I have a feeling we might be," Senneth said, pausing at the front door to hug Carryl goodbye. "I think the king might be about to send me out on a mission somewhere, and you know I like to bring Tayse with me for protection."

A compliment to her son always set Carryl to beaming. "Yes—you'll be safe no matter where you go, if Tayse is with you."

"That's what I think, too."

"Well, if you leave, let me know you're going, and try to come visit as soon as you get back."

"We will," Tayse said, giving his mother a farewell kiss. "Take care."

And they were free.

A quick walk back to the palace, and Senneth invited Tayse to accompany her to her meeting with the king. "He knows if he wants me to go anywhere, you'll be with me, so you may as well come listen now," she said. He grinned, nodded, and followed her through the gilded corridors.

The king was seated in his study, a small, cluttered room of tall windows, blue furnishings, and piles of maps and papers. Baryn himself was a lanky man, with the good-natured smile and unkempt white hair of a lunatic inventor. His brown eyes peered out through smudged spectacles on a world he seemed to find perpetually entertaining. He appeared to be perusing a complex letter when Senneth and Tayse entered, and without even looking up, he motioned them to two seats across from his desk.

"Yes, yes, in a minute—I just wanted to read this again—exactly." He dropped the paper and gave them a bright smile. "How is my favorite mystic? I cannot call Tayse my favorite Rider, you know, because that would cause jealousy among my loyal guard and no end of conflict and recriminations."

Senneth grinned. "Well, if Kirra were to hear you call me your favorite mystic, I think there would be just as much rage and envy."

He waved a thin hand. "Oh, I whisper to her that *she* is my favorite, but that I am forced to placate you so you don't burn down my palace."

"Such a wise king," she said. "So adept at keeping his subjects happy."

"And I am about to make you happier," he said. "You're a most restless woman, and yet you've patiently stayed here in Ghosenhall for how many weeks, not complaining about boredom! I appreciate your restraint."

"You want me to go on a mission for you."

"To Coravann Keep, if you would be so kind."

She nodded. "Surely. What's the news from marlord Heffel? Is he recovered?" There had been a convocation of marlords at Ghosenhall just a week ago, but Heffel had not been among those present, prevented from traveling because of a lung infection.

Baryn picked up the paper again. "He says he is improving every day, but that's not the most interesting part of this letter. He writes that some of his wife's relatives have come to visit for a few weeks. His wife's relatives, in case you didn't know—"

"Are from the Lirrens," Senneth supplied. "I did know. Some of them were visiting last summer when we passed through."

"Apparently there is an endless stream of them, crossing the mountains and trading their goods. One group comes and leaves, then another. I don't understand how *any* woman could have had so much family."

Senneth was laughing. "They're not all related by blood, I'm sure. There's a close-knit clan network, and any of the Lahja alliance—I think it's the Lahja who claim Heffel as kin—would consider themselves to be part of the same family."

Baryn put up a hand. "Please. I cannot keep all the feuds and families straight when it comes to the Lirrenfolk. But I thought you might find it interesting to talk to some of these fellows."

Senneth leaned back in her chair. "What would I be talking to them about?"

Baryn made a delicate motion with his head. "War may be coming. We might need allies. The people of the Lirrens don't have many ties with the people of Gillengaria, but I have met some of their young men, and they are certainly a contentious breed. Perhaps a few of them would be interested in throwing their lot in with our armies. At any rate, I would rather secure them for *our* troops then let them be wooed away by Halchon Gisseltess for *his*."

"They might fight for us," Senneth said. "I've considered it before. But you might not raise more than a few hundred men from their ranks."

"Better a few hundred with us than a few hundred against us," Tayse commented.

"And they are skilled fighters," Baryn added. "Worth recruiting."

Senneth arched her eyebrows. "And when have you been privileged to watch Lirren men showing off their battle skills?"

"Pella and I traveled across the Lireth Mountains about a year before she died," Baryn said. He always spoke the name of his first queen very calmly, but Senneth sometimes wondered what it cost him. By all accounts, he had loved her a great deal. "We found the people fierce but polite. Pella was completely captivated and she made several close friends there."

Senneth tilted her head. Pella's death had come quite suddenly; few people had known the queen was even sick. But perhaps Baryn and Pella had known. Perhaps they had crossed the mountains looking for a cure. Among the Lirren women were healers so gifted they could save almost any life, no matter how far gone. Had Baryn known that? Had the queen?

"I'm glad they treated you well," she said. "They don't always take kindly to strangers. Even strangers who call themselves king."

Baryn was smiling. "But I'm a most gracious king," he pointed out. "In any case, perhaps you could persuade them that I'm worth fighting for. Play on whatever sympathies you think they have, and recruit some of those ferocious men for my armies."

Senneth nodded slowly. "All right. I don't know what success I'll have, but I'm happy to meet with Heffel's in-laws and mention the idea."

"But before you get to Coravann," he said, "you might want to stop in and visit Rafe Storian."

Senneth laughed in disbelief. "Storian City is in entirely the opposite direction!"

"I know. But Rafe was so outspoken when he was here last week. He might appreciate a chance to express his views a second time, rather forcefully, to a smaller audience."

"I don't have much rapport with Rafe Storian," Senneth said dryly. "I don't envision him confiding in me."

"It's the gesture that counts," the king said. "It will please him that I am willing to hear him out, no matter what messenger I send."

"All right. Anywhere else you'd like me to go?"

"Not that I can think of at the moment," he said.

"You realize this is a trip that will take a certain amount of time. It could be weeks before the journey is concluded."

"I understand that, but *you* must understand that I will be sitting here, impatient to hear what you've learned," he replied. "So come back to Ghosenhall as soon as you have anything to report."

She widened her eyes. "Of course."

The king was not convinced. "I know you! Once you escape from the strict confines of the palace, you'll be reluctant to ever come back. If I let you go now, you won't return for months."

Laughing, she closed her fingers around the pendant she always wore, a flat gold disk meant to represent the sun goddess. That and a moonstone bracelet were the only pieces of jewelry she actually owned. "I'll be back the minute my mission is discharged," she promised. "I swear by the Bright Mother's red eye! What could possibly keep me?"

THE evening was taken up with packing a few clothes, visiting the great kitchens for a supply of dried food and other travel essentials, and planning their best route. And bathing. Again. Who knew when they would next be indoors at a facility large enough to offer a tub and plentiful water? Senneth washed her hair twice, short as it was, just to make sure it was clean.

In the morning when Tayse opened the door, he almost fell over Cammon, who was sprawled on the floor before their room. Catching himself before his heavy foot came down on the boy's stomach, Tayse merely gazed down at Cammon with no apparent expression of surprise. "What are you doing here?" he asked.

Cammon scrambled to his feet. Senneth noted his worn travel clothes and the scruffy leather bag slung over his shoulder. "I'm coming with you," he said cheerfully.

Tayse raised his eyebrows, utterly expressionless. But Senneth could tell he was deeply amused. "You are? Where are we going?"

Cammon waved a hand. "Somewhere. South, I think. I couldn't tell exactly."

She could hardly contain her laughter as she came to gaze over Tayse's shoulder. "What makes you think we want company?" she asked. "Perhaps we were looking forward to a leisurely, intimate trip. Just the two of us. Since we so rarely have any time alone."

Cammon was not abashed in the slightest. "I'll get my own room when you stay at an inn. And you know I'm useful when you have to camp out."

Tayse glanced back at Senneth. "Well? Should we bring him?"

"I always earn my keep," Cammon said.

Completely without inflection, Tayse repeated, "He always earns his keep."

She couldn't keep the smile back any longer. "Indeed he does. And I'm sure they'll be happy to see him again in Coravann. Let's saddle up three horses and be on our way."

CHAPTER

10

I⊤ seemed, at least the first week they were back at the convent, that the Lestra had forgotten Ellynor's existence. For which Ellynor was profoundly grateful. The new moon slowly resumed her gauzy silver garments, and every night more novices joined the group outside in the courtyard, singing the Pale Lady's praises. Ellynor's work shifts rotated between kitchen duties, clean-up duties, a stint in the laundry, and many days spent in the fading garden. They had a spell of cold weather that made everyone else shiver but turned Ellynor hopeful. Winter could not come soon enough for her.

She spent much of her free time thinking about her trip to Neft, which had held so many new experiences. The sumptuous Gisseltess mansion—the fine foods so casually served—the exhilarating walk *alone* through the city streets, marveling at all the shops.

The encounter with Justin. That was what she thought about most of all.

She was almost relieved when sickness moved through the convent and half the novices succumbed to cough and fever. Finally, an important task she could focus on that would require all her skill and energy. No more thinking about handsome young men who could end up dead if they so much as touched her hair.

Darris was the senior Daughter in charge of their day-to-day health, so she was the one who ran the infirmary. Anyone who volunteered to tend the sick was immediately relieved of other duties, but even so, there weren't that many girls who had the patience for nursing. Darris was always glad to get Ellynor's assistance—gladder still when Ellynor offered to take the night shift. As she always did.

"But wake me up if Lia gets any worse," Darris said, after running through a list of instructions that covered the five girls currently in the infirmary. "Everyone else is mostly just uncomfortable, but her fever is high enough to frighten me, and I don't think she's swallowed anything since noon. I don't think—but I've seen cases before—well, I'm worried, that's all."

"I'll sit with her," Ellynor promised.

"And Astira's none too strong, either," Darris continued. "But the others should all be well enough to go to their rooms tomorrow." The plump older woman turned her head aside and produced a wheezing cough.

"You're sick yourself!" Ellynor exclaimed.

Darris waved a dismissive hand. "No. Not sick. Too busy to be sick."

"Sometimes sick doesn't care about busy," Ellynor said.

"I'll be better in the morning."

After a few more exchanges, Darris left. Ellynor moved through the infirmary, checking the patients. Everyone sleeping, except Astira, who sighed deeply when Ellynor approached. "I feel horrible," she whispered. "And I'm hot. And I can't fall asleep. Is there something you can give me? If only I could sleep."

"Let me see what Darris left behind." Ellynor picked through the pressed herbs and medicinal concoctions that Darris had mixed up, and then handed Astira a glass with a rather nasty-smelling liquid. "Drink that. I think it'll help."

She didn't really think it would, of course, but most people liked to believe they were drinking some kind of potion that targeted their illness. "Lie back," she said next, and ran a cool cloth over Astira's warm forehead, sponging off her neck and shoulders.

All the while, feeling the power of the Black Mother tingling through her fingertips, drifting over Astira's skin, sinking toward the bones.

Astira sighed. "I do feel better," she said. "I'm going to close my eyes. Will you be here when I wake up?"

"If you wake before morning."

"All right then," Astira said drowsily, and not another word.

Ellynor checked the other beds again, then settled beside Lia. She was probably no more than sixteen, a slight, delicate, fair-haired girl with a dreamy manner on the best of days. She was thin enough to make Ellynor suspect she had come from poverty, though she knew little about Lia's history. Frail enough to have a hard time fending off disease. Had probably seen brothers and sisters die of just such a fever, might have barely survived a similar illness a time or two in her past.

"Great Mother," Ellynor whispered, laying her hands on either side of Lia's face, "use my body to save this child."

She felt it again, the jolt of power, the steady stream of warmth and courage and strength. The waxing moon had set already; all Ellynor could see when she looked out was spangled night. The only goddess she could sense in the room with her was the Dark Watcher, hovering just at her back, her broad palms laid on Ellynor's shoulders. Ellynor felt a richness in her blood, coloring her skin, making her glow with an opal darkness.

She pulled the fever from Lia's body into her own, and her hands felt momentarily hot. She drew the congestion from Lia's lungs, and briefly, Ellynor could not breathe. She stole the illness from Lia and held it tightly in her own arms, until the Great Mother siphoned it away. Out into the cool night sky to dissipate between the stars.

Lia stirred and seemed to smile, then turned on her pillow, her hand underneath her cheek. Ellynor felt the Dark Watcher withdraw, flowing from the room as if a wind had blown backward. Her own body felt curiously light, as if her bones had been ground up fine, and curiously heavy, so that she could scarcely move. She settled as comfortably as she could in the chair beside Lia and promptly fell asleep.

In the morning, Ellynor woke when someone impatiently shook her shoulder. "Have you been sleeping here all night?" Darris demanded. "Look at you! Have you gotten up *once* to offer anyone a drink of water or another potion? I thought I could expect better of you, Ellynor. I am very disappointed."

Ellynor was groggy enough to wonder, for a very brief moment, exactly where she was. When she remembered, she felt a thin spiral of panic down her spine. She *had* slept the night through! Lia had been sicker than she realized, because healing her had required enough energy to sap much of Ellynor's strength. She made a weak defense. "No, I—I checked on everyone when I first arrived, and then I—"

"She gave us most excellent care," Astira spoke from across the room. She was sitting up in bed, yawning, and she looked completely recovered. "I had water several times in the night, and so did the others, didn't you?" Lia still slept, but the other three patients murmured quick agreements. "I feel quite well, thanks to Ellynor," Astira added, and again the other three nodded. Indeed, they looked like they had never known a day's illness in their lives.

"I just fell asleep here by Lia very late in my shift," Ellynor said, lying, but not too worried about it. "But she was resting so comfortably that I thought I could close my eyes—"

Darris looked slightly mollified. "Well, if she still has a fever, you'll be back here tonight, and you *won't* be sleeping."

But Lia, when examined, was so noticeably improved that even Darris's sour mood improved. The girl's breathing was easy, her temperature was down, and when she woke, she could only produce a minor cough. "You'll stay here one more day, even so," Darris decided. "Ellynor, if you want to redeem yourself—"

"I'll watch her tonight," Ellynor said quickly.

"Good. Then you go get some real sleep now, and I'll see you back here this evening."

But late that night when Ellynor returned—rested and fed, since she had been absolutely starving once she left the sickroom—she found a little crowd gathered in the infirmary. Lia was awake and fretful in the way patients sometimes got right before they were completely well—tired of lying in bed but not quite so recovered that they had the strength to leave it. Lia's best friend, a short, pudgy redhead about Lia's age, was sitting cross-legged on the patient's bed, filling her in on events that had transpired while Lia battled a fever. Disposing themselves in various attitudes of relaxation on the other empty sickbeds were Astira, Rosurie, and two other girls who clearly were bored enough to try for any kind of diversion.

"I don't think Darris would be happy to see all of you here, running the risk of getting infected," Ellynor said with some concern.

"We'll be fine," Astira said. "Most of us have already caught the fever and recovered."

Rosurie, who had not, merely shrugged. "I'm not afraid of getting sick," she said.

"Oh, please don't make them leave," Lia begged. "I'm so *bored*. There's been nothing to *do* all day, and Darris just kept telling me to rest some more. I'm tired of resting."

"How are you feeling?" Ellynor asked, and laid her hands on Lia's clear skin. No heat; no clutter in the blood. "Much better, I think."

"So can we stay?" the redhead asked.

Ellynor settled on the sickbed next to Astira. "I suppose so." She glanced over at her friend. "Thank you for what you told Darris this morning," she said. "I don't know why I slept like that. I never do in a sickroom. And I'm glad everyone else survived the night while I was snoring!"

Astira shrugged. "I felt so much better that I got up a few times and made sure everyone else had something to drink," she said. "You were sleeping so hard. But I could tell you'd done something to help Lia." She splayed her hands and put a look of mischief on her face. "Some of that spooky Lirren stuff, I guess. You're always so good in a sickroom."

Ellynor was silent, not sure how to answer, but Rosurie offered a little laugh. "The Dark Watcher," her cousin said. "Ellynor has a special place in her heart."

"What's the Dark Watcher?" Lia asked. Astira already knew, since they had talked a little about their families when they first became friends.

Before it had occurred to Ellynor that the Lumanen Convent might not be the place to talk about other gods.

Everyone waited for Ellynor to answer, so she smiled and tried to look completely guileless. "The Dark Watcher is also called the Black Mother, like the Pale Mother is sometimes called the Silver Lady," Ellynor said in a light voice. "In the Lirrens, the Dark Watcher is the goddess that most people revere. She wraps her hands around us to keep us safe—she hides us from our enemies—she counts us every evening to make sure no harm has come to us while she was away on the other side of the world." She glanced around the room. Rosurie was yawning, and Astira was faintly smiling, but the other girls were wide-eyed and fascinated.

So Ellynor continued her story, telling it like some old half-forgotten myth. Instead of the reality she lived with every day. "There are certain women who have always seemed to have a deep connection to the goddess," she said. "Who seemed to carry a special power of healing in their hands—a gift directly from the Black Mother. It is said that all these women are direct descendants of Maara, whom the goddess loved above all others."

"Why did she love Maara?" Lia asked.

Ellynor leaned her back against the wall to get more comfortable. "Well. One day many, many, *many* hundreds of years ago, Maara got up early to tend her garden. The sun had just risen and none of the birds were stirring. No one else in the whole world was awake! But as Maara stepped into her garden she saw a strange sight—a little girl lying in the dirt, so motionless that she might be dead. Maara hurried over and found the child still breathing, but in very bad shape. She seemed to have fallen when she twisted an ankle, and hit her head and maybe broken an arm. She was unconscious, she was bleeding, she was having trouble breathing. She was very close to death.

"Maara forgot all about her gardening. She carried that child inside and laid her on her own bed, and she tended her the entire day. She wrapped the girl's wounds and put honey on her tongue and sang her lullabies when the girl started crying. Once, when it seemed the child had almost stopped breathing, Maara put her mouth against the girl's and offered her own breath. When it seemed her heart might stop beating, Maara put her hand on the girl's chest and pressed that heart back into motion. From sunup till sundown, Maara did nothing but keep that girl alive.

"The minute the sun dropped below the horizon, a magnificent dark-skinned woman strode into Maara's house. Maara had never seen her before, had no idea who this woman could be, yet she instinctively fell to her knees in awe. 'You have saved my daughter's life,' this woman said. 'All day you have cared for her, when I was far away and could not come to her side. Yesterday she was playing, and she ran from me, and I could not catch her. I saw her fall, but I could not reach her. Already the sun was rising, and I had to flee to the other side of the world. I thought she would die before I could return. But you have saved my daughter's life.'

"Well! Then, of course, Maara realized that this terrifying stranger was the Dark Watcher herself! She bowed her head even lower to the floor and babbled out some kind of answer about how she was happy to be of service to the Black Mother. And the goddess said, 'Hear me, Maara. For the gift of my daughter's life, which you have given me, I will present you a gift in return. For as long as you live, and the daughters born to your body, and their daughters, and theirs, you shall be able to call on me. If you find someone bleeding and broken—or fevered and ill—you may raise your voice and pray, "Great Mother, give this one a single night." And I will keep that soul alive one night. One night, so that your human medicines have time to take hold. No matter how close to death that person is, he or she will live at least until the next sunrise—longer, if your skills succeed. I have promised this, and it is true.'"

Ellynor paused, but there was utter silence in the room. Rosurie still looked bored, but the younger girls were rapt, and even Astira seemed intrigued. "And does that happen?" Lia asked. "Are there women among the Lirrenfolk who can keep someone alive like that?"

Ellynor smiled. "Well, it's just a tale," she said. "I don't know anyone who's ever called on the goddess that way. But there *are* a number of gifted healers among the Lirrenfolk, and all of them give credit to the Black Mother."

"Do you?" Astira asked abruptly. "I mean—Lia—and that old woman in Neft. She was so sick until the night you nursed her—"

"*We* nursed her," Ellynor said sharply.

"Well, I don't think I did anything except wipe her face down. But you were in the room with her first. And everyone knows how good you are in a sickroom. Do you—do you think you get some ability from this Dark Watcher? This Lirren goddess?"

Rosurie was picking at her fingernails, not even interested in the conversation. It was still a wonder to Ellynor that her cousin could have so completely renounced the Black Mother within weeks of stepping inside the Lumanen Convent. Rosurie felt no fugitive fear, held no divided loyalties in her heart. Was not at all worried that someone might discover she loved a goddess other than the Silver Lady.

"I think that maybe the goddesses are sisters and hold each other in affection," Ellynor said. She did not have to pray that the Black Mother would forgive her for what she was about to say. The dark goddess understood all about secrecy; she knew there were things best not confessed. "But only the Pale Mother has any power in Gillengaria. It is she we worship at Lumanen Convent and she who spreads her glory around us."

Astira sat back, seeming satisfied. Rosurie flicked Ellynor one look of quick, sardonic amusement—she understood both the answer and the unspoken words—and returned her attention to her hands.

"I don't think Darris or Shavell would want to hear us talking about other goddesses," Lia said hesitantly.

"Certainly not!" Ellynor exclaimed, exaggerating her reaction so the other girls would laugh. "So if you don't want to get me in trouble—"

"It's just a story, after all," the redhead said.

"Just a tale," Ellynor agreed. "So, Lia, are you sleepy yet? Should I chase everyone out of the room? That's right, all of you, better go. And tonight I will *not* fall asleep at my patient's bedside."

In a few minutes, the room had cleared and Lia was drowsing on her pillow. And Ellynor was sitting upright in her chair wondering what the jealous Silver Lady had thought of her story and whether or not she would whisper tales in the Lestra's ear.

Two days later, the Lestra summoned Ellynor to her office. Ellynor's first thought, which left her tight with fear, was that Lia or Astira or one of the other girls had repeated her account of Maara and the Dark Watcher. But she was almost immediately relieved of this dread.

"Sit down, Daughter," the Lestra invited her in a kind voice, and Ellynor took a seat. She tried to look around without being too obvious; it was rare a novice had a chance to see the Lestra face-to-face or be inside this closed sanctum. The room was large and shadowy, swathed with black velvet hung from the ceiling and creating what was almost an indoor tent. Although there were candles placed in strategic corners, a large yellow-glass globe in the center of the room was the primary source of light. Ellynor guessed it held four or five candles inside, although their light was so evenly dispersed that the sphere looked like a single round ball of creamy color. Dangling from the velvet overhead were silver chains hung with star-shaped charms and milky moonstones. Bookshelves and cabinets and storage chests made bulky shapes against the walls. The Lestra herself sat behind a large desk carved from some ebony wood. Ellynor faced her, perched primly in a straight-backed chair, Shavell beside her in a chair that looked just as uncomfortable as Ellynor's.

"I have a special task for you to do," the Lestra continued. Her voice was so beautiful it was almost hypnotic; Ellynor found herself leaning forward a little just to hear it. "I need you to return to the bedside of Paulina Nocklyn." She must have noted Ellynor's mystified expression, for she added, "Serra Paulina is Jenetta's mother. The sick woman you tended."

"Is she better?" Ellynor asked.

"Indeed. So much so that she has been up and about the house, which proved to be unwise, since she lost her balance and fell."

"Oh, no! Did she hurt herself?"

The Lestra nodded. "Broke her leg. A not insignificant injury for a woman her age, though the doctor says it will heal in time." The Lestra glanced briefly at Shavell, who sat there silent and thin-lipped. Ellynor thought Shavell must not approve of whatever was coming next, which made Ellynor even more curious. "The serra has requested the attendance of one of my novices, to sit with her while she recovers and to help her with her prayers. Jenetta said her mother was most adamant and will not be satisfied with the services of a maid or a girl from town. It must be a novice." The Lestra inspected her. The hard, square face was impassive, but the black eyes were bright with intelligence. "She specifically requested you."

"Me? I don't think we spoke more than three words. The first night she was sleeping the whole time I was in the room. The second night— she asked for a drink of water, and then she wanted me to open the window. I didn't even tell her my name."

"Nonetheless, she remembered you, and she described you to Jenetta. I am not normally eager to send my novices into the world to suit the whims of the nobility—"

"It's ridiculous," Shavell snapped. "Any servant girl would do to tend that old lady's wounds."

The Lestra inclined her head, as if in acknowledgment of Shavell's words, but spoke as if they had not been uttered. "And yet, Jenetta is my cousin and very dear to me. Her mother is sister to the marlord of Nocklyn—a very rich man. I think it would enable us to win powerful friends if we could grant this small request."

The musical voice held a questioning note, as if the Lestra was actually asking Ellynor if she was willing to take up this commission. Ellynor wouldn't have expected to have a choice in the matter, but if she did, it was certainly clear. To return to Neft! Unguarded and unwatched! "I would be happy to sit with your cousin's mother and help her raise prayers to the goddess," she said formally. "When would you like me to leave?"

"As soon as you gather your things," the Lestra said.

Shavell turned to Ellynor, her pinched face even tighter with warning. "You will not speak with the guards who accompany you, except as required by courtesy or your own direct needs," she said. "You will remain inside the Gisseltess house at all times. You will consider Jenetta Gisseltess to stand in my stead, and obey her, and give her respect. You will serve the Silver Lady with all honor, so that every report we hear of you will be full of praise."

"How long do you think I will need to stay there?"

"A week, perhaps," the Lestra replied.

"I am happy to go," Ellynor repeated.

"Good. Then pack your bags and meet Shavell at the front door as quickly as you can. Carry the light of the Pale Mother with you so that she shines on the ill, the infirm, and the sick at heart. Go gently with the goddess."

As it turned out, serra Paulina was not much interested in singing the Silver Lady's praises or having a convent novice say prayers with her while she lay, shivering and suffering, on her sickbed.

"You can pray all you like, but do it when I can't hear you," the old lady said five minutes after Jenetta had left Ellynor in her mother's bedroom. It was early dark, since Ellynor's small party had arrived in Neft just as the sun was going down, and Jenetta had wasted no time delivering Ellynor to her mother. Ellynor had set her travel bags down in the corner of the room, made a little curtsey when Jenetta departed, then lit a single candle to set in the room's wide window. This would signal the Pale Mother that a soul of piety resided within.

Then she had turned to the bed where the old woman sat, one leg curled beneath her, the other one stretched out, wrapped to immobility between a pair of splints. "If you give me your hands, I will pray with you," Ellynor had said in a quiet voice.

Serra Paulina had made her extraordinary reply. Now Ellynor sat down in her chair and tried to think what she should say next.

The old woman snorted. She looked much better than she had the last time Ellynor had seen her. She was still thin and pale, with high cheekbones so sharp they looked ready to cut through the skin, but her eyes were clear and remarkably blue. And her mouth was twisted in a grimace of disdain, not pain. "I know, I told my daughter to fetch you so you could weep and moan over me, call down moonlight or whatever it is Coralinda claims she can do, but I just said all that so they'd make you come. Never cared much for that Silver Woman, Silver Lady, whatever they call her. Never thought too much of Coralinda, if it comes to that. Arrogant and dangerous, and more ambitious than anyone realizes. Don't understand why no one can see that."

Ellynor just stared at the old lady, too astonished to speak.

Serra Paulina made another sound that could have been a cough or maybe a chuckle. "Guess you're not used to hearing anyone say such things about your precious Lestra, are you? Strange little deal she's got set up there—all these people bowing and scraping to her, everyone calling her by some fancy name. It's like she's her own little queen on her own little throne, and she's got everyone there believing it! Well, what happens when a queen realizes she's not the only royalty in the country, hey? When the king tries to shut her down? Baryn's a damn fool. He never should have let Coralinda run on like this for so long. He'll be sorry when she starts her own revolution."

Baryn. That was the king's name, Ellynor thought. This mad old woman was saying the king should fear that the Lestra would start some kind of uprising.

It was something Ellynor could instantly believe.

But. "The Lestra cares only to celebrate the goddess," Ellynor said in a soft voice, dropping her eyes, keeping her face demure. "She sent me here at your request. If you did not want my prayers—"

"You're the one who made me well," the old woman interrupted, and Ellynor's eyes flew to her face. "I was so sick I was going to die. No one would say it, but I knew. And then you were here—you and that other girl—and I got well. You're the one who saved me. I could feel the power in you that second night, just when you walked in the room."

Ellynor felt a little shaky. This was treacherous ground. Heretic this old woman might be, but her daughter wasn't, and Ellynor was here on convent business. "I have only the power that the Great Mother chooses to lend me," she said, still softly, the words deliberately ambiguous.

The serramarra snorted again. "Call it a gift from the Pale Mother if you like, but you're a skilled healer, girl. And I've got a damn lot of pain in my leg, and I don't like it. I want to be well. I want to be up and able to walk out of this room. And I don't want to *hurt*. I'm tired of hurting. You have no idea how long it's been since I've been free of pain."

Ellynor's sympathy was quickly roused at the slight break in the old woman's voice, and she studied her patient for a moment. Paulina was watching her, the blue eyes intense, the thin mouth drawn tight. Ellynor thought that, for all her scornful words, the old woman actually was a little afraid—that Ellynor did not possess the power she thought, or would not use it.

"It would seem very odd," she said carefully, "for your leg to be healed overnight. For you to get up tomorrow morning, whole. Your daughter and your physician—everyone—would think it was strange. And troubling."

Paulina sat back against the headboard, still regarding Ellynor. Her eyes were even brighter. "If you healed me," she said, "I'd stay in bed another two weeks. I'd pretend to be in pain. I would. I would make sure you'd been gone for days before I started to remark how much better my leg was."

"People still might wonder."

An unholy smile came to the old lady's lips. "I'll credit the doctor. He's fool enough to believe he can work miracles! Think of the patients who'll be begging him to come to *their* bedsides then."

"Think of the people who might call him a mystic," Ellynor said bluntly.

That made the old lady pause. Some of the excitement left her face. "That's a word that'll get you stoned to death in Neft," she admitted. Her bright gaze fixed itself on Ellynor's face. "Is that what you are? A mystic?"

Ellynor shook her head, genuinely surprised. "Oh, no. I don't know anything about magic. I don't have any power of my own. It's just that the Great Mother chooses, now and then, to pour her strength through my body so I can help the sick and wounded."

"The Silver Lady is not much of one for healing, not that I ever heard," scoffed the serramarra.

"I call on the Black Mother," Ellynor said in a low voice. "She's the one who watches over the Lirrenfolk."

Now Paulina looked deeply interested. "You're a Lirren girl, are you? What brought you across the Lireth Mountains—and to Lumanen Convent, of all places?"

Ellynor smiled. "Oh, I had many reasons. And I am happy to be at the convent. I admire the Lestra greatly and I am learning to love the Silver Lady, though she is so different from the goddess I know."

"She's elegant and spiteful, if she's anything like the woman who worships her," Paulina said dryly. "But we won't quarrel about Coralinda! Indeed, I should be thanking her right now, for agreeing to send you to me. That is—you have not said—if you are willing . . ."

Ellynor smiled and hitched her chair closer. "Indeed, if you will promise some discretion, I am willing," she said. "Let me get close enough to lay my hands on your leg. I will ask the Great Mother to mend you in the shortest possible time."

A couple of hours later, back in the bedroom she had shared with Astira, Ellynor found herself unable to sleep. She had placed her hot hands on Paulina's legs and felt the bones and tissues reknit beneath her fingers. She had secured the old woman's promise to sleep now and to lie abed a good while longer, and she was pretty sure Paulina would keep the promise because she did not want to jeopardize Ellynor. But it was still a risky move, summoning the Black Mother in a household such as this, when someone else was awake and watching.

Ellynor could not be sorry, but she could not be entirely easy, either.

Unable to sleep, she knelt on the floor before the window and gazed past her candle at the limitless night sky. The waxing moon was remote and a little offended; she seemed to turn her glowing face deliberately away from the supplicant at the window. But the Black Mother was expansive and comforting, spreading her hands over the sleeping city, the slumbering land, holding everyone close and safe. She approved of Ellynor's actions. She had answered at the very first call.

Ellynor crossed her arms on the windowsill and rested her chin on her wrists, watching the scene below. Like Paulina's, this bedroom overlooked the front of the house, the sweep of lawn, the wrought-iron gate, the street beyond. It was late—past midnight, she guessed—and almost no one was abroad. Ellynor could see moths congregating near the glass, anxious to get to the candle. Occasional shapes made distinctive patterns against the sky—spiky bats, feathered owls. Something crept across the lawn below, some small nocturnal creature looking for scraps or vermin. A shadow moved slowly up the hill, big enough to be a man on foot.

Someone coming home late from an evening of pleasure, she thought with some envy. A man who had toasted his friends at the tavern or lain with his sweetheart in secret inside her father's house.

He slowed as he crested the hill, came to a stop as he turned to appraise the Gisseltess house. He wrapped his hands around two of the wrought-iron bars and stood there a long moment, gazing up at the windows.

It was Justin.

CHAPTER

II

NOT even pausing to ask herself what Justin might be doing at the Gis-seltess mansion at this hour of the night, Ellynor gave a little squeal and pushed open the window. She waved both her arms, still clad in her white novice robes, hoping to catch his attention, since she didn't dare raise her voice to call him. For a moment, he didn't see her—she could tell the exact instant that he did. His head jerked up and his smile swept across his face, utterly transforming it. He waved back.

For a moment, they grinned at each other like fools across the whole distance of the lawn, Ellynor and this young stablehand about whom she knew nothing at all. Then he stepped back and made a motion with his hand, first pointing at the house, then sweeping his arm down toward the street. *Can you come outside?* he seemed to be asking. *Can you join me here?*

Of course she shouldn't. For so many reasons she could hardly list them all if she took the rest of the night to try. Of course she wanted to. She leaned farther out, held up a single finger. *One minute.* Then she ducked back into the room, pulling her shoes off, checking to make sure her hair was tied back.

There was no question that she could move through the sleeping house in complete silence. The children of the Black Mother were utterly at ease in the dark, skilled at stealth, adept at crossing unfriendly territory without drawing attention. Torrin was proud of his ability to turn almost invisible, a talent he used when hunting game or engaging in feuds with hostile *sebahta.* He had taught Ellynor to glide soundlessly through any terrain, wrapped in the Dark Watcher's cloak.

She negotiated the stairs without a sound, tiptoed past the single footman dozing in the hall, let herself out of the door without any noise at all. Then she flew across the yard and slipped out the front gate, laughing. She was so delighted at this unexpected rendezvous that she wanted to throw her arms around Justin's neck for the sheer joy of it.

She didn't, but she did allow him to take her hands in a warm clasp as he peered down at her. It was unlikely he could see in the dark as well as she could, but he had sharp eyes even so, for she could see the changing expression on his face as he looked her over and assessed her mood and well-being. He was probably used to night maneuvers himself, she thought. He was not someone who was afraid of events that unfolded in the dark.

"What are you doing here?" he asked in a low voice.

She gave a light laugh. She felt ridiculously happy. "The old woman I met last time I was here? She hurt herself and asked for me to come nurse her. I just arrived tonight. This morning when I woke up I had no idea where I would be by moonrise! But what are *you* doing here?"

He grinned. "Looking for you, of course. Thinking how much I enjoyed meeting you, and wishing you would come back, and wondering if I'd ever run into you again." He shook his head. "I never expected to see you at the window."

"Have you walked by *every* night since I've been gone?"

He looked a little self-conscious. "Not every night. Every day, though, probably, at one time or another."

"The rest of your life must be very dull," she said.

He gave a rather hollow laugh; the expression on his face made her think he was reviewing some recent incident that had been anything but boring. But before he could comment on that, she shifted position as she pulled away from him, and he glanced down at her feet.

"Where are your *shoes?*" he exclaimed, still keeping his voice quiet. "You shouldn't be walking out here barefoot! In the dirt—and the horse droppings—and the *cold.*"

She laughed. "This isn't cold. What kind of pathetic winters are you used to wherever you come from?"

He grinned, but still looked concerned. "Ghosenhall, and it gets plenty cold there," he said. "But you can't stand here barefoot. Let's—here—let's sit down and you can wrap your feet up."

Wrap them in what? she wondered, but that was quickly solved. He drew her to the side of the road, where a strip of grass looked inviting even in the dark, and they dropped down and made themselves comfortable. Then he stripped off his overshirt and proceeded to bundle it around her feet.

Laughing, she tried to pull away—"Justin! Don't put your clothes on my dirty toes!"—but he dragged her knees across his lap and held them there with one hand, his other hand around her ankles. The set of his face was intractable. She was both touched and a little annoyed.

"You remind me of my brothers *so much*," she informed him.

"I don't think your brothers would allow you to wander around bare-foot in the cold at night."

"Well, there you're wrong! Who do you think taught me to do it?" He just looked at her, and that made her laugh again. She put her arms behind her to brace herself. It actually felt rather nice to have his hands touching her—impersonally enough, through the layer of clothing, but warm for all that. It was a novel sensation to be fussed over by a man and not resent it highly. Rather, to find it flattering. "My brothers are night hunters," she informed him. "They can move through the dark as easily as most people can move through the light. We used to play games when we were children—hiding from each other, or sneaking past a pretend campsite. When the whole family was together—dozens of children, all about the same age—we would stage these very complex feuds where we would have to attack each other under cover of night. No one ever caught Torrin. And I think Hayden only was taken captive two or three times. I wasn't as good as they were, but I can make my way through the dark. And to sneak out of a house at night," she summed up, "you have to take off your shoes."

"You must be really close to your brothers."

"To my cousins, too. To all of them. The way I grew up, nothing was more important than family. If someone needed something from you—an aunt's second husband's son by a former marriage—you gave it to him. You never turned your back on a family member. Which meant no one ever turned his back on you. If I needed something, even now, I would just have to raise my hand—" She lifted one arm, held it before her a moment, then put it behind her again to take her weight. "And brothers and cousins and uncles would be at my door."

"Sounds wonderful."

"Wonderful and oppressive," she agreed. "Sometimes you don't always want quite that much attention."

"Really? I like the idea of raising a hand and having a whole contingent of brothers at my back."

She studied his face in the dark. He had strong features, quick to show a smile or a sneer, but otherwise fairly watchful. Not giving much away. Not instinctively formed for trust. "And you've never had that?" she asked softly.

He considered. "I have that now. In a manner of speaking. I have friends who would come if I called—no matter why I called them or where I was. People who would not abandon me. I miss them."

Her voice was so soft it was scarcely louder than a breath. "Did some-one abandon you, Justin? Did your family?"

He looked at her, maybe trying to read her face the way she had read his. She wondered how much he would tell her, this man who clearly was not made for sharing secrets. "I never really had a family," he said.

"Three sisters. You told me."

A quick smile, instantly gone. "So you remember that."

"Well, of course I do."

"They weren't around very long."

She sat up, drawing her feet back toward her body so she could sit cross-legged beside him. As she made no move to uncover her feet, Justin allowed her to pull away. "What happened to them? What happened to *you?*"

He spoke with absolutely no inflection in his voice. "My mother was a whore in Ghosenhall. Four children by four nameless fathers. I was the youngest, and all my sisters were gone by the time my mother died. I was ten." He shrugged. "A long time ago, it seems."

Ellynor felt like she had been dropped in fire. Her skin was melting; her heart was ablaze. Her eyes had been scalded—no, that came from the sudden tears. "*Justin.* How did—but that is—you are—"

"Not a pretty tale," he said, and his voice was gentle. "I don't tell it to get your sympathy. Just so you know how different my own life has been."

"But then—what happened to you? How did you—how did you *survive?*"

"Oh, for a while I lived on the street." Another swift smile, this one a little devilish. "Where I learned some of my skill at fighting. I bet I could show your brothers a trick or two I learned during those days. Then I had some luck—met some people who took me in and trained me in a profession. Now I'm a soldier, and a good one. I don't have family, but I have friends—friends who won't fail me."

"Friends you miss. You already said that," Ellynor replied. "So why are you here, now, and not with them? They didn't turn against you, did they?"

He hesitated for a long time, and she knew he was trying to decide how to answer her question without lying. She was intrigued both by the thought that he felt he had to lie, and the realization that he wanted to give her the truth. "They didn't turn against me," he said at last. "They know I'm here. They'll come for me in a while."

Which was the least helpful reply he could have given. She leaned forward, her elbows on her knees. "You have secrets, don't you, Justin?" she said softly. "You're in Neft for reasons you don't want to reveal."

He looked at her silently in the dark, weighing his answer, weighing her. "Everybody has secrets," he said at last.

She swayed even closer, put a hand on his arm as if she could, through touch, discern the true composition of the man. "You're not a bad man, Justin, are you?" she whispered. "You aren't cruel? You aren't here to bring anyone to harm?"

Almost unconsciously, it seemed, he lifted his own hand to cover hers. "No," he said instantly and with such conviction that she believed him. "That I can swear to you, Ellynor. I never lift my sword except in defense. I have my cause, but it's virtuous—I believe that with all my heart. I am never violent just for the sake of violence. Or for personal gain. I am—you can—don't be afraid of me."

"I'm not. Oh, Justin, I'm not afraid. I just—I wanted to hear you say it."

"I wish I could tell you my secrets, but they're not mine," he said. "Or at least the biggest one isn't, and it affects all the other little ones."

She was almost laughing now. She realized she was still touching him, so she casually withdrew her hand and folded it in her lap. "I have secrets, too," she offered. "Big ones. And I can't tell them, either."

His face assumed a mock sternness. "And are you cruel? Will these secrets bring anyone else to harm?"

To her surprise—and, clearly, his consternation—her face suddenly crumpled with tears. He reached out for her, his eyes wide with concern, but she waved his hands away and drew her legs up to make a sort of barrier between them. Then she rested her cheek against her updrawn knees until she had composed herself again. Justin didn't move, didn't ask questions, but she had the feeling he would prevent her if she tried to simply get up and run back to the house.

Not because he was so curious to uncover the truth about her. But because he thought her tears meant she was deeply afraid, trapped and endangered. And he was the sort of man who liked to confront danger and defeat it.

"I'm sorry," she said after a moment and lifted her face. She still kept her knees pulled up, her hands wrapped around her ankles. "That was stupid. I didn't think I would start crying."

"You're afraid of something," he said flatly. "The Lestra?"

"I'm a little afraid of the Lestra, but that's not it," she said. "I was—oh, Justin, don't hate me. I was thinking that my secret is I shouldn't be friends with you."

Something flickered across his face and was quickly hidden. "You're married? I didn't think they allowed wives into the convent."

"No! Of course I'm not married. It's just that—my brothers, my family—" How to tell this without giving it all away? And what did it matter if he knew she was from the Lirrens? But she didn't want him to know, somehow. Didn't want him to have all the pieces. She did not have all the pieces about him, after all. "The men of my family are very protective, and they don't like to see their women—spending time with other men—men that aren't approved by the family, I mean. They would—you would—if Torrin saw me talking to you tonight, he—well, he—there would be a fight."

Now Justin was wearing his most sardonic smile. "I think I can handle myself in a fight."

She took a deep breath. "Yes. I'm sure you can. But I think—I feel that I—it's not right that I'm sitting here talking to you, and putting you at risk, and you don't even know you're in danger. I shouldn't be talking to you at all, and I know that. So it's unkind of me to keep this secret. That's what I was thinking."

"I think you shouldn't worry about me," Justin said.

"I think you have no idea how angry my brothers can get."

"If I say I'm not afraid, will you keep seeing me?" he asked.

"I shouldn't."

"But you want to?"

She was silent a moment. He waited. He wasn't patient so much as stubborn, she thought. If silence didn't produce the answer, she thought he might try other methods. "I want to," she said at last. "I've never had a—a friend—who was outside the circle of my family. Someone who thought so differently from the people I know. It's so intoxicating! No wonder I was thinking about you all last week. But I know that it's a risky friendship, and I know it can't continue—even if your secrets weren't so great that they'd probably keep us apart anyway. I know that I should just go inside right now and not even look out my window again." She gazed at him a moment, thinking how quickly she had come to like him, how sad she would be if she never saw his face again. "But I don't want to."

He was silent for a beat. Then he said, in a carefully neutral voice, "So you were thinking about me all last week?"

It was not what she had expected him to say, and she was surprised into a laugh. "I was. But only because you're such a novel experience. Don't get all conceited."

He bowed his head as if rebuked. "I'll try not to think too highly of myself. I'll try to keep in mind that you would find any stranger equally fascinating."

"See, that's the sort of thing that would send Torrin into a frenzy," she scolded. "He can't stand the idea that someone would flirt with his only sister." Justin laughed, and Ellynor bristled a little. She said, "Why is that funny?"

"I didn't even realize we were flirting." His face was full of mirth. "I don't know enough about women to realize when it's just a conversation and when it's—" He made a motion with his hand. *When it's something more.*

Ellynor was flustered. Sweet Mother, had she assumed too much? Had there not been that undertone of romance in some of the things they said? Had she just been so caught up in the dark appeal of doomed lovers that she believed Justin felt the same sparks and energies? "Oh! Well, I— I mean, certainly you—and, of course, *friends* is what I want us to be—all we can be—"

He stopped her with a hand on her arm. She didn't think she touched her cousins or her brothers in a whole day as often as she and Justin had touched each other in an hour. "I thought of you all last week, too," he said quietly. "I haven't known that many women and I don't know how a man is supposed to treat them. I have a friend, and he's in love with a woman, and he is so good to her that she knows she is safe and cherished no matter where she goes in the world. If I was in love with someone, that's how I'd want her to feel when she was with me. But I don't know anything about falling in love or the steps people take to get there. I thought we were friends, too. Maybe that's how it starts. Maybe only some people go on from there. But I think that's where we are."

She smiled at him, feeling her eyes mist up again. "I think that's where we are, too, Justin," she said. "But I'm glad we're that far."

"How long will you be in Neft, this visit?"

"I don't know. About a week, I think. The Lestra didn't really want me to come, but she wanted to please Jenetta Gisseltess. I don't think she'll want me gone too long."

"Will I be able to see you again?"

"I hope so," she said swiftly, and they both laughed.

"I can come back tomorrow night. About this time. If you can get free."

She nodded. "That shouldn't be a problem. Most everyone else is asleep."

He lifted an eyebrow. "*Most* everyone else? You snuck out of a house where someone was on watch?"

"Just a footman. And he was half asleep."

"Like to see you running an ambush," he commented.

"My days of playing pretend war games with my brothers are long over."

His expression said, *I wasn't talking about pretend games*, but he didn't pronounce the words aloud. For a moment, her heart misgave her. Who *was* this man she was admitting so blithely into her life—no, that she was running after in a headlong fashion, demanding to be admitted into his? She knew nothing about him except that he was dangerous and had a story he refused to tell.

And that he was funny and kind and impatient and thoughtful and stubborn and, at the oddest moments, vulnerable. And that she was about to walk away from him right now and already she missed the sight of his smile, the casual touch of his hand.

He had decided to say something else. "If you can get free during the day instead, I'll most likely be at the stables," he said. "Do you remember how to get there?"

"I think so," she said cautiously.

He grunted. "I'll make a map for you. I'll bring it back tomorrow and leave it—" He looked around. "By that fencepost. I'll dig a little hole. You'll know it by the fresh dirt."

She could feel her eyes light up with excitement and intrigue. "All right. But I don't know what they'll have me doing during the day. I'm supposed to be nursing serra Paulina. Who doesn't need that much nursing," she added.

"And then I'll be back tomorrow night. Around this time."

"Or I could come to you at the stables tomorrow night. If you've left me a map."

He looked at her as if she was crazy. "At *night*? By yourself?"

"I told you. I can practically see in the dark."

"I think you must not be remembering what happened to you last time you were wandering around Neft on your own."

"But there's nobody out at night! Look! We're the only two people on the street."

"Believe me, there are people out in some of the districts you'd be crossing through. And you *don't* want to come across them while you're alone. Night *or* day." He studied her in the dark. "Promise me you won't try it. Or I won't leave the map."

"You're as bad as Torrin," she said.

"Maybe." He just waited.

"Oh, fine, I won't try to come alone at night."

"Good. Then I'll see you tomorrow, one way or the other."

She pushed herself to her feet and he rose nimbly at the same time. "Something to look forward to," she said with a smile. Her feet were tangled in his shirt. She rested a hand against his shoulder as she un-wrapped herself and handed back his clothing. "You'd better wash that before wearing it again."

"Bring your shoes with you tomorrow night," he ordered. "Unless you want me to get all my shirts dirty."

"You're very bossy."

He shrugged. "Never thought of it that way. I'm practical."

"You're extreme."

"Sometimes."

She shook her head. "I'll bring my shoes. Justin, it was so good to see you."

"Tomorrow then, Ellynor."

It could have been awkward, for it almost seemed as if she should hug him good-bye. Instead, she smiled, gave him a little wave, and hurried back through the gate. Through the door, past the drowsing footman, silently up the stairs, into her own room.

Across the floor so she could gaze out the window. Yes, as she'd expected, Justin was still there in the street, waiting to make sure she'd safely navigated the nonexistent hazards of the house. She waved again. He lifted a hand in a brief salute, then turned and headed back down the hill. She watched him till he was out of sight.

CHAPTER
12

Most unexpectedly, it turned out that serra Paulina had a soft spot for forbidden romance.

Ellynor had, understandably, slept late—and found herself encountering Jenetta Gisseltess's frown when she checked the sickroom at noon the next day.

"You're supposed to be here nursing my mother, and yet you sleep the whole morning away?" the noblewoman exclaimed. "A girl from the kitchens would do as well, and so I will tell Coralinda! Why we had to send all the way to the convent for such sloppy work—"

"Oh, hush, Jenetta. This young woman has been a great help to me," Paulina interrupted. "She was in my room till nearly dawn, after traveling half the day to get to my side! I think she deserves an extra hour of sleep in the morning."

Jenetta looked even more furious at being scolded in front of a virtual stranger. Her cheeks were red with rage or embarrassment as she glanced at her mother. "You said you were still in pain this morning," she said stiffly.

"I imagine I will be in pain for a great many more days," Paula said tartly. "But I'm *better*. I told you that the minute you came in. All due to this girl and her kindness."

Ellynor judged it time to speak up. She assumed a most contrite expression and dropped a small curtsey in Jenetta's direction. "I'm sorry. I got to bed very late. The serramarra assured me servants would be in this morning. I could sleep in the room with her so that she would never be alone—I would be happy to do that if—"

"Mercy, no!" Paulina cried. "It's bad enough I have to have people hovering over me at all hours, helping me with the most intimate things. Can't I sleep in private, at least?"

"Truly, I did not mean to abandon her," Ellynor said humbly.

Jenetta was a little mollified. "I suppose I can see why you might be so tired after a day like you had. It's just that I hate to think of my mother suffering—"

"Oh no," Ellynor said earnestly. "I will do everything I can to help her."

There was then a brief consultation about how serra Paulina was feeling, what Ellynor might do to aid her this afternoon, and what duties Jenetta had that would keep her from her mother's sickroom the rest of the day. Finally, Jenetta left, and Ellynor and the old woman were left alone together.

"And are you really still in pain?" Ellynor demanded.

"No! In fact, I feel amazingly good. Strong enough to tear these splints off and go dancing down the hall."

"You promised you wouldn't do that," Ellynor said.

"I won't. I wouldn't want you to get in trouble."

"Well, and you could get in trouble, too! Just because your leg is feeling better doesn't mean the bone is truly healed. It will take some time to regain its full strength and be able to bear your weight. And as for *dancing*. I think it will be a while before you should attempt anything so energetic."

"It has been a while since I have attempted to dance, but I am thinking now I should give it a try," Paulina said. Her voice sounded amused; she was watching as Ellynor eyed the remains of her breakfast tray, still laden with fruit and pastries. "Are you hungry? Eat whatever you like."

"I'm famished," Ellynor admitted, picking up a flaky roll and devouring it. As soon as she'd swallowed, she added, "I didn't stop in the dining hall to get a meal—and just as well, or think how late I'd have been then!"

"Still, I do wonder," the old woman said in an innocent voice, "what kept you abed so long this morning? It was midnight when you left my room. And you couldn't get up till noon?"

Ellynor had not thought to prepare an excuse, and for a moment her mind was empty. She had picked up an apple and now she just held it in her palm. "I was—well, the trip was long, and I was more tired than I thought I'd be—"

Paulina was watching her, the blue eyes bright with curiosity. "Tell me, Ellynor. Do you have a lover in Neft? Did you sneak out to be with him last night?"

Ellynor had taken a bite of fruit and now she almost spit it out. "A—a *lover?*" she exclaimed, when she was done coughing with mortification. "Serra Paulina!"

The serramarra waved a hand. "Oh, perhaps someone you have not actually taken to your bed," she said with the unconcern of the very old and the not easily shocked. "A boy you fancy. Someone who makes your heart race and your dreams turn dizzy."

That describes Justin well enough, Ellynor thought. She said, "Novices at the convent are discouraged from forming attachments to young men."

Paulina snorted. "Yes, and all young women are encouraged to be demure, but how many wayward girls do you know? I've come across plenty in my day. I was just wondering how to account for your time. I could help you, if you like." Ellynor gave her a swift, hopeful look, and the old lady burst out laughing. "Oho, so there is somebody, isn't there? I thought there was."

"I met this man only once before," Ellynor told her. Half of her wanted to keep the secret, half of her wanted to spill the tale, share some of her excitement and fear. She was being recklessly honest with this old woman on so many topics; she would be in dire trouble if the serramarra decided to repeat a word. "He seemed—I like him so much—I didn't know if I would ever get a chance to see him again."

"He's here in Neft?" Paulina asked. Ellynor nodded. "Hmm. That shouldn't be too hard. I have errands I will insist that only you can run. Jenetta will think it improper but she won't mind if you don't squawk about it. Her own servants have their hands full keeping up with her orders."

"I would be happy to run errands for you, serra."

"Well, give me a few moments. I'll think of something I'm dying to have. And, here, eat the rest of this bread. Now, what do I want?"

A few hours later, Ellynor was once again braving the streets of Neft all by herself, feeling the same illicit thrill she had the first time. Actually, this time, an even greater level of excitement was mounting inside her chest, leaving her both tense and smiling. She clutched Justin's map in one hand and consulted it at every crossroads. He had drawn it with painstaking detail, sketching in recognizable buildings and particularly visible plots of vegetation. He must have worked on it last night and returned to the Gisseltess house before dawn to put it in place.

He must have hoped to see her again.

Still, she felt the pressure building up around her heart as she approached the stables where he worked. How did you talk to a man coolly by daylight once you had gazed on him by starlight? How would he seem different? How would she?

She hesitated a moment, then pushed open the wide door and went in. Instantly she was surrounded by the rich smell of horse and hay. From the direction of the stalls, she could hear the sounds of animals shifting, snorting, and nervously pawing at the ground. No one was in the front area where new arrivals were received.

She took a deep breath. "Justin?" she called, and pushed through the connecting double doors. A few broad, curious faces swung over the gates to investigate her, the big liquid eyes looking wise and kind. She knew better, though; horses could be skittish and stupid, though she had a fondness for the ones she regularly rode back home. She patted a few noses as she moved down the row of stalls toward a back door open to a small corral. "Justin?"

He came striding through the door, a bucket of water in each hand, and almost dropped them both as he saw her. "Ellynor!" he exclaimed, setting down his burdens and hurrying up to place his hands on both her shoulders. His eyes had not yet made the transition from sunlight to shadowy interior; he bent down to examine her as if she was hard to see. "Is something wrong?"

"No, nothing. My patient sent me out to run some errands and made it clear I didn't have to hurry back, so I thought—I'm probably interrupting you, I'm sure you have work to do—"

"Always work to do at a place like this," he said with a grin. "But give me a few minutes and I'll take a break. Sit here and talk to me while I water the horses."

Obediently she dropped onto a rough bench in the middle of the aisle. "I don't suppose you have any food," she said. "I ate off of serra Paulina's breakfast plate, but I missed lunch."

He was emptying the bucket into a trough, but he glanced back at her. "We could go to the Golden Boar for something to eat," he said. "There's even a restaurant that's a little nicer, though nothing like the places you'd find in Ghosenhall. I've got plenty of money if you don't."

"I passed some of those places the other day!" she exclaimed. "People just go there? To eat? Food that someone else made for them?"

He laughed. "What part of the world do you live in that there aren't taverns and restaurants?" he asked. When she didn't answer, he just went on, as if there had been no break in the conversation. "Not sure what the Lestra would think about that, though. One of her novices dining out in public with a strange man."

"Not to mention my brothers."

"They're farther away. And anyway, here in Neft no one has to know *who* you are to realize *what* you are. Everyone knows the novice's robes."

Ellynor glanced down at her white skirt, feeling mutinous and resentful. He was right. Anyone would recognize her, and no one would think it was appropriate for a Daughter of the Pale Mother to be consorting with a stablehand in a public place. "I don't have any other clothes with me," she said in a brooding voice. "Even back at the convent, I only have the clothes I wore when I made the journey here."

Justin hunkered down next to her, shaking his sandy hair back from his face. He was grinning, and his brown eyes were full of mischief. "Well, I don't think you'd fit in my clothes, but Delz—man who owns the stables—he's pretty small. There's an old shirt of his in here, a pair of pants. You'd have to belt them up tight, but—"

She stared at him a minute, unable to believe her ears. Dress up like a *man*? To go out dining in *public*? Shaming herself, her *sebahta,* and her religious order? He had to be joking. "Nobody would do such a thing," she said faintly.

Again, that touch of deviltry in his smile. "I know some women who would. Your brothers wouldn't like it, though."

"No, I suppose they wouldn't!"

He immediately looked repentant. "Sorry. I didn't mean to offend you. I can go fetch us something to eat and bring it back."

"You were *serious*? Not just teasing me?"

"A little teasing. A little serious. But I don't want you to—"

"How would we do it? What about my hair? Do you really think anybody would be fooled?"

He tilted his head back, assessing her. She thought he was trying to gauge if she was angry, if she was feeling reckless, if she would later regret any rash action embarked on now. Ellynor herself was flushed with exhilaration, sparkling with rebellion. She couldn't believe it, couldn't *believe* she was considering such a thing.

Couldn't believe how much she wanted to do it. What an adventure in a life that had held so little!

Justin had no idea how flattered she was that he would even make her the offer, believe that she had the nerve and desire to carry off such a wild masquerade. Would be willing to make her a partner in such a lark. Would give her the chance to take such a risk.

"Got a cap I wear on cold days—you could shove your hair up under that. You're so small and your skin's so smooth. Everyone will think you're my little brother. Just don't say much. Oh, and let me see your shoes."

She lifted the hem of her robe. Plain and sturdy boots, good for walking. She'd worn them for the trip in from the convent and forgotten to bring any others. Justin nodded.

"Those'll do. Let's get you changed." He stood, then hesitated a moment, looking down at her. "Only if you want to. Don't let me talk you into something that's going to make you hate me later."

She rose, the motion almost turning her dizzy. Or maybe it was the emotion. The excitement. The blissful terror. "I won't hate you. Now I have to do it or I'll hate myself forever for the missed chance."

In fifteen minutes, she was transformed. Delz's clothes were too big on her, but they helped hide her figure and left her looking, or so Justin said, like an underfed urchin. She had to rely on his assurance that she could pass for a boy, since there was no mirror here for her to check. Still, she had trusted him this far; accepting his assurance on this point was a minor act of faith. The knit cap fit rather sloppily over her coiled braids, and Justin adjusted it so it covered her ears, tucking a strand of hair back in place.

"You look like you're about twelve," he said. "Just keep that wide-eyed expression on your face and everyone will think this is your first time in from the country."

"It may as well be," she retorted.

"And don't talk too much, at least to anyone but me. I'll order for us. What do you like to eat?"

"What are my choices?"

They discussed possible menu items during the short walk to the Golden Boar—a taproom where, Justin said, her somewhat disreputable appearance was less likely to be noticed than it might be in a more formal establishment. It was some time past the usual lunch hour, so company was sparse and they got a table to themselves in a corner of the room. Justin sat with his back to the wall, but she only had to turn her head a little and she could survey the whole scene. The individual tables, some still littered with dirtied plates and glasses. The wide smooth bar near the front entrance, lined with high stools on one side and kegs of ale on the other. The men gathered in twos and threes at various points in the room, eating in silence or arguing in idle voices. Two women were there with men who seemed to be their husbands. A pretty girl about Ellynor's age approached their table and gave them a tired smile.

"Eating or drinking?" she asked.

"Eating," Justin said. "What's available?"

Within another fifteen minutes, they were both happily consuming a hearty meal of soup, bread, potatoes, and roasted vegetables that was much better than convent fare, though not nearly as good as feast food at a Lirren household. Ellynor didn't care. She had been starving ever since drawing on the Great Mother's power to heal Paulina's leg last night. She didn't think she could ever fill the cavern of her stomach.

"Don't know how someone as little as you can take in so much food," Justin observed.

"Am I being vulgar? It's just that I missed breakfast—*and* lunch—and we had cold rations on the road last night—"

"I'm hungry, too," he said, cutting himself another slice of bread.

"I love it here," she told him, so earnestly that he started laughing. "I do! We just ask for more food, and she brings it, and we don't have to do any of the work—we don't have to wring the chicken's neck or pluck the feathers or roll the dough or chop the vegetables. Oh, and we don't have to scour the pans afterward or haul water up to soak the dishes—stop laughing," she said, but she was smiling, too. "You don't know how much work it takes to prepare a meal."

"Oh, yes, I do. I've cooked plenty when I was traveling. Hunted my own game, too, *and* dressed it. I'd wager that's as hard as picking a chicken out of a coop or separating a cow from a herd for slaughter."

"Do you travel a lot?"

"Goes in cycles. Sometimes yes—weeks at a stretch. Other times, I sit at home for months."

"Which do you prefer?"

He shrugged. "I don't like to sit still. If I'm at home, I'm up and doing something. Practicing bladework or prowling the city. So the traveling's good, because it keeps me occupied."

"Gives you a way to focus your energy."

He nodded. "How about you?"

She shook her head. "Oh, I think I'd like to travel awhile—see everything there is to see—and then go home again. I think my heart is made for contentment, and that I'm happiest with familiar things around me. But not just yet. Lately—right now—I've been so restless. I've felt so confined. I want to see everything! Gillengaria first and then, who knows? Arberharst. Karyndein. All the lands beyond the ocean. Then I think I'd want to wander home."

"Maybe home wouldn't look so good then."

"Maybe not. Maybe I'd want to stay someplace else that I'd found along the way. But I'm pretty sure I'm the type to settle, once I've found the place I like the most." She took another bite of bread. She was starting to feel almost full. "So where have you been? What places did you like best?"

"Ghosenhall's where I've spent most of my life, and I tend to like cities. Especially the ones around the marlords' estates—Helvenhall, Rappen Manor, Coravann Keep. More going on there. A lot more energy. Rappen Manor's a fortress—so's Coravann Keep, when it comes to that." He described them at length, dwelling longer than he probably realized on such details as the reinforced battlements, the well-equipped training yards, the degree to which the owners could protect themselves from assault.

Oh, yes, he was a soldier to the core.

No matter what role he had taken on for the moment.

"So how do you see your life going forward?" she asked him when he'd stopped talking to take a final bite of potatoes. "Do you think you'll go back to Ghosenhall? Hire on as a guard somewhere? Do you think you'll settle down, look for a wife, raise children?"

He made that sound that seemed so characteristic of him—a snort or a laugh or a little grunt of disbelief. "Men like me don't usually start families."

"Men like you," she repeated.

He spread his hands as if to indicate his body, as if to say, *Take a look*. "Sometime mercenary, sometime vagabond, always moving on to something else. Not the steady sort."

She watched him a moment. "You seem pretty steady to me," she said at last. "Not quite the drifter you pretend to be."

He gave her a half smile, somewhat mocking. "Good man in a fight," he said. "Not so good with a baby."

She smiled back. "Now, you don't know that," she said, teasing. "I'll bet you've never held an infant in your life."

He laughed. "Well, that's true! I wouldn't even know what to do if somebody handed me one, all wrapped in blankets and probably squalling its eyes out." He thought for a moment, and then added in a hard voice, "Though I'll tell you this much. If any woman ever *did* have a child of mine, I'd take care of that baby—with my own hands, if I had to, or I'd pay somebody. I wouldn't just leave. I wouldn't just walk away, knowing some baby I had fathered, some child who was part of *me*, was roaming the world somewhere utterly abandoned."

Ellynor felt her throat tighten and had to resist the urge to reach out and touch his arm. Not dressed like this, not in such a place. "I think you'd make a charming father," she said as lightly as she could. "You'd be very fierce and protective if you had a daughter, and if you had a son—well, I'm guessing you'd teach him how to use a sword before he was even two years old."

Justin's face had lost its bleak edge. "I'd teach a girl the same thing," he told her. "I know plenty of women I'd trust to take my back in a fight."

"Someday you're going to think about something besides fighting," she said.

"Sure," he agreed, "when the world has changed so much that you don't even recognize it."

She was going to answer, but a noise made her turn in her chair. Justin's eyes had periodically gone to the door the whole time they'd been sitting here; he hadn't missed a single entrance or exit in the past hour. Now both of them watched the small party that entered in a manner that seemed, oddly, both bold and stealthy. There were five of them. Three looked like guards, and one was a small, blond woman who appeared faint with exhaustion. One was a strong-featured, dark-haired man whose impatient movements and brusque demand for "food, *now*" made him appear the clear leader of the group. Ellynor didn't like his face—it was harsh yet sensual, and she imagined that he got most of his pleasures from large and small acts of cruelty.

A ridiculous thing to think. About a total stranger.

The proprietor hurried over and ushered the man and the woman to a table on the other side of the taproom. Their guards settled themselves nearby, their poses as watchful as Justin's, their backs to their master, their faces turned toward the door. None of them wore any insignia that marked them as being from a noble House, but Ellynor was betting that this was a marlord or a serramar, traveling in disguise.

"What an interesting-looking man he is," she said in a low voice, turning her attention back to Justin. "What do you think he—"

Her words trailed off as she realized Justin had not even heard her speaking. His hands were fists on the tabletop; his eyes had darkened with anger colored by a good deal of surprise. So this was someone her new friend recognized. Someone he obviously despised. And had not expected to see in Neft.

"Who is it, Justin?" she asked. "Who's that man? The lord whose service you left? Are you afraid he'll see you?"

Justin's grunt was half amused and half disgusted. "It doesn't matter if he sees me. He doesn't know who I am."

"Then why do you hate him?"

That caught his attention; he finally looked at her. "Only some of it's hate," he said. "Some of it's fear."

She felt her eyes grow wide. "Why? Who is he? What has he done to you?"

He shook his head. "He's never done anything to me, only to people I care about. He's dangerous. He's ambitious. And, last I heard, he'd been confined to his estates. He shouldn't be out riding around at will, working on his rebellion."

Her breath caught. "His rebellion?"

Justin nodded. "He wants to knock the king off the throne so he can take it for himself."

"Who is he?"

Now his sardonic expression was very pronounced. He watched her as though curious to see if she would believe him. "Marlord Halchon Gisseltess. Brother to the Lestra."

CHAPTER
13

I T seemed to Justin that Neft was suddenly the most popular destination in Gillengaria.

First, Ellynor had been there an entire week, and every day she had managed to get free and come spend a little time at the stables. Justin couldn't believe how much he looked forward to her visits, how much they found to talk about. He was not used to having long conversations with *anybody*, let alone someone he scarcely knew, let alone a woman. And yet there was so much to tell her. There was so much to learn. Every time she left he remembered something else he'd meant to ask, something else he should have said.

Every time she left, he was afraid he might not see her again.

Every time she returned, his relief was almost as profound as his delight.

She was gone from the city now, but she had seemed hopeful she would be able to return eventually. "Serra Paulina told me she can sense that she'll have a relapse as soon as I'm back at the convent," she had said with a laugh. "I hope the Lestra will feel obliged to humor her."

"I'll miss you."

"Oh, and I'll miss you, too! I'm so sad already, and I haven't left yet!"

"Stay away from Halchon Gisseltess," he recommended. "If he's at the convent now? Keep clear of him."

"What do you think he'd do to me? Does he have a reputation for hurting young women?"

"I don't know about that. Just—stay away from him. He's a bad person. A terrible man."

She didn't laugh at him. She didn't ask him how he knew or what, exactly, the marlord was guilty of. "All right," she said. "I know how to make myself disappear. He won't notice me."

"Good."

Neither of them had known how to say good-bye—surely they should not hug, and a handshake seemed faintly ridiculous—so he had just put his big palms on her delicate shoulders and smiled down at her. "Take care. And I mean that truly, watch yourself."

"You, too. Don't get into any fights defending some other girl's honor."

Another laugh, a wave, and she was gone. He'd felt a little off balance ever since.

But her arrival and departure, much as they'd disturbed his peace, didn't shake him up as much as the appearance of Halchon Gisseltess. What was he doing off his estates? Why was he in Neft? Stopping here briefly on his way to see his sister, no doubt—to discuss what? Formulate what kind of dreadful plans? Justin had to get word to Ghosenhall. He was reluctant to put sensitive news in a letter and send it with a courier he did not absolutely trust. Fortunes had changed hands many times because of a dangerous missive gone awry. He would have to be careful about committing any words to paper.

Fortunately, two days after Halchon passed through, one of Tayse's messengers arrived. He was a young man from the king's civil guard—not a Rider and probably never good enough to be a Rider, but earnest and enthusiastic and eager to do his best. Justin sat with him an hour, giving him concise details about the things he'd seen and guessed so far, and sent him on his way the next morning. It chafed him to have to sit still in Neft, awaiting word from Tayse. Surely he had seen enough by now to know Coralinda Gisseltess was plotting against the king? Surely the fact that men of her guard were murdering nobles in their homes was reason enough to have King Baryn move against her? Surely there was very little else Justin needed to stay here to learn?

But if he was called back to Ghosenhall, he would never see Ellynor again.

He didn't want to stay. It was so strange to realize that, even more, he didn't want to leave.

Three days after Ellynor left, another visitor arrived in Neft, this one even more welcome than Tayse's messenger.

Justin was alone in the stalls, checking a horse's legs for injuries, when he heard an imperious voice raised outside. "Hey, there! Boy! Boy! Isn't there anybody who works here? Will someone come take my horse?"

He straightened, left the stall, and hurried out toward the front, a grimace on his face the whole time. It sounded like some rich, fat, old noblewoman who wasn't used to waiting, who was about to leave him with some high-strung animal that would take half the night to settle. Hard to believe a woman like that would be traveling alone, wouldn't have servants with her who could lead the horse to its quarters for the night while she made herself comfortable in the only truly respectable inn the city offered.

But when he emerged into fading daylight, he found that the new arrival was indeed all alone. He'd been wrong about the fat part, but he'd gotten the rest of it right. She was an elderly woman, white-haired and scowling, but sitting poker-straight on the back of a magnificent night-black stallion. She was dressed in silk and velvet, a fortune in jewels around her throat, and even the horse's bridle looked expensive. When she saw him, she tossed her head and allowed a look of distaste to cross her patrician features.

"Are *you* the only one here?" she asked in accents of disgust. "You don't look like you could be trusted to run the kennels, let alone manage a spirited animal like mine."

Justin had the lowest possible opinion of the nobility, but such rudeness was almost unprecedented. "I can be trusted," he said in a level voice. "How long will you be staying?"

Her scornful glance swept over what part of Neft she could see from this admittedly inferior district. "As short a time as possible. A day, perhaps two."

"We'll be happy to feed and water your horse for you. Groom him, too, but that's extra."

Her attention returned to him. She appeared to be sneering. "I can pay for any services you might see fit to offer," she said bitingly. "Now help me from the saddle, gutter boy."

Justin had automatically raised his arms to lift her down, but at that, he froze. Impossible to tell by looking, of course, but he stared up at her a moment, letting his arms drop to his sides. "Kirra?" he asked in a disbelieving voice.

"Kirra? What? Is that some kind of insult, boy?" she demanded, but she couldn't restrain the laughter anymore. "Help me down, I said! Or I'll turn you into a field mouse, and you'll be eaten by some kind of horrid creature."

"Kirra!" he exclaimed. Now he grabbed her from the saddle and hauled her down, swinging her around in a circle so wildly that she actually squealed. "Who'd have believed that I'd actually be happy to see *you*? What are you doing in Neft?"

"Put me down! Ow—you're bruising my ribs! Put me down!"

He did, but not until he'd given her a little scare, tossing her up in the air a few inches and catching her. He spun around to give the black horse an appraising look. "And is this Donnal? I suppose it must be." The horse gave a whinny and pulled his mouth back, the equine version of a smile. "You shouldn't let her treat you this way," he said, leaning in, as if to whisper a secret in the horse's ear. Donnal was Kirra's constant companion, no matter what shape he took. "You're her horse, you're her dog—you need to remind her once in a while that you're a man."

"Oh, we were both wolves just this morning," Kirra said. She had looked over her shoulder as if to be certain that no one was close enough to be watching, and even as she spoke she began a gradual transformation. The white hair turned gold, the pinched features grew youthful and gracious. When Donnal changed shapes, the alteration was so quick it was almost instantaneous, but Kirra shifted slowly enough that you could watch her body melt and reshape and redefine. "We only donned our present disguises for your benefit."

"What are you doing in Neft?"

"Tayse said if we happened to be down by Nocklyn we should drop in on you," she said carelessly. "And I said, well, it's out of my way, of course, and I don't much like Justin, but if it's important to *you*, Tayse—"

He felt himself grinning. Kirra Danalustrous was an amazingly beautiful woman once she stood there inhabiting her own skin. But she was so wayward and so irritating that Justin had always been able to overlook her physical attractions. Indeed, the first three months he'd known her, he would have said he hated her. He still didn't understand how it was that they were actually friends. Of a sort.

"Well, if you're returning to Ghosenhall, you can take a message for me," he said. "I just gave a report to one of Tayse's men, but you could probably make it back more quickly."

"Probably not," she said. "We were just in Ghosenhall, then Rappengrass, and I think it's time to head back to Danan Hall." She glanced around. "Is there any urgent news from sleepy little Neft?"

"Halchon Gisseltess passed through a few days ago," he said, and had the satisfaction of seeing her grow instantly serious.

"He *did*? But isn't he under guard at Gissel Plain?"

"Apparently not. And there's been all sorts of action down at the convent. If you—"

She stopped him with a lifted hand. "I want to hear it all. I do. But I'm starving. Can you tell me over dinner?"

"Of course," he said. "We can go to the taproom, but—hmm." He debated a moment. "Are you going to go as yourself?"

"What? Why shouldn't I?"

"Well, the story I put out when I got here is that I left some marlord's service because of a fight over his daughter." He saw the look of mocking delight on her face and added, "It was Cammon's idea. Anyway, if someone sees you, they might think you're the one I was trying to seduce."

"But, Justin, I've just been waiting for you to try," she said soulfully. "All this time I thought, oh, if only Justin would notice that I'm a woman, and a woman who cares about him—"

He grinned. "Particularly as one day someone asked me *which* serramarra I'd been involved with, and the only ones I really know are from Danalustrous—"

"My father will be thrilled," she informed him. "A match with a King's Rider, while shockingly unequal, would still be better than a match with a peasant's son." She glanced at Donnal. "Who looks like a horse."

"And then a few weeks ago I made friends with a novice from the convent, and I've seen her a few times," he went on, a little self-consciously now. "So if *you* show up all of a sudden and start going to taprooms with me, well, people might notice how many women seem to be in my life."

She had stepped back and was now gazing at him with a lurking smile. "Justin. A novice? From the *convent*? You *have* exceeded expectations! Come instantly and tell me everything. I'm starving, but this is a story I absolutely must hear."

He gestured at the horse. "What about Donnal? He can't exactly come like that."

She was laughing. "Lead us into the stables, gutter boy. We'll both change into shapes a little more appropriate."

Twenty minutes later Justin was back at almost exactly the same table he'd sat at with Ellynor, sharing a meal with yet another woman masquerading as a man. Kirra's disguise, however, was more convincing. She'd kept her fair coloring and aristocratic features, but taken on weight, added some stubble, altered her clothes, and deepened her voice. It was amazing how easy it was, still, to think of her as Kirra. Perhaps because Justin had seen her take so many shapes and retain, through every modification, her essential personality, sunny, charming, and lawless.

Donnal, on the other hand, was dark as the horse he'd first appeared to be, but far sleeker. He was of medium stature, with dark hair and eyes, a close beard, and a taciturn nature. He was almost as unlikely to talk whether he was fashioned as man or beast. His quiet intensity was a welcome counterfoil to Kirra's bright restlessness.

"So," Kirra said. "What's been going on here?"

He described in detail the days he had spent spying on the convent and following the Lestra's guardsmen the night they went burning down houses. Kirra looked exceedingly grim at the news. "I hadn't heard that story yet. I wonder if it's made its way to Ghosenhall? Do you know whose house it was?"

"Southern Nocklyn. I can describe the place and the people I talked to, but"—he shrugged—"I don't know the nobility."

"Well, this is proof, if Senneth wanted any, that the Lestra is engaged in murder. I can't imagine that Baryn can just overlook such actions!"

"But if royal guards can't keep Halchon on his estates, how will the king be able to control the Daughters?" Justin demanded. "When so many people worship the Pale Mother and would do anything the Lestra demanded?"

Donnal looked up. "There are a few who fear the Pale Mother, too, *and* the Daughters," he said in his quiet voice. "If they fear the goddess more than they fear the king, they will act for the convent and not for the crown."

"And what's going on in Ghosenhall, anyway?" Justin said, a note of complaint in his voice. "I haven't heard any kind of important news."

"Well," Kirra said, folding her hands around her glass of beer. "There was a summit recently—most of the marlords were there and Thirteenth House lords from all over the realm. It was organized by the regent."

She gave Justin a fleeting glance and returned her attention to her hands. Last summer, Kirra had fallen madly in love with Romar Brendyn, the king's regent and a married man. The affair had almost ended her friendship—or whatever you'd call it—with Donnal and had most certainly broken her heart. In fact, Justin had not seen her since she had broken off the relationship with the regent and returned to Danalustrous, Donnal at her side.

Time had healed some of the worst wounds, it seemed. Justin didn't feel he could ask her for all the details as long as Donnal was sitting next to her.

"Nothing of any real significance was decided at the conference," she went on. "The marlords, as might be expected, strenuously resisted any notion of giving up control of even the smallest portions of their lands. The king remained entirely neutral. But—there seemed to be—the overall feeling was one of hope, I thought. Hope that things might begin to change, now that there were actually public discussions of the topic. Romar encouraged the marlords to make lists of properties they might be willing to sign over, and the lesser lords to make lists of the properties they most coveted. I have no doubt at all that nothing on these lists will match. But it's a start."

"So someday we might have Fifteen Houses, or Twenty," Justin said. "That will seem strange to you."

"Yes, I can see why a street urchin such as yourself would care that the social order was about to be upended," she said in an affable voice.

He grinned. "And your father? How did marlord Malcolm express his views?"

"You just simply never know what my father will do or say. Give up control of an acre of Danalustrous? I couldn't imagine him willingly doing such a thing. But he sat there and wrote four names on a piece of paper and handed it to Romar while the rest of the marlords were still muttering into their wine. All I can think is that he doesn't really believe the transfer of ownership will occur. Otherwise, why would he be so tame? My father would fight to the death to protect Danalustrous."

"What about your sister? Was she there?"

"Casserah to cross the border and leave Danalustrous? Are you mad?" Kirra exclaimed. "Of course she wasn't there. I assume she and my father discussed matters before he left. Or not. They think alike in the strangest ways. Sometimes I don't understand either of them."

Donnal shrugged. "They think a strong Thirteenth House makes the realm content, and a content realm keeps Danalustrous undisturbed," he said. "Not so hard to understand."

"And that actually is the only thing that makes sense," Kirra said with a sigh.

Justin sipped his beer. "So you went to this conference with your father?" he said. "I thought you were off someplace doing miraculous healing."

She smiled at that. "Dorrin Isle. We were there almost three weeks before I met my father in Ghosenhall."

"So? All those people who were sick? Could you cure them?"

"All except the stupid ones," Donnal said.

Justin glanced between them. "What's that mean?"

Kirra made a motion with her hands. "There were a few who were afraid to undergo my form of treatment. Which, I admit, was rather extreme. They were afraid to be turned into dogs and horses so the other healers could administer drugs that worked."

"Afraid of mystics." Donnal growled. "Or despising them."

Kirra nodded. "Those who agreed all recovered."

"That's wonderful!" Justin exclaimed. "You must have felt pretty pleased with yourself by the time you left."

She laughed. "You know, I did. I felt like I had done something worthwhile and important and *good*. Not all my days hold such unselfish rewards."

"There's a price though," Donnal said. "People left the island carrying the tale. Who knows, maybe even the Lestra has heard it by now. One more reason for people to fear us."

Kirra sighed. "They feared us anyway. Maybe now a few more people have reason to love us."

The serving girl came by their table to see if they wanted more to drink. Kirra and Justin both said yes, but Donnal said no. "I'm tired," the dark-haired man said, shaking off a yawn. "I need to sleep."

"Where are you putting up?" Justin asked. "I've got a room if you need a bed. Not very plush, but tolerable."

"Thank you. I bespoke accommodations at an inn before I came looking for you," Kirra said. She tossed Donnal the room key. "I'll be back within an hour. Just the idea of sleeping on a real bed—I don't think I can resist much longer."

Donnal nodded and left the table. Justin waited until their glasses had been refilled before he asked another question. "So. How does it go? Between you and Donnal?"

He hadn't been sure Kirra would answer—they were not exactly used to confiding in each other—but she didn't respond with either a jest or a sarcastic comment. Instead, her face became thoughtful, a little rueful, and she tapped her fingers against her glass. "Mostly it goes very well," she said at last. "I know him better than I know any person, any creature, in the kingdom. He knows the thoughts in my head before I express them. I cannot imagine anyone more suited to me, anyone who could love me more." She looked up, her blue eyes direct. Even in the partially disguised face, her eyes were still unmistakably Kirra's. "But I can imagine other ways, other lovers. I remember how I felt about Romar—even if he does not remember how much he loved me. It is hard to give my whole heart. Donnal has such a very, very big part of it—but I have kept a little bit for myself."

"Maybe he's kept a fraction of his own heart and decided not to give it to your careless hands."

She smiled then. "Maybe. But Donnal has never been very good at keeping anything from me if I decided I wanted it."

"And Romar?"

"We haven't talked. Or—no more than our social positions required. During the summit . . . Sometimes he would look at me and I would see this sort of puzzlement in his eyes. Like he knew there was something about me he'd forgotten—something important—a secret I told him once or a dreadful thing he saw me do. But he couldn't remember." She shook her head. "It's better that he doesn't remember."

Justin didn't have all the details, but he did know that Kirra had used some potent spell to erase herself from the regent's heart. He found it a little frightening that it was something she was able to do. Was willing to do. "And what if the magic wears off someday? What if he suddenly sees you—and every memory returns?"

"I suppose I'll deal with that day when it comes. But I don't think it will be soon." She sipped from her glass, but did not look as if she tasted the beer. "Anyway. He will have much else to preoccupy him soon. His wife is expecting their first child sometime next year. And perhaps more will be on the way after that."

Justin drank from his own glass, thinking. "Don't ever do that to me," he said finally. "Go into my head. Change things around."

"Justin, you're impervious. Nobody's magic could get past your thick skull."

He grinned. "I know enough about your magic to know that's not true."

She shook off the pensive mood and gave him one of her wide, mischievous smiles. "But let's talk about something far more interesting! Tell me about this girl! This—this novice. *How* did you meet her and *what* is going on?"

"Rescued her on the street one day when a drunkard tried to steal a kiss. We made friends."

She widened her eyes and nodded in an encouraging way. "Yes? And? I need more details."

He fidgeted. He wanted to pour out the whole story, recount every conversation and dissect the significance of every one of Ellynor's sidelong glances. He needed someone with more experience to explain to him what all of this might mean. And yet he didn't want to repeat a word; he wanted to hoard every sentence, every laugh, in the closed storeroom of his heart.

"She came to the convent to be with her cousin. She's not a fanatic like the Lestra and so many of the novices. She's never been away from home before—not this far, anyway—and she comes from some back-country part of the world where they don't have much in the way of shops and restaurants and commerce. She thinks Neft is a big city! But she's not—that makes her sound like some kind of yokel, but she's—she has a sort of wisdom. There's a kind of peacefulness to her. Oh, and kindness. The Lestra sent her back to town last week to take care of this sick old woman, and I could tell how gently she's treating this old lady, how she's come to care for the woman even in just a few days. Everything interests her. Everything she sees in Neft—everything I tell her. She just absorbs everything. I wish I could talk to her every day."

He fell silent, conscious of doing a poor job, of not describing Ellynor with any accuracy at all. *She makes me talk about myself. She makes me like talking,* he wanted to add, but that seemed stupid. Irrelevant. That wasn't about Ellynor at all.

Kirra was smiling at him, the expression on her face wondering, with only the faintest trace of teasing. "But, Justin! You sound like you've fallen in love with her!"

Maybe she expected him to vehemently deny it; she looked surprised when he showed her an anxious face. "Does it? I don't know," he said quietly. "I don't know what it's like to fall in love. I don't know how you're supposed to feel. But I can't remember feeling like *this* before. Around any of the women I ever knew. You, or Senneth, or the women among the Riders—I like you all. Well, not *you,* not all the time, but you're all my friends. This girl is my friend, too, but somehow it feels different."

"What's her name?"

"Ellynor."

"What does she look like?"

"Dark. Small. I guess you'd say she's delicate. She has the littlest hands. Her face is—at first I thought she was only pretty, but now when I see her, I think she's beautiful."

He looked at Kirra as if daring her to call his comment ridiculous, but she merely nodded. "Where does she come from? What part of Gillengaria?"

He shook his head. "I don't know. I don't think she wants to tell me."

Kirra raised her eyebrows. "Secrets? That's not so good."

He snorted. "Well, it's not like I'm not hiding things from her."

"Yes, but secrets can get you killed. And, Justin . . . she's a novice. At the *convent.* Where people like her are trained to hate people like me."

"I don't think she hates mystics," he said.

"You don't sound so sure."

"We haven't discussed it. Exactly."

"Well, you might see if you can find out how she *does* feel about magic. Exactly."

"I think—I think she's a little uneasy at the situation she's found herself in," he said. "I think she's not sure the Lestra will ever let her leave. Will let any of them leave. And she's feeling a little trapped."

"So. A trapped, desperate, beautiful woman—with secrets—turns for help to a solitary man who appears to be something of a drifter, who obviously has some skill with a sword, and who's already proved he's willing to fight for her honor. If I were a more cynical woman, I'd say you were being carefully manipulated by someone with a deep agenda. As it is— Wild Mother watch me! Justin, these are troubled waters."

"You don't know her," he said. "How can you say something like that? She's—I'd bet my life she's exactly as she seems."

"That's exactly what you could be betting," Kirra said. "Make sure you know the stakes."

He gave her a long, serious look. She stared back at him from her boy's face, waiting for whatever he would say next. "I can't see that it matters," he said, trying to keep his voice casual. He even shrugged. "I mean—you think I'm falling in love with her and maybe that's true, I don't know. But why would she fall in love with me? Who am I? What would I even have to offer a woman? I'm nothing but a sword arm and a pack of muscle. I've never been anything else. Never *will* be anything else. I don't know why she'd want to be with me."

For a moment, Kirra's disguise actually wavered. He saw her true face flicker across her cheeks as her eyes softened and she laid a hand on his arm. "*Justin.* Don't say such a thing."

He pulled away because people might be watching. "It's true."

"It's *not* true. You have so much more to offer than a sword! Intelligence. Loyalty. You have—you are—you don't give up. You're—well, I've always thought of you as *dogged*, but I mean that in the best sense! If something matters to you, you can't be turned aside. And if this girl matters to you—" She shook her head. "Nothing I say will keep you from her. I just hope she deserves your heart if you decide to lay it at her feet."

"I don't know if I'll get the chance to find out. I don't know if I'll see her again. She's back in the convent now, and who knows when she'll get a chance to return to Neft? And it's not like I can go visit her there."

Kirra had her facade under control now, but she was still watching him. He thought he had rarely seen her so serious. "If you want to see her again, Justin, I'm sure you'll find a way."

* * *

IN the morning, Justin told Delz he had business to attend to, and he joined Kirra and Donnal a few miles outside of town. Neft was situated in the middle of flatlands that offered little vegetation besides spiky trees and cluttered undergrowth. They had to go some distance to be out of sight of the main road. When they were in a small, brushy valley that seemed completely safe from observation, they dropped their belongings and their basket of food.

"You realize Tayse will kill me if he ever realizes I've done this," Kirra said cheerfully.

"Any number of people want to kill you for any number of reasons," Justin replied. "Let's not worry about Tayse."

Last night before they had parted, she had agreed to practice her shape-changing skills on him—again. It was strictly forbidden for shiftlings to transform any humans but themselves, and in fact most shiftlings didn't even have the magic necessary to do so. But Kirra had learned the spells, and she had obviously turned them to good account this summer as she visited the patients on Dorrin Isle. Justin was the first person she had ever changed from man to beast, and she had twice turned him into a shaggy yellow hound. He had loved the sensation of being four-footed and fleet, bounding across a field with a wholly foreign kind of energy. He had loved the rich scents that tickled his nose, the distant sounds that played distinctly across his ears.

Today they were trying something else. Kirra was going to turn him into a bird.

"It won't do you any good to watch Donnal transform, but watch him anyway," Kirra instructed, and almost before the words were out of her mouth, Donnal was a crow. His obsidian feathers glinted in the weak sunlight; his eyes were an unblinking black. "Now watch the way he moves. See him lift his wings. Pay attention to how he moves his weight. Notice the placement of his eyes? On either side of his head? You won't see things the way you normally see them. You won't be looking straight in front of you."

"All right," said Justin impatiently. "Just change me. Now."

She laid her hands on his shoulders and pushed him down so they were both crouching in the yellowed grass. He could feel the heat in her hands, saw the intense strain on her face as she called up her power. His own body strung with a sudden tension, then his chest was crushed with pressure. He felt himself gasping for breath, unable to take it in. His hands balled into fists—or tried to—his fingers wouldn't curl, he had no fingers, he had no hands. The world whirled and shifted, grew monstrous, grew strange, he couldn't see, he couldn't think, he couldn't speak.

He opened his mouth to cry out and only a harsh cawing noise ripped from his throat.

Then suddenly he felt fine. Light, hollow, warm, but insubstantial.

He twisted his head, trying to get a look at himself, but it was hard to see more than a sweep of black, a thin mottled leg. His body was so weightless that almost any movement set him in motion, hopping to one side, unfurling his wings to keep his balance. *His wings!* He had wings! He was a bird. There were two other birds nearby, chattering at him as if trying to communicate, but the sounds would not resolve themselves into sense. One was a crow, one some rare red-feathered creature clearly too glamorous to exist in such a meadow.

That one had to be Kirra.

The crow flapped its wings and took off in a smooth glide, circling once over the clearing and coming in for a flawless landing. The scarlet creature chirped at Justin as if to say, *You see?*, and did her own graceful takeoff, swirl, and landing. It didn't look hard at all. Justin ruffled his feathers, hopped again (he couldn't seem to help it), and threw himself into the air.

And careened wildly through a mild breeze, almost crashed into a squat tree, somersaulted over a boulder, and fell awkwardly onto the soft earth. Instantly, the other two birds crowded around him, pelting him with incoherent exclamations. He was afraid that Kirra would decide this stunt was too perilous and turn him back into his natural state, so he righted himself quickly, gave them both a baleful stare from his left eye, and practiced a little strutting walk over the uneven ground. He was fine; nothing was broken. He just did not understand the principles of flight yet. Kirra was still following him, asking him urgent, indecipherable questions, but he ignored her. He spread his wings to their fullest, tried to gauge their power. He was used to working in utter harmony with his body; he knew exactly what his strengths and limits were. Just not *this* body. He would try again.

His second attempt at flight was slightly better—still clumsy but more controlled. At any rate, he landed where he wanted to, head up and every feather intact. All right. That time it had made a little more sense. He could do this. He just needed more practice.

Over the next two hours, Justin took progressively longer and more successful forays around the clearing. He still looked like a drunken bumblebee, he thought, at the mercy of any strong wind and wholly incapable of such maneuvers as landing on a tree branch, but he was getting the trick of it. Give him a few more days and he'd be able to take this shape to travel across Gillengaria.

"I think that's enough for one lesson," Kirra said, materializing in human form as Justin took a somewhat longer break. He tried to explain to her that he wasn't ready to change back yet, but his words came out as an agitated twitter. She didn't seem to have any trouble guessing what he was trying to convey, however. "I don't care what you want. I want to turn you back into a man while you're still more or less whole."

He didn't move away fast enough, and she cupped her hands around his small, trembling body. Again, that sense of heat and pressure, and then the world seemed to tilt and melt around him. He closed his eyes, taking a hard breath against a searing discomfort, and suddenly he was kneeling on the ground, his head resting against Kirra's palms, every bone and muscle of his body stretched with pain.

"Ow," he said, not opening his eyes. "This hurts more than I thought it would."

She pulled her hands away and knelt there until he opened his eyes. "I think you got pretty battered. I probably let that go on too long," she said. "Look. You've already got a bruise on your arm."

He tugged back his sleeves to do a quick inventory, then sat and turned up the legs of his trousers. Oh, yes, nicks and bruises everywhere, and the soles of his feet felt like he'd stomped across broken glass. He gave Kirra a sideways look. "Does this happen to you every time you change shapes?"

She shook her head, laughing. "I'm better at it. When I was younger and first learning, I had a few unfortunate incidents, but these days the transitions are always very smooth."

Donnal came to rest in the grass beside them, cawed once, and then shifted into his natural state. "Not too bad though," he said in an approving voice. "It's hard to master flying. Even harder to do it as a moth or a butterfly. It's just so different from everything you know."

"Can we come back tomorrow and practice again?" Justin asked.

Kirra was amused. "I am continually amazed that a man who expressed so much disdain for magic when I first met him—"

"That's before I understood how useful it could be," he answered, grinning.

"Before you found out how much you enjoyed it," she countered.

"That, too."

She rose to her feet and Justin followed suit, repressing a groan at the ache he felt in his thighs. "We can't stay," she said. "I'm already a week overdue in Danalustrous."

"But you'll come back? I want to do that again."

She was still amused. "We'll come back. Or maybe you'll be in Ghosenhall again before long. I'm sure we'll be heading there once we've left Danan Hall."

"Till then, I suppose."

"Till then."

She glanced at Donnal, who nodded, and the dark man flowed into the shape of a wolf. Kirra's own transformation followed, more choreographed, in some ways more unnerving. So much for a civilized good-bye. Donnal had already turned his head north and was scenting the air, checking for danger on the route ahead. Kirra stepped forward and butted her sleek, pointed head against Justin's leg, and he leaned down to pet the brushy fur.

"Travel safely," he said. "Thanks for coming by."

She nudged his hand again, then trotted to Donnal's side. Without a backward glance, the two went racing off, chasing each other through trees and bushes. Justin untied his horse and rather carefully hoisted himself into the saddle. The return trip to Neft seemed even longer than the trip out.

CHAPTER

14

FOUR days later, Ellynor was back. The intervening time had not been without incident, for more visitors had arrived in Neft. One was a serramarra of Nocklyn, come to visit her sick aunt at the Gisseltess house. She was accompanied by her husband, a dark and intense man that Justin was pretty sure Kirra and Senneth disliked. The second day they were in town, he left his wife's horse at the stables, took his own animal, and was gone a night and most of the next day. Justin found himself wondering if he had ridden out to Lumanen Convent. And whether Halchon Gisseltess and his entourage were still there. They had not come back this way.

A red-faced and unpleasant-looking fellow passed through the next day—no one Justin recognized, though he heard someone call him marlord Rayson. Justin guessed he was the man who held most of the lands in Fortunalt and was commonly believed to be allied with Halchon Gisseltess in a desire to take the throne.

Justin thought this must be the busiest little city in the south.

He actually said something of the sort that night to Faeber, who joined him in the Golden Boar for a beer as Justin was finishing his meal. The magistrate often worked his way around the tavern at night, having drinks with one table of men, playing a hand of cards with another group. Justin admired his style. A good way to get a sense of the mood in your town, a good way to show you were aware of what was going on.

When Justin made his remark about the recent wave of noble visitors, Faeber ran his hand through his unkempt gray hair, mussing it even more. "We get all kinds of traffic through Neft," the older man said, giving Justin an unreadable smile. "Even some Daughters today."

Justin kept his expression neutral. "Daughters? Oh, you mean from the convent?"

Faeber nodded, watching him. "Saw them ride in this afternoon.

So if you're feeling chivalrous and you see any of them on the streets to-morrow—"

Justin pretended to laugh. "I'll get my sword ready."

Faeber toyed with his glass. "You want to be careful about getting too close to those convent girls," he said at last.

Justin narrowed his eyes. "You warning me away from them, or warning me against them?"

"Wouldn't seem as though they could do any harm to you, would it?" Faeber said. "You'd think it might be the other way around. Man like you could take advantage of a young girl. But I don't think the convent guards take too kindly to anyone who gets interested in those novices."

"Well, I guess I'll just have to watch myself then."

"I guess you will."

Justin paid his bill, returned to his attic room to sleep for a couple of hours, and shook himself awake at midnight. Out into the crisp night air—they were well into autumn now, and the nights were brisk—to move with a catlike care through the quiet streets of the city. No matter what Faeber had said, Justin had read it as a warning. *I will be watching you.* His own men might be out prowling the streets tonight, patrolling past the Gisseltess house, under orders to make sure Justin did not loiter there.

But Justin was fairly confident that he could outwit any half-trained city guards who didn't know a damn thing about true combat.

At any rate, he only encountered a few other late-night wanderers, none of them in the uniform of the city guard, most of them drunk, and none of them near the Gisseltess house. He stood in the shadows and watched the windows, knowing by now which one overlooked serra Paulina's room and which one was the guest room commonly assigned to Ellynor. She would not be sure he knew she was in town, but she would look for him anyway; she would hope.

In fact, he had only been at his post about twenty minutes when he saw a haze of white at the serramarra's window. He stepped forward, still half in shadow, but knowing that Ellynor's keen eyes would pick him out just by motion. He did not want to risk waving or making himself too visible in case the form at the window was not her.

But it was. The glass was pushed back, and a body leaned out over the sill, gesticulating enthusiastically. He saw her turn her head back, as if to speak to someone in the room, and then she faced him again, holding up a finger. *Give me one minute.* She disappeared back inside and pulled the window shut behind her.

Justin drew back into the shadows to wait, imagining the stealthy route she must take through the sleeping house. Who might be awake at this hour? The old lady, obviously, and probably a footman or two. Anyone who was restless or troubled and could not sleep. Justin hoped Ellynor had a story ready if someone caught her.

No one did. A few minutes later she was creeping out the front door, flying across the yard, and letting herself noiselessly out the gate. Her hands were extended, so he took them in a strong clasp. She did not seem to mind.

"Justin! How did you know we were here? I looked for you when we rode in, but I didn't see you anywhere."

"Someone mentioned Daughters coming to town. So it's not just you this time?"

"No, there are five of us. This time I'm not here to take care of serra Paulina, though she did ask to see me while I'm here. But we've all come to proselytize in Neft tomorrow and the day after."

"What do you mean?"

She casually pulled her hands away as she answered. "We'll walk through the town square and offer the benediction of the Pale Mother to anyone who wants it. We'll stop people who try to hurry by, and we'll explain that the Silver Lady can see their souls, don't they want to do her honor? We'll give out moonstones to people who want them—and you'd be amazed how many people do."

Justin remembered riding through Neft many months ago, when the way was blocked by Daughters who wanted to lay their hands on every passerby. Donnal and Kirra and Cammon couldn't endure the touch of those hands, covered with moonstones; there had been a short, ugly scene when the Lestra's men came asking questions. "Do the convent guards come with you and watch to see who shies away from the Pale Mother's benediction?" he asked, a bitter edge to his voice.

"Yes," she said. "I hate it. I don't mind sharing the blessing of the Silver Lady—in fact, I rather like it, and so many people are quite grateful! But when people turn away, or hurry past, or look over at us, so afraid, and I see the guards watching them—I get anxious. I'm afraid of what might happen next."

"And have you seen it?"

"Seen what?"

He made a motion, as if he had suddenly pulled a hilt into his hand. "Seen what happens when the guards track down a nonbeliever."

"I'm not sure they do," she said, troubled now. "They're with us all day—most of the day, anyway—and surely they don't—I mean, there must be plenty of people here in Neft who—not everyone loves the goddess."

"I think your guards are looking for mystics," he said in a hard voice. "And they think anyone who won't take your benediction is suspect. And I think they follow some of those poor folks and question them in a pretty brutal way. I'm wondering if there aren't a few dead bodies littering the alleys on days after the novices come to town."

"Oh, no," Ellynor said, seriously distressed. "That can't be. The Lestra and her men abhor mystics, of course, but—I mean—they don't *harm* them. They don't—what are you saying? That the Lestra has them *killed*? Mystics? Justin, that can't be true."

"You're living under her roof and you don't know what she's capable of?"

"But, Justin—! You're talking about murder! Yes, she despises mystics— all the Daughters do—I listen to the rhetoric but I don't know that it means anything. It's like my brothers talking about the men they don't like and how they want to hurt their enemies, but it's mostly just muttering and posturing. The Lestra doesn't—I mean—"

He spoke in a gentle voice, because she was really upset, but his tone was uncompromising. "Throughout Gillengaria, for the past few years, there has been a rising tide of distrust toward mystics. Your Lestra has been the source of much of that distrust. She has spread her doctrine of hate across the Twelve Houses and to every small town and backwater farm from here to Brassenthwaite. Mystics have been stoned to death in city streets by common men enflamed by the words of the Daughters. But the Lestra is more direct than that," he said, raising his voice when she tried to speak. "As I rode into Neft five weeks ago, I came across a hut in the woods where a mystic woman was being tortured to death by five men. They all wore convent livery. They were there under the Lestra's orders."

Now Ellynor was staring at him as if he had told her the worst possible news. Her house had been burned down, all her family was dead. No one she loved was left alive. "What happened to her?" she whispered.

He did not particularly want to recount this tale, he suddenly realized—did not want to tell his part in it. "She escaped," he said shortly.

"And the men? The convent guards?"

He watched her a good long moment before answering. Well, it had been inevitable. She was used to violent men, but she had made it clear she did not condone their ways, and if she knew him long enough, she would learn just how ruthless he could be. And then, even if she had liked him before, she would like him no longer, and he might as well tell her now and watch her walk away. If not tonight, some other time. Some other wretched day or night.

"Dead—four of them, at any rate," he said.

She swallowed. "You killed them?"

He just nodded.

Then she surprised him. "Why not the fifth one?"

He looked away. "He was a boy. He looked—sick. Horrified at what was being done. I didn't think he had a hand in her torture. I thought he wanted an excuse to run. I let him go."

"Great blessed Mother," she breathed, and fell forward into his arms.

His hands came up automatically to enfold her; she was weeping bitterly against his chest. He didn't know what to say, how to console her, how to explain himself or apologize. He could not believe she had not picked up her skirts and raced back inside the house, away from him and his bloodstained hands. Instead she clung to him for comfort, and he cradled her against his body. *Bright Mother burn me*, he thought. *She is so tiny and frail. If I hold her too closely, she will break.* And yet he drew his arms around her even more tightly.

"I'm sorry," he whispered into her dark hair. "I thought you knew. I thought everyone knew. I'm sorry it was me who told you. I'm sorry I'm the one who—who stopped the guards. I'm sorry this is the truth of the world."

It was a few moments before she was calm enough to speak, and by that time Justin had pulled them both to the ground and settled Ellynor across his lap. He had never done such a thing before, and yet it seemed entirely natural. He noticed that her feet were not bare tonight, though she wore only thin slippers. Still, better than nothing on a chilly night like this.

"I wish I didn't believe you," she said finally. She was sitting sideways across his legs, her head against his chest, and he had to lean down to hear her quiet voice. "But I do. I'll ask Astira tomorrow, and maybe she'll tell me that you've made it all up, it's not true, but somehow I don't think you'd lie to me. I mean, I know there are things you're not telling me, and I don't count that as lying. But about something like this—I don't think you'd mislead me."

"I'm so sorry, Ellynor."

"Anyway, I know it's true. We heard that five guards were missing, and that some of the bodies had been found. Someone said something about mystics, but I thought—I thought it was mystics who killed them. I didn't know the guards were trying to do the killing."

"The Lestra wants to destroy them all. I'm sure there will be more murders." He thought of the scene he had witnessed, the convent guards burning down a nobleman's house, and decided Ellynor could not bear to hear that story tonight. "Coralinda Gisseltess says she is carrying out the divine will of the Pale Mother."

Ellynor stirred in his arms but did not pull away. "That's not true," she said.

"What's not true? It is what she says."

"Maybe, but—I don't think—it doesn't seem to me—I don't think the Pale Mother is so cruel. She's a vain and fickle goddess, yes, but there's a sort of—childlike quality to her. She wants to be loved and admired. She'll do anything she can to draw attention. But demand that people be killed—any people? I don't think so. I just don't believe it."

Justin found himself, unexpectedly, amused. "And what would you know about the Silver Lady?"

A sound from Ellynor, almost a laugh. "Well, they're sisters, aren't they? All the goddesses? Where I come from, people worship the Dark Watcher, the goddess of night. And she is complex and difficult, and she hides terrible secrets, and I have known her to be cruel a time or two. But she doesn't call for anyone's murder. I don't believe the Pale Mother does, either. I think the Lestra must have misunderstood."

Ellynor's hair had come loose from its knot while she rested her head against Justin's chest, and now he ran his hands through it, slowly, absently, straightening out the tangles. The sliver of the moon had already set; there was not enough light to see the variegated patterns dyed into her hair, but he remembered them clearly enough. "Most people talk only of the Pale Mother," he said cautiously. "Only lately have I heard references to any of the other goddesses—the Bright Mother, the Wild Mother—I think there are others. But no one seems to know anything about them."

She seemed to tense slightly, as if afraid she had given something away. "I only know anything about those two," she said rather quickly. "The goddess of night and the goddess of the moon. I couldn't answer any of your questions."

He had plenty of questions, none of them about deities. He continued stroking her hair until she grew calm again, relaxing against him. "So you think the Pale Mother does not hate mystics as much as the Lestra does," he said. "That's interesting."

"All the Daughters seem to hate mystics," she said.

He kept his voice casual, his hand gentle, so she could not know how important this question was to him. "How do you feel about mystics, El-lynor? Have you been influenced even a little by the Lestra's hate?"

But something in his tone gave him away, because she tilted her head back as if trying to see his face more clearly. "I don't think I hate anybody just on principle," she said. "But why do you want to know?"

He chose his words carefully. "I have friends who are mystics—good friends. They will be in my life always, I think. If you and I are to be friends, I can't be afraid that you will denounce them. I can't be worrying that I put people I care about at risk."

She was quiet long enough for him to imagine various cold responses. *You don't know me well enough to be worrying about how I fit into your life. Or, Are you telling me you would put other friendships above mine? Why would I want to continue this relationship then?* But she did not offer those observations. "So it's true," she said quietly. "You protect the people you love even when they're not right in front of you."

He wasn't sure what that meant. "I just want to know how you feel about mystics," he said earnestly. "It's important to me."

She gave a soft laugh. "I'm not even really sure what mystics *are*," she confessed. "I don't think I've ever come across one in my life."

"They can do magic."

"But what does that mean? Magic? What kind of magic?"

"It depends on the mystic. Some can call fire. Some can change shapes."

"Change shapes—you mean, change from human form? To what?"

"They become animals, mostly. Birds, wolves, dogs. I think they can even turn themselves into insects if they want."

She sounded intrigued. "How exciting and frightening that would be! Can they still think? Are they still themselves? I don't think I'd like that."

He splayed his hand and let rivulets of dark hair trickle between each finger. "They say they are still themselves even in their altered forms. And, after all, they're able to change themselves back, so they must re-member who they really are."

"Are there more kinds of magic?"

He nodded. "There are readers—men and women who can sense what you're thinking and what you're feeling. There are healers who can make you well if you're sick."

Ellynor laughed. "Oh, that's not magic. That's just the grace of the goddess."

"Well, some people think sorcery is a gift from the gods. That each goddess has a particular strength or skill, and she's passed this on to a few special people."

"If that's really true, think how angry the gods would be at the Lestra! For trying to harm the people that the deities had singled out!"

"So maybe the gods will go to war right alongside the marlords," he said, slightly amused. "Think what a battle we would have then."

She pushed away from him, a hand against his chest. "What do you mean, a war? You mentioned rebellion once before—and serra Paulina talked about an uprising—what's happening? What are you afraid of?"

He was sure that, even in the dark, she could see the grimness on his face. "Some people believe that Halchon Gisseltess is gathering the marlords in a bid to take the throne. And that his sister—your Lestra—is in league with him. So far they haven't made any overt moves, but the king is watching them. And everyone is afraid of what might happen next."

She was still staring at him. "And you? What will you do, if there is a war? You're a fighter. You must be planning to fight for somebody."

He tried to pull her back against his chest, but she resisted, flattening her fingers against his vest and keeping her arm rigid. "I will fight with those who side with the king," he said. "Which means I will be at war with Halchon Gisseltess and his sister. I hope that does not mean I will be at war with you."

Now her face looked as troubled as it had earlier, when he told her about the hunting and murdering of mystics. "I do not want to go to war with anybody," she said.

"You may be forced to choose," he said gently. "If you cannot countenance what the Lestra does, what she says, you may have to leave the convent. In fact, I think you should. You are—"

"I can't leave," she said quickly. "Not now. Not with Rosurie still there and my family convinced that I am safely within the walls of Lumanen. If I could talk to my father or my brother—I have to think about this. I can't just leave."

"If you're afraid of the Lestra, I could help you," he said, pressing her a little. "I could hide you in Neft and help you get clear of the city."

"And take me all the way back to my family?" she asked skeptically.

"Yes. I would do that."

"No, you wouldn't, because if Torrin saw you riding up with me by your side—oh, you don't know what kind of trouble that would cause! Justin, I have to think about this. I am appalled by everything you've said but I—I have to understand it before I decide what to do next. I have to think about everything."

"Think about it," he said. "And come see me tomorrow."

To his great disappointment, she drew herself clear of his arms and came to her feet. He stood beside her, thinking, as always, how small she was next to him. "I'm not sure I can," she said. "Come to you tomorrow, I mean. There are five of us, and we'll be together the entire time. I don't see that I'll be able to get free."

"Tomorrow night then? Here?"

She gazed at him, her expression uncertain. "I probably shouldn't."

"Why? Why not?"

She hesitated and then gave a candid answer. "I think maybe you've upset me too much. I think maybe I'm too confused to see you again so soon."

He felt a sudden gust of something that felt like panic, though it seemed a strange time to experience a battlefield emotion. "But I have so little time to see you," he said. "Only the minutes you can steal during the few days you're in Neft. I hate to lose any chances to talk to you. I'm sorry I said the things I did—even though they're true and I think you should know them. Don't stay away from me."

She stood undecided in the dark. "We'll see," she said at last, and put a hand on the gate.

He grabbed one of the wrought-iron rods to keep the gate from opening. "I'll come by," he said. "Tomorrow night. I'll be here. If you want to talk."

"Maybe," she said. She pushed on the gate again and he reluctantly released his hold, allowing it to swing open. Ellynor made as though to step through, paused, and turned back to him. Reaching up with one hand, she drew his head down, and kissed him lightly on the cheek. "It was good to see you, Justin."

And then, before he could move or speak or respond in any way, she gathered her skirts and flew back to the house. Almost immediately, she disappeared from view. He watched the windows for ten minutes, for thirty, but she did not appear at any of them to wave goodnight. With a heavy heart—that bounded with unexpected lightness every time he remembered that kiss—he headed home.

THE workday was long and full of minor frustrations. Delz was in a foul mood and shoveled manure as venomously as if it had offered him a personal affront. An irate traveler claimed that he had already paid for his horse's accommodations upon arrival and refused to pay again as he left. A mare in the back stall had nicked herself badly with her own clumsy hoof, so Justin prepared a poultice and kept her leg wrapped most of the day. They were busy enough that he missed lunch and devoured his dinner.

He was tired enough that he climbed to his third-floor bedroom and fell instantly asleep.

Near midnight, he came awake suddenly and completely. From Tayse he had learned the ability to wake when he wanted, prepared to take the night watch. He dressed in the dark, crept downstairs and outside, and moved silently through the streets to the Gisseltess house.

Where he waited for two hours alone.

Ellynor did not come down to join him. She did not appear at any of the windows and wave. If she watched him from the shadows of the house, she stood back far enough that he could see no flicker of movement, no flash of white. If she was awake and thinking of him, she gave no sign.

After the second hour passed, Justin pushed himself to his feet and made his way slowly back to the boardinghouse. His thoughts were chaotic, but the line of his mouth was hard. He had never been the sort of man who gave up easily. Now would not be the time he began.

CHAPTER

15

In the morning, Justin was at the stables ahead of Delz, forking down the hay, watering the horses, and cleaning out the stalls. "Got somewhere to be for a little bit this afternoon," he told the stablemaster when Delz commented on his industriousness. "I'm going to be gone a couple hours. Thought I'd get a little ahead on the work."

"Fine," Delz said with a shrug. "But you'll be back for the evening shift?"

"I will."

After eating a quick lunch, Justin washed his hands again, changed into a fresh shirt, and set out looking for evangelists in the streets of Neft.

It took him nearly thirty minutes to track down the Daughters. He'd thought they'd be near the crossroads where most of the shops were congregated and where the majority of traffic passed through, both on foot and by horse. But that part of town, though clogged with carts and pedestrians, held no cluster of smiling young women clad in white robes and sparkling moonstones. No, and no escort of silent men, wearing black-and-silver livery and watching every stranger who passed by, trying to guess his secrets.

He found them, eventually, at the west edge of town, not far from a small shrine set up to honor the Pale Mother. They had positioned themselves on the edge of the main road that led into Neft from the southwestern parts; anyone bent on traveling into the city from Rappengrass or Fortunalt was bound to pass this way. Justin loitered behind one of the scattered buildings found this far from the city center, trying to get a sense of how successful their day had been so far. While he watched, most of the open carts and gigs that came through pulled to a halt. The drivers, with every appearance of satisfaction, accepted the novices' prayers and blessings. Two closed carriages bowled on past without stopping; one of them was allowed to go unmolested, but the other one was immediately followed by two of the Lestra's guards. Justin watched them go, wondering what would happen next. A confrontation here in the middle of Neft? Surely not. More likely the guards would ride behind the carriage till it cleared the city, and possibly make some kind of move once they were past the crowded streets. Or they might mark where the carriage came to a halt inside the city limits, and note which house entertained guests who were not eager to take the blessing of the Daughters.

Even once those soldiers had vanished in pursuit, there were still seven convent guards stationed on both sides of the road near the novices.

Justin slipped from his hiding place, headed back toward the middle of the city, then left Neft by a northern route. After making a wide loop, he came out on the main road and began a steady walk eastward toward town. A couple of carts passed him, and he waved when the drivers seemed friendly. A group of horsemen clattered by, clearly in a hurry. Two riders came the other way, leaving the city. He was close enough now to notice that they paused, bent their heads, and held out their hands to receive the benediction of the goddess.

In a few minutes, he was strolling straight toward the sacred roadblock, five girls strung across the road with their hands lifted and their faces serene. A cart rolled up behind him just as he arrived, so there was a little flurry of motion, horses whickering, voices calling, the sound of wheels grinding to a halt. White robes fluttered as the girls circled and murmured among themselves. Who would approach the cart, who would see to the man on foot?

Justin put his hands in his back pockets and a bumpkin's grin on his face, and beamed at the assembled company. His eyes were making quick appraisals. There was Ellynor, staring at him in something like fear; there were four other girls of various ages and sizes. One of them looked enough like her to be her cousin Rosurie. Just beyond them was the ring of convent guards, watchful, ready, unsmiling.

A tall girl about Ellynor's age was giving directions. "Rosurie, there's another cart coming! You and Lia talk to them. Semmie, help me with this one. Ellynor, can you talk to that man who just walked up?"

"I'd sure like the blessing of the goddess today," Justin said in a hearty voice.

Ellynor made no move in his direction, so the other woman gave her a slight nudge. "Hurry! I see another carriage down the road. I never thought we'd be this busy." And she and a very young girl approached the open gig, their hands upraised, moonstones dangling from their wrists. "The blessing of the Pale Mother upon you this afternoon!"

Still looking a little unwilling, but conscious of many pairs of eyes on her, Ellynor stepped up to Justin. She put her hands up and Justin immediately moved forward to press his own palms against hers. "The blessing of the Mother upon you," she said in a low voice.

She would have dropped her hands right away, but Justin curled his fingers over hers to keep her in place. It was clear she did not want to make a scene, not with so many people watching, so she did not try to jerk free. "Thank you for your kindness," he said. "Could you do a favor for a penitent?"

She had avoided his eyes at first, but that made her look at him and frown. "What favor?"

"I have no moonstone, nothing by which to call the goddess. I understand that convent novices sometimes hand them out. I would be grateful if that were so—if I could take one from your hand."

Wordlessly, Ellynor nodded and pulled out of his light hold. She reached into a pocket of her robe and produced a moonstone, small and milky and attached to a silver chain. When she laid it in his outstretched palm, he quickly lifted his other hand to imprison hers between both of his. He thought she flinched, almost as if the moonstone between their hands burned into her flesh. Certainly the gem seemed hot to the touch, scalding his own skin.

He barely noticed. "Thanks be to the Great Mother," he said piously. "I will treasure this always."

She nodded and tried to free her hand. When he did not release her, she gave him an indignant look. "May she watch over you all your days," she said, but her tone was cold.

"Come to me tonight?" he breathed, still giving her the idiot's smile he expected any man who loved the goddess to wear.

"You have to let go of me," she replied, her voice almost inaudible.

"Tonight?" he repeated.

"Yes," she said, and tried again to break his hold.

He hung on. "A promise?"

"Yes."

He let her go. "Praise be to the blessed lady," he said. He gave her another broad smile, bobbed his head at one of the other novices who happened to glance his way, and carefully stowed the moonstone in the pocket of his shirt. Whistling now, he continued down the main road, into the heart of Neft, and made his way back to the stables.

* * *

THAT night, Ellynor practically burst out of the doorway and flew down the walk to where Justin was waiting outside the gate. Her passage was utterly silent, but she was clearly furious. "Justin! How dare you come to me in public like that? Don't you know how dangerous that was? Don't you know that everyone was watching—all the novices, all the soldiers?"

Her hands had been outstretched as if to give him a good hard shove, but he caught them in his and then kept them when she would have yanked away. "I was careful. I didn't do anything anyone would notice. I wanted to see you."

She twisted her hands, unable to free them. "Well, I told you I wasn't ready to see you! I needed time to think."

"But that's not fair," he argued. "Why should you get to choose? Why shouldn't I be able to decide? What if I have things to say even if you don't want to hear them?"

She was silent a moment, and she stopped struggling. Then she sighed. "I suppose you're right," she said. "We're in a very strange position, both of us, and we cannot give in to moods and tantrums."

He grinned. "I never have either."

"Well, you make me want to have both."

She tugged at her hands again, and he dropped one of them, but kept the other and tucked it into his elbow. "Let's walk a little," he said. "I know the front of this house by memory, from staring at it so long."

She fell in step beside him willingly enough; indeed, he felt her fingers tighten upon the crook of his arm. They strolled forward, following the downward slope of the hill. Justin let the silence run on a little, because Ellynor was clearly thinking about something, and then she spoke abruptly. "I asked Astira, and she said you were right."

"Who's Astira?"

"One of the other novices. She was there this afternoon—the tall girl. Well, she said she didn't think the soldiers *killed* mystics, but that they tortured them, trying to get them to renounce magic. And when I said, 'But that's terrible!' she gave me this very strange look and said, 'But mystics are evil. They have to be destroyed.' And I think all the novices agree."

"So you believe me now?" She nodded. "Does it make you want to leave the convent?"

The sound she made was half a laugh, half an exhalation of despair. "There have been days I've wanted to leave the convent ever since I arrived," she said. "But it's not so simple."

"But you'll think about it? I could help you leave."

"I'll think about what I should do next," she said, a note of finality in her voice.

So he changed the subject. Sort of. "How long will you be here this time?"

"Only another day, I think. But I might be back. Serra Paulina is doing very well but she told me she starts feeling listless and weak when I'm not around. At first I thought she was teasing, but she's very frail. I think she could fall sick again at any minute—you know how old people are always catching every cough and fever that comes along."

"I wouldn't wish anyone a fever, but I hope she'll find a way to call you back."

She laughed. "Yes, because I'm sure your life is quite dull when I'm not around."

He grinned. "Mostly. Though Kirra and Donnal passed through last week, and it's hard to ever be bored when Kirra's nearby."

She turned her head to look at him and spoke in the coolest of voices. "Oh? Kirra? Who's that?"

"One of my mystic friends. She was curious about you, too."

Ellynor came to a complete halt and pulled her hand free. He was so surprised he let her go. "You were talking about me? To someone else? You were gossiping about a novice from the convent?"

She was angry, but he wasn't sure why. "I know, the Lestra wouldn't like that, but you can trust Kirra. It was months before I could actually stand her, even though she's so beautiful that most men are practically falling at her feet. But now I consider her one of my closest friends. I know she'd do anything for me if I needed help."

"I certainly hope she's within call if you're ever in trouble," Ellynor snapped, and began stalking down the street.

Dumbfounded, Justin caught her arm and didn't let go when she tried to jerk from his hold. "Wait, wait! What? I'm sorry, what did I say?"

"Well, why are you standing here talking to *me* at midnight when this beautiful, delightful woman is your *closest friend*? The person who entertains you when you're bored—the person you rely on most—why aren't you off somewhere visiting with *her*?"

He stared at her. He had heard people describe jealousy before, he had just never expected anyone to feel it in relation to him. "Ellynor. Don't be silly. I—"

She wrenched away and clutched her skirts in her hands. "I have to get back to the house," she muttered and took off at a run.

Justin caught her in three steps. This time she really was fighting him, but he was much too powerful for her. He turned her in his arms, crushed her against him with one arm so that she had no chance of breaking free, and used his other hand to force her chin up. "Ellynor," he said sternly. "What are you thinking?"

"Let go of me," she panted.

"Kirra's my friend. She'd laugh if she thought you could be jealous of her—"

Wrong thing to say. Ellynor uttered a little cry of outrage and struggled furiously in his arms, kicking at him hard enough to leave bruises, trying to get her hands loose to claw or slap him. He didn't know what to do. He tightened his hold, lifting her completely off the ground, and when she opened her mouth as if to scream, he kissed her.

For a moment, everything stopped. Ellynor's struggles, the sounds of the night, Justin's thoughts, Justin's heart. For a moment, he lost himself in wonder and sensation as he kissed the girl who lay so calmly in his arms. It was like holding formed silk, tamed fire; it was like heat and luxury and excitement all at once.

Then she broke the kiss and made a mad scrabble for freedom and, cursing himself, he let her go. How many times had she told him she despised ruthlessness, how often had he heard her talk about her brothers and their friends, so rough and domineering? He didn't want to be like the men she railed against. He didn't want her to think he was the kind of man who took what he wanted from a woman just because he could.

She was backing away from him, her blue eyes wide and dark, hands out to push him away if he tried to touch her again. He followed, his own hands up as if in surrender, as if showing her he was innocent of weapons. "I'm sorry," he said, over and over, as she continued to back away, as he continued to follow. "Ellynor, I'm sorry. Please. Wait. Talk to me."

Against all hope, she halted, and he halted a few paces away, still penitent. "I'm sorry," he said again.

Her eyes were huge, but even so, she bent forward a little, as if she was having trouble seeing him—she who could read manuscripts in the dark. "Why did you stop?" she asked in a low voice.

"Because I shouldn't have started. Because that was wrong, that was unfair. I don't want to be that kind of man. I want to be the kind of man—" He paused and took a shuddering breath. "I'd rather be a man you trusted. A man you felt safe to be with. Ellynor, I'm so sorry."

She stepped closer, close enough to touch. "I do trust you," she said, and kissed him on the mouth.

This time, when his arms encircled her, he held her as if she was breakable, as if he could mar her skin unless he was careful. She put her arms around his neck, pulling him closer; her mouth clung to his as if she was afraid he would desert her. The part of him that was not alive with physical pleasure was drunk with marvel—that he could be holding such a woman, that she could be kissing him, that she could seem to want him as much as he suddenly wanted her.

There was a jingle, a hoofbeat, a horse's snort, and Justin was suddenly slammed with combat adrenaline. Riders approaching, and he had not heard them till they were almost upon him! In a few rough motions, he had torn away from Ellynor, thrust her behind him, and drawn his sword. He could see the three mounted men picking their way up the hill, turning their heads this way and that as they peered into the shadows. Within seconds, they would spy Justin and Ellynor, foolishly standing like landmarks on the edge of the road without a shelter in sight. Running would only draw more attention to them. He tightened his hold on his hilt.

"Don't worry," Ellynor breathed in his ear. "They won't see us. Stand very still and they will pass us by."

Before he could ask what she meant, a filmy black shadow seemed to settle over the spot where he and Ellynor waited. It was as if an errant drift of night sky piled around them, dense and opaque, but light as air. Ellynor's hands stole around his waist and he felt her lean against his back, but otherwise she was frozen in place. Justin stood motionless, listening intently, since it was difficult to see through the haze of black. The slow clop of horses' hooves, the low murmur between men, the creak of saddle leather. Coming closer, moving on, finally disappearing altogether.

Justin drew a deep breath and seemed to inhale all the black fog, or else it dissipated in a single instant. Sheathing his sword, he turned slowly, careful not to displace Ellynor's grip, and put his hands on her shoulders. "What did you do?" he asked quietly.

She was smiling. "I told you. My brothers taught me how to creep from a house—or cross a mock battlefield in stealth. Torrin can call a darkness so profound it covers an entire valley. I can only do little tricks, like that one."

He wasn't even sure how to ask the question. "What kind of magic is that?"

She shook her head. "Oh, no. It's not magic. It's just—I told you, my family worships the Black Mother, and she responds when we send her our prayers. I prayed for darkness just then—and you see, she answered!"

His thoughts were in a complete jumble. He didn't know enough about magic to know if this was the way it worked for other mystics—if, indeed, this sort of skill would be in their repertoires. But it seemed like power, nonetheless, and something Coralinda Gisseltess would view with great suspicion.

"You don't want to say those kinds of prayers when you're in the convent," he said urgently. "You say it's not magic, but it might look mystical to the Lestra. You don't want to call darkness or even talk about how the Black Mother helps you heal sick people. You don't want to put yourself in danger."

She had been smiling, pleased with herself, but now her face took a somber expression. "I won't. I haven't. I mean, I've helped out in the infirmary, but I've been careful what I've said—mostly—" Her voice trailed off.

His hands tightened on her shoulders. "Ellynor, I'm not sure you're safe there," he said. "The more I learn about you, the more I think you shouldn't be living there."

She dropped her arms and stepped back, and he let his own hands fall. "I know what you think," she said. "I need to decide that for myself."

He sighed, unwilling to have an argument again. He glanced back over his shoulder, but the men were truly gone. "Who were they, could you tell?" he asked. "I couldn't see through your—haze."

"Soldiers from the convent," she said shortly. "They would have been most unhappy to find me out with you."

Kissing in the dark. Yes, Justin could imagine how unhappy the guards would have been. "We'd probably better get you back then," he said, "in case anyone else comes looking for you."

They turned in the direction of the Gisseltess house, no more than a quarter mile away. But they moved slowly, neither of them eager for the night to end. Experimentally, Justin reached for Ellynor's hand, and she allowed him to take it. She even squeezed his fingers as if to make certain he was real.

Outside the gate, they stopped and regarded each other by insufficient starlight. "I think some things have changed tonight," Justin said hesitantly.

Ellynor nodded. "I think so."

"I'm not good at this. I don't know how to do this. But Ellynor, I—I have to see you again. This has become too important to me."

She nodded again. "It's important to me, too, Justin. But I don't know—there are so many reasons—I don't think there are any promises

I can make. I *want* to see you, please believe that. If I stay away, it's because I don't have much control over my comings and goings or—or—because it seems better for both of us that we're not together."

"It won't be better for me," he said immediately.

She smiled, but he thought the expression was a little sad. "Someday we'll tell each other our secrets," she said. "And everything may change again."

She lifted her face, an invitation, so he bent to kiss her one last time. When he lifted his head, her fresh smile was a little brighter. *"There's something to dream about,"* she said in a whisper. And she slipped away from him before he could kiss her again. A few moments later she had disappeared inside the house.

CHAPTER
16

ONE more night when Ellynor met him in secret—one more rapturous interlude of shy smiles and stolen kisses—and then she was gone. Justin was watching from the side of the street when the cavalcade rode by, five novices and nine guards. If Ellynor saw him, she made no sign.

Justin found himself wondering how soon he could go out to Lumanen again. Convince Delz he needed another two or three days off, then creep through the forest and find himself a convenient perch to spy on the convent. How could he communicate with Ellynor if she was inside the walls and he outside? If she knew he was loitering in the forest, could she make up some excuse for going outside the gates? Why hadn't he thought to ask these questions, make these preparations, before she left town again?

Too many kisses, not enough plans.

He was glum and sullen for two days, until he noticed how carefully Delz was avoiding him, and he realized he was behaving like a man who would start a fight without provocation. So he forced himself to improve his mood, at least outwardly, and was relieved to see Delz relax. Faeber came up to him that night at dinner and talked breezily for twenty minutes, and the magistrate hadn't said a word to him for days.

Justin supposed he could seem fairly ferocious when he was in a foul mood. None of the Riders, of course, was afraid of him, so he wasn't used to the effect his scowl might have.

And, anyway, he was rarely ill-tempered, at least as he saw it. Sarcastic and disdainful, yes, much of the time, but he never felt like *this*—like he wanted to pummel someone, anyone, merely for the crime of breathing. He expended his considerable energy by doing extra work around the stables. When Delz wasn't around, he took off his boots and shirt and practiced bladework in the barn. His body hadn't lost any of its conditioning during this enforced exile from the training yard, but his hand might be a bit slower on the feint, he thought. He pulled his dagger into his left hand, kept his sword in his right, and practiced thrusting and parrying against insubstantial opponents. If only there were another Rider here to train against! He hated the thought that he might be losing an inch of ground, a fraction of his speed.

As if a particular goddess watched over him and heard that prayer, the very next day his plea was answered.

IT was evening, but the greatest rush of night traffic was over, and Delz had just told Justin he could leave to get his supper. Justin stepped outside into the gathering dark and noted that the temperature had dropped considerably from the sunny afternoon. Three riders were approaching at a lazy trot, angling toward the stables in a way that made Justin think they were looking to house their horses for the night. He paused, willing to do Delz a favor by taking in these last stragglers. A woman and two men, the one man good-sized, muscular, about the build of Tayse—

Justin slapped his fist against his thigh and hurried forward, smiling broadly. It *was* Tayse—and Senneth and Cammon—all of them wearing warm smiles to match his own. "What are you doing here?" he demanded, catching at Senneth's bridle as they got close enough to stop. Her hair was in even greater disarray than usual, as if they'd ridden through windstorms at breakneck speed. Or as if she'd merely failed to comb it that morning. He looked over at the other Rider. "You said you'd send messengers, but I didn't think you'd be coming yourself."

"We've got business in Coravann and decided to ride through Neft," Tayse said. "Cammon said he wanted to come."

"Should we have some kind of alias ready?" Senneth inquired. "Or would people expect you to actually have friends among the king's men?"

He grinned. Tayse wasn't displaying his royal insignia, and Senneth never wore anything that showed off her Brassenthwaite heritage. It would be easy to pass them off as mercenaries or drifters. "I'm not sure anyone would believe that tale. We'd better find another one."

The three of them dismounted and looked around. "Where does a person sleep in this town?" Senneth wanted to know.

"I'm in a boardinghouse up the street. I've only got one extra bed, but there might be more rooms to rent. If not, I can sleep in the stables."

"Where do we *eat*? I'm starving," Cammon said.

Tayse gave Justin one quick, serious look. "We have much to talk about that is best said in private," Tayse said quietly. "Perhaps it would be better to buy food and bring it here. If that's allowed."

Justin nodded. "I'll tell Delz—the owner. He won't care. It's a couple more hours he won't have to mind the stables."

"Come on, Cam, you and I will go find this boardinghouse," Senneth said. "Tayse, you'll go foraging for food?"

He nodded at her and pulled a pack from the saddle, jingling with coins. Justin gathered up all the bridles.

"I'll settle the horses and tell Delz to go home," he said. "See you soon."

HALF an hour later they were all disposed around the front room of the stables, sitting on benches and bales of hay. Tayse had brought back more food than they could possibly eat, so they were all feeling full and happy. Outside, the night air was chilly, but inside, Senneth's magic made the room comfortably warm. She'd also lit tapers at strategic points to give them more light than Justin was used to indoors at this hour. Place looked a little grimy when you could see it this clearly. Maybe he should spend a few hours cleaning next week.

Tayse hadn't received Justin's message, since his party had left Ghosenhall before it arrived, so Justin filled him in on Halchon's arrival and the Lestra's nighttime depredations. The other Rider was deeply displeased to learn that the marlord had slipped away from Gissel Plain a second time.

"He'll have to go back, though, won't he?" Justin said as he finished up his meal.

"I assume so, since I would think that's where he keeps both his money and his manpower," said Tayse. "Unless he's craftier than we realize and has set up armies and stores of gold in secret locations."

"I'm betting on him being crafty," Senneth said pessimistically.

"No reason some of that gold couldn't be in the convent," Justin said. "Since he was there. And it's fortified. And defended."

"Actually, that seems to be a likely hiding place," Tayse said.

"And if it is," Justin added, "anyone working with Halchon Gisseltess could ride up to the convent and get access to some of the gold. Rayson Fortunalt, for instance. He was here the other day, or at least I think it was him."

Senneth was frowning. "What would Rayson need with more money? He's got plenty of his own—and taxing his vassals at a rate that's causing plenty of complaints, I might add. A half dozen of the lesser Fortunalt lords were in Ghosenhall for the summit with the regent."

Tayse gave her a long, considering look. "Why would Rayson Fortunalt need more money?" he repeated. "Who might he be paying?"

"Soldiers," Justin said promptly.

"Can't he afford his own army?"

Justin glanced at Senneth, who was still frowning. "Hiring from somewhere else?" Justin guessed. "Freelance mercenaries? Malcontents from the loyal Houses? How much money would that take?"

"This is worrisome," Senneth said. "All along we've been assuming Halchon is raising an army of zealots—people who hate mystics, who think the king is too old to rule, people who are genuinely afraid for the future. I believe they're misguided, but they have some personal stake in a war, if it should come. But if Rayson is raising an army of mercenaries—with Halchon Gisseltess's money—"

"That ends up being an even bigger army than we thought," Tayse said.

"Exactly."

"Well, we're just speculating about the gold," Justin said.

"It's a speculation that has the unfortunate ring of truth," Tayse replied.

Cammon, who had been quiet during this whole discussion, stirred on his seat of hay. "I wonder how we can find out if there's a store of money at Lumanen Convent," he said.

Senneth glanced at him, faintly smiling. "Can you ride by the gates and concentrate? Try to sense great piles of gold locked in one of the empty rooms?"

"No," he said regretfully. "I never get a sense of *things*. Only people."

Justin was laughing. "Well, maybe you can sense if any people there are planning how they can break in and steal a fat handful of coins."

Cammon looked intrigued. "That I might be able to do."

"Seems risky and not particularly useful," Tayse said. "I'm willing to assume the money's there."

Justin considered. "I wonder if Ellynor could find out."

There was a moment's silence while the other three all looked at him. "Ellynor?" Senneth said in a neutral voice.

Justin tried to look casual. "A novice from the convent. I've made friends with her."

"On the face of it, an impossible task," Tayse said.

Justin shrugged, as if the tale didn't matter. "She was walking the streets of Neft until she was attacked by a man who was interested in something other than a moonstone. I stopped him, and we fought—well, it wasn't much of a fight—then I brought her back here. We talked a little bit. I couldn't see *what* good it could do, exactly, but I thought it might be useful to have someone who lived inside Lumanen and had some goodwill toward us."

"Have you seen her since that first time?" Tayse asked.

"Actually, yes. She's been sent to Neft a few times to nurse an old woman. Wait, let me see if I've got this right." He couldn't keep all the Twelfth House bloodlines straight, but he knew Senneth would instantly be able to recognize the names. "There's a woman here in town named Jenetta Gisseltess. She has a big mansion. I can show it to you. She gives a lot of money to the Lumanen Convent. So Coralinda tries to keep her happy and brought a bunch of the novices in to pray over Jenetta's mother when they thought the mother was dying. She's still alive, though, and she's someone from Nocklyn—a serramarra, I think? Is that right? Paulina, that's her name."

Senneth was nodding. "Els Nocklyn's sister. Mayva's aunt." Justin remembered now. Marlord Els was sick and his daughter, Mayva, was running his estates—but Mayva was married to a Gisseltess man, and so Kirra and Senneth had figured Nocklyn would side against them in a war. "Interesting information, but I don't see how it helps us any."

"Ellynor says Paulina doesn't care much for Coralinda and her religion."

That caught Senneth's attention. "So you've discussed some rather delicate subjects with this Ellynor?"

He nodded. "Yes. We've had pretty long conversations. I feel like I know her."

"You think she's someone you can actually trust?"

"Well—I do," he said.

"Have you told her who you are?" Tayse asked.

"No. But we've—talked about things. I don't think she likes being at the convent. She's a little afraid of the Lestra. But she doesn't seem too sure she can leave."

Tayse was grinning. "Not an easy place to break free of, unless you have assistance."

"I've offered to help her escape," Justin said.

That brought another short silence. "So, Justin," Senneth said softly. "Why don't you tell us exactly what your relationship is with this girl?"

He felt a flare of anger and defiance. Was Senneth going to berate him now, warn him against making rash friendships with mysterious women? Was she going to scold him about risking his mission, risking his life, endangering the kingdom? He swung over to glare at her, but her wide gray eyes were filled with a cool compassion.

Senneth was unlikely to ever moralize about falling in love where it was least expedient.

"I don't know—I mean, I'm not sure I understand it myself," he said a little jerkily. "She is—I like her very much—I'm worried about her. I don't think she should stay at the convent. I can only meet with her when she's in town, of course, and she says the convent guards wouldn't like it at all if they saw us together. I think she's in danger, that's all, and I want to help her. I *will* help her, if I get a chance and she needs me."

He expected Tayse to say something grave like *Make sure your feelings for this girl don't interfere with your responsibilities*, but the big man was watching Senneth, reading something on Senneth's face that led him to keep quiet. It was more than Justin could do; he could not guess what Senneth was thinking.

Still, when she spoke, her voice remained gentle. "What kind of person is she? What makes you like her so much?"

Kirra had asked this question and he hadn't answered it very well. "Why does anybody like anybody?" he said irritably. "Just because you do."

Cammon spoke up in an encouraging voice. "You like her hair," he said.

Sweet gods, and had Cammon just picked *that* up from his thoughts? Senneth was laughing. "Go on, Justin, tell us about her hair."

He grinned reluctantly. "It's long—way past her waist. Dark. With this—" He waved a hand over the back of his own head—"this light pattern dyed into it. These flowers and bird shapes—I've never seen anything like it."

Surely it was his imagination that Senneth, for a moment, seemed truly aghast. Cammon glanced at her curiously, but Tayse was the next one to speak.

"Did you learn anything about her at all? Where she comes from? What her family is?"

"I don't think *I'm* the next one who's going to fall in love with a serramarra," Justin said, trying to joke. "Pretty sure she's not from a noble House. If I had to guess, I'd say she's from deep in Merrenstow or Tilt or Storian, from some tiny farm community miles from any big town. She has a large family—brothers and uncles and cousins—one of her cousins is at the convent with her, in fact. She seems very close to all of them. I think she's more homesick than she expected to be."

Senneth was nodding, as if everything he said tallied with something she had expected to hear.

"What have you told her about yourself?" Tayse asked.

"A little bit about my own family." That surprised the other Rider, he could tell; Justin never discussed his mother and sisters. "A little bit about—oh, soldiering that I've done. Said I used to ride in a lord's private guard. She knows there's something I'm not telling her. I don't think she wants to ask in case I turn out to be someone horrible. She'd rather think I'm chivalrous and kind."

"Well, if she's seen you in a brawl she knows you're not *always* kind," Cammon said, laughing.

"I think her brothers are fighters, too. At any rate, she wasn't that impressed."

Senneth abruptly got to her feet. "Maybe that's because you've lost your edge a little, skulking about Neft, not working out every day. Maybe you're not as fearsome as you used to be."

Surprised and a little wary, Justin grinned up at her. Were they done talking about Ellynor then? He was relieved but not quite sure why the conversation had taken a turn. "Still better than *you* are any day," he said, making it a taunt.

Her face wore that lurking smile that meant she was thinking something she would never tell you. "Do you think so? You've been gone eight weeks, and I've been training with the Riders all that time. I just might be able to defeat you. Grab a sword. Let me see."

He didn't move. "Can you beat Tayse yet?"

"No."

"Well, you won't be able to beat me, either."

"I bet I can. You'll be surprised at how much better I've gotten."

He glanced at Tayse, whose own face was unreadable. Was it really possible the other Rider thought Justin's skills had waned during the days he'd been gone from Ghosenhall? "Practice swords or real swords?" he asked in a silky voice.

Senneth laughed. "Real."

"Practice," Tayse countermanded. Senneth rolled her eyes, but didn't bother arguing. No one contradicted Tayse. The older Rider nodded at Cammon. "You pay attention at the door. Make sure no one comes in unexpectedly to see vagabonds practicing Rider tricks."

Senneth tossed Justin one of the wooden swords and then, before he'd properly gotten his hold on the hilt, rushed him with her own blade extended. He dodged and parried, laughing, but she wasn't through. She followed up with a quick series of slashes and feints, still trying to catch him off guard, pressing him hard before he'd even gotten his footing. She hadn't been joking; she'd improved tremendously in a few short weeks, and her control was impressive. He let her set the pace at first, devoting all his attention to defense, noting where she was strongest, where she was weakest, gauging her true level of ability. Ah, she'd learned that trick from Coeval—and *that* little sidestep from Brindle—but she hadn't quite mastered that forward lunge, that deadly stroke—

He backed away from her, still only defending, tiring her out, though her energy didn't flag nearly as quickly as he'd expected. She'd been training in wind and weights, too, he guessed; she could probably keep this up half the night. What interested him was that she was really trying to land a killing blow. She wasn't just practicing on him, enjoying the hard workout and the chance to show off new moves. She really wanted to see if she could break through his guard, bring him to his knees, prove she was a better fighter.

He might have been out of the training yard for two months, but he could still defeat a middle-aged mystic who wasn't bred for combat.

He stepped forward and smashed three times through her fierce but inadequate defense. "Dead," he said, as his wooden blade rested briefly against her throat. "Dead," as the tip pressed against her heart. "Dead," as he traced a line on her chest from her navel up to her neck.

She fell back, panting and covered with sweat. He dropped his swordpoint to the floor and folded his hands across the hilt. "Did you *really* think you might be better than I am?" he asked.

She was laughing; something about the exhibition had pleased her deeply. "I always hope," she said, and pushed back strands of pale hair that clung to her wet forehead. "But didn't you think I'd improved?"

He nodded. "Oh, yes! If I was a great lord and I was hiring for my civil guard, I'd take you on in a minute."

Tayse spoke up. "Have you been practicing? Doesn't look like you've lost a step."

Justin shook his head. "No one to practice with. I've done some fencing with shadows here in the stable, but that's mostly just to keep my muscles in shape." He handed Senneth his blade so she could put the wooden swords away. Turning away from her, he happened to catch sight of Cammon still watching Senneth, a slight frown on his mild face.

If Cammon was perplexed by someone's strange behavior, then there was no chance Justin would be able to figure it out.

He took a seat on the floor in front of Tayse where the big man sat on a bale of hay, looking completely relaxed. Of course, if the door rattled or a shout was raised outside, or if Cammon cried out advance warning of an assault, Tayse would be on his feet with a sword in his hand so quickly no one would be able to see him move.

"So what's in Coravann?" Justin said. "Why there?"

Tayse indicated Senneth with a jerk of his head. "The king wants her to talk with marlord Heffel about his connections with the Lirrenfolk."

Senneth dropped beside Tayse and leaned against him. Tayse's arm went around her waist almost absently, as if settling in its proper place. Justin couldn't imagine ever being so casual about touching Ellynor, so certain that when she was beside him, that was where she belonged.

"Maybe you don't remember this, but last summer there were Lirren-folk in Coravann. Heffel's got relatives across the Lireth Mountains," she said. "Baryn thinks maybe we can convince the Lirren men to fight for us if the country truly goes to war."

"I thought the Lirrenfolk weren't too keen on outsiders. Why would they listen to you?"

She was grinning now. "Can't you remember anything you've ever been told? I lived in the Lirrens a few years back. I was a member of the Persal family of the Lahja *sebahta-ris*."

Nonsense words. "As the what?" Justin asked.

She waved a hand. "Oh, I guess you'd call a *sebahta-ris* a closely linked network of families. Providentially, Heffel Coravann's in-laws are also Lahja. That makes me kin. That means they'll at least listen to me. That doesn't mean they'll agree to raise an army for Baryn."

"I thought Heffel Coravann had decided to be neutral if there is a war," Justin said.

Senneth sighed. "Yes. That's another reason this probably won't work. But it seemed worth a try. Worth the ride out to Coravann Keep and back."

"When do you leave?"

"In the morning," Tayse said.

Justin knew his face showed dissatisfaction. "Not much of a visit for me."

"You weren't our destination," Senneth said. "You were just a small detour along the way."

"Justin doesn't like it here," Cammon informed them while Justin scowled. "He thinks it's lonely."

"Justin will stay here as long as it will do us some good," Tayse replied.

"Yes, but—what else is there to learn?" Justin said a little hesitantly. He was not entirely sure he wanted to leave Neft, after all. "I've already been able to answer two key questions—the Lestra *is* sending her guards out to murder mystics, and convocations of rebels are gathering at the convent. What else do you need to know?"

"Not sure," Tayse said. "But we need you here a few more weeks."

Senneth yawned and pulled away from Tayse. "Bedtime for me," she said, standing up. "Anyone else?"

Cammon glanced at Tayse, glanced at Justin, and came to his feet. "Me, too," he said.

"I'll stay awhile," Tayse said.

So Cammon had sensed that the two Riders wanted to talk privately. And Senneth had just figured it out on her own. They promised to come by the stables before they left in the morning, and then they departed, leaving Justin and Tayse alone with a single candle burning. All the mystic light had departed with Senneth—much of the warmth, too.

"What's going on back in Ghosenhall?" Justin asked.

Tayse changed position and looked even more relaxed. "Preparations for war, mostly. The Riders practice all day. The king's expanded the royal army and sent troops to Merrenstow for the regent to house. Kiernan Brassenthwaite sends messages daily about the money he's raised, the soldiers he's training, the stores of food he's laying in to feed his army. We have renewed oaths of fealty from Kianlever and Merrenstow and Helven and Rappengrass, but there are still question marks beside the names in Nocklyn and Storian and Tilt."

"Danalustrous?"

Tayse shrugged. "Like Coravann, currently neutral. Kirra is working on her father, but I don't know that anyone has ever had any luck influencing Malcolm Danalustrous."

"So the king expects a war."

"As does everyone else."

Justin stirred restlessly where he sat on the hay-strewn floor. "I feel tucked away here—useless," he admitted. "I could do more if I was back in Ghosenhall."

Tayse's dark face was hard to see in the poor light. His voice was soft. "Tonight I formed the impression that you were of two minds about leaving Neft."

Justin gave a sharp bark of laughter. "It's stupid. I scarcely know Ellynor. I don't know why she has such an effect on me." He glanced at Tayse through the dimness. "No one ever did before. I never cared about girls particularly."

"Which might be why this one matters so much."

"I was sure you were going to lecture me about putting my mission at risk."

"I have too much faith in you to think you would ever do that, no matter how you might be seduced by a young woman's charms." There was a smile in Tayse's voice, and Justin laughed, but instantly Tayse grew serious. "But I would tell you to be careful, Justin. Love is a patient enemy and it strikes from ambush. Nothing else can lay you so low so quickly. Or fill you with more strength and courage."

"But how do you know?" Justin asked in a quiet voice. "If it's something that matters and not just some passing emotion?"

"What would you give up for her?" Tayse said. "Would you resign your post as Rider?"

"No!" Justin exclaimed, appalled. When Tayse didn't speak, he added reluctantly, "Is that what it would take? Giving up so much?"

Tayse did not answer directly. "Would you defy a direct order from me to save her life? Would you turn your back on the king?"

Justin was silent a moment. "Would you do such a thing for Senneth?" he asked at last. "Give up your life—or everything that *was* your life before you met her?"

"I don't know," Tayse said. "I didn't have to make that choice. I think love should make you more of who you are, not less. A better Rider. A better man. But I think sometimes love changes your choices." Justin could hear the sudden smile in his voice. "I think, if you believed I would hurt this girl, you would fight me to the death."

Utterly bewildered, Justin instantly realized that was true. But what he said was, "Why would you want to hurt her?"

"To keep her from hurting you."

Justin shook his head. "She won't. She wouldn't. She is—you have every reason to be suspicious of her, but she is the opposite of a harmful person. She's a healing person. She's good—you would know that right away if you met her. Or, well, Cammon would." He looked directly at Tayse across the gloomy darkness. "She trusts me, Tayse. She thinks I'm a worthwhile man. It makes me want to be the person she thinks I am, or that I could be. She's the only one who's ever believed in me—except you. But I don't want to give up what I have—I don't want to leave the Riders—I don't want to change so much that she's the only thing left in my life."

"Love always changes you," Tayse said, "but you have to change enough to allow it in. You'll have that moment of choice, I'm sure. You'll know when it comes."

"I know what you chose," Justin said.

Tayse nodded and came to his feet. For such a big man, he moved with a silent grace. He replied, "And never regretted it a day."

CHAPTER

17

JUSTIN looked so woebegone the following morning as they prepared to ride out that Senneth wanted to kiss him like a bruised child. She had never considered the burly fair-haired Rider an object of compassion before; he was as competent and self-complete as they came. But he was not happy overseeing a lonely outpost. He was a man who truly enjoyed having his comrades around him.

And he was so flummoxed about this girl. Tayse had repeated to her most of his conversation with the younger Rider, but he hadn't been able to answer Senneth's foremost question. "Is he really in love with her?"

"I don't know. I don't think he knows. But he seems well on the way."

Clearly, asking Justin point-blank would do no good. So Senneth merely gave him a warm hug, smiled at him, and said, "Take care of yourself."

"How long will you be in Coravann?" he asked. "Maybe you could come by on your way back."

She swung herself into the saddle and laughed down at him. "Maybe a week. But Neft is hardly on the way for a return trip to Ghosenhall."

He shrugged. "All right. Well, practice against Tayse while you're traveling. Maybe you'll be able to beat me next time I see you."

"I will," she promised. A few more words passed between the men, and then they were on their way.

They headed north and a little east, passing through Nocklyn country with a certain amount of caution. King Baryn seemed to believe that Els Nocklyn would never betray him by siding with Halchon Gisseltess, but Senneth was far less optimistic. And it was clear that, whatever side the marlord took in an upcoming war, someone in this House was anticipating a battle. Soldiers in the wheat-and-ochre livery of Nocklyn could be encountered on every stretch of road, were always to be found riding through the larger towns they passed through. Her own small party was incognito, for Tayse was not displaying his sash of royal lions, but still every guard captain who passed weighed them with a wary eye. She and Cammon were always dismissed as being of negligible threat, but every soldier gave Tayse a pretty thorough looking over.

Right to fear Tayse, she thought. *Wrong to overlook Cammon and me.*

Tayse, as was his habit, rode slightly in the lead. When they went single file, Cammon took the rear, but most of the time the younger man brought his horse alongside Senneth's and chattered happily away. She let him talk partially because she was genuinely interested in what he had been learning as he studied magic with mystics in Ghosenhall—and partially because listening to Cammon was effortless and soothing. Sometimes she thought he had no idea that she just let his words wash over her like so much effervescent distraction; sometimes she was sure that was exactly why he talked without ceasing. Cammon's way of easing her mind.

They had been riding for about two hours, and Tayse was out of earshot, when Senneth interrupted Cammon's tale about a trip through the Ghosenhall merchant's district. "So how serious is Justin about this girl?" she asked abruptly.

Cammon gazed at her, his flecked eyes at their widest. "How serious do *you* think he is?" he countered.

"I know you don't want to tell secrets," she said.

"It seems wrong to pick up someone else's emotions and then discuss them behind his back."

She nodded. "I agree. I would hope you wouldn't do such a thing to me. But this is important, Cam." She gave him a very serious look. "It's worth his life."

Now Cammon appeared even more uneasy. "She could hurt him? How do you know that? He didn't seem to think so."

"I know something he doesn't."

Cammon rolled his eyes. "You always do."

"So can you tell? Is he genuinely in love with her?"

Cammon brooded a moment. "I don't think he's sure yet," he said slowly. "But I think he is. If he thought she was in trouble? I think we would see Justin turn rash." He gave her a half smile. "And dangerous."

"Justin is always dangerous."

"So—is it because she's from the convent? I never thought about it much, but I suppose Coralinda Gisseltess doesn't really like her novices going out and falling in love with strange men. Especially Riders."

"In this particular case, Coralinda Gisseltess is the least of Justin's problems," Senneth said shortly.

"Then Justin is really in trouble," Cammon said, somewhat awed.

Senneth made no answer, merely rode on in silence. After a while, Cammon began his endless chattering again, but this time he didn't seem convinced that he was offering her any real comfort.

THEY reached Coravann Keep three days later, having traveled with very few stops. The forested countryside of northern Nocklyn gradually gave way to the scrubbier hills of Coravann. The marlord's stronghold was a grim, dark, massive building, though much more welcoming inside than its exterior would suggest. They were greeted by Heffel's daughter, Lauren, a tall, dark-haired girl who exuded both serenity and natural graciousness. She was the one who showed the newcomers to their spacious quarters.

"You asked for two rooms close together," she said, ushering Senneth inside the first one and seeming momentarily startled when Tayse followed. "You are—I assumed the men of your escort would share a chamber?"

Senneth smiled at her. "We will sort ourselves out as suits us best," she said. It was unusual enough to ask to have one's guards housed on the same floor as nobles, but the Riders had been well-treated here earlier in the summer, and Lauren was not likely to forget that Senneth preferred her swordsmen within easy call. Still, no reason to shock the young serramarra by explaining exactly what the sleeping arrangements would be.

"Come down for dinner when you've had time to change," Lauren said. "My uncle and cousins are here and they're looking forward to meeting you."

Lauren escorted Cammon to the room next door. Such was his charm that Senneth could hear Lauren laughing as she showed him around, though the sound was muted by the walls. Tayse was watching her with a little smile.

"Ashamed to claim a lowborn lover?" he asked.

Senneth came up and put her arms around him, resting her head briefly against his broad chest. As always, no matter what her struggles or preoccupations of the day, a moment in Tayse's arms helped restore her to a sense of balance. And made her feel obscurely safe. Despite the fact she could protect herself very well on her own. "Hoping not to embarrass a gently bred young woman," she replied.

Tayse threaded his fingers through her short hair and tugged her head backward. When she tipped her face up in response, he kissed her. "I'm not sure how much longer you will be able to lead a dual life," he said.

"Serramarra of Brassenthwaite who meets with lords and nobles. And consort to a King's Rider, who does not."

Senneth tightened her arms and kissed him back, hard. "Then I shall just be a consort to a King's Rider."

He smiled, but he seemed serious. "If my presence makes it more difficult for you to carry out such commissions for the king—"

"If ever I feel that is the case, I will consign you to the barracks for the duration of our stay. But don't try to pretend you're worried about my honor when what you really want is to hear me say I love you and would give up anything in the world for you."

He was laughing now. "Can't I be feeling both things at the same time?"

She kissed him again. "I love you and would give up anything in the world for you," she whispered. "And you're going to sleep next to me here tonight."

SENNETH did not, however, bring Tayse with her to Heffel Coravann's dinner table. Even she was not as abandoned to all sense of decorum as that, though it irked her. It irked her merely to have to play the role of noble ambassador, draw on her Brassenthwaite heritage so that she could be accepted in the dining hall of any marlord in the realm. She had renounced Brassenthwaite nearly eighteen years ago. It seemed mighty hard to have to claim it again when she didn't want to.

But she would do anything she could to avert war. Or, if war came anyway, to win it.

There were about thirty people at the dinner table, and Lauren made sure Senneth was introduced to all of them. Some Senneth already knew, of course, particularly the large, affable, lumbering Heffel Coravann, who seemed so vague and was really so shrewd. Lauren and her brother were there, and a few of the Coravann vassals, who seemed pleased enough to meet a Brassenthwaite serramarra. They didn't realize Senneth had been there earlier in the summer, escorting Princess Amalie on a tour of the southern Houses. But Senneth had tried to be very inconspicuous then. This time out, she was not going to be so lucky.

Also at the table were seven Lirrenfolk, clustered together around Lauren and her brother, and looking ill at ease and suspicious in this company. Senneth was not acquainted with the whole story, but understood that, more than twenty years ago, Heffel had eloped with a girl from the Lirrens. She knew very well how those tales tended to turn out, so she was convinced someone had died in the process. Yet, here were the bride's brothers or cousins or uncles or other members of the *sebahta*, maintaining what for them was a friendly relationship with an outsider. Someday she would like to hear the details of that romance and marriage.

It was the Lirrenfolk Senneth had come to see.

She managed to get through the evening uttering the usual polite inanities, though Heffel's vassals were interested in discussing the potential new charters for selected Thirteenth House lords and wanted to know what she thought of the regent. Senneth glanced at Heffel a few times to see how he liked such talk at his table, but he didn't appear to mind. He was a man who seemed to value peace over almost anything and was probably willing to sacrifice some of his personal acreage if it meant staving off conflict.

On the other hand, she always had the sense that, if he ever *were* roused to action, Heffel could bring the Lireth Mountains down with his rage.

Once the meal was over, Lauren ushered them into a medium-sized drawing room, and, with great skill, managed to steer individuals into smaller groups. She had been hostess of this house since her mother died a few years ago; she was certainly better at the social niceties than Senneth would ever be.

Senneth found herself, as she had hoped, sitting in a small group that comprised the seven Lirrenfolk. Lauren listed all their names again— Wynlo, a compact, dark-haired, intense and watchful man; his sons, Torrin and Hayden, who looked exactly like him except twenty years younger; his brother; his brother's son; and two men who appeared to be from the *sebahta-ris*. Senneth shook hands all around; smiled, though not too widely; and settled beside Torrin.

"We are kin," she said. It was the formal greeting exchanged by individuals who had worked out a relationship, however torturous, with people they had met for the first time.

Wynlo looked interested, but Torrin wore a scornful expression. "We do not acknowledge clan networks among the Gillengaria Houses," he said. "So even if you are sister to marlord Heffel, you are no kin to us."

The others were all nodding agreement, but Wynlo gave Senneth a straight look. "How are you kin to us?"

"I am the adopted daughter of the Persal family, who claim the Domen as brothers. We are all Lahja."

That changed everything. Even Torrin looked a little friendlier. "How did you come to be adopted by the Persals?" Wynlo asked. "Which family took you in?"

"I crossed the Lireth Mountains more than ten years ago and I wandered for some time among the *sebahta*," she said, giving the tale a storylike rendering. As they would expect. "I was a stranger but not a despised one. The Persals allowed me to stay with them, but gave me no status, because I was a woman and unproved and alone. But one day I went hunting with Ammet Persal and his sons, and I was the one who brought down the boar that was charging in to trample Ammet. His family honored me for my skill and my courage, and allowed me to live with them for a year to test my honor and my heart. And by the end of that year, they were satisfied, and they adopted me. And now throughout the Lirrenlands I am known as Senneth Persal, of the Wafyn *sebahta*, of the Lahja *sebahta-ris*."

"I have not seen Ammet Persal for a good five years," said Wynlo.

His brother stirred. "I have. We met in my cousin's house, three summers back." He glanced at Senneth. "He told the tale of his adopted daughter when I inquired after his family. We are kin."

So that was nicely settled. "I have not crossed the Lireth Mountains in many years," Senneth said. "I would ask for news of my family and those they love."

Wynlo's brother got comfortable. This might take some telling. "Here are tales of the Persal family," he said, his voice slipping into a sort of singsong. "Tabbet has died and his son, Meltis, taken over the land. Meltis has three sons of his own. . . ."

As she had expected, the recitation took more than an hour, though the others chimed in to add tales of their own friends, all bound together in complex kinship. Nothing particularly startling was revealed; most of the stories revolved around birth, death, marriage, property lost, property gained, alliances formed and broken. What she really wanted to know, and what she eventually learned, was that the Lahja *sebahta-ris* was even stronger than it had been when she had lived in the Lirrens, since it had absorbed the small but feisty Cohfen *sebahta*. Two key marriages had cemented that bond, followed by a new baby in each household, so now there were blood ties as well as ties of affection inextricably linking the families.

She was only guessing, but she estimated that, among its many farflung branches, the Lahja *sebahta-ris* boasted a couple thousand men of fighting age. A considerable army, should any of them be roused to war.

If men from one family joined, men from all families in the *sebahta-ris* could very well follow suit.

But then Senneth would be responsible for every one of those deaths, if any of the Lirren men should fall in combat.

As was custom, her new kinsmen saved till last the details of their own recent lives. A marriage here, a failed crop there, a son born, an infant sadly dead from fever. "And my daughter and my niece have come to stay for a short time on your side of the Lireth Mountains," Wynlo finished up.

Senneth allowed herself to look surprised. "That's unusual," she said. "Have you fostered them with kin in Gillengaria?" She glanced over her shoulder. "With marlord Heffel, perhaps?"

"No, but he is the one who suggested where we might place them," Wynlo said. "My niece Rosurie—" He shook his head. From the undisturbed look on his brother's face, Senneth inferred that this was not the man who'd had the pleasure of siring the wayward girl. "Too wild to tame."

"She tried to run off with a Bramlis man," Torrin interpolated.

"Not to be thought of!" Senneth murmured.

"But she was so devious. So clever," Wynlo continued. "Impossible to keep her apart from him. Then Heffel suggested we send her to live in the house of the goddess under the supervision of one of your noble ladies. A place of both safety and sanctity. My brother-in-law made the arrangements."

Rosurie was not the name Justin had pronounced with such pleasure. "You sent her to Lumanen Convent? With your daughter, you say?"

"Yes, and together they will find it easy to remember the ways of the *sebahta*."

Senneth nodded. "That is good. No one should be without family. Are they children of Gillengaria now, or will they return across the Lireth Mountains someday?"

Wynlo smiled as if that was a silly question. "Of course they will return to us. Soon, I think. My wife misses Ellynor."

Ahhh . . . "I did not realize that the Lestra of Lumanen Convent happily allowed her young women to come and go," Senneth said, speaking carefully. "I thought perhaps once a novice joined, she stayed for life."

"That might be as the Lestra prefers," one of the other men said gravely, "but our women will return to us in time."

"Do you know her?" Wynlo asked Senneth, watching her closely. "This Lestra? Heffel speaks of her very highly."

Impossible to answer this question as she'd like. "I have met Coralinda Gisseltess many times," Senneth said. "She is a most devout lady. Any young women under her protection will be closely watched, I'm certain. I believe marlord Heffel has long had a close relationship with her and she views him with great esteem."

That seemed to satisfy them. "When they return to us, they will no longer have their heads full of men that their families cannot abide," Wynlo said.

Senneth wished she could be more certain of that.

"It is good to hear we have chosen an excellent guardian for our women," his brother added.

Senneth turned the conversation. "I am less fond of her brother, Halchon," she said, and *that* was certainly the truth. "You might say I despise him."

She had their attention now; they knew all about hatred and the feuds it could prompt. "Has he dishonored you or your kin?" Hayden asked.

She glanced at him, then let her gaze roam the entire circle. "He plots rebellion," she said. "He wants to unseat the king."

They responded with murmurs of surprise and excitement, but it was all a sort of remote interest. Gillengaria was not their concern; what they cared about lay across the Lireth Mountains. "Rebellion and war—very ugly," Wynlo's brother said. "Are you certain?"

"Entirely. He told me to my face. He believes the king is old and weak and his daughter not fit to rule after him."

The men exchanged glances and offered a series of incomplete rejoinders. "Well—a woman on the throne—he might be pardoned for having some doubts—"

Their reaction was no less annoying for being wholly anticipated. Senneth cloaked her thoughts and said, "No doubt the king will see her married well and the mother of a promising son very soon. And doesn't *that* boy deserve to hold on to the property that is his by blood heritage?"

Now they were all nodding in agreement, instantly throwing the weight of their opinion behind the unborn heir who should never be deprived of a birthright.

"Always wrong to try to usurp the position of a proven leader," Wynlo's brother said with finality. "Unless the man is evil or mad or incompetent, and even then, it is his family who steps in to move him aside. The family is there to keep the family strong."

"What sort of *sebahta-ris* does this Baryn have?" Wynlo wanted to know.

The Bright Mother knew she would not be able to break down the bloodlines of the Twelve Houses for them in anything under a day. "Alliances are forming among the noble families of Gillengaria," she said. "We don't reckon kinship as you do—sometimes, with us, friendship matters more than blood. But when I tally the numbers, I see them close to equal. Which frightens me. We could be headed for a war that devastates the entire country."

"We have not had true war in the Lirrens for a century," Hayden said, his voice almost wistful.

Senneth looked straight at him. "Nor we," she said. "But in past times, the men of the Lirrens fought side by side with men of Gillengaria."

The younger men all looked intrigued at the thought, the older four disturbed. "Gillengaria's troubles are not ours," Wynlo said. "The mountains are between us for a reason."

"If Halchon Gisseltess seizes the throne, I think he is the kind of man who will look around and see what else he might want to take," Senneth said. "The Lirrens are the closest thing at hand."

"I think he might find Lirrenfolk difficult to subdue," Wynlo said.

"I hope he does not have the chance to try," Senneth said. "I hope quarreling friends and brothers can find a way to mend their differences. I hope war never comes. But if it does, I hope the king's forces can win against a rebel army." She swept her gaze across all seven of them again. "I would hope that rebel army would not be swelled by Lirren swords."

Wynlo's brother shook his head. "We do not take up arms against our own leaders. If we had a reason to fight in this war of yours, we would fight on the side of your king. But we have no reason to fight."

She glanced at the younger men again. "But if some of your sons and nephews wanted to join our war? Would you stop them?"

Wynlo and his brother exchanged troubled looks. "No one ever stopped a young man who wanted to fight," his brother said shortly.

Hayden laughed. "It would be exciting to be in a war," he said. "There is nothing to fight for across the mountains."

"Maybe not for you, brother," Torrin said, taunting a little. "I have fought for a woman's honor or the slight to a cousin's name."

Senneth turned to survey him. "Did you actually duel the Bramlis rascal who courted your cousin Rosurie?"

He nodded, his dark face lighting with pleasure at the memory. "I did. And you may be sure I beat him so badly he will not come calling on her again, even once she is home among her family again."

"That was a good fight," Hayden said. "Too fast, though."

Torrin looked contemptuous. "And at that I had to hold myself back so I didn't defeat him too quickly. I wanted him to feel every blow, to remember for the rest of his life what the punishment would be for trying to seduce a Domen woman."

"Are you the champion of your family?" she asked. "The one who would be chosen to fight if there was an insult to avenge?"

They were all nodding. "Though Hayden, here, he's almost as good," Torrin's uncle said.

"I've never beaten Torrin," Hayden said—half ashamed of himself, half proud of his brother. "But almost no one else can defeat me!"

"When Torrin took on the Bramlis boy. *That* was a fight worth seeing," the uncle said.

It didn't take much prompting for Torrin to begin recounting, in tedious detail, the duel he had fought with the unfortunate Bramlis fellow. Senneth listened, deliberately allowing a smile to come to her face, but she didn't say anything until Torrin began to dislike her expression.

"Why do you look that way?" he demanded with a scowl. He was hotheaded and sure of himself, and probably with reason. He was slim and small-boned as most of the Lirrenfolk were, but he was also quick and well-muscled. She imagined he was an exceptionally dangerous man in a fight. Not one to hold back. Not one to allow any fear for his own safety to slow him down.

"I was thinking, you are probably one of the most skillful swordsmen across the Lireth Mountains," she said. "But there are fighters here in Gillengaria you would not be able to defeat."

"I would," he said instantly. "Show me any man here that you think can wield a blade! I'll take him on."

"I think I could defeat you," she said deliberately.

There was, for a moment, absolute silence among her listeners.

"*You?*" Torrin exclaimed, while Hayden and the other young man laughed. The older men, however, looked more thoughtful. Senneth saw Wynlo give her a second, more careful inspection, noting her height, her reach, the breadth of her shoulders. The sleeves of her dark blue gown concealed the muscles in her arms, but his gaze lingered on her wrists, her long-fingered hands.

She smiled and her voice became soft, almost dreamy. Back to that storytelling singsong. "Do you hear, even across the Lireth Mountains, tales of the King's Riders?" she inquired. "Fifty men and women whose lives are dedicated to protecting the crown. They train all day—on foot, on horseback—they practice with swords, with crossbows, with daggers, with bare hands. It is said that it takes two men to hold a Rider at bay, three men to kill him, four men to find the courage to drag his body to a grave. And a whole battalion to run in fear from his fellow Riders who come to avenge his death."

"I've heard of King's Riders," Wynlo said quietly. "They are respected for their bravery and their skill, but they are legendary for their loyalty."

She nodded. "No Rider has ever betrayed his king."

"But they are still men," Torrin argued. "They can still be defeated."

She looked at him. "Men and women," she said.

He looked her over, something like a sneer on his face. "And you are one of these Riders? You?"

She shook her head. She was smiling again, mostly because she could tell it annoyed him. Somewhat against her will, she rather liked this arrogant and abrasive young man. This must have been what Justin was like when he first joined the Riders. Was still like, except somewhat less extreme. "I have not had the honor of being named a King's Rider," she said. "But I have friends among them. I train with them. I have lifted my sword against a Rider's sword many times in practice—and I have given a good accounting of myself, too, though I have never yet defeated a Rider."

Hayden was frowning. "In the Lirrenlands, women do not fight battles," he said.

"We are in Gillengaria now," she said serenely.

"But if you are Lahja," he persisted, "you should behave as a Lirren woman would."

And surely *that* had been coming since the conversation opened. "I am *bahta-lo*," she said very gravely, and they all looked surprised and then nodded. Then they inspected her again.

She had explained this carefully to Tayse and Cammon one night as they camped on the road. Tayse had wanted to know why she thought the Lirren men would listen to anything she had to say if they held women in such low esteem. "They don't despise their women, you've got that wrong," she had said. "They love their women—too much so, maybe—they protect their women almost single-mindedly. They think women must be kept safe at all costs."

"You don't exactly behave like a woman who allows herself to be taken care of," Tayse had pointed out. "Aren't they going to think you need to be cowering on a farm somewhere, following the orders of a father or brother?"

"I am *bahta-lo*," she had told him. And when both he and Cammon demanded to know what that meant, she had said, "That means 'above the clan.' A woman apart. Every once in a while—it's very rare—a

woman chooses to leave the protection of her family and become a wan-
derer. Often these women are skilled healers who feel compelled to go
wherever there is great sickness, no matter what clan has been affected.
Sometimes they are older women who have demonstrated uncanny wisdom over the years, and they become mediators, particularly between
warring clans. Sometimes, to tell the truth, they're completely mad, and
they roam from one corner of the Lirrens to the other, and no one harms
them, and everyone shows them respect. The Persals accepted my claim
of *bahta-lo* when it became clear I wasn't going to turn into a docile
woman and marry some domineering Lahja boy. They loved me anyway,
but this allowed them to set me free."

It was clear that Wynlo and the rest did not entirely approve of kinsmen who had been weak-willed enough to let an adopted daughter slip
out of their hands. "We do not have any *bahta-lo* among the Alowa,"
Wynlo's brother said.

"A family does not choose to name a woman *bahta-lo*. A family ac-
cepts that that is what a woman has become," Senneth said. "And a
woman does not choose such a path lightly. She chooses it because that
is the will of the goddess. The Black Mother has set this restlessness in
her heart, and she must give in to that urge to wander, or die."

Wynlo nodded reluctantly. His brother looked thoughtful. Torrin's
mind was quickly back on other matters. "*Bahto-lo* or not, you still cannot
defeat me in a duel," he said.

She smiled at him. "I'm sure I can."

He tilted his chin up at her. Oh, *so* like Justin. "If you have a weapon
with you, I would like to prove you wrong," he said. "Is it permitted here
at Coravann Keep that we match swords?"

"There is a training yard on the grounds. Heffel will be happy to allow us to use it. And indeed, I have a weapon with me. I never travel
without it."

Torrin's eyebrows rose. He looked excited and scornful all at the same
time. Nothing like the prospect of a little bloodshed to improve a young
man's mood. "Then let us meet tomorrow to test our skill against each
other."

"Let us do so. May we invite anyone we choose to be our witnesses?
Or do you prefer to limit the audience?"

"Anyone may attend," Torrin said.

"And should we set rules? Decide beforehand what constitutes a win?
I am not looking to strike a death blow, you understand—as I hope you
are not, either!"

He nodded with some semblance of graciousness. "You are kin. We are merely determining who wields the best sword. Shall we say the fight ends at first blood or at the killing thrust—that is not driven home, of course?"

Tayse was not going to be happy to learn that she had essentially goaded this intemperate young man into challenging her to a duel, and he would be even less happy when she told him she would not be able to explain why. But he wouldn't be afraid for her. He would stand on the sidelines and watch her, silent, unalarmed, knowing full well that she could defend herself. Afterward, win or lose, he would calmly tell her what she had done wrong, where she needed to improve her technique, what moves she might try next time she found herself facing a similar opponent.

She was not entirely certain she would be able to defeat Torrin, but she absolutely had to discover if she could.

"Oh, let us fight to the pretend death," she said to him now, smiling. "I think neither of us will be satisfied with anything less."

CHAPTER

18

ONCE she was back at Lumanen, Ellynor found it almost impossible to breathe.

Partly because, after the open streets of Neft, the high, walled compound seemed too small, too closed in, too inescapable. The forest pressed in too hungrily, and even though most of the trees had lost their leaves by now, their thick, tangled branches were too dense to allow enough air to sift through to the convent.

Partly because there was not enough room in her chest for breath. Everything else was crowded out by fear.

How could she have done it? How could she have kissed Justin there in the streets of Neft—not just once, an accident, a momentary spell of lunacy—but a second night? For hours? Her body pressed against his, delighting in his shape and bulk, her bones already memorizing the specific size and weight of his hands against her back. Her mind a dizzy, incoherent whirl. Her heart a skipping child, overcome with laughter.

Great Mother, she had allowed him to think he could love her, and now he could die.

She had not been able to keep away, that second night. Had not been able to make herself lie motionless in bed, listening to Astira and Lia quietly breathing, knowing that Justin waited for her outside by the gate. *Don't go don't go don't go don't go,* she had told herself, over and over again, and yet there she was. Rising to her feet. Slipping on her shoes. Creeping from the room, down the stairs, past the guard.

Out into the chill, enchanted night.

She could never see him again. She had to cut the connection now, avoid him for the rest of her life. He could not fall in love with her, not now, not truly. He could not believe he had a chance to win her. He would not understand when she tried to explain—he would laugh—he would claim he was good enough, fast enough, cruel enough, to best her brother in a duel. But no one had ever beaten Torrin. And instead of kiss-ing her in the dark, Justin would be lying dead at Ellynor's feet.

Or standing over Torrin's lifeless body, a bloody sword in his hand. El-lynor could not bring herself to decide which was worse. She only knew that both outcomes were unendurable.

How could she have let things go so far? How could she have been so stupid, so selfish, so reckless, so abandoned? How could it matter what *she* wanted? Weighed against the possibility of Justin's death, her desire for him was a light thing, paltry, unimportant.

But, oh, sweet Mother, if he was standing before her now, she would want to kiss him again.

This was why women were not allowed to roam the world without su-pervision. Because when they did, they made terrible mistakes. Because they had no judgment. Because they were incapable of choosing wisely when it came to love.

Well. She was back in the convent now. Safe behind those white walls, that let in no air and very little light. Justin could not come to her here. She just had to make sure she never left again.

THE first week back passed in something of a blur. The other novices were whispering, half excited and half afraid, because the Lestra's fierce brother had returned to the convent, his wife and about twenty soldiers in tow, but Ellynor couldn't bring herself to care. It was not like she ever saw them, anyway. The Gisseltess soldiers kept mostly to the barracks, while the marlord and his wife rarely strayed from the suite of rooms re-served for the Lestra's most exalted guests. And Ellynor had plenty of other more important things to think about. Whether she was working in the kitchen, singing in the nightly rituals as the moon swelled back to full, or simply walking the grounds, trying to breathe, she spent her time thinking. About what she should do next.

She and Rosurie had been here more than a year now. How long did their families intend them to stay? Even though it was clear that the Lestra expected them to reside here for the rest of their lives, she was sure her father had a different idea. When would he come for her? Was there any way to get a message to him?

Would Rosurie be willing to go?

Despite her own preoccupations, it had not escaped Ellynor's atten-tion that Rosurie had been very quiet lately. When Ellynor had returned to the room they shared, Rosurie had greeted her listlessly and failed to supply any gossip about events that had transpired during her absence.

Over the next few days, her normally vivacious cousin had been almost taciturn, clearly lost in thought. Rosurie had never been one to keep her own counsel for long, so Ellynor bided her time, certain that the other girl would confide in her soon. But as the week slipped by, her cousin became even quieter.

"Is Rosurie sick?" Astira whispered to Ellynor at dinner one night. "She's hardly said a word all day."

"I've been wondering that myself," Ellynor whispered back. "I'll see if I can get her to talk to me tonight."

But first there was the meal to get through, and then the singing. With the moon about three-quarters full, most of them were needed to stand in the courtyard, gathered in the shape of a not-quite-circle, their white robes shimmering with starlight, their voices ethereally high.

Almost, in the dark, in the cold, her chilled heart warmed by the Black Mother's presence, Ellynor could breathe.

Then she remembered everything, and her throat closed up, and for a moment she could not sing.

For once, she was happy to go inside and up to her room. Rosurie was already in bed, sitting with her back against the wall. She had lit the candle in the window, but the rest of the room was in darkness.

Moving quietly, Ellynor readied herself for bed and then slipped under her own covers. The single candle was just bright enough to see by; it was like trying to view a landscape by the light of a high full moon. Rosurie was still upright, apparently staring at the opposite wall. Her hands were two small fists laid in her lap.

Ellynor lay on the mattress, facing the other bed. "Rosurie," she said in a soft voice. "You've been so quiet the past few days. I'm worried about you. Is something wrong?"

For a moment Rosurie didn't answer. "I'm just—I'm thinking," she said tightly.

"About what?" No answer. "Are you worried about family back home? I got a letter today. You can read it."

"No. I mean, yes, of course I'll read it. But no, I'm not worried."

"I've been a little homesick lately. Have you?" Ellynor continued, still in that soft voice, inviting confidences. As she talked to sick children in the infirmary, or old women on their deathbeds. "Getting a letter from my mother made me miss them all even more."

"I don't miss them," Rosurie said in a jerky voice.

Ellynor shifted on her bed. "*Really?* The harvest feast is already past, and the midwinter feast isn't that far away. I was thinking about the salt bread and the sweet fried cake—I was thinking about winter ale made with the first snow—"

"We have plenty to eat here at the convent."

"Well, of course we do," Ellynor said a little blankly. "It's just that it's been so long since we had holiday fare—we were gone last winter, too. I miss the customs. I think I took them for granted all those years, and now I wish I was back with the *sebahta* for midwinter."

"That's the problem," Rosurie said, and her voice held a low note of intensity. "With you—with Astira and Lia—with so many of the girls. We miss our old lives. We want to be back with our families. We don't know—we don't realize—we don't give enough to our new life." She took a deep breath. "We don't offer enough to the goddess."

Sweet Mother of the midnight skies. "We sing her praises under the moon," Ellynor said calmly. "We light a candle in every window. We pray six times a day. We wear her moonstones everywhere we go, and pass them out to strangers who want to learn to love her."

Rosurie made a sudden sharp gesture. "Those are—those are acts we perform. Duties we observe. Ways to carry out her will. They are important, yes, but they have no deep meaning. They are not *sacrifices*."

"Sacrifices?" Ellynor repeated doubtfully.

Rosurie turned to her, suddenly eager. "Yes! An act of great and personal significance done to honor the Silver Lady. To prove how much we love her."

"What kind of act?"

Rosurie kneaded her hands together. "Something difficult. If it is hard to do, the Pale Mother knows how important it is."

"Yes, but—"

"Shavell cut her arms and legs with a crystal dagger. Did you know that?" When Ellynor shook her head mutely, Rosurie plunged on. "She did. Three years ago. She stood under the half moon after the ritual was sung and dug great wounds all over her body. Then she stayed there, all night, bleeding, her hands raised to the goddess. When they found her the next morning, she was so faint she could not walk under her own power, and so cold they thought she would die by noon. But *she* knew she would not. *She* knew the Pale Mother would keep her safe, because Shavell had sacrificed her body to the goddess. She became a Split Moon Daughter. She bears the scars still—see if you can't get a glimpse of them sometime. Mostly her robes cover them, though."

"Well—Shavell is very devout. All the dedicants are. I hope you're not thinking of—"

"It would have to be something different," Rosurie said, a note of brooding in her voice. "Something unique to me. Darris gave the Lestra her gold—and there was a lot of it, apparently. She comes from a merchant family and she was the only one to inherit her father's wealth. And she gave it all up to the goddess. But I don't have any money."

Ellynor was trying hard to throttle her alarm, but it galloped around inside her constricted chest like a panicked pony. Rosurie had always been such a passionate girl; why had Ellynor not foreseen this? The Silver Lady loved a fanatic. "I'm sure if you pray hard and give it a lot of thought, something will come to you," she said, trying to speak soothingly. "But I don't think that the Silver Lady or the Lestra requires that—"

"No, of course they don't *require* it," Rosurie said. "That's why it's so powerful. It's done of your own free will. You give of yourself to the goddess."

"I can see giving money, but blood? Does she really appreciate a gift so extreme?"

Rosurie was brooding again. "They say that Nadia denounced her little brother as a mystic," she said in a quiet voice. "That was *her* gift to the goddess. And she had loved her brother very much."

Ellynor felt sick. "What happened to Nadia's brother?"

Rosurie flicked her a look and went back to staring at the wall. "I don't know. What I heard was that the Lestra thanked her and said the goddess would deal with him as he deserved. And then Nadia cried and said he was too small to be punished. And the Lestra said, 'The goddess makes allowances for youth. But the goddess is greatly pleased with you.' And so Nadia stopped crying."

"I still want to know what happened to the brother."

Rosurie shrugged irritably. "Your problem is that you think too much of people, and not enough of the goddess!" she exclaimed. "Your mind is not focused on the Pale Mother. Your heart is back with the *sebahta*."

"It is," Ellynor agreed. "I love my family. I miss them. Why is that a dreadful thing?"

Rosurie gave a long, shaky sigh, and finally stretched herself out on the bed. Ellynor thought she was still wide awake, though. She appeared to be staring in some concentration at the ceiling. "It is not dreadful," she said. "Most people would miss their families—I did, at first. But now I am—I am different, somehow. I am filled with moonlight and wonder. I feel like my blood is running silver in my veins—like I have been possessed by the goddess. And I have this—this—tension inside me, telling me to do something splendid and terrible to prove I love her. I don't expect you to understand. You're an ordinary woman, like most of the novices. You haven't been singled out. You haven't been marked, like I have."

Worse and worse. "Rosurie—don't do anything too drastic," Ellynor said.

"How can it be too drastic if it is in service to the goddess?" was the immediate response.

"Yes—well—I mean—just don't hurt yourself. Don't stand in the moonlight and bleed, like Shavell did. I wouldn't want anything to happen to you. I wouldn't want you to *die*. I mean, how would I explain that at the next gathering of the *sebahta-ris*?" She ended up on a light note, making a joke of it, and Rosurie actually laughed.

"No, none of them would understand," her cousin agreed. She imitated her father's voice. "'What? She died for a principle? Not in a fight over land or honor or love? There were no weapons involved at *all*? How can this be?'"

"The Lirrenfolk understand death, but it has to behave properly, in a manner they understand," Ellynor said, still lightly.

"Well, don't be afraid. I don't want to die. I won't do anything that will make you worry."

"I am very impressed by your devotion," Ellynor said, trying to make her tone admiring. She was appalled, more truthfully, but it had always been pointless to try to turn Rosurie away from any course of action. You supported her, or you lost her confidence forever. "I'm sure the goddess will smile on you, whatever you do."

"Thank you," Rosurie replied, her voice finally sounding sleepy. "I feel so much better having talked about it! It is always easy to tell you things."

"You can always talk to me, you know that."

An indistinguishable reply, and then they both lay in silence for a few moments. But Ellynor was far from sleep—concern over Rosurie now added another layer of pressure on her chest, which was already leaden with fear for Justin and depression at her own unhappy situation. But before Rosurie had gotten caught up in this religious ecstasy, she had been just as passionate about a young man who was every bit as unsuitable as Justin was.

"Rosurie," she whispered, in case the other girl was asleep. But the "What?" came back instantly, just as quietly, and so Ellynor raised her voice just the tiniest bit to ask, "Do you ever think about him?"

"Who?"

"That Bramlis boy. The one they would not allow you to marry."

A long silence, and Ellynor almost expected a disdainful reply. *Women who devote themselves to the goddess do not remember unworthy men.* But finally Rosurie let all her breath out in a wistful sigh. "I think of him," she said at last. "When I can't help it. I don't suppose I will ever stop thinking about him, though now there are more and more days between the times I remember and the times I'm able to forget."

"Do you want to forget?"

She heard the sound of Rosurie nodding her head against the pillow. "I want to forget the look on his face when I told him I didn't love him. I lied, of course—I love him still, even now. But I didn't want him following me, starting a clan war. Dying. I knew he would only give me up if he believed I had given him up first."

"Maybe that is what you have sacrificed for the goddess," Ellynor suggested. "Your love for this boy. Maybe there is nothing else you have to relinquish."

"I didn't give him up for the Pale Mother," Rosurie said, and even in a whisper, her voice sounded hard. "I gave him up for the men of my family. Maybe it is the men of my family I will give up for the Silver Lady."

ANOTHER week passed; the moon flowered toward full. Almost every night, Ellynor managed to be among the novices left behind to sing to the waxing Silver Lady. But she managed *not* to be in the group of women sent to Neft to hand out moonstones and benedictions on the city streets. Justin would see the white-robed girls. He would circle them eagerly, looking for her face, but he would go back to the stables disappointed. Ellynor would not be there; he would not see her again.

He would never see her again.

Ellynor would never see *him*. Never gaze on his strong features, his sandy brows drawn down in concentration, his brown eyes narrowed as he puzzled something out. Never watch his quick changeover from watchfulness to merriment as she said something that made him laugh. Never see the surprised wonder in his eyes as he kissed her and pulled back to stare down at her and find that her expression matched his own.

There were moments she hated her brother Torrin.

But not enough to risk his life.

Rosurie recovered some of her usual animation, though it was clear she was still mulling something over. The days were cold but sunny, so Astira and Ellynor worked in the gardens, clearing out the old stalks and roots, and whispering secrets. There was a young guard named Daken from a half-noble family in Brassenthwaite; he was lonely and homesick and so very sweet. He and Astira had been meeting in secret down by the barracks. It was wrong, Astira knew it was wrong, and yet she was so fond of him. She would be circumspect, no one would find out, didn't Ellynor think it would be all right as long as they didn't allow the situation to go too far?

I am the wrong one to ask for advice, Ellynor thought. "Just be careful," she said. "What will the Lestra do if she finds you've been consorting with a guard?"

Astira shook her head. "I don't know. Will I be thrown out of the convent? Will he? I know there have been indiscretions before, you always hear stories, but no one ever says what *happened*."

"Just be sure you know what you're risking," Ellynor said. "Make sure it's worth it."

Ellynor was tempted, but she resisted the urge to reciprocate with her own confessions. Bad enough to trade kisses with one of the Lestra's own guards, who at least professed to love the goddess and belonged inside the convent walls. But to play at romance with some idle stranger? About whose background you knew nothing at all? Even the lovestruck Astira would cavil at that.

Lia stuck her head out of the kitchen door, which overlooked the garden. "Can you two come help? The supply horses have arrived and there's no one else in the kitchen and I can't carry everything in by myself."

Always glad of an excuse to get away from gardening, Astira and Ellynor jumped to their feet. "They're late," Astira observed. "I noticed we were running low on flour."

Packhorses came every three or four weeks from Neft, a small caravan of five or six animals led by a couple of freighters. Ellynor supposed wagons, which would have been more efficient for hauling bulk quantities, couldn't force their way through the overgrown forest path. Of course, the Daughters grew and canned some of their own produce within the compound, and the soldiers often hunted for fresh meat, but there were necessities they relied on the city to supply.

"Are they out front?" Ellynor asked. It was a tedious chore to carry baskets and bags all the way from the courtyard through the great receiving hall and down progressively narrower corridors to the large kitchen at the rear of the main house.

Lia shook her head. "I told them to come around back," she said a little defensively.

Astira looked reproving. "You know the guards don't like it if they can't see visitors from the gate."

"It's two men! And seven horses! I think we're safe. Anyway, my foot hurts. I can't walk that far twenty times in the next two hours."

Ellynor smothered a laugh. From around the side of the building, she could hear the sound of horse hooves clopping on the dry dirt, and a man's voice raised in a soothing tone. "Easy there, girl. Just a shadow. Come on, you've made it this far. That's right." She saw a stocky, middle-aged man round the corner, leading a skittish gray horse by the bridle. It was late in the day and the bulk of the convent itself instantly covered him in shadow, but Ellynor could see him clearly enough. Behind him were three horses on a lead rope. The rest of his party had not yet pulled into view.

Astira was eying him with some disfavor. "That one seems too high-strung to be a packhorse," she said. Ellynor grinned. At times like this, Astira's haughty noble roots were most evident.

"Her first time out. Well, second," the freighter grunted. "She'll get quieter. Here, is there someplace we can tie them up while we start to unload?"

Ellynor and Astira hurried forward to help situate the animals. Lia turned to greet the second man as he stepped into sight, leading his own string of horses. The first man started unbuckling straps on one of his packhorses and hoisted a canister of flour out of a pouch, handing it to Ellynor. "It's heavy," he warned.

"I've got it," she replied, and pivoted back toward the kitchen.

And then she almost dropped the canister in a moment of dizzy shock.

The second freighter was standing by his lead horse, securing the reins, but he glanced her way as she turned. It was Justin.

CHAPTER
19

I<small>T</small> was impossible to speak to Justin—impossible to *look* as if she wanted to speak to him—with so many other people around. Not just the novices and the other freighter but, within five minutes, two convent guards, who showed up to oversee this interaction between the novices and city folk. But Ellynor was acutely aware of him—every gesture he made, every word he uttered, every glance he sent her way.

How could he come here? How *could* he? Perhaps there was no risk to it, not really, for all sorts of visitors came to the convent and left again and didn't make a ripple in their calm lives. But there was something about Justin that was not calm. There was an inherent challenge in the way he stood, in the way he carelessly swung bundles down and settled them into Lia's arms, or Astira's. In the way he looked around, *really* looked, as if curious to know the exact layout of the compound, the square footage given over to gardening, the number of guards visible on the walls.

In the way he gazed at her, when she had the courage to glance his way. *You might stay away from me*, his expression seemed to say, *but I will not stay away from you.*

It terrified her. It exhilarated her. Sweet Mother, look at his face, alive with laughter at something his companion had said. Watch the way he tossed back his fair hair. See his muscles bunch under his shirt, then smooth out as he handed over his burden. She was almost staring at him, despair and longing in her face. She forced herself to glance away.

The freighter was squinting up at the sky and wearing an expression of concern. "Be dark in an hour or two," he said. "We got such a late start—not a chance we'll make it out of the forest by nightfall."

He handed Ellynor a heavy, shifting bag. Dried beans, maybe. She altered her grip on it, pretending she didn't have a secure hold, and then set it on the ground and adjusted her robes. She wanted to hear the rest of this conversation.

"You afraid of traveling in the dark, Jenkins?" one of the convent guards asked, sounding amused. "Even when the moon's practically whole?"

"Damn it, I am!" Jenkins replied, a little ruefully. "Almost got killed by a wolf one night—three, four years back—ever since, I just don't care for journeying by moonlight."

"Room in the barracks," the other guard said thoughtfully. "You couldn't go roaming, though."

"No, no, we'd stay put," Jenkins said.

"Well, you could step outside the building, maybe as far as the training yard. No farther."

"You sure about this?" the first guard objected. "Don't recall that we've housed visitors before."

"Oh, sure. Mostly in winter, when the roads are bad and daylight's so short. You can check with Koban first if you want, though."

"I think I'd better." He hurried off toward the back of the compound where the barracks and the training yard could be found.

"Don't worry," the remaining guard said nonchalantly. "You can stay the night."

"Thanks. I appreciate it." Jenkins glanced at Justin. "That do for you? Do you need to hurry home? Forgot to ask."

Justin shook his head. "I'm clear. Not expected back till tomorrow afternoon."

Ellynor thought she didn't draw a single breath during the next fifteen minutes, as she and the other girls carried bundles into the kitchen, then went back outside for more, and everyone waited for final word on whether the visitors could spend the night. Finally, finally, the first guard came jogging up, his expression relieved.

"Koban says they can stay," he reported. "Bunk in the barracks. Eat with us, too."

"Good news," the freighter said. "Damn, it'll be dark in an hour! I hate winter. Don't mind the cold so much, but I can't stand the dark."

Ellynor, who all this time had helped Jenkins unload his packhorses, now turned casually toward Justin's string and watched as he hauled down a package wrapped in brown paper. It was solid but not too heavy; a round of cheese, she thought. She held her arms out for it and he carefully handed it over.

She allowed her eyes to lift to his face for just a second, knowing he would be watching her, waiting for her signal. *Midnight,* she mouthed. He nodded infinitesimally and turned instantly away, pulling out something else from his saddlebags. Ellynor carried the cheese into the kitchen and stood there a moment, shaking. If her heart were to beat any faster, any harder, it would hammer its way out past her ribs and she would die of fear right here, right now.

Fear. And excitement.

IT was a simple matter for Ellynor to leave the courtyard with all the other novices who had formed the moon shape—tonight, just a sliver past full—and step inside the building with the rest of them. Simple for her to mention that she was hungry and head on back toward the kitchen while the others turned for the stairs. Any number of people were still awake in the convent at midnight. They were, after all, women who worshipped a night goddess. Some of their prayers and rituals could only be performed in the darkest hours. The Lestra, it was said, often stayed awake the whole night through, scribbling in her study or wandering the grounds under the direct eye of the Silver Lady. Surely Ellynor did not want to run into *her.*

So she cloaked herself in a veil of secrecy, the Black Mother's gift, and drifted through the hallways like an only slightly corporeal shadow. Now and then she heard voices, a few rooms back, and footsteps from overhead or down another hallway, but she did not encounter anyone. The kitchen was empty and the door yielded silently to her hand. No one stood in the denuded garden, breathing in the star-chilled air. No one lurked along the pathways that connected the great hulking structure of the convent proper to the scattering of buildings in the back of the compound, where the guards were housed and the horses were kept.

Where novices were not supposed to go.

Justin would not have strayed far from the barracks, a long, low, utilitarian building that looked out over the training yard. If he had managed to win free at all, which he might not have, he would have stuck close to the territory outlined for him as permissible. This was hardly the time and place to go exploring, no matter how curious he might be about his surroundings. If a guard came across him, outdoors at this hour, he would have to appear as innocent as possible.

But he might not have been able to creep out. He might have been too closely watched—he might not have the skills of stealth that came so naturally to her. He might not be there at all.

But he was.

She saw him before he saw her, even though she was moving and he was standing still. He was leaning against the slatted fence that enclosed the training yard, staying as close to the stables as he could to take advantage of what cover the building afforded. He was in profile to her, so that half his attention could be on the barracks in case anyone was searching for him, and half of it could go toward listening for her approach. She paused a moment, just to take the chance to truly look at him, drink in the sight of the face that she had been so certain she would never see again. Sweet Mother, when had he become so dear to her? When had she fallen in love with him?

She moved closer, silently, she thought, but he turned his head as if a sound had caught his notice. She could see his eyes scanning all approaches—he even looked straight at her—but the goddess's power was stronger than human eyesight. He could not see her. Ellynor stepped closer, even more daintily, and saw a frown cross his face. He was concentrating so hard that he could hear her slippered feet in the brown grass, or her breathing, or her heartbeat. He knew she was near.

But she was still invisible to him as she placed a hand on his arm and spoke his name. She had thought to startle him, but she guessed wrong. His hand closed over hers and he drew her against him so swiftly she didn't even have time to gasp. She loosed and reformed her night-dark cloak, and now he was standing inside it with her, both of them safe from the eyes of outsiders, sheltered in the arms of the goddess.

"Ellynor," Justin said, and bent in to kiss her.

She couldn't help herself; she pressed herself into that kiss as if he was light and air and she had been deprived of both for a lifetime. Only for a moment. She pulled back, hard, her hands against his chest. He caught her by the shoulders before she could move too far away.

"Justin, what are you *doing* here?" she demanded in a furious whisper. "Don't you know how dangerous it is?"

"Dangerous how?" he shot back, raising his chin and showing every evidence of stubbornness. "A man asks if he can hire me to help deliver goods, and I accept on good faith, and I do my part of the job. I'm here, and no one cares that I'm here. What's wrong with that?"

She stared at him in the dark. His face was as clear to her as if they were standing under a noon sun. "Don't pretend," she whispered. "You came here to see *me*. Don't pretend you didn't."

He grinned. "Well, of course. Wouldn't have taken the job if you weren't here. But I didn't do any harm by coming."

She wanted to hit him, or shake him, or scream out her fear and fury.

But the first two options wouldn't have budged him, and the last would have had dire consequences. "Justin. *You can't come here to see me*. You can't. You have to stay away from me. You have to stay away from the convent."

He shrugged. "Well, I won't. I want to see you. I want to know you're all right. You don't have to talk to me. You don't have to meet me in the middle of the night. Just stand in the window or the courtyard or the kitchen garden and let me get a look at you, make sure you're still breathing and you've got no broken bones. And I'll deliver my goods, and mount back up on my horse, and ride on out."

He would, too. She could tell by the set of his mouth, his obdurate stance. This was a man it was impossible to turn aside once he had decided on a course of action.

What would he do, what would he say, when she told him she could never see him again?

She could not have that conversation, now, tonight, on the convent grounds, with so many hostile parties so close and probably wakeful. She could not warn him away, she could not lie to him, she could not make him believe that she did not love him.

"You shouldn't have come," she said, but now her voice was gentle, full of some of the wonder she felt. That he would come so far just for a glimpse of her, just to assure himself that she was safe. "Whoever you are, I can't rid myself of the feeling that you are no friend to the Lestra, and that she and her men would do something terrible to you if they found you inside this compound."

Now his face showed amusement. "I was here once before, and they didn't like me much then," he admitted. "But I'm being more careful this time."

"You can't come back."

"Then you have to come to Neft."

She shook her head. "I have no control over that."

"Then I'll be here again. Look for me."

"Justin—" she said, having absolutely no idea how to finish the sentence, but she didn't have to. He pulled her back into his embrace and kissed her, and she lost any interest in forming a coherent sentence. Nothing mattered except his arms around her body, his lips against her mouth. Nothing moved, nothing breathed, nothing lived, except the two of them in their dark and secret circle.

Eventually they broke apart, just a little—pulling back just enough to watch each other's face—it was cold enough that they actually needed each other's body heat to stay warm. Idly, they began to talk, sharing the tales of their recent days. More friends of Justin's had passed through Neft, and he was careful not to use their names, for some reason, but she got the impression one of them was a woman. Oddly, she didn't feel the same hot jealousy she had felt when he mentioned the beautiful Kirra. Maybe he had a different relationship with this particular woman—or maybe Ellynor no longer worried that Justin's heart was bestowed elsewhere.

She told him about Rosurie and her unnerving desire to offer a sacrifice to the Pale Mother. "Is she the kind of person who just talks about things and never does anything, or is she the kind who follows through?" he wanted to know.

"Follows through. Usually in the most dramatic fashion possible."

"Then nothing you say is going to be able to stop her. Just step back. Don't let her drag you with her into whatever conflagration she starts."

Better advice than she had been able to give herself, and she was comforted by his practical words. Imagine how restful it would be to always rely on Justin to help her solve problems big and little. "I'll hope that this time it's a small and personal fire," she said, joking.

He had loosened her braid so that her hair fell free all the way past her waist, and now he was stroking his hands slowly, rhythmically, down her back, allowing plaits of hair to slip through his spread fingers. He had done the same thing back in Neft; he seemed fascinated by the feel and texture and pattern of her hair. "It doesn't sound to me like she's going to be ready to leave the convent anytime soon," he said, his voice as slow and deliberate as his caress. "Would you be willing to leave without her? If you decided you wanted to? If you became uneasy enough about unfolding events?"

"I don't know," she replied. She rested her forehead against his chest, feeling the chilled leather of his coat smooth against her cold skin. He smelled like horse and sweat and something indefinable. Maybe just himself. "My family might not want me to leave her behind. And I would find it hard to abandon her, I admit. She is—she doesn't always make good decisions. Without someone to watch her, her choices might be even worse."

"Well, it's something you should start thinking about," he said. "How you can leave the convent. And, if you won't walk out without her, how you can persuade Rosurie to come, too."

"I've thought about writing a letter to my father," she said. "To tell him it's time to bring us home. But I'm not sure—well—it's possible the Lestra has our mail read. I mean, I don't know that for a fact, but—"

"But it would seem entirely in character," he finished up. "I can take a letter for you and send it on its way."

And then be struck dumb when he realized it was directed to her family in the Lirrens. "I don't have one ready just at the moment," she said, forcing a light laugh. "Perhaps I will by the next time I see you."

"And that will be when?"

"I told you, I don't know."

"In four or five weeks, maybe," he said. "If I bring in your next supply of goods."

She was alarmed. "Justin. Won't it seem strange if you keep showing up here? Won't someone notice?"

He shrugged. "Far as I can tell, Jenkins has been hauling goods in for the past six months, and no one seems concerned about *him*. No one should pay any attention to me as long as I behave myself."

She lifted a hand to his mouth and traced the full lips. "And this is what you call behaving yourself?" she murmured. "Seducing novices under the moonlight?"

He caught her hand in his and pressed a kiss into the palm. "And this is what you call seduction?" he asked. "I must have missed part of it."

She giggled and tried to free her hand but he held on tighter, sliding his other arm around her waist to hold her in place. His lips moved from her palm up to her fingertips, back to her palm and down to her wrist. The sleeves of her robe fell back; her moonstone bracelet slid down her arm toward her elbow, every glowing gem hot against her skin.

His mouth paused in its travels and his hand closed with unexpected pressure around her fingers. "*Ow.* Justin!"

Now he lifted his head and twisted her arm so he could try to see it, but the light was too poor. His grip shifted; he ran his fingertips back and forth over the rough patch of skin encircling her entire wrist. "What's this?" he asked, his voice quiet but holding a note that struck her as ominous. As if he believed someone had offered her great physical harm and he was determined to discover who. And then set off on a mission to strangle that person or run him through with a sword.

She tried without success to pull her hand away. "What's what?"

His finger, for a moment, pressed harder against the band of roughened skin. "*This.* You've got a scar around the base of your hand. Feels like—doesn't feel like a knife wound, so I guess nobody tried to slice your hand off. Feels more like a burn."

She sighed and stopped tugging on her hand. His fingers continued investigating, gentle now, checking for the extent of damage. "That's what it looks like, too. I wear my sleeves long, so it doesn't show. And most of the time I try to keep the bracelet off my skin, wearing it outside the cloth of my robe, but sometimes it—"

"Wait," he interrupted. "Wait. Are you saying your bracelet is burning you? Your moonstones are hot to the touch?"

She felt her heart skip in sudden fear. He knew something she didn't and he was suddenly, deeply alarmed. "Yes," she said cautiously. "I just assumed—aren't they always? Don't they burn everybody?"

Now he was staring at her in something like horror, and it took her a moment to realize he was not terrified *by* her, but *for* her. "The touch of a moonstone only bothers people with magic in their blood," he said, his voice low and urgent. "A moonstone will only burn your skin if you're a mystic."

CHAPTER
20

JUSTIN and Jenkins accomplished virtually the entire trip back to Neft without saying a word. The freighter attempted a few conversational gambits, but gave up when Justin didn't respond; even their stops for food along the way were passed in silence. Not until they reached Jenkins's barn and property on the edge of town did Justin rouse himself to speak.

"If you need me again, I'd be happy to ride out with you next time you're going to the convent," he said, as the freighter counted into his hand the money he'd promised for the job.

"Got a trip up toward Nocklyn Towers later in the week," Jenkins said hopefully.

Justin shook his head. "Not interested in any route except the one to Lumanen."

If Jenkins thought that odd, he gave no outward sign. "Well, I might need you at that. I'll let you know."

"Appreciate it."

Justin hiked over to the stables to tell Delz he was back and ready to work. Indeed, he shoveled manure and hauled down hay with more vigor than most men would have mustered after a long ride and a virtually sleepless night. But he had to work off some of the ferocious energy building up in his muscles. His body had braced itself for combat and now had to launch itself into action or explode.

A mystic. By the grace of the Bright Mother, *a mystic?* In Lumanen Convent? That explained Ellynor's ability to heal sick old Paulina Gisseltess—that explained her eerie skill at practically making herself disappear. That explained almost all of the mysteries about her, but added a whole new layer of conundrums.

She hadn't believed him. *Justin, don't be ridiculous, I'm not a mystic. I scarcely even understand what that means!* He had tried to explain—*A mystic is merely someone who has been granted magic by the gods, and surely you have*—but she just shook her head and laughed. *I'm not a mystic. I'm an ordinary woman.*

In the end, it didn't matter if she believed him or not, if she acknowledged that her power was in her own blood, and not granted on a random basis by a careless goddess. What mattered was that she understood how much danger she was in now. Real, mortal, immediate danger.

"If the Lestra sees this burn on your arm," he had told her, speaking slowly and deliberately, "if she knows it was caused by your moonstones, she will believe you are a mystic. If she believes you are a mystic, you will die. Do you understand me, Ellynor? She is on a campaign to systematically eliminate mystics from the realm. It will not stop her that you say you have no magic. It will not stop her that you say you didn't know. Nothing will stop her. She will kill you. You will be dead. Do you understand me?"

She had understood. She had believed him, and she was frightened. All good things. But she would not, even so, agree to leave as soon as she could gather her clothes and slip out into the darkness. He had urged her to leave right then, that very night, creep past the guards at the gate and loiter in the forest until Justin and his companion could pick her up as they left the following morning.

"You could sneak out. I've seen what you can do. No one would know you were leaving," he argued. But she would only shake her head.

"No. Justin. No. I'm not ready to leave yet. I've kept my secret for a whole year and I didn't even know I had a secret to *keep.* Now I'll be twice as watchful. I won't make any mistakes."

"Everybody makes mistakes," he said. He had regarded her speculatively by moonlight, trying to decide if he could take her by force, steal a horse and escape with her this very night. His mood favored the plan, but his cooler intellect recognized it as suicidal.

"I won't. I'll be fine. Just trust me."

Since he'd had no choice, he had left her behind, but he was already scheming about how and when to return and what sorts of persuasions he could bring to bear when he did. He would go back with the freighting man; that was a dead certainty. Maybe sooner, if he could think of a way to get inside the compound.

Sweet Mother of the burning sun. Ellynor was a mystic.

She could not have found a more dangerous place to stand if she had searched every acre and plot in the entire country of Gillengaria looking for one.

* * *

"YOU'VE been quiet lately," Faeber remarked to him two nights later as the magistrate joined Justin in the taproom. Justin was almost done with his meal and couldn't have said what he'd eaten. He had no attention to spare for inessential details these days; he only bothered to eat because he intended to keep himself as strong, as ready for action, as humanly possible.

He didn't make much effort at a smile. He was finding it hard to keep up this game of pretending to be harmless. "You'd rather I started breaking tables and throwing chairs through windows?"

"I'm thinking you've done some damage in your time."

Justin shrugged and took a swig of ale. He didn't particularly care if Faeber thought him rude. Who cared what anybody thought about anything? Ellynor was in danger. "Not lately," he said.

"Not so sure about that," Faeber said in a soft voice.

Now Justin gave him a quick, level stare out of narrowed eyes. "What have you heard about me?"

Faeber settled himself more comfortably in his chair. Clearly Justin's hostility wasn't having much of an effect on him. "There was a story some weeks back. Fancy house burned down a few miles up the road in Nocklyn territory."

"And you think I had something to do with it?"

Faeber shook his head. "I think it was burned down by convent guards trying to smoke out mystics," he said bluntly.

Plain-speaking for someone as roundabout as Faeber. Justin remained noncommittal. "Is that right?"

"Trouble is, they seem to have missed their target," he said. "Young boy was staying at the house—everyone thinks he's got magic in his blood. Everyone thought he died in the fire. Turns out he didn't. The story I heard—just today—is that some stranger happened to be riding by, and he helped the youngster get clear of the soldiers. Turned the boy over to people who could be trusted. Never told anyone his name."

Who would have expected nobility to be gossiping with the magistrate of Neft? "Depending on how you feel about mystics, that was a stroke of either good fortune or bad," Justin commented.

"I think the young serramarra who's running Nocklyn thought it was good fortune," Faeber said. "Serra Mayva? That boy's related to her somehow, and she's very fond of him. She was ecstatic to get the news, they say."

"Well, that's interesting," Justin replied. "What about you? Pleased or disappointed?"

Faeber stretched out his legs. "I'm not one who sanctions outright murder," he drawled. "I can think of a few men I'd like to see dead, but I wouldn't set their houses on fire in the middle of the night."

Which was as close as Faeber had ever come to admitting he disapproved of the persecution of mystics. Still, that didn't mean Justin should share his own views. He wasn't ready to trade confidences just yet. "No," Justin said. "If I'm going to kill someone, I want him to be armed and staring me straight in the face."

Faeber chuckled. "Just the sort of thing I'd expect you to say," he said. "Even so, I have to wonder why you were out roaming the countryside the night that house burned down."

Justin grew very still. "Who says I was?"

"No one. It just seemed to me like the man who saved that boy sounded an awful lot like you. From the description I heard."

"Well, I can tell you this," Justin said with a little more heat than he'd intended. "Anyone who *had* been riding around that night and *did* happen to see that boy running from the fire *should* have helped him to safety. Doesn't take a good man to do something like that. Takes a bad man not to."

"I didn't think you'd admit it," Faeber said, satisfaction in his voice. He sighed heavily and climbed to his feet as if the act took a great deal of effort. But he lingered a moment before walking away. "It wouldn't hurt you to trust me," he said quietly. "Sometime if you needed to."

"How do you know you can trust *me*?" Justin replied.

Faeber only smiled and shook his head. Still smiling, he strolled away, stopping to speak at another table full of diners. Justin finished his meal, finding it a little tastier than he had a few minutes ago. Seasoned with something like friendship.

THE next day was extremely chilly but bright with sun. Delz was sick, so Justin handled the stables by himself. He didn't mind the extra work, for he still felt driven by that instinct to act, to stay in motion. When he'd finished with the normal chores, he began working at the tasks they never got to, sweeping out the main room, hammering down a loose board, replacing a smashed stall gate that had been kicked in by a fractious horse.

Dark had long since fallen, and he had run out of make-work, when he heard one of the front doors creak open. He was in the back half of the building, checking a gelding's legs for nicks, and he lifted his head and waited to be summoned. But no one called for an ostler. There was no sound of footfalls, either human or horse, from the main room. Maybe the wind had just blown the door back.

Justin didn't think so.

He released the gelding's foot, backed out of the stall, and silently latched the gate. His dagger was already in his hand. There was a lantern lit in here, but the front room would be dark; anyone could be lurking in the shadows. Who had come calling? Convent guards, not deceived by Justin's air of innocence? Faeber and his men, not so fond of mystics and their champions after all? A thief, come to steal a saddle or a traveler's horse?

Justin moved noiselessly across the floor, paused at the connecting doors, and listened closely. Someone was breathing, hard and fast, as if he'd been running. Or sobbing. There was a rustle of clothing, the sound of a body dropping onto a bale of hay as if it was the softest, safest sanctuary in the world. More rustling, as if a cloak had been unwrapped—or a skirt had been rearranged. A long sigh, half vocalized, the voice sounding in the upper register.

A woman waited on the other side of the doors.

Justin wasn't stupid enough to think all women were useless in a fight—he knew plenty who weren't—but there were only a handful of people who could beat him in one-on-one combat, and none of them were female. He didn't think he would risk much by confronting this one head-on.

In three swift movements, he'd snatched the lantern from its hook, swung open the connecting doors, and burst into the main room. The woman sitting there leapt to her feet, one hand pressed to her heart, one pressed to her mouth, and visibly held back a scream.

They stared at each other.

Justin didn't know what he'd expected, but it wasn't this woman: small, pale, blond, and very clearly noble. She huddled inside a thick, fur-lined coat and stared at him, eyes wide with terror. The look on her face said she knew he was going to kill her.

He lowered his dagger but kept the lantern lifted high. "Who are you?" he asked in a quiet voice.

She shook her head and didn't answer.

"I won't hurt you," he said, though he found himself wondering how

many attackers claimed the same thing seconds before they leapt forward
to cut someone's throat. "You look afraid. Is someone coming after you?
Someone who wants to harm you?"

She dropped her hand from her mouth, but kept her other hand
balled up against her throat. Or—no. She was clutching something in her
fingers, a necklace or an amulet, perhaps. "My husband," she whispered.
"He wants me dead."

Time to get practical. "How many men does he have with him? What
direction did you come from?"

She opened her mouth as if to speak, but no words came out. Clearly
she was not used to good fortune; she wouldn't believe she could trust
him. Justin made his voice softer. He kept remembering how Cammon
had told him not to intimidate Delz. This lady was probably even more
unnerved by his size and ferocity. "How close are they? Do you have a
guess?"

She moistened her lips. "I don't know. No one was paying attention,
so I just left. I don't know when they got back or when they started to
miss me."

"Where were you? Did you come on foot?"

"Yes. Well—someone gave me a ride in a cart this afternoon. I was
walking yesterday."

So she'd been on the run or in hiding for a full day or more. He wondered what had made her trust the driver of the gig. "Where were you?"
he repeated.

She tried twice before she could answer. Her eyes were desperately
scanning his face, trying to read in it some promise of compassion. "The
convent," she said.

"The *Lumanen* Convent?" he repeated, more forcefully than he intended. She swayed backward and almost fell over the bale of hay. What
in the name of all the goddesses in Gillengaria was drawing half the nobility of the realm to this one small corner of Nocklyn?

"Yes," she whispered. "I was there with my husband."

"And your husband is—?" he said, but his voice trailed off. He studied her. He had seen her before; he knew he had. Dressed in a fine gown
and gracing some sumptuous ballroom, but looking just as fragile and
afraid as she did right now.

And more recently. Here in Neft. Standing in a tavern with a group
of soldiers who had ridden in with—

"Halchon Gisseltess," he said abruptly, and the terror on her face
ratcheted up a notch. "You're his wife."

She didn't answer. He thought fear might kill her where she stood.

"You don't have to be afraid of me," he said, trying to remember the tale. He sat down a few yards away from her on a rickety stool, and set the lantern near his feet. They had been in Nocklyn last summer—Senneth guarding Princess Amalie, Kirra and Queen Valri along to give her consequence, Justin and Tayse and two other Riders there to protect the women—and Halchon Gisseltess had shown up at a grand ball. With his wife at his side. He was, of course, supposed to be under arrest at Gissel Plain. Soon enough, the regent had produced enough royal soldiers to send the errant marlord, and his wife, back to their estates. But before they had left, Halchon's wife had managed to meet with Senneth and whisper secrets about the war her husband was planning. . . .

So that was a name the shivering marlady might recognize. "I won't hurt you," he said again. "I'm a King's Rider. I'm a friend of Senneth's."

It was the talisman he'd hoped. She caught her breath and then seemed to crumple, falling all in a heap back on the bale of hay, her hands over her eyes, her whole body shaking. By the Bright Mother's red eye, she was crying. What was he supposed to do now?

"We don't have time for tears," he said, raising his voice a little so she could hear him over the sound of her weeping. "We have to figure out how to keep you safe."

"I'm not safe, I'll never be safe," she said on a sob. "He'll find me, and he'll kill me, and I don't know what to *do*! I'm so tired—I'm so tired of being afraid—"

"Well, he'll find you for certain if you're here," Justin said, not wanting to sound unsympathetic but wanting her to pay attention. "Stables'll be the first place he and his men come looking. We have to find someplace less likely."

"It doesn't matter," she said hopelessly. She seemed to have stopped crying, but Justin couldn't see that this brightened her attitude any. "He'll find me no matter where I go."

He shook his head. "Not if we're smart. Not if we hide you before anybody sees you . . ."

His voice trailed off again as he considered and discarded options. Obviously, he would have to take her to his room. She was much too exposed in the stables, and she would attract notice if she tried to rent a room for herself. But how to transport her from here to there? She was about the same size as Ellynor. She could borrow Delz's clothes as Ellynor had—except the clothes were off their accustomed hook, taken home for cleaning, he supposed. He could parade her boldly through the front rooms of the house, pretending she was a doxy he'd brought home for the night. Though that might seem out of character since he hadn't indulged in such entertainment in all the weeks he'd lived here. He could try to sneak her into the house, hoping he encountered no one on the stairs, but any air of furtiveness was sure to draw attention just when he didn't want it.

"Here's what we're going to do," he said. "I've got a room in a building not far from here. You're going to walk there, openly, head up, not looking around like you're afraid someone's going to grab you from behind. You'll go in the front door—if anyone looks at you, just nod your head like you know right where you're going. If someone asks you if you need help, say, 'I'm picking something up for a friend.' If they ask who, tell them Justin. You'll take my key—" He dug it out of his pocket and passed it to her in an underhand throw; she actually caught it. "You'll go up to my room and you'll let yourself in. And then you'll wait for me. I'll come in twenty or thirty minutes later so no one sees us together." He considered. "It would be better if you didn't have to use my name," he conceded. "But don't get flustered if someone asks who you're seeing. Just be nonchalant. Just act like you don't have a thought of trouble in your head."

"Is that your name?" she asked timidly. "Justin?" He nodded. She said, "I'm Sabina."

That made him smile at her, because it was so politely said. The expression she showed him was almost an answering smile. "Don't worry, Sabina, everything will be all right."

She nodded. "When you come—would it be possible—is there any chance you could bring some food?"

"Good idea. I'll stop by the taproom and pick up something to eat." He looked around. "If you're that hungry, I've got an apple in here somewhere."

"Yes," she said.

He rose, crossed the room, and dug through the pockets of his overcoat to find the fruit. She took it from his hand and bit into it instantly, daintily enough, but clearly starving. He'd have to bring her more than bread and cheese if he could manage it.

"Let me know when you're ready to go," he said. "I'll tell you exactly how to get to my place. And don't worry, I'll just be a few feet behind you. If someone tries to grab you, I'll be at your side in a couple of seconds."

She nodded but did not answer; she was still eating. Her free hand crept up again to close around her necklace. He had had a chance to see what it was, though—an onyx stone set with a small garnet. Pretty and probably valuable.

Unexpectedly, she noticed that something had caught his attention, and even figured out what it was. She swallowed the last bite of apple, licked juice from her fingers, and gave him the faintest smile. "She was right, after all," she said.

He was lost. "Who was? Right about what?"

"Senneth. She told me she could enchant my pendant. She told me that if I took hold of it when I was afraid and weak, that I would find comfort and strength. Senneth laid her hands on this worthless symbol of Gisseltess and made it the very thing that would save my life." She gazed at him with a great deal of intensity. "It led me to you. To her friend. It has kept me safe, just as she promised."

Well, now, that was something he'd have to ask Senneth about sometime. He'd never seen magic transferred to inanimate objects before. Then again, he had come to accept as an article of faith that Senneth could do pretty much anything she wanted to. And anything that helped keep Sabina Gisseltess calm had to be something he approved of.

"Excellent," he said. "Are you ready? Let me tell you where you're going."

CHAPTER
21

JUSTIN and the marlady slipped out into the darkness, the crooked streets in this part of Neft lit only randomly by the few shops and houses where candlelight glowed through the windows. He had thought she might be too rattled to remember his instructions, and was prepared to repeat them several times, but she had listened carefully and repeated them back to him without a mistake. He let her get a few yards ahead of him, then crossed to the other side of the street, appearing to stroll casually along, glancing in windows, nodding at passers-by. No one molested the marlady, though one or two passing men gave her suggestive smiles or offered a warm greeting. She didn't let them distract her. She walked on, her posture very straight, her face no doubt drawn in concentration.

Within ten minutes, they were at the boardinghouse, and Justin idled by. Not too far; he wanted to be within sight if she came rushing out, if some part of his plan failed. He allowed her enough time to climb the two flights of steps at a fairly slow pace, pausing to have a brief conversation once or twice, and then come running back downstairs in a panic. But she did not emerge.

So he hied himself over to the taproom, groused that he'd had to work late and, damn, wouldn't have time for lunch tomorrow, could someone wrap him up some meat and bread and maybe some cheese? Another ten minutes, and he had a couple of fairly hearty meals put together and was back on the street.

Back in the boardinghouse. A few souls were gathered in the common room, but no one looked up from the card game when he stepped in. He bounded up the stairs, knocked twice on his own door, and stepped inside.

The room was in darkness, but he could instantly see the small shadow that was Sabina Gisseltess, pressed against the far wall. "It's Justin," he said, in case she couldn't tell. "Did you have any trouble?"

She came toward him. "No. I didn't speak to anyone at all. There were some men downstairs when I came in, but they looked like they were gambling and they didn't pay any attention to me."

"Good. Draw the curtains and I'll find a candle. Then you can eat. Then we can talk things over."

In a few minutes, he'd lit two candles, built up the fire—a luxury he rarely bothered with, but he'd paid for the wood already, so why not?— and laid out Sabina's meal. In no time at all, she was sitting on the floor before the hearth, eating her second piece of bread, and actually smiling. Warm and fed and more or less safe for the first time since she'd left her husband's care. Justin guessed she was probably on the edge of euphoria.

"Now. We have to figure out what to do next," Justin said. The room offered no furniture besides a dilapidated chest of drawers and the two beds, and he felt a little peculiar sitting on a bed while he was entertaining a woman he didn't know, particularly a marlady. So he just dropped to the floor and sat facing her. "You can stay here a few days, but you'll need to find a more secure destination, and we'll have to decide how to get you there."

She swallowed a piece of meat. "I was thinking, probably, I should go to Ghosenhall. And meet with King Baryn."

Justin nodded. "And if you can tell him what your husband's been up to lately, I'm sure he'll be even happier to see you. But Ghosenhall's a pretty far trek for a lone woman on foot. How are we going to get you there?"

She took another bite and waited. Clearly, she wasn't the one who was going to try to come up with plans.

Another messenger should come from Ghosenhall soon enough; maybe this one would be a Rider. Would it be safe to send Sabina Gisseltess back to the royal city with only a single armed escort? Justin reviewed the likely envoys. With Tayse or Tir or Hammond or Coeval, yes—with himself, of course. But he wasn't sure he would trust any other solitary soldier, even a Rider, to protect this particular cargo for such a long journey.

Well, then, he'd just keep the runaway wife safe in his room and send an urgent message back with whoever came calling. That would disrupt his life for days, maybe weeks, longer than he'd like; but there didn't seem to be much choice about it.

"I think maybe you'd just better stay here until I can get a message to the king," he said. "Might be a week or more—and you'll have to stay out of sight that whole time—but I think it will be safest."

She nodded. "I don't care. I'll sit in this room a year, if I have to. Just to be free of him—" Her voice broke off.

Justin nodded. "I've met him once or twice. Not a man I'd care to spend much time with."

"I've been married to him more than fifteen years," she whispered.

He didn't know what to say in answer to that. "So. I'll bring you food and water every day. You'll have to stay quiet. Take off your shoes—glide across the floor when you walk. I'll show you the boards that creak. No one comes up here because that's how I got cheap rent—I haul the wood and the water and take down the linens every couple of weeks. That bed," he added, pointing, "is the one I haven't slept in, so it's got clean sheets. Well, Cammon slept in it twice, so—"

"I don't care," she said again. "I would have slept in the stables. I would have slept in the woods. I can't believe I'm so lucky as to be inside. Warm. Taken care of. I can't tell you—I can't thank you—"

He was afraid she'd start crying again. "Don't. I'm in service to the king, and he will reward me, I promise you, for taking you in. He knows Halchon Gisseltess is his enemy, and he can use you as a weapon against him. I'm just acting on the king's behalf."

She swiped at her eyes. "I think you're better than that," she said in a low voice. "I think you would have helped me anyway."

He was silent, thinking about that. A year ago, he might not have. Probably would not have, unless he had been able to see, instantly, how this frail marlady could so quickly become a dagger in the king's hand. He wouldn't have turned her over to the Gisseltess soldiers, he might even have let her sleep in the stables, but he wouldn't have rescued her. Wouldn't have thought it was important enough to do.

Senneth had changed him—Senneth who tried to save everybody, no matter how insignificant. Senneth who had no sense of priorities. She would jeopardize her mission for the king in order to keep some peasant girl from dying. Until Justin had seen Senneth fight for the nameless and the wretched, it had not occurred to him that anyone would choose to do so.

That he could do so. And be damn good at it, just because he was so good at fighting.

He rose to his feet. "I'm going to get a change of clothes and head on back to the stables to sleep. Lock the door behind me. I'll check on you in the morning."

Now alarm returned to the face that had looked, briefly, content and actually pretty. "You're going to leave me?"

He was surprised. "I thought—you'd rather—you don't know me, and it's a small room—"

"Please. You'll be more comfortable in your own bed. And I—I—I think I'll be less afraid if you're here. I understand you'll be gone during the day, but at night—tonight at least—if you'd stay—"

He could hardly refuse. He had no problem sleeping with a stranger nearby. He could wake in an instant if someone came creeping toward him in the night, bent on murder. Not that he thought she would. Not that she even had a weapon that he'd seen. Still. He was confident in his ability to repulse her if he had to.

"All right then. I'll stay," he said, and her thin shoulders relaxed in relief.

"Thank you," she whispered. "I will never be able to repay you."

A few minutes later, as they blew out the candles and took to their separate beds, Justin thought that over, too. What kind of payment would he ask for, if Sabina Gisseltess had the power to grant it? Or if the gods decided to liquidate human debts and level all accounts, what kind of reward would he request? He wasn't much for material things—a fast horse and a set of good blades were the only things he really cared about—so he wouldn't particularly want gold. He loved his life as a Rider, so he wouldn't ask for land. He had friends; he had status, of a sort. All he wanted was for Ellynor to be safe—for the gods to guide her to shelter and a champion as surely as they had guided Sabina Gisseltess to him.

If he believed in the gods, he might now think he had the right to ask them a favor. *Bright Mother, Black Mother, Pale Mother, whichever one watches over Ellynor, keep her safe tonight. Keep her safe always.*

He heard Sabina rustle in her bed and he listened, in case she was about to ask him for something, but she said nothing. He put a hand briefly to his forehead, thinking about everything that had happened in the past week, everything he needed to sort out or take care of. Everything he wished he could tell to someone he trusted, or hand over to someone who would deal with it most efficiently.

Senneth, he thought, the words sounding fierce even in his own head. *I wish you were here. I wish you could tell me what to do next.*

THE next three days were as strange and tense as any Justin had spent in Neft so far. Gisseltess men showed up the very next morning, dressed with no attempt at subtlety in the black-and-red colors of their House, and began prowling through the town. The minute he saw the first one clatter down the street, Justin put down his shovel.

"Delz," he called. "I've got business to do. I'll be gone an hour or two."

"Gone where?" Delz replied, sounding irritable, but Justin didn't bother answering. He just snatched up his coat and left.

Up in his room, he found Sabina Gisseltess sleeping, though she woke with a start when he spoke her name. Her face instantly showed fright; he guessed it was her most familiar emotion.

"What's wrong?"

He jerked his head toward the window. "Your husband's men just arrived. I wanted to be here in case they headed this way."

Her pale face whitened even more. "And if they do?"

He sat on his bed and pulled off his boots. He'd already laid his jacket aside. "If they do, I think I crawl in bed next to you and cover you entirely with the blankets. You're so small and I'm so big, I don't think they'll notice there's another body on the mattress. There's really no place else to look—not even a closet to hide in. If they think I'm alone, maybe they won't come in."

"But if they do come in?" she whispered.

He gave her a confident grin. "Then I guess we'll end up with a couple of dead Gisseltess soldiers in the middle of the room."

"Yes, but if that happens—!"

"It gets dicey," he admitted. "Then we run. Maybe we try to find Faeber, I don't know."

"Who's Faeber?"

"Magistrate. Runs the local guard and so forth. He'd like me to trust him, but that's my option of last resort."

She was silent a moment. "If you kill them—kill some of my husband's guards—you'll be in trouble. You'll be arrested, won't you? I can't ask you to do that for me."

Justin shrugged. He was back on his feet and over at the window, looking out. So far, none of the guards had made it to this street. Seemed like they were being slow and thorough. He wondered how many had arrived and how they had split up to search the city. He had a strategic advantage against greater numbers only if they crossed the threshold of his room one at a time.

"By the way. In case I didn't say so before. Stay away from the window," he said over his shoulder. "You don't want anyone seeing you look out. I don't just mean Gisseltess guards, I mean anyone. The whole time you're here."

"That won't be hard," she said. "All I want to do is sleep anyway."

"That'll wear off after a while."

She gave a small laugh. "I don't think so."

There. Justin flattened himself against the wall and peered out at an angle. Looked like the guards had broken up into teams of two and were taking their own sweet time about conducting their search. Damn. One pair had just stepped into the building next to the boardinghouse; another had entered the shop across the street. Maybe fifteen minutes and one set would be walking through the door downstairs.

Justin pivoted from the window and surveyed the room for anything that would give away the marlady's presence. Small, expensive shoes on the floor; fur-lined coat folded neatly by the bed. That wouldn't do.

"You get under the covers," he instructed. "Completely under—I don't even want to see your hair. I'm going to mess things up a bit."

She complied without comment, though she did peek at him from under the sheets while he created a systematic havoc. He hid her shoes under her coat, then pulled out one of the dresser drawers and dumped its contents on top. His own boots he lobbed in the general direction of the pile. He wanted this room to look like it was lived in by a man who just threw all his clothes on the floor. There were two dirty plates and two glasses left from yesterday's hasty meal. He placed one set on top of the dresser and hid the other set inside the drawer that was now empty. No other traces of Sabina were evident.

Back to the window to watch. Soon enough, soldiers were stalking through the door of the boardinghouse. Concentrating closely, Justin thought he could hear a snarl of outrage from the patrons downstairs, then the tread of heavy footsteps. He crossed the room to listen at the door, turning the lock slowly so it fell in place without a sound. Voices on the stairs—loud knocks, raised protests, what could have been a door slamming open and hitting an interior wall. The soldiers were still on the first level. More argument, a small crash, the sound of something hard falling to the floor. Footsteps on the stairs.

The soldiers were on the second story.

Justin turned and smiled at Sabina. It was clear she was deathly afraid, but he felt a fine and pleasurable energy running through his veins. "Looks like they're coming all the way up," he said. "I can still see your hair. Scoot down."

He fetched the pillow and blanket from his own bed and bunched these up on top of Sabina. Stripped off his shirt and socks, so all he was wearing was a pair of trousers. Laid his sword just under the bed, in easy reach. Kept his dagger in his hand as he carefully climbed in next to Sabina, trying not to push too close. There was no way to escape a certain sense of intimacy. He turned so his back was to her and he was facing the door. He lay entirely still, every sense strained to hear what was happening.

Heavy footsteps on the stairs, a low exchange of voices, then an impatient pounding on the wood.

"Is anyone inside? Open the door."

Justin didn't answer. He quickly ran a hand through his hair, trying to make it look as messy as if he'd been sleeping on it for a few hours.

"*Anyone inside?*" The query came more loudly, then there was a rattling at the door. "Locked. Someone's in there."

"Does one of the keys fit?"

"Too damn many keys to this place! I'd rather break the door in."

"Knock again."

"*Is anyone in the room?*"

Justin let his voice sound rusty and ill-tempered. "What is it? Who's out there? I'm trying to sleep!"

The door rattled again. "Let us in! We're men of the noble House of Gisseltess, searching for an escaped outlaw."

"Nobody in here but me," Justin said, slurring his words like a man on the point of falling back asleep. In reality, he was as alert as he'd ever been. The knife felt like an extension of his own hand.

Pounding on the door again. "We want to see for ourselves."

"Go away!"

More muttering at the door, the jangle of keys, the sound of the lock clicking back. And suddenly the door swung open and two men burst inside.

Justin pushed himself up on his elbow and reared back, half-crushing Sabina under him. "Wha—I told you!" he said furiously. "There's nobody in here! What time is it? I've been asleep an hour, do you understand that? Pale Lady curse you, I have to be on the road again in four hours, and you come breaking into my room—"

Unmoved by his tirade, the soldiers made a show of looking around. One of them even bent enough to see under the beds, while the other strolled over and kicked at the pile of clothes. Justin kept up the bitter monologue, fighting back a yawn, pulling himself upright in bed, and leaning his shoulders against the wall. He was trying not to actually sit on Sabina, but he could feel her compact shape against the small of his back. His hand with the dagger he kept concealed under the pillow.

The guards exchanged glances. One shook his head and the other shrugged. "No one here. Our apologies. Get back to sleep."

"Back to *sleep*?" Justin repeated. "How am I going to manage *that*?" He threw a pillow at the door as they closed it behind them, and he heard one of them laugh. He sat forward enough to remove any pressure from Sabina, but otherwise did not move as he listened to the soldiers tramp down the stairs. When he judged they were on the ground story, he slipped out of bed and stood by the window, once again just peering out from the side. In another minute, he saw them leave by the front door and head to the next house.

"They're gone," he said, swinging around to look at Sabina and tucking his dagger back into its sheath. "You can come up for air."

Rather slowly, she folded the covers back and sat up shakily. Her eyes were huge and her face was almost bloodless. "They would have found me if you hadn't been here," she said in a strangled voice.

He nodded. "Probably. But I don't think they'll come back."

"You don't *know* that."

"I don't know that," he agreed.

"Then—will you stay with me? All the time? Not just at night?"

"I'm sorry, Sabina, but I can't. I have a job to do—a couple of jobs—and they're important. I think you're safe for a day or so. I don't think they'll come back and search all the rooms they've just been through."

She was kneading her hands together. "I can't stay here. I need to get someplace safer. Someplace he can't find me."

"You do," he said. "If help doesn't come soon or I can't think of a better plan, well, then, I guess I'll have to try to take you to Ghosenhall myself." He read the look on her face and added, "Don't try to go without me. You won't get very far. And I won't come after you if you run, because I don't have the time. You have to trust me, Sabina. I won't let harm come to you, not if you do what I say."

"I trust you," she said in a very faint voice. "It's just that—I'm so afraid."

He nodded. "I know. But you'll make it through. Just give me a few days to hope that a messenger from the king arrives."

He sat on the floor and began pulling on his discarded clothes and boots. "You're leaving now?" she said, trying not to sound panicked.

"For a while. I'll be back later with a meal. Don't make any noise. Don't look out the window. I'll be back sometime after dark."

"I'll be here," she said.

He had to be careful as he made his way back to the stables. He didn't want to run into the two guards who had questioned him, who might wonder why he wasn't still in his room, trying to sleep. But he also wanted to get a sense of how much territory the Gisseltess men were planning to cover. So he made a hasty circuit through town and found the soldiers everywhere. *There must be thirty of them,* he thought, and they were forcing themselves into all kinds of establishments, from lace shops to barrooms to brothels. He even spotted some of them quartering the finer district of town, as he climbed the hill that took him to Jenetta Gisseltess's place.

He stood for a moment outside the wrought-iron fence, looking up at serra Paulina's window. Then he turned on his heel and headed back to the stables.

Delz seemed less annoyed at his absence than excited by the disturbance turning this into an out-of-the-ordinary day. "You see those Gisseltess men all over town?" the owner demanded. "Just came inside like they owned this place, looked in every stall, climbed up to the hayloft. Who are they hunting? Did you hear?"

Justin shrugged. "Outlaw, somebody said."

Delz made a skeptical noise. "Someone Halchon Gisseltess isn't too fond of, more like," he said. "Man thinks he can ride around any of the southern properties and do anything he pleases. People are afraid of him. They hate him, but they let him do what he likes. People who stand up to him end up dead."

Justin nodded. "That's the way it happens sometimes."

"Well, I hope they're gone soon and they don't come back," Delz said. "Bet they don't even leave their horses here if they decide to spend the night. Wish they'd go."

Justin grinned a little at the juxtaposition of righteous anger and commercial greed. But he wished the soldiers would go, too.

He put some extra effort into his chores that afternoon, to make up for missing part of the morning, but his mind wasn't on his work. What was he going to do with Sabina Gisseltess? What if no envoy arrived for another week—or more? He would not be able to hide her forever, and she would slowly go mad from terror if she had to cower alone in his room for too many days. Should he, in fact, abandon his post in Neft and risk the long journey to Ghosenhall? What if one of the Riders came looking for him? What kind of message could he leave that would make it clear a new imperative had superseded his original instructions? What if Ellynor needed him? He had *no* way of leaving her any information about his whereabouts. What if something critical happened in the city that he was supposed to be observing, and he missed it? He was fairly certain both Tayse and the king would agree Sabina was a prize worth changing their plans for, but he did not like the idea of leaving his post. Still, it might be his best choice. It might be his only one.

Should he leave? And if so, how quickly? Was there anything to be gained by lingering in Neft even another day?

For a moment, he paused in his act of sweeping out the back room and let his hands lie idle on the broom handle. A single pulse of pain drove an ache deep into his skull, and he briefly closed his eyes. When he opened them, he was seized with a sudden conviction. He would stay in Neft another two days. He would know then what he was supposed to do. It was almost as if he had heard a voice, echoing and disembodied, in the back of his head. *Wait,* that voice had said. He didn't understand it, he didn't know if it was real, but he had made his decision. For now, he and the marlady would stay put. If no answer became clear in two days, they would hazard the journey to Ghosenhall.

THE Gisseltess soldiers did not reappear, and Sabina grew a little calmer. True to her word, she seemed likely to sleep away her entire sojourn in Justin's room, for she was never awake any time he returned—at night, or in quick checks during the middle of the day. He realized she really had nothing to do except sleep, but he thought there might be more to it than that. He thought she might have spent the entire span of her marriage in a heightened state of readiness, prepared for the next insult, the next blow, the next threat against her life. He wondered if she had ever been able to relax for a minute.

No obvious solutions to his dilemma had occurred to him by the time that second day was drawing to a close, and Justin found himself uncharacteristically at a loss. The evening rush of customers had already passed, and Delz had quit for the night; in a few more minutes, Justin would head to his own room. He did not want to leave Neft, but he had to get Sabina Gisseltess to safety. He supposed he'd better look into getting them a week's worth of provisions and tell Delz the bad news: He had to take a significant leave from this job. He would be back—no doubt about that—but he would understand if Delz wouldn't want to keep his position open for him—

"You look so deep in thought," said an amused voice, and he whirled around to see a tall, slim woman standing just inside the main doorway. "If I'd been an enemy, I'd have cut your throat for sure."

"Senneth!" He had never been so glad to see anyone in his entire life. He crossed the room in three strides and enveloped her in a bone-crushing hug. "You have no idea—where's Tayse? Where's Cam?"

"Back on the road a bit. We weren't sure exactly what kind of trouble you were in, so we didn't know if we should all come rushing here at once."

He stared at her. Her returning smile was mischievous. "How did—you can't possibly—what makes you think—?"

Her smile widened. "Well, now, how exactly *do* you think I'd be able to know something was wrong with you?" she teased. "From a hundred miles away and with no particular reason to worry?"

Now he felt his bones prickle with disbelief. "Cammon? He could feel—*Cammon* told you I needed you? Where were you?"

"Halfway through Nocklyn on our way back from Coravann."

"And he could tell—that boy is spooky-strange."

Senneth nodded. "He is. But useful, in his own special way. What's wrong? You don't appear to have any broken bones. Well, I didn't expect you to. He said you weren't hurt, just uneasy. And I said, 'Justin? Are you *sure* you're picking up emotions from the right person? Because I've never seen Justin unsure of himself for even five minutes.'"

Now he was grinning back at her. Bright Mother blind him, but he was happy to see her. And he couldn't wait to see the expression on her face when he shared his news. "Well, now, you tell me how *you'd* handle this situation," he drawled. "Three nights ago a woman took refuge in the stables. Told me she was running away from her husband and any men he might send looking for her. Turns out her husband is Halchon Gisseltess."

Senneth looked every bit as astonished as he'd hoped. "Sabina Gisseltess is *here*? She's left him? I didn't think she had the nerve." She glanced around, as if expecting to see Sabina's blond head poking up from behind the hay bales. "Where is she? Did you find someplace to keep her safe?"

"Barely. She's in my room. Soldiers did come through a couple days ago, but I was able to hide her. I've been trying to decide if I should risk taking her back to Ghosenhall on my own—but I didn't particularly want to leave Neft—couldn't decide what to do." He thought a moment about that voice in his head. *Wait.* "Did you tell Cammon to try to think something at me?" he asked slowly. "Because I had decided I should leave, and then I just felt this compulsion to stay a few more days."

She was grinning. "You felt that, did you? Cammon said he wasn't sure you'd pick it up, you not being too sensitive to mystics and all. So he made the message as simple as he could."

He felt the skin on his back tighten and release. "I got it. I didn't understand it was a message from him, but I got it. That's—I don't know that I really like that, Senneth. I have to think about it."

"You think about it," she said amiably. "And I'll go talk to marlady Sabina."

THEY spent one night in Neft, and then Senneth and her group were back on the road, their party augmented by one. It was clear to all of them that their trip required equal parts speed and stealth, so they covered ground quickly, efficiently, and with a great deal of caution. Once again, Senneth thanked the Bright Mother for the impulse that had made her agree to bring Cammon along on this trip. Not only had he been the one to steer them back toward Neft when he picked up on Justin's disquiet, but his heightened senses would alert them to danger if they crossed the path of Gisseltess soldiers—or anyone else bent on doing them harm.

Sabina was a better traveler than Senneth would have expected—but that, too, might have been due to Cammon's presence. He rode beside the marlady for most of the way, talking to her in a low, calm voice that even Senneth found soothing, and she wasn't particularly nervous. As a result, Sabina was docile, even helpful when they broke the journey to camp at night. She didn't whine about keeping up the pace, sleeping on the ground, or running low on water. She did what she was told and seemed heartbreakingly grateful that Senneth and her friends had effected her rescue.

"You're not safe yet," Senneth wanted to say that second night on the road, when Sabina thanked them again, but she couldn't bear to add any tension back to Sabina's pinched face. Still, a quick look at Tayse let her know he was thinking exactly the same thing. Instead she said, as gently as she could, "We're glad we were near enough to be able to help."

Tayse had questioned the marlady fairly closely about what she and her husband had been doing at the convent, but Sabina had not had many details to offer. They had traveled to the convent many times before. Yes, even after the king had placed them under arrest on Gissel Plain. No, she didn't know how Halchon was so easily able to slip through the royal guard sent to Gisseltess to keep him in place; she suspected some bribery and some cunning. They had left in the middle of the night and cut across the back lawns of the estate, guarded by a few loyal men. She rather believed that one of Halchon's cousins had remained behind in the mansion, pretending to be the marlord. They looked somewhat alike if viewed from a distance. She had no idea if the Ghosenhall guards were even aware that her husband was gone.

"I can't help thinking that the marlady is peculiarly ill informed," Tayse said to Senneth that night. They were lying curled up together on one side of the fire; Cammon and Sabina were asleep in their separate blankets. Tayse had just returned from his habitual midnight circuit of the perimeter with the report that all was well. "She has told us very little."

Senneth grinned and settled her back against his chest. His hand came up to rest on the curve of her hip. "I was thinking the same thing. But I don't believe Halchon has ever taken her into his confidence and anything she does know she has learned by eavesdropping. And this past year or so I think all her energy has gone into keeping herself alive, knowing that her husband had been considering the advantages of seeing her dead."

"Why run now?" Tayse asked. "Was it just the opportunity? An unguarded gate, a city close enough to reach? She doesn't seem to have thought out her escape too well."

"She said something about that. She heard Halchon tell his sister that the time had come to do away with her," Senneth said. "She seemed to think that there would be a riding accident of some sort when they left Lumanen. So if she was going to die anyway—" She shrugged. "Might as well die fighting to live."

"She'd have been dead anyway, if Justin hadn't found her."

"And aren't you proud of him?" she murmured. "Not just that he figured out what he had to do to keep her safe, but that he was moved to do so. I didn't think Justin would ever be soft enough to care what happened to strangers."

"And you think that's what I like?" he asked in mock outrage. "For Riders to be *soft*? For Riders to be easily distracted from their commissions?"

"Well, I'm proud of him, at any rate," she said, smiling. "I wonder if this is Ellynor's influence. If finding himself in love with her has made him feel more kindly disposed to the world at large."

He was amused. "I'm not sure that's how it works for most men," he said. "I think love makes them more ferocious with the rest of the world—determined to keep that one woman safe."

Now she sighed. She laid her own hand over Tayse's and his fingers interlaced with hers. Strange how she wasn't able to sleep these days unless this man was beside her, his hand folded over hers. And she knew perfectly well that she could keep herself safe without help from anyone. "I'm not sure he's going to be able to manage it in Ellynor's case."

"What did he tell you? I saw him draw you aside."

She debated how much she could repeat and decided she could tell Tayse what Justin knew, at least. "He thinks she's a mystic."

"A *mystic?* At the convent? How did that happen?"

"Apparently she's not even aware of it. Doesn't recognize that the things she can do are any kind of magic."

"What can she do?"

"Heal people, for one thing."

Tayse considered. "So can you. So can Kirra. That seems like a kind of magic."

"Indeed, it does. A gift from the gods—though not from the Pale Lady."

"Any other tricks?"

"Yes, a most useful one. She can hide in the dark. I mean, literally create some kind of scrim that no one can see through, and she can use this to conceal herself and someone standing close to her. Justin said she hid both of them one night while they were on the streets of Neft and soldiers rode by. You can imagine how impressed he was by a magic with such practical application on the battlefield."

She heard the grin in Tayse's voice. "Always seeking the advantage in combat."

"At any rate, apparently it never occurred to her before that these abilities were out of the ordinary. Justin thinks he managed to convince her to be careful, but he didn't convince her to leave the convent. Which I must say," she added, "seems like a really good idea to me."

Tayse's mind was still back on blithe sorcery. "So none of Ellynor's friends or family ever found her powers unusual? Where does she come from that skills like these are simply accepted without comment?"

Again, Senneth hesitated. "She hasn't told Justin."

His hand closed harder on her fingers. "But you've guessed."

"I guessed the minute he described her."

Tayse, who never forgot anything, reviewed that conversation of three weeks ago. "Something about her hair?"

"Very good. And her particular brand of magic is familiar to me as well."

"Not to me. Although, I suppose, *you* can choose to disappear also—

but not by wrapping yourself in some kind of darkness. What kind of goddess offers that kind of power?"

It was no use. She had to tell him. This was weighing too heavily on her mind. She had decided Ellynor should be able to choose what to confide in her lover and what to keep secret, but this was becoming too dangerous a game to play. "The Dark Watcher."

"You're the only one I've ever heard mention her name. What kind of people worship her?"

"Lirrenfolk."

"You think this Ellynor comes from the Lirrens?"

"I'm positive she does."

"But don't they—you told us a tale—they forbid their women to marry outsiders. And if a girl falls in love with an unsuitable man anyway, they . . ." His voice trailed off. He had remembered the story precisely.

"They duel to the death. Yes."

"You have to tell Justin."

"I wanted her to do it."

"Sounds like she won't be ready to tell Justin anything till her brother or her father shows up with sword drawn."

She could hear the roughness in his voice and turned in his arms to place her hands against his chest. "Don't be angry with her."

"She's put Justin's life in very real danger."

"She fell in love," Senneth whispered. "Against all reason. Against all judgment. Against everything she was ever taught. She probably didn't realize it would come to this. She probably thought she could control it—just taste it, the sweetness of forbidden romance. She didn't know how quickly that would become the only thing she lived for."

"You don't know that she loves Justin. Just because he loves her."

"No," she said, snuggling her head under his chin, wanting to be even closer to him. His arms came up and tightened around her. "But I don't think she would be this careless if she didn't."

"What are we going to do?"

She sighed. "First, we're going to take Sabina to safety. Then—I don't know. I'm not worried for Justin's life. I think he can take on any swordsman from the Lirrens and come out the winner. But I'm worried for his heart. If he kills one of Ellynor's brothers—I don't see love surviving that disaster."

"Do you want to return to Neft once we've taken the marlady to Ghosenhall?"

She was silent a moment. "I don't actually want to go to Ghosenhall."

Tayse pulled back a little, trying to see her face. "Why not?"

"I don't want to give Halchon an excuse to declare war on the king because Baryn has given Sabina sanctuary. So I want to leave her somewhere else that's well-defended and not easily accessible. Among people Halchon used to call his friends and might hesitate now to call his enemies, though he knows they hate him. I want to take her almost as far from Gisseltess as possible."

Now Tayse was laughing. "And you want to drive such a deep wedge between Halchon and your brothers that they would never agree to offer you up to him as a bride."

"Yes," she said. "I want to take her to Brassenthwaite."

SABINA seemed pleased, confused, and even more nervous at the idea of journeying all the way to the northeasternmost territory of Gillengaria. "Are you sure? Your brothers—they won't mind? That I'm there? I knew Nate fairly well once, but Kiernan—I'm not sure he liked me. I would hate to be in the way."

Senneth gave her a cynical smile. "Kiernan will see you as the political prize you are. Don't worry. He might not greet you with warmth, because Kiernan is incapable of warmth, but he'll be civil. And he'll keep you safe."

"And Nate won't mind, either? You suppose?"

The two of them were alone in the hasty camp. Tayse had gone off to hunt and Cammon was refilling their water bags. Senneth had started a fire, merely touching her hand to a bundle of wood, and Sabina was assembling their leftover food. They would have to stop in a day or two to get more provisions in some small town. Particularly if they were going all the way to Brassenthwaite.

"No, I'm quite sure Nate won't mind," Senneth said. She was watching Sabina out of the corner of her eye, wondering how much the marlady would reveal. "He's not very comfortable with women in general, you know—maybe because he never married. In any case, he doesn't have much in the way of social graces, but I'm sure he'll do his best to make you welcome. Try not to be offended if he seems rude."

A small smile touched Sabina's lips and was gone. "Oh, I wouldn't think he was rude. I think he's just unsure of himself. He's really quite a sweet man if you give him a chance."

Senneth had always found Nate to be completely sure of himself and the farthest thing from sweet. It hadn't bothered her at all not to speak to him for seventeen years—a period of time which, by all appearances, had encompassed some kind of friendship with Sabina Gisseltess. Well, well, well. This trip was going to be even more interesting than she'd expected.

THEY arrived at Brassen Court close to sunset on a miserably cold day that had had the added disadvantage of intermittent rain. Once across the Brassenthwaite borders, they had felt free to abandon caution, so they cut over to the main road and made even better time than before. Despite herself, Senneth felt a sense of familiarity, of completeness, as they rode through the hilly countryside, the slate-black mountains always visible on the southeastern edge.

I have left Brassenthwaite. I don't belong here anymore, she told herself firmly. *No one and nothing I love is here.*

But she still felt a fugitive joy upon returning.

Brassen Court loomed out of the gray sky, itself just as gray, a sprawling stone house of many wings and levels. It had a great deal of stubborn personality but no particular charm, Senneth had always thought, and it put her irresistibly in mind of her brother Kiernan. It appeared as unyielding as the Lireth Mountains in the distance, as indifferent to weather, as able to withstand attack. It was not a place to inspire love; it was neither restful nor beautiful. But it was secure. It would endure. She had to give it, always, her reluctant admiration.

They were greeted at the door by Reesen, an expressionless, efficient, and highly intelligent steward who was probably the person Kiernan trusted most in the world, after Nate. Two snaps of Reesen's fingers sent footmen out into the rain to commandeer the horses and brought maids scurrying in from the back hallways to take the travelers' wet overcoats.

"Good evening, serra," Reesen greeted Senneth, personally lifting her cloak from her shoulders and not indicating by the flicker of an eyelid that he disapproved of the man's trousers she wore for travel. "Are your brothers expecting you?"

"Hello, Reesen. Since I only realized a few days ago that I needed to come to Brassen Court, no, I don't believe they are. Is Kiernan home?"

He nodded. "All of them are, except ser Harris."

Senneth indicated the rest of her party. "They'll need rooms. Except Tayse, of course. He'll stay with me." She dared Reesen to show any outrage at that, but she was much too late, of course. If he'd allowed himself to be shocked by the fact she was sleeping with a soldier, he'd have worked through his uncharacteristic emotion the first time she brought her lover to this house, almost six months ago. "My brothers are going to want my traveling companion given the very best quarters."

That did catch Reesen's attention; his eyes went quickly to Sabina. Who was looking around the severe hallway as if it was just as she remembered it, the most delightful spot in the world. Senneth wondered when Sabina had been here before and if Reesen would remember her.

He did not disappoint her. He offered the new arrival a very faint bow. "Marlady Sabina," he said. "We are most happy to welcome you back to Brassen Court."

"I'm going to find Kiernan," Senneth told the others. "You go up and change clothes."

Cammon gave her a curious look, and even Tayse was watching her as though she was behaving oddly. "What's so funny?" Cammon asked her.

She showed him a serious face. "Am I laughing?"

"Inside you are."

Tayse nodded. "You're very pleased about being here."

She smiled and just waved them toward the sweeping staircase. "Up to your rooms. I'll see you at dinner."

Reesen must have discreetly sent an underling to inform Kiernan she had showed up, for when she found him in his study with Nate and Will, they were all expectantly watching the door. She paused a moment to look them over. Kiernan resembled their father, with thick dark hair, a closely trimmed beard, heavy features, cold eyes. He was of middle height but thick-set and relatively powerful. She knew for a fact that he spent part of every day working out in the training yard to maintain his strength. Nate had the same coloring but a slighter build and a face perpetually showing an expression of anxiety or distaste. Will, like Senneth, favored their mother. He was taller than either of his older brothers, more loose-limbed. His hair was an indeterminate brown, his eyes were gray, and his mouth was formed for smiling.

He was the one who saw her first—or, at any rate, jumped up to acknowledge her. "Sen! What are you doing here?" he exclaimed, crossing the room to give her a hug. He was the youngest of all of them, but hardly the boy she remembered. He had been the only one who seemed truly happy to see her last summer when she made her first trip across the Brassenthwaite border in seventeen years. He released her and looked down, concern on his pleasant face. "I hope nothing's wrong?"

"I don't think so," she said, smiling at him, and then glanced at the other two. Kiernan gave her a curt nod and merely waited for what she would say next. Nate, of course, was frowning. "I think I may have brought you a bargaining chip. I'm not sure. I might have brought you a packet of trouble. I can always turn around and leave it in Ghosenhall—but I thought you might want to see it first."

Nate's frown deepened. "What are you talking about?"

"Don't play games," Kiernan said. "What do you have?"

But she was enjoying the game and she was going to play it for just another minute. She gave her second-oldest brother a long, considering look. "I have always wondered, Nate, why it is you never took a wife. Never found anyone in any of the Twelve Houses who quite suited you. I mean, you're something of a catch, or you were until Kiernan's boys were born, but even though you're not the heir now—"

"Senneth," Kiernan said in his measured voice. Not even annoyed. Wanting to get to the point. "Why are you here?"

Will, though, was intrigued. He glanced from Senneth's smiling face to Nate's scowling one. "He was in love once, Harris told me," he said helpfully. "But she married someone else. I don't know who she was."

"I'm betting she was a Gisseltess girl from the Thirteenth House who was forced to marry an ambitious serramar," Senneth said. "When *I* turned out to be an unwilling bride."

Nate caught his breath. Even Kiernan looked surprised. Nate came a few steps closer and demanded, "Are you speaking of Sabina Gisseltess? Have you heard news? Has something happened to her?"

Senneth looked at Kiernan. "I'm also betting you would give the marlady sanctuary if she decided suddenly to leave her husband."

Kiernan considered. "It might be just the excuse he needs to force us to go to war."

She nodded. "One reason I didn't want to take her to Ghosenhall. I thought Brassenthwaite might be safer."

Nate was now almost on top of her. With a visible effort he refrained from reaching out to shake her by the shoulders. "Are you saying you have brought the marlady to Brassenthwaite? Where is she? Is she safe?"

"Risky no matter where she lands," Kiernan decided. "But I am not averse to offering her shelter—in exchange for learning what she knows."

Now Nate did take hold of Senneth's forearm, none too gently. "Senneth. Where is she? Can I ride there before nightfall?"

Who would ever have thought she'd feel compassion for Nate? "No need," she said. "She's upstairs. Reesen can tell you which room he's assigned her."

For a moment, Nate stared at her, and then he bolted through the door without another word. Will and Kiernan gazed after him, Will dumb-founded, Kiernan thoughtful.

"I've never seen Nate move that fast unless there was a meal at the other end of the course," Will said, shaking his head and giving Senneth a wide grin. "I think you guessed right."

She returned her attention to her older brother. "Kiernan could tell us."

Kiernan gave an indifferent shrug. "There was almost a match be-tween them, but then one day we got word that she had eloped with Hal-chon. Everyone nodded and said that Sabina had chosen the higher title, for now she would be marlady. Nate was convinced she had been ab-ducted and forced to wed. Our father was furious—following so closely on the heels of *your* refusal to marry Halchon, it was a second time he had been thwarted in an attempt to arrange a marriage between Brassen-thwaite and Gisseltess. Before he could try again, he had died."

"And all these years Nate has nursed a broken heart," Will said.

"Hardly that," Kiernan said, very dryly. "But he had no incentive to wed."

"Well, I never thought Nate was the type to inspire undying love in anyone, but the marlady seems to hold him in affection still," Senneth said. "She grew all giggly and shy at the idea of seeing him again."

Kiernan's eyes narrowed. "That could create an unfortunate situation."

"Or a fortunate one!" she said gaily. "Think far into the future, Kier-nan! Imagine war over and Halchon dead—wouldn't you like to marry off one of your brothers to the widowed marlady of Gisseltess? Acting as stepfather to Halchon's young sons?"

Will laughed and Kiernan gave her a wintry smile. "A lot of ground to cover before we could celebrate those nuptials," Kiernan said.

"Well, I see interesting days ahead," she replied.

Will took her arm and drew her deeper into the room, and they all sat. Senneth glanced around. This study used to be their father's favorite room and the place she hated most in the world. Kiernan—or, more likely, his wife—had refurbished and rearranged the decor so that the room was now far more pleasant. It was still very masculine, with its green upholstered chairs and matching curtains, innocent of any pattern. The walls were covered with maps of Gillengaria and a detailed sketch of every acre of Brassenthwaite. The desk was piled with papers and opened mail packets. Senneth was willing to bet that, if she had the time and in-clination, she could read through all the items collected in that one place and come away knowing everything there was to know about

Brassenthwaite—from the souls under its protection, to the taxes owed, to the number of men of fighting age currently undergoing training on some vassal's back property.

"I still can't believe you're here," Will said. "Tell us where you've been and what you've been doing! You're always so mysterious."

"I was just in Coravann, trying to make deals with Heffel's in-laws," she said.

Will didn't make the connection, but Kiernan did. "His Lirren relatives, you mean? Were they interested in joining our war?"

"Not particularly. Well, the old men weren't. But the young ones—a few of them could be tempted. From what I can tell, the *sebahta* are fairly quiet right now, and some of the young men are restless. I drew them maps and told them to come to Brassenthwaite or Merrenstow if they wanted to join an army."

Kiernan nodded. "And do you think they will?"

She stretched her legs before her. Will glanced at her trousers then back at her face, grinning; Kiernan completely ignored her attire. "I think a few will. Maybe not in great numbers. But the Lirrens were always a long shot. If we get a hundred of them in our ranks, we'll be lucky."

"And can they fight?"

She shrugged. "As with any group of soldiers. Some are good, some are not. But they *like* to fight—that makes them valuable, to a degree."

"I'd like to meet one of these Lirren men," Will said. "They sound very intense."

"That's the right word," she agreed.

"So who came with you, besides Sabina Gisseltess?" Will wanted to know. "Tayse?"

"Of course. Also a mystic named Cammon. A young man who's about twenty years old."

"What's his family?" Kiernan asked.

"Mongrel. No noble blood at all. But he's astonishingly powerful."

Last summer, Senneth had noted that while Nate still sneered at the concept of magic, Kiernan was beginning to accept it, to consider it as something that could be turned into a weapon. Tayse's philosophy exactly. It depressed her to think her older brother and her lover might have some attitudes in common. "What can he do?" Kiernan asked now.

She gave him a wicked grin. "Read your mind. Not the words in your head so much as the emotions and inclinations in your heart. He can tell if you're lying, most of the time. And he can sense when his friends are in pain or in trouble—sometimes from many miles away."

"A useful skill, but limited," Kiernan said.

"What? Aren't you worried about him reading your thoughts?" Will demanded. "I am! It's unnerving."

Kiernan was unmoved. "I rarely bother to conceal what I'm thinking, so it scarcely matters."

Which was so true that Senneth gave a snort of laughter. "Nate won't like him, at first, but Cammon will win him over. Everyone loves Cammon eventually. Well, *you* won't. But you don't love anyone."

Kiernan looked faintly amused at the barb. "If he is as powerful as you say, I will respect him. I would expect that to be good enough."

"From you, certainly."

Kiernan shifted in his chair and changed the subject. "How long do you stay in Brassenthwaite?"

"I don't know. Until Sabina is settled, I suppose."

"And where do you go after that?"

"Back to Ghosenhall. I have a report to make to the king."

"I wonder if you might be induced to visit your friend Kirra instead."

"Here we go," Will said, and rolled his eyes and laughed.

Senneth was mystified. "What? Why? Is she in Danalustrous?"

"I believe so," Kiernan answered. "I have been exchanging letters with her father."

"How ironic that we were just discussing political marriages," Will said. "Since that's what's on the table now."

Senneth glanced between her brothers. "Will and Kirra?" she said, and shook her head. "Kirra will never agree to it."

"Will and the heir to Danalustrous," Kiernan corrected.

Now Senneth felt her eyebrows rise. "Will and Casserah," she said, and turned the idea over in her mind a few times.

"Malcolm is willing, and he seems to believe he can persuade his daughter to do his bidding."

Senneth laughed. "Well, he can't. No one can tell Casserah what to do. On the other hand, she's a very plainspoken girl. If she didn't want to marry Will, she'd have said so by now." She looked at her younger brother. "What do you think of this scheme?"

He shrugged. "I'm twenty-eight and haven't made a love match yet." He grinned. "Though I've had a chance to explore some possibilities and would not feel too cheated if I had to give up the bachelor life."

She flung up a hand. "Spare me the details."

He sobered. "And I'm willing to marry for the sake of an alliance. I'm not going to inherit here, and there are days I feel—" He shrugged. "Not entirely valuable."

"Your brothers and I value you highly," Kiernan said, but Will ignored him and continued speaking directly to Senneth.

"So I would do it and feel it to be—an honor, I suppose. Something important I could do for my family."

"You'd have to leave Brassenthwaite," she warned. "Casserah didn't like to step outside of Danalustrous *before* she was named heir. You could visit, of course, and travel wherever you wanted but—she would expect your life to be at Danan Hall."

Will shrugged again. "That wouldn't bother me. But I want to know—what's she like? Would she even be interested in marrying a man like me? I've never met her."

Senneth made an equivocal motion with her head. "What's Casserah like. . . ? Very focused. Very serene. I have seen her laugh quite easily but she is not a whimsical woman. If things don't interest her, she simply puts them aside." She lifted her eyes. "She is not entirely dissimilar from Kiernan, when it comes to that. They both have a single-mindedness to them. I suppose it comes from considering themselves stewards of their particular plots of land."

"It comes from knowing what's important and what isn't," Kiernan said.

Senneth ignored him and turned toward Will, suddenly animated. "I think she *would* like you, Will. And I think, more important, that you would understand her. That you could make a decent match with her. And think how powerful the alliance between Danalustrous and Brassenthwaite would be then! The more I consider this, the better I like the idea."

"You're very political all of a sudden for someone who refused an arranged marriage on her own behalf," Will pointed out.

She laughed shortly. "I suppose I am. These days, everything I do—every thought I have—revolves around preventing war. And if I can't prevent it, I want to win it. What bargains can I strike, what allies can I find, what weaknesses can I bolster up? And if that means finding a way to control every House in Gillengaria, than I am all in favor of it. Yes, I would love to see you married to Casserah Danalustrous! I would love to see Nate sitting next to the marlady in Gisseltess. I would love to see Brassenthwaite tie up the four corners of Gillengaria."

"There is still Fortunalt," Kiernan reminded her. He did not seem at all discomposed at the thought of amassing power. Had probably been thinking along the same lines himself these past ten years.

She looked over at him. "Rayson's daughter is fourteen, isn't she? Not a bad match for your oldest son."

"Rayson Fortunalt will never make an alliance with Brassenthwaite," Kiernan said. "Unless he, too, has died off in this war you're so eager to prevent."

She gave a twisted smile. "You're right. Then let's marry your son to Ariane Rappengrass's oldest granddaughter. Kirra met the girl last summer and liked her a great deal."

Kiernan nodded. "I'll write Ariane in the morning."

Will tugged on her arm to get her attention. "So will you come? To Danalustrous? Kiernan wants me to go in the next week or two to meet Casserah. It would be easier if you were along to smooth the way."

"I think I will," Senneth said. "I would like to see Malcolm's face when Brassenthwaite comes calling."

CHAPTER

23

MARRIAGE turned out to be the topic on everyone's mind that night, though Senneth had hardly expected that to be the case. Dinner was an intimate family-style meal, held in the cozier but still rather imposing smaller dining hall. Her three brothers were there, of course, as well as Kiernan's wife, two sons, and daughter. Senneth had informed Kiernan that she expected Tayse and Cammon to have places at the table, and he had nodded curtly, so they were present as well. Cammon had scrubbed his face and worn his best clothing but still looked like a vagabond charitably rescued from the street. Tayse wore Rider regalia and kept his expression severe, though Senneth privately thought he was enjoying himself immensely. The children, who had met him once before, still had not lost their awe and watched him unwaveringly throughout the entire meal.

Sabina sat between Will and Nate and barely said a word, though she smiled the whole time as if at a particularly enjoyable party. She'd had scarcely a rag of decent clothing to change into, so Kiernan's wife, Chelley—five inches taller and forty pounds heavier than Sabina—had scrounged up some hideously ill-fitting, outdated, but expensive castoff gown for Sabina to wear to the dinner table. Senneth thought it might even be something that had belonged to *her* when she was seventeen, which meant it was way too long on Sabina but just about the right size through the bust and shoulders. Still, Sabina was not complaining. She looked happy merely to be alive, safe—and sitting next to Nate. Every once in a while she would glance at him, blush, and glance away.

For his part, Nate could not have been more considerate toward the runaway marlady, offering her more food, asking frequently if she was too hot, too cold, too tired to be sitting at the table. Had she tried this dish? It was a delicacy rarely found outside of Brassenthwaite—he was sure she would like it. More wine? From Brassenthwaite vineyards. It had a delicate flavor she would certainly appreciate.

Senneth glanced from Nate to Kiernan and lifted her eyebrow just a fraction. His lips turned up in the slightest smile, and then he looked away.

Oh, there would be a match between Gisseltess and Brassenthwaite yet. If only they could get rid of the inconvenient marlord . . .

Kiernan addressed Tayse as directly as he might address Reesen. Kiernan was highly aware of class distinctions but firmly believed that every individual had a role to play and deserved the respect of his position. "Have you been to Merrenstow to see what success Romar Brendyn is having at training new troops?"

Tayse looked up and nodded. "They've brought in another thousand men, mostly from the northern regions, and split them into divisions. The regent has farmed them out to some of the top vassals of Merrenstow, but he rides between properties every week, checking that the training is going smoothly."

"Does the king plan to keep them all in Merrenstow?"

"At the moment. The thinking is, if there's a war, it will come immediately to Ghosenhall. And Merrenstow is close enough to allow a quick deployment."

"What about the royal guard in Ghosenhall? Have those numbers been increased?"

"To some degree. But there is limited space to house more soldiers in the royal city. Baryn has been looking into renting land on the eastern edge of Storian and making that another training camp."

"Not a bad idea," Kiernan said. "That would give Rafe Storian a reason to think twice before siding with any rebels."

Tayse smiled. Wearing the full black of the Rider livery, relieved only by the parade of golden lions across his sash, he looked wickedly lethal. The smile somehow only enhanced that impression. "That consideration was not lost on the king," he said.

"Set up a base in Tilt, too, while he's at it," Nate suggested. "Gregory Tilton is a sure bet to change sides a half dozen times before this war is over, but he might be more wary if there were guards in his backyard."

Chelley leaned forward. She was a plain-featured, strong-willed, absolutely imperturbable woman whom Senneth had come to greatly admire during the few times they had been together. But Senneth was impressed with the imprints of grace and ease that Chelley had left on Brassenthwaite. She was impressed with the well-behaved children. She was impressed by the fact that Kiernan actually seemed to listen to her.

"Let's talk about something other than war," she said now.

"It's all anyone is thinking about," Kiernan said.

She said gently, "Because that's all anyone is talking about. Let's discuss something else at least for a few minutes, just to prove to our guests that we can." She turned smoothly to Cammon. "I understand you've been traveling with my sister-in-law. Tell me a little about your own family."

Cammon never minded being the focus of attention and was never intimidated by anybody else's rank and title. He shook back his shaggy hair and smiled at her. "My parents were wanderers," he said. "I spent a lot of time in Arberharst and Sovenfeld. Have you ever been to either of them?"

No one at the table had. "I hear they've got good soldiers in Arberharst," Kiernan said.

"*Kiernan*," Chelley reprimanded.

"I don't know if they're any good, but there are a lot of them," Cammon said. "But I never had any dealings with them. Mostly my mother and I worked in the honey spice fields while my father did business deals."

"Honey spice! It grows in Arberharst?" Chelley asked.

Cammon nodded. "Great fields of it. In the spring, every plant has about ten bright red blossoms and the fields just stretch on forever. You can stand in the middle of a honey spice field and everywhere you look, all you see is red."

Between Chelley's promptings and Cammon's willingness to talk, much of the rest of the meal passed in a travelogue of sorts. Senneth was fairly certain that her brothers were bored with the conversation, but the children were fascinated, and even Sabina seemed to like the tales. But it wouldn't have been a meal with Cammon if he hadn't then started asking questions of his own, guilelessly and with complete sincerity wanting to know where Chelley was from, what the children were learning, who was the oldest, where they had traveled. Soon enough, Cammon, Chelley, and the heirs to Brassenthwaite were chatting happily among themselves, while her brothers and Tayse began a sotto voce discussion of war strategy again.

Worse ways to spend an evening, Senneth supposed. She was not particularly interested in either conversation, so she played with her food and thought over the prospect of a trip to Danalustrous. Well, it would be good to see Kirra again, if indeed the flighty serramarra could be found there. She was even more restless than Senneth and could hardly be counted on to spend two nights in the same location. But Malcolm

Danalustrous would make Senneth welcome, and so would Casserah, in her cool way.

Will and Casserah . . . it might work. Among the serramar and serramarra, sometimes the best you could hope for was that an arranged marriage would not be disastrous.

As a wedding between Halchon Gisseltess and Senneth would have been. Senneth didn't even want to think about what Sabina's life had been like these past fifteen years. Although Sabina was no mystic. She would not feel, as Senneth did, her sense of magic drain away the moment Halchon put his hand anywhere on her body. Sabina might hate him for his cruelty, for his coldness, for his driven ambition, but any wife might hate a husband for those reasons. Senneth had had other reasons to fear and despise the man who had been heir to Gisseltess. . . .

Kiernan pushed his chair away from the table. He was done with the meal. "So!" he said. "We have no entertainments planned, since we weren't expecting your arrival. You can make yourselves free of the house, of course. But if you have no further need of me, I'm going to retire to my study and go over accounts."

Tayse rose deliberately to his feet, and everyone reflexively turned to look at him. He appeared relaxed, but Senneth noted the placement of his hands—lightly resting on his belt, inches from his sword and dagger—and the way he was balanced on his feet. Ready for combat if combat came. She stared at him, completely nonplussed, then glanced at Cammon. Who was looking down at his plate to hide his expression and trying hard not to laugh.

What, by the Bright Mother's golden hand, was Tayse planning to say?

"Marlord Kiernan," Tayse began formally. "A minute of your time, please."

Kiernan, never caught off guard, merely nodded. "We can withdraw to my study, if you like."

Tayse glanced around the room. He met Senneth's eyes fleetingly and returned his attention to his host. "I would like to speak before the entire family, if I may."

"Certainly."

"I'm forty years old. I have spent the last twenty-two years as a King's Rider, like my father and his father before me. The king would trust me with his life, and every man who knows me would tell you I am honorable. There is not a chapter in my life that I would be embarrassed to have you read. But I do not come from noble stock."

Senneth was motionless in her chair. Her body was alternately weighted like stone and blazing with fire. She could not lift her hand to hide her face; she could not have spoken no matter what the incentive. Around her, she could hear the others shifting in their seats, could catch the quick looks that passed between Will and Nate, between Kiernan and Chelley. But she could not move. She could not look away from Tayse's dark, stern face.

"I realize that it would benefit you to arrange a marriage between your sister and a son of the Twelve Houses," Tayse went on. "I believe you tried such a match some years ago, and it did not succeed, and that you might be hoping to persuade her to consider another marriage now. I understand that any lesser match degrades her in the eyes of your world. I understand that I am not good enough to marry her."

Now Senneth was able to move one hand, and she used it to cover her mouth. In a minute, she would be using it to wipe her eyes. She still could not speak.

"And yet I love her, and she loves me," Tayse continued. "And I will marry her if she will agree. But you are her brothers. You are her family. You are all of a noble House. Before I ask her, I would want to know that you look upon my suit with favor. I know you will not believe I deserve her, but perhaps you will agree to let me have her even so."

He stopped, and there was absolute silence in the room. From the corner of her eye, Senneth could see Nate's black frown, Will's delighted smile, and Chelley's look of surprise and pleasure. Not often anyone got to witness such a declaration; almost any woman would let it melt her heart.

Kiernan, as befitted the marlord of the most powerful House in Gillengaria, carefully thought over the proposition before he replied. He did not look either surprised or offended; Kiernan never bothered with pointless emotions. He was actually, Senneth thought with some indignation, considering the advantages and disadvantages.

"When the king dies, what happens to you as one of his Riders?" Kiernan asked.

Inquiring into job prospects! Senneth thought, repressing the urge to laugh hysterically. *As if I needed someone to feed me and take care of my household expenses!*

Tayse nodded, as if this was a fair question. "Princess Amalie, upon becoming queen, dismisses all the Riders. That is tradition. And those she wishes to reengage, she then hires back. Thus they make their oaths of fealty directly to her. I have no way of predicting if I would be among the Riders she would choose to keep. My hope is that I would."

"And if you are not?"

"I have some skill with a sword. I would be able to sell my services elsewhere."

"Besides the king and your fellow Riders, who would vouch for your character and your ability as a fighter?"

"I believe the regent, Romar Brendyn, would speak of me highly." Tayse inclined his head slightly. "And you yourself have had a firsthand opportunity to judge me. I have stayed in your house and eaten at your table. You must have formed an opinion."

"Indeed, I have been most impressed by your intelligence, your steadfastness, and your loyalty," Kiernan said.

"Then will you allow me to wed your sister?"

"Serramarra do not marry King's Riders!" Nate burst out, unable to contain himself any longer. "Not even the best of the Riders, as we all know you to be!"

Kiernan gave Nate a quelling look. "But we have long ago given up any notion of marrying Senneth off for political gain," Kiernan said.

"Well, we never thought she'd be willing to marry *anyone*," Will interposed. He was laughing.

He received a quelling look, too. "And we have long recognized that, whatever our plans for Senneth, she would do whatever she desired, so our opinions have never mattered much to her."

"Your opinions matter to me," Tayse said.

Kiernan nodded. "You are the king's man, and Brassenthwaite serves the king. It would be an honor to welcome you into our family as my sister's husband." He stood up, his wine goblet in his hand, and saluted the Rider. "You have the blessing of the House."

So there was, after all, entertainment for the evening, despite the fact that the host and hostess had not thought to provide music or dancing. Everyone ignored Nate's black looks and joined in a celebration. Chelley called for more wine, and even let the children raise a toast to Aunt Senneth and her unconventional suitor. Will came around the table and lifted Senneth off her feet in a rib-cracking hug, while Cammon ran up to Tayse and pounded him on the back. Kiernan stepped up to shake Tayse's hand, but no one else had the nerve to get too close to the Rider, even when he was clearly in a benevolent mood.

Senneth herself did not want to come near enough to touch him; she was afraid she would combust.

Sabina made her way around the table and took Senneth's hands in her small, cold ones. She was smiling wistfully. "I feel like I should be very shocked," she said. "A serramarra and a King's Rider! And I am, a little bit. And yet I think—is this a chance at happiness? I did not have such a chance myself. I would very much like someone else to be able to. If you love him, Senneth, marry him."

"I love him," Senneth said in a choked voice.

Sabina pushed herself to her tiptoes and kissed Senneth on the cheek. "Oh, then I am so happy for you. And I envy you from the bottom of my heart."

Chelley pulled Senneth aside next. "Shall you be married from Brassenthwaite? Kiernan would like that, I think. We could invite all the Twelve Houses."

Senneth could imagine few things more horrible. "Oh—Chelley—I don't think so. A quiet ceremony, probably in Ghosenhall. I haven't— trust me, this is something of a shock to me, I haven't thought it through. But I would not be planning on some event at Brassen Court."

"Well, if you change your mind, let me know. I would be happy to help you plan."

Cammon came up behind her and put his arms around her waist. "You should have seen your expression," he said. "You would have thought Tayse was asking permission to cut off your head."

She turned to face him and he dropped his arms. He was grinning widely. "You could have warned me he was planning this."

"I didn't realize it till he stood up. Anyway, I wouldn't have told. It was more fun this way." He laughed. "I've never seen Tayse nervous before. I didn't know he could *get* nervous. Justin won't believe it."

"Someday I hope to see you endure great public humiliation," she said, her tone heartfelt.

He laughed again. "Probably won't happen. I almost never get embarrassed. I mean, I don't even know when I'm *supposed* to be embarrassed."

"Well, then, I hope you fall in love with the wrong person and everybody stares and whispers about you."

"Now *that* might happen someday. Seems like the sort of thing I'd do."

At last, everyone had had enough opportunities to exclaim and congratulate and offer good wishes. It was almost winter; the sun had long since gone down. Sabina yawned and said she was exhausted, and the others all expressed the intention of seeking their beds. Senneth did not look at Tayse as she kissed the children goodnight and promised to talk more with Chelley in the morning. By the time she was heading toward the stairs, Tayse had collected Cammon and the two of them climbed up behind her, Cammon talking with great animation.

Tayse, like Senneth, was mostly silent.

She stepped inside their bedroom first, while he paused a moment in the hall to exchange a final word with Cammon. The cool air warmed merely from her presence; she bent at the grate to kindle a fire with her fingertips. Pacing across the room, she lit candles on the armoire, before the window, beside the bed.

Tayse stepped inside and set the lock, then stood unmoving before the door. She was halfway across the room, and both of them were in partial shadow.

He was the first to speak. "It hardly does me any good to abase myself before the marlord if the woman I love will refuse to have me."

"Oh, that's a risk, it is," she said in a soft voice, staying where she was. "Serramarra are notoriously fickle. They toy with men's affections because they only play at love."

"Although they play very well," he said judiciously.

She was surprised into a laugh. She reached up and began slowly unbuttoning the front of her dress. She had changed from her travel trousers into more ladylike attire for the meal, so at least she looked properly soft and womanly for this momentous occasion. Still, the dress must have twenty-five buttons; what had she been thinking? She undid the ones down to her waist, and then shrugged out of the sleeves.

"I am not entirely clear," she said, "on the king's policy toward his Riders. I know some of them are married, but very few. Is there any prohibition in place?" She pushed the dress down to her ankles and stepped out of it, leaving her shoes behind as she did so. Now she was wearing a chemise and an underslip borrowed from Chelley. She took a few steps closer to Tayse and began pulling at the lace holding the chemise together.

He stayed where he was, but she could see him smiling in the candlelight. "The formal policy is that Riders are not *encouraged* to marry," he said. "Thus, the tradition is that all Riders elope, theoretically to avoid risking the ire of their king by asking permission to wed. In reality, Baryn has always been quite delighted when his Riders have found themselves husbands and wives. He has always been most extravagant with wedding gifts."

There—the chemise was off. The underslip was balled up and thrown in a corner. Senneth was standing there entirely nude except for two pieces of jewelry—the glowing moonstone bracelet around her left wrist, and the golden pendant around her throat. Both of them seemed hot against her skin this night; both of them were pulling fire from her own wakened magic.

Four more steps and she was inches away from him. He had not moved or attempted to disrobe. He had not so much as lifted the embroidered sash of lions over his head. She placed her hands on his shoulders and let him feel the heat in her palms, all the way through the layers of his clothing to his taut flesh beneath.

"Yes, Tayse, I will marry you," she whispered, and lifted her mouth to kiss him. "If you will have me, I will be entirely yours."

That was all he had wanted to hear, apparently. He swept her up and carried her to the bed, kissing her so hard she gave up on any hope of breathing. The candles guttered and flickered; the fire hissed and leaped up; but they lay on the bed together, a conflagration of their own between them, and did not look away from each other for the whole of that long night.

CHAPTER
24

THE last two weeks had crawled by at a glacial pace, and even the gathering dark of oncoming winter could not cheer Ellynor up. She felt confused and restless and uneasy and lonely and, just the tiniest bit, at risk.

Justin had called her a mystic. She was sure it wasn't true—and yet it could be true—he knew more about such things than she did. Ellynor had explained to him very earnestly that the goddess had conferred small magics upon her and he had replied impatiently, "Yes, of course. Magic is a gift from the gods." Which no one in the convent had ever said, or seemed to believe, so perhaps he was wrong.

It was not like she could ask. It was not like Darris or Shavell would sit down with her and kindly delineate what constituted sorcery and what did not. *Oh, your ability to heal with a touch? That's not magic. We don't mind such displays. The Lestra would not be at all disturbed to learn you had such powers.*

The Lestra would be unhappy indeed.

Ellynor began to think Justin was right. She needed to leave the convent.

She began formulating letters in her head, during the days while she was cooking in the kitchen, during the nights when she could not sleep. *My dear Father: I miss the family. I miss the feast days. Please, may I come home for a visit? Rosurie does not want to leave, but please, may I come home?* That might not be strong enough. Neither her father nor her uncle would want her to leave Rosurie behind, and a little homesickness would not seem, to them, to merit the long trip across the mountains to fetch her.

Maybe she should write Torrin instead. If he believed she was unhappy, he would sail across the world to find her. He would battle the guards at the convent gates. He would bundle her up across his horse and go pounding back out into the forest, racing away till they were free of pursuit. *My brother: Come for me. They are cruel to me here.* That would fetch him for certain. He wouldn't even balk at leaving Rosurie behind— or, more likely, would drag her along with them, screaming and protesting that she didn't want to leave.

Still, Ellynor didn't believe she could actually write such a note. She had no proof that the Lestra—or Shavell or Darris—read their outgoing mail, but she had often suspected they did. Certainly letters that arrived for them had been opened. *The Pale Lady sees all; there are no secrets from her,* Shavell had told them all when Astira complained about this practice.

Well, the Black Mother kept plenty of secrets. That was what she did best.

There was a letter Ellynor could send that was guaranteed to bring both her father and her brother dashing across the border. *My family: I have fallen in love with a man of Gillengaria. . . .* That would drive them across the Lireth Mountains in record time. But that was the very last letter she would write.

If she decided to leave the convent, she would have to do so on her own, in secrecy. But she would have to have a plan in place—somewhere to go, somewhere to take refuge if the guards came after her, as she thought they might. Neft would be the first place they looked. Could she make it all the way to Coravann on her own? Would marlord Heffel take her in? Would he help her get safely back to the *sebahta*?

She was not worried about escaping the compound itself. She knew it could be done. Just a few days ago, hadn't she aided in the escape of that poor, sad creature—marlord Halchon's wife? There had been such an uproar when it was discovered she was missing, and Ellynor had felt a peculiar satisfaction in knowing she had been the one to send the whole convent into a frenzy. Not quite so helpless as she sometimes felt.

She hadn't thought it through, though, before she did it. It had been a cold, sunny afternoon, and the novices were spending the day in the forest "gathering." That was what they always called it when they streamed out in large, untidy groups and went ranging through the forest for whatever they could find. Most of the younger girls just brought back armloads of wood for the fires. The country girls, the farmers' daughters, hunted for mushrooms and nuts, knowing what was edible and what was not. The more frivolous ones brought back bouquets of wild flowers— useless but beautiful.

And this went on all day. They poured through the open convent gates, fanned out through the woods, and returned, laughing and flushed with the exercise. Ellynor loved the "gathering" days—most of them did. They offered welcome breaks from the precise routines of everyday life.

On her second or third trip through the gates, in company with Rosurie and Astira and a half dozen of her other friends, Ellynor had noticed the marlord's wife standing to one side, watching them. She had been here for quite some time, this visit, she and her husband and a whole troop of men. The Gisseltess soldiers, of course, stayed mostly in the barracks, and the novices only got a glimpse or two of the Lestra's fearsome brother. But the small, pale woman had drifted around the compound, clearly at loose ends, looking fragile and lost. On this particular afternoon, she stood near the gates as the novices flitted to and fro, a wistful expression on her face. As if she did not think she would be allowed to set foot outside. As if she had forgotten what freedom felt like.

On her third trip back in through the gates, her baskets heavy with nuts, Ellynor had casually brushed past the marlady. "We're going to make one last trip out into the forest," she said, her voice so low almost no one would have been able to hear it. "Would you like to come with us?"

The blond woman had looked both pleased and frightened. "Oh—I would—but I shouldn't." She glanced over her shoulder where two men in black-and-red livery stood talking with some of the convent soldiers. There to guard the marlady, no doubt.

"Come with us as we drop all this inside," Ellynor said. "No one is paying attention. Then just come back out with us as we leave again in a few minutes. It will do you good to get some air and exercise."

"Oh—" the marlady said again, still indecisive, but she followed Ellynor and Astira to the kitchen at the back of the convent. And she followed them to the front of the compound again and stood quietly listening while Astira and Lia giggled over something Semmie had said. Not sure such a trick would work in the daylight, Ellynor invoked a little of the Black Mother's power—oh, very well, call it magic—to make the marlady virtually disappear. When Rosurie and two other girls finally joined them at the gate, Astira said, "Let's go," and they all stepped outside. The marlady was in their midst, and no one noticed her. Not the convent guards, not the Gisseltess soldiers, not even the other novices beside whom she paced in utter silence. Clearly, this magic was even more powerful than Ellynor had realized, if it could cloak a grown woman who stood in the direct sun.

They spread out as they pushed deeper into the woods, the younger girls looking for kindling, Astira and Ellynor more focused on seeds and nuts. The marlady slowed down—fell behind—backed away. Ellynor tried not to watch her. When, twenty minutes later, Ellynor looked around, the marlady was nowhere in sight.

No one knew when she had gone, or where. Soldiers were sent out that very afternoon, and the next day, and the next, but they never came back with the errant wife. Astira whispered that Lia had overheard a great shouting match between the Lestra and her brother. She had not been able to catch the words, but that he was furious at his wife's escape there was no doubt.

Ellynor was pleased rather than sorry. Hopeful that the poor, frightened, exhausted woman had found sanctuary.

Wondering if she could find haven herself if she decided to run.

THE night before the dark of the moon, Ellynor was one of the handful of novices chosen to sing the Pale Mother's praises. They formed the merest sliver of white as they stood in the courtyard and lifted their faces, lifted their voices, mimicking the thin curve of a fading moon. It was cold out, and Lia was shivering, but Ellynor felt the chill night air wrap her in calm and stillness. Almost, her mind was clear. Almost, her heart was serene. The Black Mother seemed much closer than the Silver Lady.

As midnight struck and the girls turned toward the convent, Shavell stopped Ellynor with a touch. "Stay a minute," the older woman said, and Ellynor obediently paused and waited until all the other novices were inside.

"Tomorrow night the Lestra must ride to make an appointment," Shavell said in an unfriendly voice. "She wishes you to travel with her and guide her on the path. She says you are Dark Moon Daughter and that you will not lose the way."

Ah, the hostility came because Shavell was jealous. She hated to see anyone, even Darris, receive a mark of the Lestra's favor. "Certainly, I am available to serve the Lestra if she needs me," Ellynor said. "When shall I meet her? And where?"

"In the courtyard. Shortly after the sun goes down. It is a trip best undertaken at night."

Any trip made under cover of darkness was bound to be illicit to some degree, Ellynor thought with some disquiet. In the Lirrens, men rode to war at night, or carried out raids against a hated *sebahta*. Rarely did someone ride at night to bring happy news.

"I'll be here."

"You may be excused from your afternoon duties," Shavell said grudgingly. "You will be riding long hours. Sleep in the afternoon while you can."

"I will."

Accordingly, the following night, Ellynor arrived in the courtyard rested, fed, and dressed for travel. In the last instance, that meant wearing a long, dark cloak over her white novice robes. If they were traveling at night, surely the Lestra would not particularly want them to be seen.

There were already a dozen soldiers milling around just inside the gate, mounted on dark horses. A young recruit was holding the bridles of three additional animals. One was the Lestra's own stallion, a large, nervous beast, coal-black and magnificent. The others were just horses from the stables, but also sporting dark coats and accoutrements that were innocent of bright ornamentation. This was a party designed to move through the night without drawing any undue attention.

A minute later, the Lestra and Shavell joined them, and the soldiers scrambled to help the three women into their saddles. No one had said anything to Ellynor, and no one said much now. "Ride out," the lead guard called in a quiet voice, and the gates were swung open. The party trotted out into the forest, into the night.

For the first hour of the journey, Ellynor was wholly ignored, riding somewhere in the center of the group. Shavell and the Lestra were in the lead, preceded only by two guards who seemed to be guiding them out of the forest. They took a path Ellynor did not know, for it didn't lead west toward Neft or east toward Coravann, the way she and Rosurie had come. Winding their way north, they eventually broke free of the overgrown trees. They intersected some road that looked like a major thoroughfare, but only stayed on it for a mile or two, before turning off on a twisty, poorly marked path that would be hard to find if you didn't know what you were looking for.

After an hour of cautious travel down this road, the whole party came to a stop. Ellynor watched a brief consultation between the Lestra and the lead soldier and was not surprised when Shavell suddenly turned and called her name. She nudged her horse forward to join the knot of people at the head of the group.

"Now is when we need your help, Dark Moon Daughter," the Lestra said in an encouraging voice. "The way is obscured, but the prize at the end is very great. Can you show us how to go? Can you follow the path even though the Silver Lady shuts her eyes?"

Ellynor's heart was pounding so hard it was difficult to speak. What lay at the end of this road? "I can," she said. "The Great Mother guides me."

The lead soldier pointed somewhere toward the northeast. "There's a path here, but I can't find it. We need to follow that another five miles."

Ellynor cast her eyes in the direction he indicated. Yes, she could see what he was seeking, a rough track that looped through a rocky valley and then lost itself in a stand of starved trees. "I see it," she said, her voice so quiet it was possible none of them heard her. "Follow me."

She turned her horse down the rocky path and slowly led them forward.

It took them nearly two hours to make their way across the valley, into the thin woods and along the unmarked trail toward their destination, whatever it was. Ellynor had no problem seeing the route they were supposed to take, but it was heavily overgrown, not often traveled, and littered with hazards. Dread also weighted her limbs. She could not come up with any good reason the Lestra needed to make this pilgrimage in the middle of the night under a blank new moon. It occurred to her, once or twice, to pull on the reins and shake her head, claim that she could not follow the track any farther, say that her vision failed. But then she would give herself a little scold. *Don't be ridiculous! The Lestra is meeting some friend or counselor, someone you do not know who is much wiser than you. The Lestra lives by nighttime, as do you, as does your goddess. There is nothing to fear. Keep going forward.*

It was somewhere around midnight when the trail ended abruptly in front of a tiny cottage in a shallow valley stubbled with small, bare bushes. The cottage was dark; no scent of burning wood escaped from the shuttered windows or thatched roof. *No one home*, Ellynor thought with relief.

Nonetheless, she expected the Lestra to ride up to the door and pound on it, demanding admittance. She did not. Instead, she nodded at the soldiers and reined her horse aside as if to get out of the way. Shavell followed her. Ellynor, not knowing what else to do, pulled her mount up beside theirs.

There was a flash of fire, brilliant in the utter blackness, and then a moment of waiting. Then the fire grew, passed from hand to hand, and Ellynor saw that the men of their party were ringing the cottage, and each of them held a torch. "Now!" the lead guard called, and, as one, the men spurred their horses closer to the cottage and touched their brands to the outer walls. In a few places, the wood was wet or stubborn and did not catch, but within minutes, small blazes had taken hold in a dozen or so spots along the bare wood.

"No!" Ellynor cried, and felt her fingers tighten on her reins as if she would ride forward and blow out the fire with her own breath.

Shavell stopped her with a hand on her arm. "No one is home," the older Daughter said in a chilly voice. "Don't be alarmed."

"But—but—this is someone's house! Why should it be burned? Shavell, why are we here?"

"Calm yourself," Shavell said icily, glancing over at the Lestra. The other woman appeared not to be aware of their voices at all. She was gazing fixedly at the leaping flames, her expression engrossed but wholly at peace. "It is the will of the goddess."

Ellynor swallowed and tried to compose herself, but she felt her hands shaking. Why travel through the night to destroy someone's home? What was the point? Who was supposed to receive what message from such a vengeful act?

And then the night was rent with an awful scream of terror, rage, and pain. Ellynor felt her whole body slivered with horror. Someone was inside! Someone was burning to death inside the cottage! She clutched Shavell's arm so hard the older Daughter hissed in pain.

"Shavell! Someone's in the house! It sounds like a woman! Look, I see a face at the window—Shavell! They must save her! *She will die!*"

Shavell shook her hand free and slapped Ellynor hard across the cheek. Her low voice was cold with fury as she replied, "The house burns as it was meant to burn."

Ellynor stared at her, and she thought her own body would go up in flames. Again, a shriek from the cottage—another one. The soldiers had pulled their horses back far enough to keep themselves from being singed, but they were close enough to stop anyone who tried to run from the blazing building.

"You said there was no one inside," Ellynor whispered.

Shavell shrugged. "No one inside but mystics."

THERE were times Ellynor truly did not think she would survive the night. Shavell's words had almost caused her to faint out of the saddle, and black spots peppered her vision, making it impossible to see. The acrid smell of smoke, the continuing shrieks of terror—the sudden cessation of screaming as a roof beam crashed into the burning house—all this combined to make Ellynor so sick she leaned over and vomited past her shoe. Twice. A third time. Nothing more came up but she stayed bent over the pommel for another ten minutes, unable to move.

In a way, it was worse when the screaming stopped; in a way, it was a relief. Dead now, or senseless, the woman inside the cottage. Gathered up in the Black Mother's gentle embrace. Still, the soldiers kept their vigilant circle around the house, waiting to see if this was perhaps a trick, if the woman was even now gathering her strength for a quick dash toward freedom.

It took forever for the house to burn low enough that the guards could bank the fire and be reasonably sure it wouldn't spread to the shrubbery in the field. A few of them were even digging a shallow firebreak to keep the blaze contained. No one seemed impatient to go. The men were all either working or watching. Shavell and the Lestra gazed at the dying flames with a sort of absorbed rapture, as if they represented a mysterious beauty of rare and divine splendor.

Ellynor sat the whole time curled in the saddle, turned into a single compact lump of pain. When the Lestra finally sighed and clucked to her horse, Ellynor was not sure she'd be able to straighten up and resume riding. The fidgety stallion had tossed his head and danced around a little while they waited, but all in all he had behaved remarkably well for such a high-spirited beast.

He must be used to nights such as this, Ellynor thought.

"We should be getting back," the Lestra said, and though her voice was quiet, all the soldiers heard her. They tugged on their own reins and fell into formation behind the women, and then, for a moment, no one moved.

Ellynor gradually became aware that everyone was looking in her direction. "Dark Moon Daughter?" the Lestra asked in a kind voice. "Are you up to directing us back to the main road? This has been a long night for you, I know, and you are not comfortable with the Silver Lady's swift justice. But you must harden your heart. You must remember that those who practice magic have put themselves outside the Pale Mother's grace. You must understand that mystics are abominations. They must be destroyed wherever they are found."

"I understand," Ellynor whispered. *I understand far better than you know.* She forced her cramped muscles to unclench, pushed herself almost upright in the saddle.

"She's been sick," Shavell said reluctantly to the Lestra.

"Yes, I know she has. But she will be stronger now," the Lestra said, her voice sounding most sympathetic. She urged her big horse closer to Ellynor's and held out her hand. In it was a small, fluid shape that Ellynor recognized as a water bag. "You will feel better if you have something to drink. Take a few sips, and then lead us on our way."

Ellynor would have liked to refuse, to fling the container to the ground at the stallion's sharp feet, but she was too thirsty. And there was so much distance left to cover. She murmured her thanks and lifted the bag to her mouth, greedily sucking down half the contents.

How could a tainted gift from such a vile source taste so sweet?

"Thank you," she said again, handing it back. "I'm better now. I'll lead until someone else knows the way."

She made herself straighten her shoulders and guide them all back toward the road. She was in front of the party, so no one could see her lips move, no one could catch her silent, desperate prayer. *Great Mother, ride beside me. Great Mother, pour your strength into my body. Great Mother, show me what I must do. . . .*

She felt the breeze stir about her so faintly that it was as gentle as a mother's breath on a baby's neck. The sky overhead grew even blacker, as clouds scrolled over the face of the night, hiding the helpless stars. A few of the men riding to the rear murmured apprehensively among themselves, worrying about a possible storm. But Ellynor knew it was no such thing. Merely, the Dark Watcher had settled in.

She felt the goddess's presence during the whole of that interminable trek. It was as if the Black Mother laid her hand on Ellynor's back and bade her lean against it for comfort. It was as if she brushed her lips across Ellynor's cold cheek and promised her the night would hold no more terrors.

Once, Ellynor saw an owl fly overhead, white and silent, a midnight hunter. Three or four times she noticed bats swooping by, dipping close enough to see her face and then clawing their way back up through the sticky air. For a good hour, she knew that a wolf paced beside them, an envoy from the goddess, protector of the Black Mother's lost children. A moth came and settled on Ellynor's hands where they were wrapped around the reins, and rested there for the whole of that endless journey.

As her body loosened with exhaustion and her ears still rang with the mystic's screams, Ellynor clung to the only thing that made sense in this whole dreadful night. The feeling that the Great Mother had enveloped her in healing hands and would carry her safely home. The belief that the idle wind had whispered actual words in her ear: *I am here. I am holding you. I will not let you go.*

FOR the first two days after she made it back to the convent, Ellynor did nothing but sleep. Darris came and checked on her three times; Astira and Lia were at the door every few hours, offering food and anxiously asking what they could do to help. It was easier to let people believe she was physically ill—not heartsick—so Ellynor allowed them to wipe her face with cold water and feed her bowls of thin soup. And then she went back to sleep.

Rosurie showed only the most cursory interest in her condition, though she did keep the chamber pot emptied and the room clean, and made sure the candle was lit and set in the window every night. "Let me know if you need something," her cousin said in such a perfunctory way that Ellynor was not moved to ask for help or advice.

"I'm fine," she said. "I just want to sleep."

But sleep brought no answers, and neither did the wakeful hours spent lying in bed, staring at the walls, trying to decide what to do. She had to leave the convent, that was certain. Where could she go? Where could she turn for aid?

If she went to Neft, Justin would help her.

If she went to Justin, and her brothers found out, Justin would die.

If she left the convent without Rosurie, her father might ban her from the house.

If she left the convent and did not return to the Lirrens, *Ellynor* would die.

She had to leave the convent, and bring Rosurie with her, and make it safely to the Lirrens without anyone's assistance.

Therefore, as she rose from her sickbed on that third day, Ellynor decided that Rosurie had become her priority.

It was impossible to talk to her cousin for most of the day, however. The novices who were Ellynor's particular friends gathered around her in the dining hall at breakfast, asking how she felt, exclaiming over her paleness.

"You look so thin," Lia said. "You haven't been sick long enough to lose so much weight!"

"I'm fine." Ellynor said. "I'm hungry now."

"You're working in the gardens today with me," Astira said. "It's cool out, not too bad. I know you like it cold. It will do you good to get sun on your face."

"Where's Rosurie working? She was gone from the room when I got up this morning."

Astira made a face. "She's off with Shavell and Darris. Some great plan they're hatching. A new ritual or something, *I* don't know. We won't see her again till dinnertime."

Indeed, the entire day passed without a glimpse of Rosurie, but it was a restful, healing sort of day even so. As Astira had predicted, Ellynor gathered strength from working outside, pulling up the dead weeds and discarded stalks, clearing out piles of leaves from the bare garden. The brisk air calmed her circling thoughts and made her skin tingle with sensation. She wouldn't have gone inside all day, even for lunch, except that she was so hungry.

Rosurie was present at dinner, but sitting too far away for Ellynor to talk to her, and then Rosurie was chosen to sing the evening devotional, while Ellynor was sent back to their room. Ellynor went upstairs, lit the candle, unbound her hair, and brushed it out with slow, methodical strokes. It had been weeks since Rosurie had last dyed it for her; maybe her cousin would have time tomorrow to add new pattern lines.

But Ellynor never got a chance to ask. She fell asleep before Rosurie returned to the room, and Rosurie was still abed the next morning when Ellynor had to hurry downstairs to help with breakfast.

The entire rest of the week went that way, Ellynor and Rosurie speaking briefly in passing but never having a moment when they were alone in the same room at the same time long enough to talk. When one of them was chosen to sing the nightly rituals, the other was sent up to her room; when one of them was assigned morning duty in the kitchens, the other had a chance to sleep in. Finally, at the end of that week, as the moon waxed toward full, a majority of novices had been kept behind to sing, and Rosurie and Ellynor were both with the group that stood in the courtyard and lifted their voices. At midnight, they climbed the stairs and let themselves into their room and quickly began getting ready for bed.

"I wonder if we could stay up and talk a few minutes," Ellynor said as Rosurie lit the candle in the window. "I feel like I've scarcely seen you! Astira said you've been consulting with Darris and Shavell on something."

Rosurie laughed. "I suppose you could call it that. I wanted to know what I had to do to take the next step—to move from a novice to proselyte. Darris and Shavell are dedicants, and, of course, I can't be one of those, not yet, though I want to be someday. But there are only ten proselytes, and Deana will become a dedicant in a few months, and so there is room for me, Shavell said. But it's a lot of work."

Every word Rosurie said made Ellynor feel more depressed and anxious. "So you think—you don't ever plan—you want to stay here. For the rest of your life," she said. "You don't ever think you'll go back to the Lirrens."

"Never," Rosurie said.

Ellynor moved on the bed, sitting up with her back to the wall. "But, Rosurie, I want to go back," she said in a whisper. "I am not—I am not as happy here as you are. And I don't think the family will let me return without you."

"Then stay!" Rosurie said. She had been perched on the edge of her bed, but now she joined Ellynor on hers. "You say you're not happy here, but you would be if you would just give yourself over to the goddess. If you would let her take over your heart and your mind—if you would make her will, your will. It's not easy, I know. I want to—I want to *push* myself into her arms, *fling* myself at the Silver Lady, but I hesitate. I get afraid. And then I despise myself for my cowardice. I want to find a way to show her I am worthy so that she will take me as her own."

Ellynor could understand a little of that devotion; so she felt about the Black Mother, whose presence was so real in Ellynor's life. But something about Rosurie's voice, her expression, made Ellynor shiver. It was as if Rosurie's love for the Pale Mother bordered on madness.

Obviously, Rosurie would not be disposed to listen to Ellynor's tale of mystics burned at the behest of the moon goddess. Or she might hear the story and react far differently than Ellynor had hoped. *Praise be to the Silver Lady for striking down mystics, burning them where they lay. . . .*

"I don't think I have your willpower, Rosurie," Ellynor said instead. "But I will hope with all my heart that you attain your own dream. That you become a proselyte and a dedicant in service to the goddess."

"I will," Rosurie said confidently. "I just have to think of a way to prove my worth."

The conversation unsettled Ellynor so much that even after Rosurie returned to her own bed and fell asleep, she could not close her eyes. Clearly, she would not be able to persuade Rosurie to leave; clearly, she could not stay. She should just plan her own escape then, slowly amass food that would take her through a couple weeks of travel, study a map, if she got a chance, so that she could visualize her route. If she left at night, it was possible no one would miss her for an entire day. Rosurie would think she had risen early to work in the kitchens and it was unlikely anyone else would sound the alarm. And she would be able to slip away under cover of darkness . . . nothing easier. . . .

That decision made, she was able to fall asleep, but she was so tired that she had a hard time waking. What eventually made her open her eyes was a long pounding at the door and the sound of Astira's voice laughing outside.

"Come on, you two, wake up! Breakfast is over and you're both supposed to be helping me in the kitchen. Were you up all night talking? I'm coming in."

Ellynor yawned and struggled to gain full consciousness just as the door swung open. Astira's shriek made her snap her jaw shut and sit up, staring around.

Rosurie lay on her back on the cold stone floor, completely nude, her arms spread out, her hands cupped beseechingly, her eyes open but unseeing. All around her, like sloppily harvested wheat, her long hair lay in patterned drifts. Her skull was imperfectly shaven, nicked here and there from a badly wielded knife or razor. A thin line of blood traced a route from her forehead down her cheek on the right side of her face.

Rosurie had sacrificed her hair—her family, her *sebahta*—to the Silver Lady. Then, apparently, had fallen into a trance from which she would not soon be wakened. Neither Astira's second scream nor Ellynor's scramble to the floor caused Rosurie to flutter or stir. Ellynor put up a shaking hand to check Rosurie's pulse, but her heart was still beating. She was still alive.

She had merely given herself completely over to the goddess.

CHAPTER

25

DARRIS allowed Ellynor to spend the entire day in the infirmary, though there was very little either of them could do for Rosurie. "But while you're here, you may as well see if you can help Deana. She's had a cough for two weeks now and she's just miserable. And you could fold these cloths for me, that's a good girl. I don't know how everything got into such a muddle."

Ellynor did everything Darris requested but only halfheartedly. She certainly wasn't going to risk calling on the Black Mother's power to see if she could help poor, wretched Deana, who sounded like she might cough her life away. Not when mystics were being burned in their houses. Not when anyone who noticed what Ellynor did would think she was mystic.

She didn't even want to summon magic to see if she could call Rosurie back from her ecstatic trance. This was a matter between the goddesses. If Rosurie had offered herself to the Silver Lady and the Silver Lady had accepted her, Ellynor had no right to ask the Dark Watcher to pull her cousin back from the brink of oblivion. Rosurie would not thank her, and the Pale Mother might not forgive her. Ellynor was already wary of incurring the Silver Lady's wrath. Now was not the time to put a foot wrong.

But she was still consumed by anxiety all day as she watched Rosurie lie motionless on her sickbed. It could not be good to lie so still, to loiter so close to death. Rosurie took no food or water all day, did not speak, did not even appear to be breathing.

Ellynor could not think what she would tell the *sebahta* if Rosurie died.

A hasty dinner with the other girls, whispering to Astira and Lia what little she knew, then Ellynor was back in the sickroom to spend the night. Deana was still coughing, and a novice had been brought in with a similar ailment, so Ellynor would have plenty to occupy her during the hours she could not sleep.

"Hope there isn't a sickness that sweeps through the whole convent, but there probably is," Darris grumbled. "I heard Shavell coughing over dinner. Next thing you know, it'll be you and me."

Ellynor found she did not much care if Shavell came down with a dreadful illness that kept her confined to the infirmary for weeks. She wouldn't lift a hand to aid the dedicant, wouldn't even whisper a prayer to the Silver Lady. Let someone else care if Shavell was sick or well. Let someone else nurse her. Ellynor would not be able to show the older Daughter any kindness at all.

She did, however, try to ease Deana and the other patient through the night, though she was still afraid to try any magic. *Magic.* How quickly she had come to accept that word to describe what she was capable of when the Black Mother moved through her body. How quickly she had come to believe that she was a mystic.

But she could not use that power, not here, not now. She stepped between the beds, administering herbs, offering water, straightening blankets. Deana and the novice alternately slept and wheezed, both of them sounding truly uncomfortable, but Rosurie did not stir at all.

Rosurie lay unconscious for the next five days. Ellynor divided her time between the sickroom, the dining hall, and her bedroom, where sleep was hard to come by. So many things weighed on her mind! Worry about Rosurie, anxiety about her own situation, ongoing horror about the midnight trip to the mystic's cottage. If only she could talk to her father— if only she could talk to Justin—no, she could not wish for Justin's advice or counsel, for that would mean Justin's presence, which she could not afford. But, oh, if only she knew which way to turn, where to go for help.

She prayed for guidance to the Black Mother every night. Invariably, she came away calmed, heartened by the conviction that someone was watching over her, but still no closer to a solution to any of her dilemmas.

When she returned to the sickroom late in the morning on that fifth day, Darris was beaming.

"Your cousin is better," the dedicant greeted her. "She woke around noon and spoke a few words. Ate some soup. She's sleeping again now, but it's a more natural sleep. I think she will make a complete recovery."

"Praise the Mother," Ellynor said. "I still think I'll sit with her again tonight."

"I would be happy if you did. And now we have three other patients. All coughing."

"You were right. *Everyone's* going to get sick."

That night was even less restful than the ones before, since the two youngest patients were fretful and impossible to please, and Ellynor was constantly bringing them water or soothing them when they started to cry. Deana, who had remained in the infirmary this whole time, seemed to be failing instead of improving. She lay almost unmoving under the covers, but her breathing was rapid, strained, and shallow. Ellynor stood a long time by the proselyte's bed, gazing down at the long, narrow face, pinched and pained by moonlight.

Deana had never been anything but kind to Ellynor. She looked stern and ascetic, but she had a charming smile, and her natural expression was happy. All of the novices liked her.

Just a little magic. Just enough to clear the lungs, ease the breathing. Deana had been sick so long. Just enough magic to heal her.

Ellynor brushed her hands across Deana's cheeks, across her shoulders, down her rib cage. Her fingers were hot; she felt the moonstone flaring against her wrist. All the candles in the room seemed to flicker, as if a shadow had passed over them, and then the room returned to its normal brightness.

Deana's face loosened and her breath grew deeper. She stirred and turned on the mattress but did not wake.

Rosurie did, though, about an hour later. Ellynor had just leaned over her cousin's bed to see if she could detect any change in her condition, when Rosurie opened her eyes. Ellynor watched Rosurie gather her thoughts, remember where she was, and take stock of how she felt.

"How long?" Rosurie asked.

"Six days."

"Just past full moon," Rosurie whispered.

Ellynor smiled. "Yes."

"I think I'll be strong again in a few more days. At the half moon."

Split Moon Daughter. Like Shavell and Darris. Like the dedicants. Ellynor leaned forward and kissed Rosurie gently on the cheek. "I'll be happy to see you improving."

Happy because, when you are well again, I am leaving Lumanen Convent.

THE next day was both much better and much worse, because it brought Justin.

Ellynor had slept till noon, then, still yawning, joined Astira in the kitchen. After giving Astira the update on Rosurie, Ellynor said, "Sorry I haven't been any help the past few days."

"Well, it's not like you weren't helping somewhere!" Astira exclaimed. "Anyway, Semmie worked with me, so it's not like I had to do it all myself. I even had a little free time."

She said the last sentence so casually that Ellynor had to ask. "Free time to do what?" She knew, though. "See that boy? That guard?"

"Daken's not a *boy*," Astira said significantly, and then they both started giggling.

It felt so good to laugh, to smile, to spend a moment thinking about something other than her constant heavy burdens. But Astira's news was not truly so lighthearted. *"Astira!"* Ellynor hissed. "Don't do anything to get yourself in trouble. I don't think—I don't know that the Lestra will be lenient if the rules are broken." She still hadn't had the nerve to tell anyone about her midnight journey that had ended in death and conflagration. She was afraid the other novices wouldn't believe her—or that they would think the Lestra had done the right thing. Her dreams, when she was able to sleep, were still haunted by flames and cries for mercy.

Astira was looking more sober. "I know. But how would she punish me? Would she banish me from the convent? Some days—some days I'm not so certain I would mind that."

Ellynor glanced around, just to make sure no one was listening at the doors, but they were entirely alone. Still, they moved closer together at the great center table where they were standing, chopping bushels full of vegetables for the evening soup. "Do you think about leaving?" Ellynor asked in a low voice. "Going home?"

"I do," Astira replied, just as quietly. "But I wonder. *Does* anyone leave the convent? Not since I've been here. Would the Lestra let me go?"

"Would she come after you if you left in secret?"

Astira nodded. "And what would she do to me then? I don't think—I mean—perhaps I'd be confined to my room—I don't think she would *beat* me. I don't know. She wouldn't—I mean—I don't think it would be anything worse. I'm not a mystic. She wouldn't *burn* me."

Very carefully, Ellynor turned her head to give Astira a sideways stare. "The Lestra burns mystics?" she repeated. As if she didn't know. But mostly just to hear it confirmed. Mostly to hear what Astira would say.

The other woman nodded. "That's what Daken told me yesterday. She goes to their houses and sets them on fire. There was one place—a mansion in Nocklyn, I think—where she was invited to come. The lord had found a mystic on his property and he wanted the Lestra to take care of the old woman. They built a bonfire and burned her at the stake."

Ellynor had to try twice to swallow. "And that is—what do you think of that? I admit I'm shocked."

Astira looked undecided. Her dissatisfaction with convent life was warring with all the principles she'd learned during two years in Lumanen. "She was a mystic," she said at last. "But that is a terrible way to die."

Ellynor drew a breath as if to reply, but she didn't have a chance. There was a quick knock on the back door, and a convent guard stuck his head in. "Packhorses here with a delivery," he said shortly. "I brought them on back to unload."

"Good," Astira said briskly, laying aside her knife and a ball of lettuce and drying her hands on a towel. "We're out of almost everything."

She stepped outside, and Ellynor followed—and then came to an abrupt halt there in the winter-bare garden.

Justin. His back to her as he began unstrapping bags and bundles from his horse. Returning as he'd promised. Refusing to stay away.

She had never been so glad and so distressed to see anyone in her life.

THEY met outside shortly after midnight, just as they had before. This time she went running to him, her feet soundless and her body without a shadow as she raced past the garden, across the compound, and straight toward the barracks. He could not see her but he must have heard her, for he threw his arms open and took her in a ferocious hug when she flung herself at him from the darkness. She was crying; she could feel the sobs wracking her shoulders, and sense his immediate, intense concern. But she could not speak, she could not explain. She just clung to him and wept.

His arms around her body made her feel safer than she had felt in more than two weeks.

"Quiet, quiet, that's right, tell me what's wrong," he whispered, kissing her cheek, pushing her hair back from her face. "I'm here, I'll help you, whatever it is. It's fine. It's all right."

Eventually she calmed enough to speak. By this time, he had pulled her down to the ground with him so that she was sitting on his lap with his arms around her waist. This was how she always seemed to end up in her encounters with Justin, she reflected.

Not so good. Not so good if she was going to be able to leave him behind.

"What happened?" he asked.

Her breath caught on a near hiccup but she refused to start crying again. Which tale to start with? "A couple of weeks ago. The Lestra asked me to accompany her and some of her soldiers. To help them find the way because I see so well at night."

"Does she know *why* your night vision is so good?"

"She thinks I'm a Dark Moon Daughter. Someone who is strongest on the night of the new moon."

He snorted. "I'd wager that's true, but not for the reasons she thinks."

"So I led them—where they wanted to go. But I didn't know—I mean, I knew it was strange to make a trip like this in the middle of the night, but I thought—I hadn't guessed—"

"You went to the house of a mystic," he said. "And burned it down."

She was so astonished that she lifted her head to stare at him. "How did you know?"

"I witnessed the soldiers doing just that a few weeks ago. I didn't know Coralinda Gisseltess ever accompanied them when they went marauding, though. Must have been someone she especially disliked."

Still wide-eyed, Ellynor shook her head. Justin had seen such a thing for himself and been able to endure it? Had he witnessed worse abuses in his life if this one left him so calm? "I think it was just some old woman living by herself in a cottage miles off the main road. I can't imagine how the Lestra even found her, let alone came to hate her."

"You have to leave the convent," Justin said.

She nodded. "I know."

He took a moment to be pleased, but then wasted no more time. "You can go with us tomorrow. Slip out the gates before we leave in the morning and wait for us a few miles down the path. We'll take you the rest of the way to Neft."

She shook her head. "I can't just yet. Rosurie—my cousin—oh, Justin, she's had this religious *fit* of some kind. She's been practically catatonic for days. Last night she finally woke up, and she talked a little, and she ate breakfast this morning, but I don't feel easy leaving her. Maybe in a few more days."

"Let's make a plan," he said. "You tell me when you think you'll be ready to go, and I'll be waiting for you. I can be right outside the convent gates if you want, or farther up the road if you think that's safer."

"Oh, you shouldn't be close! Someone will see you."

He gave her a careless grin. "I've spied on the convent before and no one noticed me. But we need to pick a spot. If I'm in hiding and you're—" He made a gesture over her head. "Disguised—well, we might miss each other."

They discussed landmarks along the forest trail, eventually agreeing on a particular bend of road near a major deadfall that they both remembered. "When?" Justin asked again.

Ellynor took a deep breath. She was afraid to do this, but she was more afraid not to. "In five days," she said. "Five *nights*. I will leave around midnight. No one will realize I'm gone for at least six hours, maybe a whole day."

"I'll be there. But if by some chance I'm not—" He debated for a moment. "There's a man in town named Faeber. He's the magistrate. Runs the local guard. Keeps order, basically. I think you can trust him. So if something happens—if you leave the convent sooner than you plan, if for some reason I'm not at the rendezvous, if you get to Neft and you need help and I'm not around—go to him. You can usually find him at one of the taprooms, just talking to people."

"What does he look like?"

"Somewhere between fifty and sixty. Not as bulky as me. Gray hair. Always looks like he just got up from sleeping in his clothes. Smart, though, if you get a chance to study his face."

Justin had studied his face, Ellynor was positive about that. Justin made it a point to pay attention to everything, everyone, in his immediate vicinity. "Faeber," she repeated. "I'll remember."

He was silent a moment, thinking. "Will you feel safe going back to Neft? Is there someplace you'd rather have me take you?"

Her heart broke—*he does not want me to stay with him*—at the same time that she felt incredible relief. She would not have to tell him, she would not have to explain to him, she would not have to try to push him away—

But he was still speaking. "I can't leave Neft, not right now, not for more than a couple of days at a time. But in a few weeks, I will. I can come to you wherever you are—at your father's house, if that's where you want to go. Anywhere. I'll come for you."

Now she felt a different kind of pain in her heart—exhilaration, *he loves me*, and terror, *he could die*. She put a hand to his chest and looked up at his dear, stubborn face. "I'm not sure you can, Justin," she said softly. "My family—they won't accept you. I told you that before. They won't accept any outsider. They would never let me be with you. They would find a way to prevent it."

He peered at her in the darkness, instantly concerned. "They would hurt you if you tried?"

She shook her head. "They would hurt *you*."

He laughed. *Laughed.* "Well, maybe. If enough of them came at me at once. But I'm pretty hard to subdue."

"Justin, you don't understand. I've been stupid—careless—I should never have encouraged you, I should never have let things go this far. I'm not free to love you, my family would never let me. I never meant to—but I haven't been able to stop myself—and it's been so sweet. So sweet. This time with you. But I can't be with you, I can't, not once I go back to my family. I'll understand if you're angry, if that means you don't want to help me leave the convent after all. I don't want you to think I'm using you, I don't want you to be hurt. But I can't put you in danger like this. I can't keep seeing you. Justin, I'll—you'll die. If I don't let you go."

When he spoke, his voice was very quiet, and of all the things she'd thought he might respond to, he picked the one she had not meant to say. "You're not free to love me," he said. "But do you anyway?"

She stared at him helplessly in the dark. His jaw was set, his mouth pressed in an unyielding line. It was impossible not to realize, as she sat within the circle of his arms, how powerful he was. This was not a man who would run from a fight, who would—because she feared for him—give her up. This was not a man who had allowed himself to desire too many things. Those few possessions he owned, those few achievements he had attained, he had acquired because he had pursued them relentlessly.

To turn him away, she would have to lie.

She was not able to lie.

"I love you," she whispered. "But it makes no difference."

It did to him. He crushed her in his arms, kissed her with a hunger that left her bruised and breathless. Somehow she was neither afraid nor sorry. She kissed him back, wrapped her arms around his neck and clung to him, giving herself up to a fearful ecstasy. Nothing mattered except this man's arms around her. Nothing and no one else in the world existed.

Oh great, oh kind, oh terrible Mother, if her brothers killed him—

Or if he killed one of her brothers—

She wrenched her mouth from him but did not try to scramble away, and they sat there a moment, both of them panting, staring at each other. "I can't let this happen," she said, an undertone of desperation in her voice. "Justin! You don't understand, but this is too dangerous."

"We'll talk about it in five days," he said. He might be breathless and strung with passion, but he was unperturbed by her dire warnings. "When you're safe in Neft—or on the way to wherever you want to go. When we're safer than we are here, at any rate."

"Nothing will have changed by then," she said, shaking her head.

She unlocked his arms and rose reluctantly to her feet. With an athlete's grace, he stood up beside her.

"Everything's changed," he said cheerfully. "You said you love me." He kissed her quickly before she knew what he was intending. "I love you, Ellynor. Whatever you're afraid of, I can handle. But I want you out of here first. One set of problems at a time."

"There are too many problems," she whispered, but he laughed.

"Maybe not," he said. "It will be an interesting day when we tell each other our secrets."

She wanted to talk more—she wanted him to leave right away—she put her hands on his arms and kissed him. Then kissed him again. Pulled back, walked a few steps away, went flying back into his arms. Three more kisses and then she really did leave. She was sure he would wait another ten minutes before going to the barracks, another fifteen, in case she changed her mind and returned.

But she couldn't have even if she'd wanted to. She was only halfway back to the kitchen door when she saw a shape moving cautiously down the path. She had drawn a veil of darkness around her and so she was not particularly worried about being seen, but she stepped into the brown grass so that the man walking toward her wouldn't collide with her invisible form. He was a convent soldier, solitary and secretive, and as he moved closer she recognized Daken, the young man Astira was sighing over. So perhaps there was more than one secret romance being conducted on this particular night.

She grinned, but almost instantly her amusement faded. His route would take him back to the spot she had just left, where Justin almost certainly would still be standing. Would Daken see Justin?

Would he guess why Justin was out late at night in a place where he was forbidden to wander?

Would he tell anyone what he saw?

CHAPTER

26

Kɪʀʀᴀ appeared delighted to see Senneth and her escort, which included Tayse, Cammon, Will, and five Brassenthwaite guards Kiernan had insisted they bring. "Welcome to Danan Hall!" she exclaimed, hugging the mystics, and even Tayse, who did not usually come in for careless embraces. "Oh, and you must be Will! You look so much like your sister."

Senneth laughed. "Since Nate has just spent the past five days telling me I look like a veritable vagabond, I'm not sure that's a compliment."

"Nonsense. You're very attractive," Kirra said. She was still holding Will's hand and smiling up at him, flirting or merely overflowing with genuine warmth, it was hard to tell. "And so is your brother."

"You, of course, are beautiful, but you must know that," Will replied.

Kirra's smile grew wider. "Well, I *do* know that. People tell me all the time."

"She's a shiftling," Senneth reminded him. "She can make herself look as beautiful as she wants. In actuality, you know, she's probably hideous."

"No, that's really what she looks like," Cammon said.

"Cammon can't be blinded by magic, so he sees me as I truly am," Kirra said soulfully to Will. She still had his hand in hers.

"But Cammon doesn't know what you look like to the rest of us," Tayse said. "I like this idea. That you're quite plain without the aid of magic."

Kirra laughed. "Help! How can I prove myself?"

Cammon pointed at a set of portraits hanging in the parlor where the steward had ushered them upon their arrival. One was of Kirra, all gold and smiling; one of Casserah, dark and serene. "Is that what you see?" he asked. They all examined the image and assented. The painter had done a good job of catching not only the shape of her face, but the mischief of her expression. "That's how she looks to me, too."

Kirra dropped her hold on Will to throw her hands in the air. "I am

vindicated! But what a sad way for Will Brassenthwaite to make my acquaintance. To have me accused of lying and subterfuge before he's
known me five minutes!"

"Better now than learn the truth later," Tayse said darkly.

Senneth and Kirra laughed. Will looked like he wanted to but wasn't
sure it would be polite.

"So how was your trip?" Kirra asked. "Oh, everyone sit down! I've
sent Menten for refreshments. I'm sure you're all hungry."

All of them but Tayse disposed themselves in the plush chairs
arranged in the center of the room. "I'd like to look around the Hall, if
you don't mind," the Rider said. "Where's Donnal? He can be my guide."

Kirra gazed up at him, not deceived. "You will not offend my father if
you sit on his furniture," she said. "Really. He's not like Kiernan. He doesn't
put much store by class distinctions. Donnal sits on his chairs all the time."

Tayse smiled. "You can have this conversation without me. I'm curious to see the stables and grounds."

Senneth gave Tayse a private smile. He met her eyes, amusement in
his own, but he kept his face grave. "Tayse is still working on being comfortable among the aristocracy," Senneth said.

"He'll have to learn, won't he?" Cammon said. "If he's going to marry
Senneth?"

"What?" Kirra exclaimed, clapping her hands together. "Tell me,
tell me!"

"Asked my brother for her hand in marriage," Will said, still clearly
relishing the memory of that night. "At the dinner table with the whole
family sitting there. I thought I was a brave man, but it wasn't something
I'd have dared."

"And? What did Kiernan say? What did Nate say? That would have
been more interesting, I'd wager."

"I see you have some acquaintance with my brothers," Will said, grinning now. "In fact, Nate thought the whole thing scandalous, but Kiernan gave Tayse his blessing." He turned his smile on Senneth. "Of course,
none of us asked Senneth what answer she gave Tayse, but we all suppose
it was favorable."

"So you're to be married! Oh, I hope you do it with great pomp—
from Brassen Court—no, from Ghosenhall! And invite all the marlords
and marladies. I will be your attendant, since I can't imagine any other
serramarra would be so debauched as to stand up for you."

"Thank you, I have not yet gotten to the stage of planning my wedding," Senneth said. "I rather think it will be a private ceremony."

Kirra was instantly serious. "But you wouldn't get married without me there, would you? Oh, promise me, Sen. Tayse—I know I'm very annoying, but *promise* you won't elope without letting me come along."

He smiled down at her. Senneth thought he might be just a little embarrassed behind his usual stoic demeanor—embarrassed, but pleased. Certainly Kirra was one of the few nobles who would genuinely wish them well. "We did not come to Danalustrous to talk about *my* wedding," was all he said. "I'm going to find Donnal. Cammon? Would you like to come with me?"

Which was Cammon's first cue that he was not, perhaps, entirely welcome at this conference. Senneth hid a smile as the younger man showed surprise, then comprehension, and jumped to his feet. "Yes, let's find Donnal," he said. "When should—will we be back for dinner?"

"No," Tayse said, but Kirra spoke over him.

"Yes, of course you will. It will just be family at the table tonight," she said. "And my father will want to get to know both of you." She flicked Cammon a smile. "I have told him a great deal about you, so he will probably try to figure out if you really have the kind of power I've described. Don't be surprised if he starts testing you some way. I couldn't even guess how."

Cammon laughed, pleased at the thought. "That sounds like fun," he said. "Then we'll see you later."

They left as Menten, the butler, was entering with a tray of refreshments. He was still arranging them on the table when the door opened again and Malcolm Danalustrous strode in.

"Senneth," he said, coming straight toward her. "Carlo told me you had arrived. It is good to see you again."

She came to her feet and let him take both of her hands in his, then stand there studying her a moment. She watched him in return, noting that the black hair was streaking with gray, but the blue eyes were as bright as ever, the firmly modeled face completely unsoftened by time. She had spent a good five years wishing Malcolm, with all his faults, had been her father. He was a strong-willed, outspoken, unpredictable but totally humane man who cared about very little except Danalustrous and the people who came under its protection. His daughters. His vassals. The few people, like Senneth, to whom he had offered complete sanctuary. *He* had not disowned his daughter when she had proved to be rife with magic. No, he had brought in tutors for her—he had honed her skills—he had forced the other marlords to accept her. If Danalustrous was going to produce magic, then Danalustrous would nurture magic as well.

"You look good," he said at last. "Serving the king agrees with you."

"Falling in love with a King's Rider agrees with her more," Kirra said.

Malcolm dropped Senneth's hands and smiled. "Well, we could hardly expect Senneth to do anything the conventional way." Will had come to his feet and now the two men shook hands. "I'm Malcolm Danalustrous. Welcome to my House."

"Thank you for inviting me. Danan Hall is as beautiful as people say."

"Father, I've invited Tayse and Cammon to eat with us," Kirra said. "You know, the Rider and the mystic? Should I go warn Jannis?" Jannis was Casserah's mother, Malcolm's third wife.

"I think she will hardly be surprised to learn you want your friends at the dinner table," Malcolm said. "But by all means, you and Senneth may leave. Will and I have matters to discuss that we can cover more profitably without you."

Kirra looked indignant, but Senneth laughed. "I'm not so sure I should leave my baby brother alone with you, Malcolm," she said. "You can be very fierce."

"Nonsense. If he can endure Kiernan, he can endure me."

Nonetheless, Senneth glanced at Will to make sure he felt up to a conversation alone with Malcolm, whose intransigence was legendary. But Will had settled back in his chair and showed a countenance that was relaxed and smiling. "I think I can hold my own," he said.

"No one holds their own with my father, but good luck trying," Kirra replied. She jumped up and grabbed Senneth's arm, towing her toward the door. "We've got plenty to talk about that we don't want you to overhear, either. We'll see everybody again at dinner."

In a few minutes, the two women were ensconced in Kirra's room, sprawled across the massive bed. Senneth was tired from the trip, but not excessively so. It felt good to lie back on the plump mattress and stare up at the flowered bed curtains, be enveloped in the subtle but unmistakable richness of Danan Hall.

"So—tell me," Kirra demanded, practically bouncing where she sat. She was still more or less upright, leaning against the pillows. It was Senneth who lay lazily on her back, running her hands over the thick fabric of the bedspread. "Tayse proposed to you in front of the whole family? Were you shocked? Or did you know he was going to do it?"

"Shocked," Senneth admitted. "And—amazed. And—overwhelmed

with love for him. That required more bravery than holding a knife to Halchon Gisseltess's throat."

"But was probably more pleasurable in the long run," Kirra said. Senneth choked with laughter and turned on her side to face Kirra.

"He did seem to enjoy the rewards," she said demurely.

"Have you told Justin yet?"

"We came straight here from Brassenthwaite. After stopping in Neft to—" Senneth sat up. "Oh, you don't *know* this! This is almost better than Tayse proposing to me at Brassen Court."

"Nothing could be," Kirra said positively.

"But listen! Tayse and Cammon and I were leaving Coravann, when suddenly Cammon says, 'Justin needs us.' He doesn't say why, of course, so we change direction and hurry to Neft and we find that Justin—*Justin*—has become the protector of Sabina Gisseltess, who's run away from her husband."

"No!"

"Yes! So we take her with us and at first I think we'll go to Ghosenhall, but then I think maybe she'll be safer in Brassenthwaite. And the whole trip—which is very fast, let me tell you, because Tayse can certainly keep a party moving when he has to—the *whole* time, Sabina keeps talking about my brother Nate. How considerate he is, what a friend he used to be to her. So I start wondering. Was there something between them, fifteen or twenty years ago? And when we arrive in Brassenthwaite, Nate practically knocks me down in his haste to find Sabina once I tell him she's arrived in our train." She gave Kirra a wide-eyed stare. "And fairly soon it's clear they were in love with each other until she was forced to marry Halchon. And they still seem disposed to care about each other. I was never so astonished in my life. I mean, *Nate*. Who could have expected that?"

"Well, she's a pathetic little thing, but that might be just the kind of person Nate needs, because he could hardly stand up to a forceful woman," Kirra said callously. "Should we now work especially hard to make sure Halchon dies in the war?"

"If there is a war," Senneth said automatically.

Kirra stretched. "I think Tayse would be happy to kill him even off the battlefield, if he gets the opportunity," she said.

"Yes, but one of the drawbacks of being civilized is realizing that you can't murder people just because you don't like them," Senneth said.

Kirra grinned at her. "What makes you think Tayse is civilized?"

"Or you. Or Justin. Or Cammon, when it comes to that," Senneth said ruefully.

Kirra bounced again. "Justin! That reminds me! If you saw him, did he talk about that convent girl? Senneth, I think he was ready to fall in love with her. And, you know, Justin has never had much time for women. Is he still seeing her? What's happening?"

Senneth instantly felt troubled. Kirra, always sensitive to mood, fell quiet and watched her. "I think Justin has gone out of his way to find the person most likely to break his heart," she said with a sigh.

Kirra surprised her by laughing. "That's what he said would happen."

"What do you mean?"

"Last summer. He said that all of us—the six of us—seemed prone to picking the most disastrous people to fall in love with. And you could hardly get more disastrous than a King's Rider and a Daughter of the Pale Mother."

"Who's from the Lirrens," Senneth added quietly.

"Who's—no! Does he know that? Does this mean—wait—that her family will require a duel to the death before he's allowed to be with her?"

Senneth nodded. "That's Lirren tradition."

"But, Sen! That can't happen! You know as well as I do that no one can defeat Justin except Tayse and some of the other Riders. I mean, he'll win this fight, but he—he—that's terrible! He'd have to kill her brother or somebody!"

Senneth nodded. "I'm hoping there's a way to avert that. But at the moment—as far as I know—he still isn't aware of who she is."

"Then how do you know?"

"He described her. I recognized Lirren signs." She shrugged. "Tayse is angry with me, but I figured it was up to her to decide when to be honest with Justin. Maybe that was a bad decision, I don't know."

"Maybe you should go back to Neft and tell him now."

"Maybe. Ghosenhall first, though, to tell Baryn about Sabina. And about our visit to Coravann, about which he still does not have my report. I sent a messenger from Brassen Court but I only sketched in the details. Some of this news is best given in person."

Kirra was still thinking about Justin. "He told me a little about the convent girl—not much," she said. "I think he was surprised to find himself confiding in me, but he was desperate to talk to somebody and no one else was around."

Senneth smiled but let it pass. Kirra and Justin were determined to believe they despised each other, or pretend they believed it. Kirra went on, "And I had the impression she was—small. Sweet. Maybe a little clingy."

"Very feminine," Senneth agreed. "The Lirren women usually are."

"But who'd have thought Justin would fall in love with a girl like that?" Kirra demanded. "I mean, look at you and me. We can defend ourselves against all comers. Look at the women among the Riders. Rough and tumble, as quick to grab a blade or knock you in the head as Justin is himself. I always thought those were the kinds of women he admired. I always thought that would be the kind of girl he'd like."

Senneth nodded. "And if you'd asked him, that's probably what he would have said, too. But I don't think so. Justin's never had much softness in his life. He's never had something precious and helpless that he felt he had to protect. No one's ever *needed* Justin. And I think maybe this girl does. And I think that that would be irresistible to him—a gentle girl who relies on his strength, but who can tame him with her sweetness. I mean, can't you just picture it? Justin standing watch over someone like that? He'd be so ferocious it would break your heart."

Kirra was staring at her, openmouthed. "Oh, yes, I can see it," she breathed. "He'll never walk away from her."

Senneth smiled, but the expression felt sad. "I don't think so, either. So let's hope these brothers can be persuaded to be reasonable."

Kirra flopped back against the pillows. "Well! This is certainly the season of inappropriate affection! You getting betrothed to a King's Rider. Nate pining after a married marlady. Justin and a *Lirren girl* from the Lumanen Convent. Oh! And there's more." She pushed herself upright again, blue eyes dancing. "Apparently Darryn Rappengrass has fallen in love with some peasant girl he met on the road last summer. Ariane is beside herself. I swung by Rappen Manor before I saw Justin in Neft, and she told me the whole story."

They talked for another hour or two, filling each other in on what they had observed in Ghosenhall and the manors of the Twelve Houses while they had been apart. Senneth had often thought she and Kirra were very different, despite the fact that they were both mystics born to noble Houses. Kirra was sublimely beautiful, completely wild, utterly confident in the love lavished on her by her sister and father. She claimed to hate the social interactions among the Twelve Houses—balls, arranged marriages, alliances of blood and commerce—but she had a passion for gossip and a natural ease with her fellow aristocrats that belied her words. Senneth, on the other hand, was serious, introspective, and willing to be wholly self-sufficient. She had been cast out of her father's home when she was seventeen, consorted with all manner of lowborn individuals, and truly despised most of the Twelfth House scions that she had been forced to meet. She had been thrust back into that world last summer, when the king commanded her to escort his daughter on a tour of the southern Houses, and she had hated the lifestyle, and the people, just as much as she expected.

Yet here she was, promoting a match between her House and Kirra's. And exclaiming over which lords had snubbed which ladies. And speculating on which alliances could strengthen the king's position and, conversely, which ones might shore up any bid Halchon made for the throne. Just like any two other serramarra, heads together, whispering gossip about their friends and enemies.

But that was not what made them so close. That was not what fostered the bone-deep connection between them. They were not, in fact, just like other serramarra. They schemed and plotted and debated—not to find highborn husbands, but to avert a war. They counted out their physical gifts—hair, skin, magic—not to secure their places in society, but to array them like bright weapons in defense of the throne. Their passions allied them. Their strengths drew them together.

And the adventures they'd had on their journeys.

And the small circle of friends they'd gathered along the way.

CHAPTER
27

IT was almost dinnertime before Senneth pushed herself up off of Kirra's bed. "I suppose I should dress," she said. "Will Donnal really join us for the meal? I've never seen him sit down to a dinner with your father."

Kirra smiled. "He doesn't like to, but he will from time to time. My *father* doesn't mind, of course, but Donnal is protective of my reputation." She snorted. "Such as it is. Anyway, on quiet nights like this my father will often invite Carlo to eat with us—that's the steward, you know—and his wife and daughter, and that seems to make everything easier across the ranks. Donnal joins us then."

Indeed, the taciturn dark-haired man was already in the smaller dining room when Senneth found her way there about half an hour later. He was very formally dressed, in a black jacket with a vest of Danalustrous red, and his serious face showed an even more severe expression than usual. But he smiled at Senneth and gave her a brief hug.

"Comfort yourself with the thought that Tayse hates these sorts of things even more than you do," she said as she released him.

"A Rider still has more status than a peasant's son."

"Well, I think Malcolm would gladly sacrifice any number of King's Riders for you after the years you have spent looking after Kirra," Senneth said.

Donnal looked amused.

The others filed in shortly afterward, and soon there were twelve gathered around the intimate table: Malcolm; his daughters; his wife, Jannis, a practical and brisk woman with a pleasant manner; the steward and his family; all the members of Senneth's party; and Donnal. Although the numbers were split evenly between men and women, there was no formal seating arrangement, so everyone just took the most convenient chair. Senneth found herself between Casserah, who sat at the foot of the table, and Tayse. Cammon sat across from her.

"How good to see you again," Senneth greeted Casserah. "I feel like we spent the whole of last summer traveling together, but it was really Kirra pretending to be you. Still, I can't shake the sense that we've been together much more recently than it's really been."

Casserah smiled in her usual cool way. She was as beautiful as Kirra, but her hair was extremely dark and her skin a creamy white. Her eyes, the same drenched blue as Kirra's, were so wide-set they gave her a perpetually abstracted air; she never appeared to be wholly engaged in anything anyone else said. She could be shockingly blunt, to the point that many people considered her rude, but she did not care about the opinion of anyone in the world. Perhaps her father, Senneth thought, and even that was uncertain.

"Well, Kirra talks about you so often that I, too, feel like I've spent time with you recently," Casserah replied. "But I think it's been nearly a decade since you lived here."

"Maybe," Senneth said. "I don't want to count the years."

Casserah took a sip of her water and gave another faint smile. "So what did you think of me last summer?" she asked. "How good was Kirra's disguise?"

"Physically, it was perfect," Senneth said, laughing. "Emotionally, she slipped now and then. But she won you many friends across the Twelve Houses."

"That would be good to know, if I ever planned to step outside of Danalustrous."

"You *never* leave?" Cammon piped up. "Don't you get bored?"

She gave him her full attention but said simply, "No."

"Don't you ever want to—" He gestured. "See new places? Meet new people?"

"No."

"She has no need to leave Danan Hall to meet new people," Senneth told him. "Look at all of us. We come to her."

"Well, I wouldn't think you could count on *that*," he said.

Casserah wore that faint smile again. "So tell me, Senneth, is your brother very much like you? I see the family resemblance in your faces."

Senneth took a swallow of wine while she considered. "Is he like me. . . ? To tell you the truth, I don't really know. He was ten when I left, and I was very close to the boy. He was funny and thoughtful and eager to learn. I like what I've seen of the man, but we've only spent a few days together, last summer and on this trip. He seems much like the boy I remember, but who hasn't changed in the last eighteen years?"

"I haven't," Casserah said.

Senneth was surprised into a laugh. "No, I suppose you haven't."

Tayse, who had not appeared to be listening, now spoke up. "I haven't."

"Maybe not, but eighteen years ago, you were already a man," Senneth told him. "Casserah was, what, three or four? And I'm reasonably certain she's telling the truth. She had the exact same personality when she was born as she does right now."

"I'm able to control my temper better," she offered.

"So am I," Tayse told her.

Senneth laughed again. "While I have *less* control over mine. I think I'll have your eighteen years instead of mine, thank you very much."

Casserah was gazing up toward the head of the table, where Malcolm, Will, and Carlo sat with their heads together, no doubt discussing something like land management or defense. "Do you think your brother came here willingly?" she asked. "I find myself wondering if Kiernan forced him to come to Danan Hall to look over the likely serramarra."

"No," Cammon said before Senneth could speak. She looked at him and tried not to laugh. He continued, "No, he's pleased that he's here and he thinks you're beautiful, but he's a little nervous. He's not sure *you're* eager to make this match. He's not sure what you want and he doesn't want to disappoint you."

Casserah's eyes were still on Will. "Well. I'll just have to make certain he understands me," she said. She looked back at the Rider. "Tayse. What did you think of the fortifications in Brassenthwaite? Is Kiernan really ready for a war?"

From anyone else, such an abrupt change of subject would mean she was uncomfortable discussing the topic. But with Casserah, Senneth thought, it meant she had simply found out what she needed to know, said what she wanted to say, and moved on to another area of interest. No subtlety, no subterfuge. Unnerving but refreshing.

Not till after the meal did Will and Casserah get a chance to exchange a few words, and then they were chaperoned by Jannis and the steward's wife. Senneth, across the room, could tell from Casserah's expression that she found the inconsequential small talk boring and pointless, but the presence of the steward's wife made her try to display some social grace. They had withdrawn into a pretty parlor with many small groupings of chairs and tables, designed to allow visitors a chance to play cards or hold more intimate conversations. Kirra and Senneth were standing with Donnal, Tayse, and Cammon, sipping sweet wine and wishing the evening was over.

"If Justin was here, we'd be all together," Cammon observed.

Startled, Senneth quickly glanced around the circle and realized he was right. "I hadn't thought of that," she said.

"He'll be mad, too, if he finds we were all getting cozy at Danan Hall while he was stuck mucking out stables in Neft," Kirra said.

"I don't think we need to keep him there much longer," Tayse said. "I'm not sure what else there is to learn."

Kirra gave him an indignant look. "He can learn if this convent girl loves him! And he loves her!"

Tayse smiled. "Not a good enough reason to leave one of the best Riders in a position of surveillance."

"I could stay in Neft awhile, if you needed someone," Donnal said. "I'd be able to get word quickly to the king if something happened."

Tayse considered. "A good offer," he said. He jerked his head at Kirra. "What if this one won't travel so far?"

Kirra tossed her hair. "I'm going to Ghosenhall in a day or two. Donnal's tired of the royal city. I think he'd be happy to have some activity planned that made him feel useful."

"I wouldn't want to stay away too long, of course," Donnal said. His face was perfectly sober, but Senneth was convinced he was laughing.

"If you're coming to Ghosenhall, you can ride with us," Senneth said.

"You're not going back to Brassenthwaite?" Kirra asked.

"No. I've had enough of my brothers for a while."

"Then, good, we'll travel with you." She scowled at Donnal. "*Both* of us will travel with you. At least as far as the royal city. Then he can go off where he likes."

"Happy to have your company," Tayse said.

Cammon was watching Casserah across the room. "I think your sister wishes someone would rescue her from her mother," he said. "She's getting impatient."

"That's my Casserah," Kirra said. "Sen, let's go pull them away. Cammon, you come entertain my stepmother. Tell her—I don't know. About new buildings going up in Ghosenhall or something. Just be polite while we steal Will and Casserah away."

Accordingly, in a few minutes, the three serramarra and the one serramar had managed to form their own small group in a corner of the room. They stood as far away from the others as they could, bunching around a window. Kirra and Senneth set their backs to the room and made it clear no one was welcome to intrude on the conversation.

"You'll never get a chance to talk to each other with Jannis around,"

Kirra said, grinning at Will. "Who likes to flirt with a woman when her mother is standing right there?"

Will laughed. "And it's so much simpler when *her* sister and *your* sister are watching instead!"

"You don't have to flirt with me," Casserah said calmly. "In fact, I'd prefer you were genuine."

"A slight touch of flirtatiousness *is* genuine with me," he said. "But I can try to be wholly serious if you like."

"I will like whatever you show me of yourself, as long as it is real," she replied.

Senneth moved as if to back away, but Kirra caught her arm and held her in place. Senneth wasn't sure if Kirra wanted to stay to guard the conversation—or to listen to it with frank interest.

Will's voice was just as composed as Casserah's. "I believe there is always some awkwardness in situations such as this," he said. "We don't know each other at all, and yet we are supposed to decide very quickly if we might like each other enough to endure a marriage."

"I rarely feel either awkwardness or embarrassment," Casserah replied. "And I am not at all of a romantic nature. I am not averse to marrying for political reasons, but I would like to have some respect for my husband."

"That seems like a good place to start."

"What would you say your virtues are?" she asked.

He considered. "I'm easygoing and diplomatic, which means I can win friends if I choose. I have an analytical mind. I know how to think things through. My brother Kiernan trusts my advice."

"Your faults?"

"I'm not a leader. I don't tend to push myself to the forefront and demand that my voice be heard. I'll take a stand, but only on issues that are extremely important to me."

Casserah seemed to think that over. Senneth felt Kirra's fingers biting into her arm. Almost, she wanted to pull back and give the young couple some privacy; more, she was fascinated enough that she could not bring herself to step away. So this was how marriages were arranged among the Twelve Houses! What had her father said to the marlord of Gisseltess as they plotted the doomed union between their children? *She's a mystic, but I'm sure your son is cruel enough to tame all magic out of her. . . .*

"The virtues are attractive, and none of the vices are repugnant," Casserah said at last.

Will smiled. "And you? What do you think are your own good points?" he asked.

"I am very strong. Very certain of myself. If I am pursuing something that is just or important, I can be relentless."

"Some people might not consider that a virtue," he pointed out.

Casserah looked surprised. "Do you?"

"I consider it familiar," he said. "My brother has that characteristic to some degree. What would you consider your faults?"

"I care about nothing and nobody except Danalustrous," she responded at once.

"Would you be able to bring yourself to care for someone you married if he came from a different House?"

"He would then be part of Danalustrous, don't you see?"

"Part of him would be," Will replied. "Part of him might still be rooted somewhere else. Would you be able to care about someplace else for his sake, if that was where part of his heart was planted?"

Casserah was quiet for a few moments, clearly trying out the concept. "I don't know," she said at last. "I have never tried to love anything but Danalustrous. I'm not sure I can." She gave him a straight look from those blue eyes. "But I would accept that *you* could love something else. I wouldn't expect all your loyalty to go to Danan Hall. Most of it, but not all."

"I would not want to be the only one giving my loyalty," he said.

She nodded, as if that was a reasonable thing to say. "I would be faithful to you," she said. "I am always faithful, unless I'm betrayed. And then I never deal with that person again."

Now he was the one to nod. "That's a bargain I can make."

"Then shall we tell my father we've agreed?"

Senneth caught her breath. Kirra actually laughed. Will smiled. "Yes, serra Casserah. I think we may tell your father that we are willing to join our Houses—and ourselves—in marriage."

He offered her his arm. Looking both surprised and pleased at the courtesy, Casserah accepted it, and they headed across the room to where Malcolm stood talking to Carlo. Senneth and Kirra stared after them.

"*Well,*" Kirra said, sounding stunned. "No wonder you and I have had such tumultuous love lives. We have expected much more—passion—and mystery—and *agony*. If only we'd spoken more plainly about what mattered to us and what we thought we could bring to the table! Think how much simpler our lives would have been!"

"I think even among the noble Houses, such a proposal must be unique," Senneth said. Now her laughter was starting to bubble up. "But I must confess, I have high hopes for this particular match! At least neither one will ever be able to complain that they didn't understand exactly what pact they were making."

"Do you know what she said to me this morning?" Kirra demanded.

"I wouldn't even try to guess."

"She said, 'If I accept Will Brassenthwaite, does that mean you will feel free to wed Donnal? Because that will be another incentive for me, you know.'"

Senneth choked. "Really? I always thought your father and Casserah just accepted Donnal's presence the way they accept Carlo's. He's here, he's part of Danalustrous, he serves the Hall. But if she actually thinks he is good enough to *marry* you—well, can I just say, it makes my own betrothal seem slightly less outrageous."

Kirra shook her head. "I don't think I'll ever get married," she said. "I don't think I want to put Donnal through what Tayse is clearly willing to endure for you. Most of our days it is just the two of us, and we're mystics, we're equals and we're content. When circumstances compel me to play the serramarra, he likes to step back. He likes to play the servant or the guard. Some people know of our relationship, but only those we trust, and Donnal would not be happy to think the great lords and ladies were whispering about me and how far I'd fallen. I can't see a day in the near future when that will change. I can't see the day he'd ever ask my father for my hand."

Senneth looked at her. "But that doesn't mean he loves you any less."

Kirra shook her head. "Or that I love him any less." She gave Senneth a small smile. "I think I own him, Senneth. I think there is nothing I could do to drive him away. That moves me and frightens me and makes me want to be very, very careful with his heart. So I will not put it on display in the drawing rooms of the Twelve Houses."

Senneth nodded. She was watching Tayse excuse himself from his conversation with Cammon and the steward's daughter and make his way toward her. He looked too big for the room, too powerful for these pretty, delicate tables and graceful, thin-legged chairs. If he put a foot wrong or turned too quickly, he could accidentally break something.

Oh, but Tayse was too graceful for that. He moved through the room as lightly as a shadow, touching nothing. He saw her noticing him, and he rewarded her with a smile.

"Whereas I will drag Tayse to any House and any battlefield I happen to find," Senneth said quietly. "If I have to endure it, then by the Bright Mother's red eye, so should he! But he never complains."

"Why would he complain?" Kirra scoffed. "That man would do anything you asked. He'd die for you."

Senneth watched him come closer, and her own smile grew. She said, "He'd better not."

Two days later, a party of five set out for Ghosenhall. They left Will behind to spend some time getting to know his affianced bride and touring the extensive grounds of Danalustrous. The Brassenthwaite guards were also left behind, though Will offered to send at least some of them along to protect the travelers.

"Will. Four mystics and a Rider hardly need anyone's protection," Senneth told him with some amusement.

He smiled and patted her hair, which was in its usual flyaway state. "Just a gesture of affection," he said. "I would sacrifice my own security on the return trip to Brassenthwaite to keep you safe."

She hugged him. "I'm safe," she said. "Congratulations on your betrothal."

"Congratulations on your own as well."

She was glad enough to be leaving Danalustrous, heading back toward the royal city. Between one unexpected trip or another, she had been gone far longer than she had planned. She didn't mind it for her own sake—she could never bear to sit still in any one place for long—but she knew Baryn had hoped she would be back sooner. She also felt a little guilty about keeping Cammon away from his studies for such an extended time.

"You'll have forgotten everything Jerril ever taught you," she said. It was late afternoon on their second day out of Danan Hall and they were heading southeast through the upper tip of Storian lands. Tayse was about a hundred yards in the lead; Kirra and Donnal were behind them on the path, talking quietly. "By the time we get back to Ghosenhall, you won't be able to read minds at all!"

"I can't read minds," he said automatically.

"Ha. Tell me how I'm feeling about my brother agreeing to marry Casserah Danalustrous."

He smiled. "You're pleased. But anyone could tell that."

"I saw you talking to marlord Malcolm the night before we left," she said. "Was he trying to hire you? He seemed very interested in discovering just what you're capable of."

"He was testing me," Cammon said. "Kirra had told him I can tell when someone is lying. So he would say something to me and I was supposed to guess whether or not he was telling the truth. He's a very hard man to read."

"Malcolm?" Senneth said derisively. "Indeed, he is! Impenetrable, in fact. Even his own daughters would tell you they never know what he's thinking. How often were you able to separate the truth from the lie?"

Cammon looked surprised. "Every time."

She started laughing. "Oh, very impressive. How much did he offer you to stay?"

Cammon grinned. "He told me I could name my price."

"You should have said, 'Let me marry Casserah.' *That* would have been interesting."

"But I don't want to marry her."

"No, the point would be—never mind. I can't believe he let you ride out."

Cammon looked a little self-conscious. "I may have told him I'd come back."

"Oh, we'll see you wearing Danalustrous red before another year is gone."

Kirra and Donnal trotted up. "Is my father trying to recruit Cammon?" Kirra asked. "I knew he would. Casserah liked him, too. Too bad my father has run out of daughters to marry off, or he'd try to bind you into the family."

Senneth glanced at her. "Don't you have cousins somewhere? Or some nice young girl born to a high-ranking vassal?"

"Not everyone wants to marry a fortune, but every man appreciates a good plot of land," Donnal put in. "Malcolm's ruthless enough to dispossess a lordling if he thought Cammon might value the estate."

Senneth and Kirra laughed, but Cammon didn't seem to think it was funny. "I don't want to be a landowner!" he exclaimed. "What would I do with property?"

"Settle down? Become rich? Acquire a little sophistication?" Kirra suggested. "I don't know how we'd ever get your hair to behave, but maybe a nice velvet suit—some expensive boots—we could polish you up a lot."

"I don't think so," Cammon said.

"Face it, Kirra, of the six of us, you're the only one who's ever going to look remotely respectable," Senneth said. "You can dress us up, you can sit us at the marlord's table, but we're all going to look like peasants, soldiers, and vagabonds."

"Well, if you'd put a little *effort* into it," Kirra said.

Donnal's voice held a grin. "Not all the effort in the world would serve to transform some of us."

Cammon opened his mouth to speak, but instead a guttural sound came out, as if he'd been punched in the stomach. Senneth glanced over and saw him suddenly jerk upright, and then put a hand over his heart with a cry of pain. She pulled hard on her reins, reaching across to him, but he was already slumping in the saddle. His horse whinnied and came to an uncertain stop; Kirra and Donnal almost rode over him.

"Cammon, what—" Senneth began, but then he cried out again and tumbled off his horse onto the hard ground. *"Tayse!"* Senneth screamed, pulling her sword and looking wildly around for any sign of attackers. Behind her, she felt rather than saw Donnal shift shape and take wing, soaring upward to reconnoiter. Kirra had scrambled out of her own saddle and was already on the ground beside Cammon as Tayse came thundering up.

"What happened? Did he faint? Was he hurt?" the Rider demanded. His own sword was out and he was raking the vistas ahead and behind for any evidence of trouble. They were passing through fairly open land; it was hard to believe they could have been ambushed by an enemy still out of sight.

"Sen," Kirra called, looking up from Cammon's prone body. "There's not a wound on him. His pulse is fast and his skin's cold, but he's untouched. Physically."

Senneth glanced at Tayse and he nodded, so she slid down from her horse and crouched beside Kirra in the dirt. "Then what happened to him? What's wrong?"

Kirra's hands were pressed to Cammon's chest, willing some of her own strength into him. Kirra possessed both healing power and some training as a nurse. Senneth's own fiery magic could be bent toward rough-and-ready physicking, though she didn't pretend to have Kirra's finesse. Still, both of them needed a wound they could see or a disease they could understand. It looked like Cammon had been felled by something more mysterious.

Senneth laid her hands on his forehead and it felt cool and clammy against her palms. "Cam," she said, her voice hard, pitched to break through a cloudy mind. "Cammon. Where are you? What happened to you?"

He opened his eyes and they seemed pale with pain. For a moment he labored to catch his breath. His lips moved, and Senneth bent down to hear whatever word he was struggling to form.

He whispered, "*Justin.*"

CHAPTER

28

ELLYNOR sat at the infirmary window and watched the rain sluice down. It was a cold, nasty precipitation, laced with ice and driven by a hard wind, and literally no one had stepped into the courtyard all morning to brave it. She wondered for the hundredth time if Justin and his companion had left at some point when she had turned away from the window, or if they were still sitting in the barracks, waiting out the worst of the weather. It was past noon now; if they didn't leave soon, they wouldn't have enough daylight left to make it back to Neft.

And if he spent another night at the convent . . .

"Ellynor." The voice from the bed was Rosurie's, and Ellynor left her post at the window to answer her. "Do you think I could try to stand up now? I feel so much stronger, and I drank all my milk this morning."

"Let's see," Ellynor said, pulling back the covers and taking Rosurie's arm. The Black Mother knew Ellynor would rejoice for a whole host of reasons if Rosurie made a fast recovery. "I think you're still a little weak, but let's see you walk across the room a few times."

Rosurie managed the feat slowly, dipping now and then from dizziness, but negotiating the room three times before dropping back into her bed. "I feel so stiff! Like all my muscles have been shredded," she said.

"Well, you should have seen yourself. Your whole body clenched tight for days. I'd think you'd be terribly sore after that."

Rosurie passed a hand over her bare scalp, where the little nicks were healed over but still visible. "It feels so strange not to have hair," she remarked. "Like my head weighs almost nothing."

Ellynor poured another glass of milk and handed it over. "Are you sorry you cut it?"

"Oh no. The Silver Lady smiled at me when I took the razor in my hand. She knew what a great sacrifice I was making, and it pleased her.

Besides, now I carry no Lirren markings at all—nothing to show I belong anywhere but here."

Ellynor watched her swallow the milk. *Drink up. Grow strong. When you are well enough, I am leaving.* "It is good to find the place you feel you are supposed to be," she said quietly.

Though Ellynor had no idea where that place would be for her.

"Do you think I might go down to dinner tonight?"

"Probably not," Ellynor said. "But I'll have someone bring you a plate of food, and if you eat it all, you can go down for breakfast tomorrow."

"I'm still a little tired," Rosurie admitted. "But I'm so bored just lying here!"

Ellynor smiled. "That usually means you're well on the way to getting better."

They talked sporadically after that, and Ellynor checked on the other three patients. All of them with that hacking cough Deana had developed, though none of them as ill as the proselyte had been. When everyone was fed, medicated, cleaned up, and resting again, Ellynor went back to the window.

The rain had abated; the sullen clouds looked as if they might grudgingly give way to a little weak sunlight. Ellynor could feel the cold seeping in past the window glass, but that didn't bother her. And it shouldn't stop a determined traveler. The roads would be wet but not impassable, not if you were willing to take your time and didn't mind kicking up a little mud on the road.

Evidently, she was not the only one to reach that conclusion. While she watched, a small caravan plodded into her line of sight, moving from the back of the convent and slowly across the courtyard. Two men and six horses. Justin and the freighter. They paused briefly at the gate, waiting until it was unlatched and swung back, and then urged their animals forward into the wet, cold depths of the forest.

Just as he passed through the gate, Justin turned his head and glanced back. His eyes searching the convent windows. Looking, Ellynor knew, for any glimpse of her. She stayed where she was, far enough back from the glass that he probably could not see her. In a moment, he faced forward again and urged his horse onward.

She was standing by the window again about thirty minutes later, feeling bereft and depressed, when she saw a second party of men go riding through the gates. There were five of them, all convent guards, and by the glitter of metal in the frail sunlight, she could see they were heavily armed. There were too many to be running simple errands, not enough to be planning a midnight raid on some hapless mystic's house. A hunting party? Maybe.

But—hunting game? Or hunting men?

For the hundredth time, Ellynor asked herself, *Did Daken see Justin last night?* Had he guessed the visitor had spent the evening wooing a convent novice? Daken was not among the men riding out through the gates, but that didn't mean much. Astira had reported he wasn't very good with a weapon. *He spends so much time practicing, he says he's getting better, but I can tell he's disappointed.* If the convent guards had decided to ride out to punish a man who had dared to romance a novice, they would send seasoned men to do the task, warriors, true swordsmen.

Oh, Great Mother, if they were truly going after Justin—

Ellynor glanced at all her charges. Either sleeping, or peacefully lying in bed, reading. Darris would be here within the hour to relieve her; no one would die if the infirmary was unattended that long. Ellynor could not sit there, could not feel this great restless terror clawing through her blood. She had to go, she had to find out, she had to see if the soldiers had set out with the intention of harming Justin.

She slipped out of the infirmary, down the hall, down the stairs. Through the great reception hall with its echoing spaces and massive chandeliers. Out into the courtyard, where the dampness of the air made the cold that much sharper. Ellynor shivered and for a moment considered going back inside for her cloak. Even for some food, in case she was gone for several hours. But there was no time. She didn't mind the chill, and she would set a brisk enough pace that her blood would heat up.

And surely she would not be gone long enough to miss more than a meal or two.

Surely nothing had really happened to Justin.

There were two soldiers guarding the entrance and three walking the perimeter, engaged in idle conversation. None of them saw her. It was trickier to pass the gate without being noticed, since she had to pull it open just far enough to slip through. She waited till the pair at the entrance got distracted by the arrival of two relief guards, and then she made her escape. The metal did not squeal; it barely moved as she made it gape just wide enough for her to squeeze out.

Then she was on the path, striding through the forest at an uncomfortably fast pace. Drops of frigid water dripped on her from the overhanging branches; now and then a squirrel ran overhead and shook a small storm of icy rain onto her head. Within twenty yards, the hems of her white robes were wet and filthy, and her feet were already caked with mud. Fortunately, her shoes were good—comfortable and sturdy—she could walk all day in these.

All day and all night if she had to.

She was not much of a tracker, not like Torrin was, but even she could tell that everyone who had left the convent this day had gone in the same direction. There were multiple sets of hoofprints in the mud; the road had been fairly churned up by the passage of ten or so animals. Bad news for anyone coming behind them on foot who was interested in keeping clean. Good news for anyone trying to follow their trail. She couldn't judge, as Torrin would have been able to, how quickly the later party was gaining on the travelers who had left the convent first, but common sense told her the soldiers had moved faster. They had better horses, none of them tied to a lead. They had a stronger purpose—

Maybe not. Maybe the soldiers were just riding into town, delivering messages for the Lestra, picking up supplies that could not be trusted to strangers. Maybe Ellynor was afraid—and cold and hungry—for no good reason at all.

She had been on the trail about two hours when daylight started to fail. She wasn't afraid of the dark, not in the least, but the onset of night would force her to make a quick decision. Keep going forward, giving up any chance of returning to the convent with some story about why she had left so abruptly—or go back. Walk on toward Neft, with no cloak, no provisions, and no hope of arriving in the city before morning—or turn back now.

She kept walking.

Another mile down the road, she saw them.

At first she didn't realize what they were, the dark shapes lying so still across the path. Fallen trees, or at least great, unwieldy branches, flung down by the earlier storm. There were half a dozen, scattered right on this bend of the road, tossed down from some tree so big and so old that it could not withstand the force of a winter storm.

Ten steps closer and she realized they were not tree limbs. They were bodies.

Seven bodies strewn across the road. Five in the black-and-silver livery of the convent. Two in nondescript traveling gear. All of them covered with blood.

One of them was Justin.

She screamed and the forest around her echoed with startled cries, but she didn't care. She didn't hear. She ran forward, sobbing, her breath fogging around her face, her hands the temperature of ice. *Great Mother, sweet Mother, dark Mother, please let him not be dead. . . .*

She knelt beside him, her hands on his chest before her knees had even settled into the mud. She could feel the blood, slick and damp on his clothes, but she didn't care about that. She had to check for body temperature, for heartbeat, for the subtle lift and settle of breath. Her seeking fingers found rents in his clothing, great gashes in the flesh beneath; she tilted her head so that her ear was just over his mouth.

An exhalation, faint and warm. A pulse, buried and weak.

Sweet kind holy Mother, Justin was alive.

Ellynor flattened both of her hands against his chest, nesting her fingers in the ripped and bloody fabric of his shirt. Her own breath slowed; her concentration became fierce and total. *Great Mother,* she prayed, her lips moving but the words silent, *fill me with your power. Make my hands your hands, my blood your magic. Heal this man. Save him. Great Mother, I love him. Save him for me. . . .*

She felt warmth trickle through her as a perceptible heat built up between her shoulder blades and slowly spread through all her bones and muscles. But there was an icy band around her left wrist, the place where the baleful moonstones on her bracelet lay against her skin. The Pale Mother's gems. The Silver Lady hated mystics. Impatiently, Ellynor paused to undo the fine catch of the slim, silver chain. She tossed the bracelet into the forest, as far from the deadfall as she could.

Instantly, she felt the heat in her blood leap higher. Her hands were almost on fire; her fingertips were conduits of flame. Justin's torso jerked slightly, as if shocked by a burning brand, and then he lay still. She felt the fever run from her body into his. She almost saw the magic arc from her closed system into his opened veins. The power pooled around her, like heavy rain on oversoaked soil, then drained slowly into Justin's chest—pooled again, and again was absorbed—again. Again.

He was so close to death that nothing, not even the Mother's energy, could sustain him for long. He was so empty of life that he could be filled and refilled and never overflow.

"Justin," Ellynor whispered. "Justin. Breathe. Force your heart to beat. Live."

And still the Great Mother's dense magic poured into her, unstinting, bottomless. Ellynor felt herself growing heavy, rich, saturated with darkness. If Justin opened his eyes, if a stranger chanced upon her on this road, they would see her face black as midnight, tears as bright as stars upon her cheeks. Her hands would look like shadows; she would appear to be nothing but a layered shape, indistinguishable from the night itself.

Justin breathed. His heart beat. He did not die.

Keeping her hands pressed against his chest, Ellynor watched his face. Pale unto death, of course, marked with bruises and blood. The dark blond hair had fallen back from his forehead and was matted with mud; every bone and angle was exposed. He was unconscious. There could be no thought process to pull his features into any kind of recognizable expression.

But she could see every pinch and flutter of his mouth and eyelids. Could read the intensity along his clenched jaw. He was struggling—straining—as if to speak, as if to sit up, as if to wake.

He was fighting. With every instinct of his body, against overwhelming odds, he was battling to survive.

"Justin," she whispered, her lips against his, her voice whispering his name into his own mouth, in case he had forgotten it. "Don't give up. Keep fighting. I love you. Do not surrender now."

Beneath her lips, his mouth took in air; beneath her hands, his heart kept beating. This was a man who did not want to die.

She must do something about his wounds. The bleeding had slowed but had not entirely stopped. Shifting her body so that one knee rested gently against his ribs—she wanted to make sure that she was touching him, always touching him, pouring her power into him in an unbroken stream—she began searching for something she could turn into a bandage.

A fallen convent guard lay within reach. Ellynor hesitated only a moment, struggling with the reality of death, then closed her heart. She felt around for the clasp of his cloak and tugged it free of his body. It came away grudgingly, muddy and bloody and already torn in half. But it would do.

Working as quickly as she could, never moving her knee from Justin's side, she ripped the cloak into smaller strips and pads and began binding the worst of Justin's wounds. That meant lifting him enough to pass the cloth under his body, an act that caused him to grunt with incoherent pain. But he seemed to lie easier once the bandages were in place. She convinced herself that the bleeding slowed and stopped.

It was hard to tell. There was so much blood already.

Not sure if it would help or hurt, she tried to tip a little water down Justin's throat. He swallowed, which she thought was a good sign, so she gave him a little more. She had no water skin of her own—no provisions at all—but Justin and the freighter had each carried water and some food. The convent soldiers as well, no doubt. Enough to keep a dying man alive for the rest of the night, the next day, the next night. . . .

But he could not lie there long enough to recover. He would almost certainly develop an infection from his wounds—and lying on the wet ground for a series of cold nights would send even a healthy man to his death. She needed blankets, clean bandages, medicinal herbs, broth, water, a bed, a fire. . . .

She needed to go for help.

Neft was the nearest place, and from this point on the road, it was probably three hours away on horseback.

That made her look up. Where were the horses? She had been so preoccupied with the bodies on the ground that she had not even thought to check for living creatures in the vicinity. But, there they were, bunched together a little distance down the road, mostly quiet now that the chaos of combat was past. She wondered why the fight had taken place on foot, and supposed the eager reach of forest branches had made it difficult to wield a sword from horseback. Or perhaps Justin had jumped from the saddle in the hope of racing off through the woods on trails a mounted man could not follow. In any case, it seemed that the horses had been abandoned in the heat of battle, and none of them had strayed yet. She counted eleven shadows standing with their heads down and their tails limp.

That presented a fresh worry. How quickly would the convent animals, left to their own devices, decide to wander back toward their familiar stables? That would be bad—that would surely signal someone at Lumanen that trouble had felled the guards. Which might not be news, anyway, if the soldiers had been expected to return immediately upon dispatching the freighter's troublesome friend.

If the guards did not return, or their horses returned without them, a search party would be on its way by dawn.

Ellynor had to go to Neft for help.

And bring the convent horses with her. Or secure them here.

She could make sure no one who traveled this road was able to find them.

But how could she leave Justin? His hold on life was so tenuous that she was certain it was only her touch that kept his heart beating, his lungs functioning. He would die if she left him.

He would die if she did not.

Great Mother, put your hands upon this man. . . .

She had been so absorbed in Justin that it had not occurred to her to wonder if anyone else had survived this day's confrontation. Experimentally, she pushed herself away from Justin's side, mere inches, close enough to touch him again if his breath faltered. But his chest rose and fell, a shallow but unmistakable movement; his lips tightened as if against pain. She could risk the ten minutes it would take to investigate the others.

Quickly she rose to her feet and shook out her ruined skirts. No need to check the guard whose cloak she had stolen. His head had been practically severed; he was definitely dead. She followed the bloody trail to the other four guards, kneeling beside each one and feeling for a pulse. Absent in every case. She tried not to look too closely, but it was impossible not to get some sense of how each one had died. Three appeared to have received wounds straight to the heart. The other was so bloody she thought he, too, had been sliced across the jugular, after sustaining gashes on his face and hands and arms. A warrior. Just not quite good enough.

The freighter was also dead, though there was no weapon in his hand or near his body. Not a fighter, not like the others. Had probably never in his life lifted a weapon to another man. Ellynor felt a fierce rush of bitter sadness at the life that had ended here so brutally, so pointlessly. This man had done nothing but try to earn a living, provide a service, carry out his commissions. He had died because Ellynor was foolish, because Ellynor loved a man she could not have.

He had died because the Lestra was evil.

That thought came from nowhere and filled her mind with a momentary blackness that had nothing to do with the Dark Watcher's presence. Hate and fear and fury flooded Ellynor's heart, and her hands clenched at her sides with her overwhelming desire to strike out. The Lestra was evil, the convent a source of violence and intimidation and despair.

But not everyone inside its walls was vicious, was tainted. Not Deana, not Astira, not Lia, not some of those laughing novices too young to understand the path they followed. The guards—some of them, like those here tonight—they were cruel and ruthless, but not all of them. Ellynor would not believe it of all of them. Hadn't that boy Kelti run away? Wasn't Daken unhandy with a weapon? Surely there were some—new recruits, young boys fresh from their fathers' farms—who would be horrified to learn how their senior officers dealt in torture and death.

And surely the Pale Mother herself was not so terrible. She was playful and vain and fickle and careless, but sometimes kind and always beautiful, and Ellynor could not bring herself to hate that charming, incon-stant face.

It was not the goddess who was to be hated and despised. It was the woman who had taken it upon herself to speak for the Silver Lady.

It was the Lestra who burned mystics and sent her guards out hunting men. It was the Lestra who was responsible for tonight's deaths—and near deaths.

Ellynor hurried back to Justin, dropping beside him in the mud. Still breathing. His skin still warm to the touch. No more blood seeping out past the makeshift bandages.

Alive. Alive. Alive.

For now.

She bowed her head so low that her forehead almost touched Justin's. Some of her hair had escaped its habitual knot, and a few locks tumbled over her shoulder, coiling on Justin's chest. She had taken his hands in hers, and she squeezed his fingers just for the pleasure of feeling his living flesh against her skin.

Great Mother, she prayed. *Dark beautiful lady. I am the daughter of the daughter of the hundreds of daughters of Maara. I call upon you now to redeem the promise you made to the women of the Lirrens. Give this man one night. Keep him alive one night. Hold him in your hands for one night. I must leave him, but I will return for him, and I beg you to keep him safe until that hour. Guard him with your body. Strengthen him with your love. Shield him with your darkness. Let no harm come to him. Let him live.*

Ellynor felt the night rustle and gather around her as the trees con-ferred and the clouds debated. The owls and the mice paused in their ceaseless game of chase and escape. Not far away, a wolf raised a liquid cry of woe and warning. A possum trotted by, an ungainly ghost; the branches overhead dipped and released a spray of water as some night bird settled in.

Invisible hands, tangible and warm, settled over Ellynor's fingers where they rested on Justin's chest. A shadow swirled around her, not quite holding a shape, faceless, incorporeal, but crackling with energy. El-lynor sucked in her breath, awe and wonder momentarily striking her motionless. She felt as if she had been drawn into a bear's cave or a wolf's lair, someplace hidden, safe, and sheltered.

She lifted her hands but Justin still breathed. The Black Mother's palms still lay pressed against his chest.

Shakily, she came to her feet, almost stumbling from weariness and a sense of marvel. "You will keep him safe, won't you?" she whispered, almost stammering the words. "No one will see him, no one will come upon him and do him harm? I will be back by dawn if I can—you will not leave him alone for a minute, will you? Someone will guard him this whole time?"

There was no answer, but a slow prickle of danger spiderwalked down Ellynor's spine. Slowly, carefully, she turned to scan the road behind her. For a moment, even her night vision could make out nothing on the path or under the trees, but then she saw it, pacing forward with a slow, menacing step.

A raelynx. The goddess's own creature, seldom found anywhere outside the borders of the Lireth Mountains. Even in the darkness, Ellynor could make out its red fur, its tufted ears, its grace and power and utter ferocity.

It stalked right by her and settled next to Justin in the mud, lending its own body heat to the fallen man. Guarding Justin from anyone who might happen upon him in the night.

It took an effort of will for Ellynor to swallow. "Thank you, Mother," she whispered. "I will be back by morning."

She bent to strip a cloak from one of the fallen soldiers and wrap it around her shoulders. She was suddenly cold, she who never noticed the chill, and she felt herself shaking from the combined effects of fear and rage and magic. She randomly chose one of the soldiers' horses, a young bay mare that looked both sturdy and swift, and led the rest of them deeper into the forest, looping their reins over low-hanging branches. No need to ask again; she was sure the Dark Watcher would make sure no passersby happened to catch a glimpse of these animals. She did not have the strength to pull the bodies from the road, but somehow she trusted the goddess to handle this detail as well. She would send her buzzards and vultures to pick the bodies clean by daybreak, or she would disguise them with an opaque sorcery. Ellynor would trust her to take care of it all.

"Keep him safe," she whispered one last time, then threw herself into the saddle and kicked the horse forward into a headlong canter. "Mother, I beg you, keep him alive."

She heard, or maybe she only thought she heard, a whispered promise in return. *Daughter, I will.*

CHAPTER

29

ELLYNOR raced through the night as if outrunning the end of the world, as if a great chasm was opening behind her, splitting the earth the instant her horse's hooves lifted from the ground. She had picked her mount well, or else the goddess had given her this one last gift and lent the bay mare speed and strength to outdistance the dawn. They flew through the forest, stumbling over no fallen logs, tripping in no muddy sinkholes. When there were hazards, Ellynor could see clearly enough to guide the horse past them, but mostly their way was smooth.

Finally—out of the dark, tangled overgrowth of woodland and onto the flatter, easier open road. Ellynor crouched low over the horse's neck, urging her on to greater speed, murmuring encouragement, offering praise. The horse never faltered and never broke stride. The miles passed, blurred by tears and motion. The stars, usually so quick to dance through their rotations, crept slowly across the night sky, as if dragging their sparkling feet, holding back the march of dawn.

The waning moon watched her from its half-closed eye as if afraid of what it might see below.

She had been running for more than two hours when Ellynor finally saw Neft taking shape on the horizon. A few dark buildings bulked up against the night sky; torches and lamplight offered a fitful, wavering il-lumination. Every shape grew clearer as she pounded closer. She could start to identify the few places she knew on the outskirts of town—a tav-ern, two ramshackle houses, a freighting office, a shop. It might not have been as late as she had thought—certainly not midnight yet. A number of pedestrians were still abroad, as well as a few other travelers on horse-back. Up ahead of her a man was slowly guiding a wagon and team toward the stables on the edge of town.

She clattered past all of them, slowing the horse only slightly and earning a couple of surprised glances. Where would the magistrate Faeber be at this hour? Justin had told her he frequented the taprooms, but she had no idea how many of those could be found in Neft. Still, she would go to the first one she could find, and start asking for him. Eventually someone would be able to tell her where he was.

There was no one else she could trust. There was no one else in Neft she *knew*, except Paulina Nocklyn, who lived in the Gisseltess house with the woman who was kin to the Lestra. No hope there.

It must be Faeber. She must be able to find him.

She envisioned a long, panicked night of running from tavern to tavern, begging strangers for aid, rousing all kinds of suspicion that might harm Justin in the long run. But the Black Mother was still watching out for her—or maybe, just maybe, the Silver Lady felt twinges of remorse and sympathy. *Someone's* divine hand tugged on Ellynor's shoulder just as she turned the mare down a short street lined with a collection of unkempt buildings. *Someone* convinced her to fling herself from the saddle in front of the second building and push her way through the swinging door into a warm, well-lit, spicy-smelling room.

It was such a contrast to the cold and dark of her journey that, for a moment, Ellynor stood frozen at the threshold, unsure of what to do next. Whom to approach, what to say. More than a few people had looked up at her entrance and now surveyed her with interest. She realized she must look a fantastic sight—her hair wild, her hands bloody, her muddy white robes only partially covered by a large, dirty cloak that she had clearly borrowed or stolen. If she had ever hoped to accomplish this part of the mission unobserved, she had just lost her last chance.

A medium-sized, somewhat rumpled man was crossing the room on his way from the bar to a table in the back. He glanced at Ellynor, set down a pitcher of beer, and came up to her with a quizzical smile.

"You look like someone who's run into a whole bunch of different kinds of trouble," he said, and his voice was rumbling and kind. "You trying to find someone? Or some*thing?*"

"I need the magistrate," Ellynor said, trying to sound calm.

He didn't look entirely surprised. "I'm Faeber," he said.

Oh, surely that was the work of the Pale Mother! She delighted in unexpected gifts. "I have to talk to you. It's urgent," Ellynor said. "Can we step outside?"

Not hesitating, he nodded and escorted her out the door. Ellynor knew everyone in the tavern was watching by now, but at least no one would be able to overhear their conversation. As soon as the door swung shut, she said baldly, "Justin's been hurt. I need someone to help me bring him to safety. In secret," she added.

Faeber's face showed instant concern. "Hurt! How? Where is he?"

She watched his face for any faint change in expression, hoping he could be trusted as much as Justin believed. "He's on the road leading out of the forest that surrounds the Lumanen Convent," she said slowly. "Five guards attacked him this afternoon and almost killed him. But he's still alive."

Now Faeber looked astonished. "*Five* guards? And he's the one who's not dead?"

She brushed that aside as of no importance. "There was another man with him, a freighter from town. He may have accounted for one or two."

"No," said Faeber positively. "I know Jenkins, and he's never held a sword in his life. Justin fought off *five men*? Killed them all? Who *is* that boy?"

"I don't know," she said, her voice growing a little ragged. "But he'll be a dead one soon if we don't go after him now."

Faeber's lined face softened as he looked at her. "Young lady, if he was close to death when you left him, there's no chance he's still alive now."

"Yes, he *is*," she said fiercely. "I swear to you—I know for certain—he will survive till dawn. But after that—if you don't help me—he will die. Or more soldiers from the convent will find him. Surely they'll come looking by daybreak. Please, please, help me bring him to safety."

He nodded. "I've got a cart small enough to fit down that forest road behind a tandem team. But we'll need guards of our own in case we run into trouble."

"No," she said. "I don't want—if anyone knows where Justin is, more soldiers will come for him. He won't be safe."

"We can trust these guards," Faeber said. "They're my sons. Come on."

He turned from the tavern and began striding purposefully down the street. Ellynor snatched up the reins of her horse and followed. She was flooded with relief—she had secured aid, she was no longer alone in this desperate misadventure—but at the same time her body was strung with tension. They were still so far away from Justin, and the minutes were skipping by so rapidly. They had to leave *now*, they should have been on the road ten minutes ago, how could they spare time to harness horses and gather up reinforcements?

It was as if Faeber could read her thoughts. "It won't take long," he said in a soothing voice. "Fifteen minutes, maybe twenty, you'll see. We'll be back on the road. Now, when we get to my house, I want you to go in while I'm fetching the cart. I want you to eat something. My wife will still be awake, she'll feed you. I want you to clean up your face, maybe change your clothes. Marney will find you something to wear. You've had a long night and it's going to get longer. Don't be stupid. Take care of yourself if you're going to take care of that young man."

Finally they arrived at Faeber's house, a rambling two-story building that radiated the same comfort and strength that Faeber himself did. More quickly than Ellynor really expected, he had called for his sons, sent them out to hitch the wagon, given Marney a brief synopsis of the night's challenge, and gone off to get his own overcoat. Marney, a large, clear-eyed, capable-looking woman, handed Ellynor a plate of food and disappeared to rummage through her closets. In just about the time Faeber had predicted, Ellynor had been fed and cleaned up, the wagon was ready, and his two sons waited outside the door, mounted on horseback.

"I figure you can ride in the wagon with me on the way out, since you'll probably be riding with Justin on the way back," Faeber said, helping Ellynor onto the bench beside the driver's place. The wagon was so narrow that they were sitting shoulder to shoulder. "We put your horse in the barn. Don't imagine anyone will find it unless they go looking pretty hard. Ready, boys? Let's be on our way."

This half of the journey seemed to take forever; there was no way a cart, even pulled by a team, could make the same kind of time as a single rider. Ellynor felt her muscles cramp with apprehension. Her lip bled because she bit it so hard to keep from crying out for greater speed.

She must trust the goddess. The Black Mother would not abandon Justin, not now. Look, it was still dark, only a short time past midnight. The goddess had promised to stay till dawn.

Their pace slowed as they entered the forest, for even this small cart was a little too wide to navigate the twists and turns of the woodland trail. Ellynor thought she would scream from impatience as Faeber carefully guided the team through a sharp angle in the road. She wanted to beg him to stop the cart, let her take one of the horses and ride on ahead. She would meet them at the place in the road where the bodies lay in a pile.

But she knew they would never find that place if she was not with them. The goddess would conceal it from everyone except Ellynor herself.

At last, at last, a dip in the road, a turn into shadows, and they came upon the site of the battle. Six corpses still lay in the road, clear to Ellynor's eyes, although Faeber's sons practically rode right over them.

"Stop! Stop! Here we are," Ellynor exclaimed, scrambling from the cart while it was still in motion. She could sense the confusion from Faeber's sons, hear one of them say, "What? Here?" as he pulled back hard on the reins. She didn't pay attention. She lit out at a flat run for the patch of ground a few yards away where a fair-haired man lay motionless on the bloody soil. She practically collapsed at his side, her hands outstretched to touch him before she had even fully come to rest.

Heart beating. Breath warm at the corners of his mouth. Alive, alive.

She heard the commotion around her as Faeber drew his team to a halt and the three men tossed each other questions. "Where'd she go? I don't see her, do you? If that isn't the strangest thing!"

"I can't see a damn thing on this road—it's like there's a mist, or something—but that's not it. It's just purely impossible to see."

They probably would be glad they couldn't see if they knew what was hiding under the Black Mother's cloak of darkness. The raelynx, lying against Justin's body across from where Ellynor knelt, now pushed himself to a seated position. He yawned, showing his splendid sharp teeth, and gazed about him as if wondering what other interesting sights this territory might hold. Then, so quickly that Ellynor did not see him move, he bunched his muscles and sprang away into the forest. She didn't even hear the slightest sounds from his passage.

One night visitor remained behind. Ellynor could sense the presence of the Black Mother still crouched near Justin's head. She was nothing more than a coil of darkness, a suggestion of weight in the formless air.

"Thank you," Ellynor whispered. "Thank you. All I ask now is that you give me the strength to do the rest. To heal him. To make him whole. And lift your magic from this place now, for these others are here to help me. I cannot tell you what is in my heart. All I know is that I will love you forever."

The shadow grew denser for a moment, and Ellynor felt the distinct shape of a kiss pressed against her forehead. A pulse of fire surged through her; she felt her blood run with heat. Momentarily, she was blinded, even her preternatural vision failing. And then suddenly the darkness lifted as if a sullen fog had evaporated in an instant. She heard one of Faeber's sons gasp and one of them curse.

"There she is," Faeber said. "And great holy goddess, there are the bodies. I didn't think it could be true."

"There're six dead men here!" one of his sons exclaimed. "And you're saying this fellow killed five of them?"

"Doesn't seem possible," Faeber said, "but I think it's so. Let's get him in the wagon, boys. Daybreak can't be more than a few hours away, and we need to be on the road quick as we can."

"I see horses back through the trees," one of the sons called as Faeber came to his knees beside Ellynor. "Do we leave them behind?"

"No. Rope them together and we'll lead them into town," Faeber said over his shoulder. Then he turned his head and gazed down at Justin's face. "And he's really still alive?" he asked, quietly enough that only Ellynor could hear. "You must possess a powerful bond with that Silver Lady of yours. I can't imagine anything but a goddess's touch keeping a man breathing when he's in a state like this."

No time to go into it all right now! "The goddess has been good to me," was all Ellynor said. "Let's get him in the wagon and go."

THAT was a nightmare journey, out of the forest, down the endless road, back to the streets of Neft. Ellynor was aware of every slow, agonizing mile they traveled. She only vaguely paid attention to her companions as Faeber's sons ranged before and behind the wagon, keeping an eye out for trouble in any form. Now and then Faeber spoke to her from the front bench, but her answers were muffled and incomplete. All her attention was on Justin. All her energy was poured into him. She lay beside him in that cramped, jarring, rocking cart, one hand on his heart and her lips against his cheek, and willed him to stay alive.

Dawn was uncurling over the horizon as they pulled wearily into Neft. The sky was actually light as Faeber and his sons carried Justin into the house and up a wide set of stairs. Marney had prepared a room for him—a soft bed, a roaring fire, a selection of clean bandages, and three basins full of water. As soon as the men had settled Justin into his bed, Marney shooed them all out the door.

"Ellynor and I will clean him up now. You three go rest."

"Ellynor needs some rest herself, I'm thinking," Faeber said.

Marney cast Ellynor one quick, appraising look. "I expect Ellynor will want to spend a little more time getting our patient settled," she said. "Now you go on to your rooms." She paused long enough to kiss her husband, and then shut the door.

"Let's get this young man taken care of," she said.

They worked together nearly an hour, cleaning and rebinding Justin's wounds, washing his face and hands, wiping away as much of the blood as they could. Marney matter-of-factly stripped him naked and redressed him in loose clothes that probably belonged to one of her sons, handling him so gently he barely grunted with the pain. Ellynor couldn't help but notice all the old scars that crisscrossed Justin's chest and arms and legs. Some of them were from clean wounds that had probably been made by a sword and had obviously been well tended. Some were still red, ragged marks across his flesh that looked as if they had been acquired in a street fight and left to fester.

"There's quite a story to this boy's life," Marney remarked as she settled him back on the pillow. "Do you know it all?"

Ellynor shook her head slowly. "Almost none of it."

"But he's worth something to you."

"I love him."

"Worth everything then." Marney hesitated. She was still perched on one side of the bed, but her hands were in her lap; she'd done what she could. Ellynor sat on the other side, patting Justin's face, his hands, the newly wrapped bandages. Checking, just checking, to make sure everything was secure, that he was still breathing, that his heart was still beating. "I'll watch him for a few hours. There's a room right next door, and I've made up that bed, too. You get some sleep and I'll take care of him."

Ellynor didn't even look up as she shook her head. "No. I'll stay with him."

"I thought you'd say that. But you've had a hard night already and you must be at your very limit. I promise I won't leave him."

Ellynor gave the other woman one quick, fierce look. "If I leave him, he will die."

"I can't believe he's not dead as it is," Marney said, her voice compassionate. "I don't want to lie to you. I think every breath will be his last."

Ellynor nodded. "I know. He should be dead. But he's not, and I won't let him die. That's why I have to be the one to stay with him."

"You think you're some kind of mystic, who can heal a man with her touch?"

"Yes," Ellynor said slowly, "that's exactly what I think I am."

A startled little silence for that. Marney was clearly remembering that Ellynor had arrived at her house wearing the white robes of a novice from the convent. Not the place you would expect to find a mystic. She obviously decided not to ask, for she came to her feet and said, "Let me know if there's anything you want."

"There is," Ellynor said. "I need food—lots of it. Milk and meat and bread and potatoes. Cheese. More than you'd think one person could eat. I'll go through it all. Blankets. And enough fuel to keep the fire going all day."

"All right," Marney said, and turned for the door. She paused with a hand on the knob. "You really think you can save him?"

Ellynor was pulling her legs up onto the bed and stretching them out alongside Justin. She arranged her borrowed skirts so they did not bunch around her knees. "I know I can," she said.

CHAPTER
30

For the next five days, Ellynor stayed beside Justin and gave him her life.

Whether she was lying beside him, half asleep, or whether she sat next to him, feeding herself from the banquet that Marney supplied, she kept one hand always on his chest. He became an extension of her, a limb, an appendage. Her heartbeat drove his pulse, her lungs pushed air into and out of his body. If he were to open his eyes, he would see only what she saw; if he dreamed at all, it was only what she was dreaming. They were a single creature animated by a single will.

With such simple needs. Eat. Breathe. Maintain a certain rhythm in the blood.

Those first few days, Ellynor was ravenous. Marney brought enough food to feed three men, and Ellynor consumed it all. Marney brought more. Even so, Ellynor could feel herself burning quickly through all the fuel she supplied her body. There was so much need for warmth. Justin had lost a great deal of blood; he could not, on his own, generate enough heat to sustain his life.

So Ellynor fed him her own heat, poured the life and energy from her body into his. She could feel the difference in temperature between his skin and hers, for her fingers lay like slender icicles on his warm chest. She wrapped herself in two quilts, in three; she requested that Marney build up the fire even more; but she did not pull away from Justin. She did not conserve her strength. She flattened her hand with more pressure on his ribs, and she felt him steal away her energy.

And she was glad.

"Look at him—face all rosy," Marney murmured the afternoon of the third day. "He was so pale when you brought him in, too, I thought there was no way he—but there. You're looking awfully peaked, Ellynor, I wish you'd let me sit with him for a while."

Ellynor just shook her head. She knew that she was the only thing keeping Justin alive.

IN the middle of the night, after the third day, she felt the infection begin to build in his body.

She woke, suddenly too hot in her cocoon of blankets, to find that Justin's skin against her palm was warming of its own accord. So far, the fever was minor, but she needed to pay attention; she needed to change her strategy. She pulled the blankets off, one by one, and pushed them down to her feet or over the side of the bed to the floor. Then she turned on her side and snuggled back against Justin, testing the temperature of his body with her own.

She remained awake the rest of that long night, watchful and afraid to sleep. Sure enough, toward dawn his fever suddenly spiked; heat lanced through his bones. Ellynor shifted her hold, lay the whole length of her arm across his chest, hiked up the edge of her dress so that her bare leg pressed against his, flesh to flesh.

Then she used herself as a wick to draw the fever from his body into hers.

For the next day and a half, his temperature raged, dangerously high, but it never had a chance to harm him. Ellynor absorbed every extra degree. Her skin felt like it was burning, her mind grew jagged and incoherent, but she would not let go of Justin. She would not pull back. Marney came by almost every hour, worried and fussing, and Ellynor let the older woman do what nursing she would. She was sure Marney dusted Justin's infected wounds with some kind of herbal mix. She knew that, several times a day, Marney washed the faces and shoulders of both patients with cool water. Ellynor tried to drink when Marney held a glass to her mouth, but she had no interest in food. It would only make her hotter.

Now and then she caught snatches of whispered conversations. Marney and Faeber, perhaps, though she wasn't sure and didn't much care.

"He's still alive, though? Never would have thought it."

"Yes, but I think she's in danger now—can't explain how—body is hot, when he's the one who's infected—"

"Some kind of mystic? But that's—"

"Mustn't have guessed at the convent—"

"You think she could die?"

"I can't convince her to leave him. I'm afraid if I force her—"

"Don't want him to die, either—"

"Nothing to do but let her be."

Ellynor rested her hot cheek against Justin's shoulder and let her eyelids close, glad when the voices faded and the door shut again. A moment's tension had tightened her muscles, forced her eyes open, when she understood enough of the conversation to realize that her hosts were debating separating her from Justin. But no one had disturbed her; she decided hazily that no one would. *Nothing to do but let her be.* She was so tired. Time to sleep again.

THE fever broke about noon on the fifth day. Ellynor, drowsing beside Justin in the bed, felt it as a distinct sensation beneath her hand. One moment a spiraling crescendo of heat, coiling from his body directly into hers. The next, a film of sweat against her palm, a sudden shutdown of that overworked furnace. She lifted her head, though it made her senses swim, and tried to determine if this was good news or bad. Had Justin's body finally given out, succumbed, lost all power to fight? Did the drop in body temperature signal an even more dangerous stage?

But no. No. She could see the color in his face, paler than it should be but reassuringly normal. His breathing was even and, for the first time in days, completely untroubled. He shifted against her, something he had rarely done while they lay embraced, as if trying to get comfortable. As if trying to wake up. She watched his face eagerly, hoping his eyes would open, hoping he would try to talk, but he was not that far recovered. He gave a small sound, like a sigh, like a whisper of contentment, and fell asleep.

Ellynor realized that Justin's body was finally beginning to mend itself. It was as if she could feel the skeins of veins, the masses of muscle, shaking themselves free of lethargy and beginning to take stock. *Wound here. Bruise over there. Hard pressure on the lung. Knit this up. Disperse this clot. Cool down.* It was as if, beneath the stolid surface of the skin, a great invisible activity was under way. Justin was busy healing.

That was her cue to raise her hand, push herself away from him, set herself free. He would be like a ravening predator now; he would snatch up any source of nourishment. Hold soup or water to his mouth and he would gulp it down. Fan air in his direction and he would suck it into his lungs. All this time, she had forced her own energy into his body, but he was strong enough now to steal it for himself. And he would—he already was. She could feel the greedy pull of his wakened desire for life. Her fingers tingled as if blood was trickling from the tips. The sensation traveled through her palms, across her wrists, up toward her elbows. In the direction of her heart.

She could not pull away.

Exhausted, she lay back against him, her head on his pillow, her arm still draped across his chest. Let him have it all then. She would gladly give him her life. It was what she owed the goddess, anyway, for keeping Justin alive. She leaned forward just enough to kiss his cheek, and fell asleep with her head against his shoulder.

Two hours later, Ellynor was wakened by commotion in the hall. She was too tired to lift her head but she listened as closely as her dreamy state would allow. Voices—shouting—heavy footsteps on the stairs. Names she didn't recognize. Nothing to do with her.

The door burst backward and two women strode into the room.

Ellynor didn't have the strength to sit up or even feel astonished. She just slitted her eyes open and watched them march purposefully to the bed. One was tall and severe; she wore men's clothing and styled her white-blond hair very short. The other was smaller, golden, and beautiful, dressed in flowing blue. It was the golden woman who came close enough to lean over the bed, laying one hand on Ellynor's cheek and one on Justin's. She gave a small exclamation of dismay.

"Wild Mother watch me! She's completely drained. Another hour or two and I believe she'd be dead."

"What about Justin?"

"I'd need to do a more thorough exam, but from just a quick look I'd say he's mending. I can't feel a fever in him, at any rate."

"Cammon said he was out of danger."

"Well, Cammon didn't say anything about this one. Look at her, Sen—look at the way she's lying here—it's like she's transfusing him with her blood. Except there's no blood."

A momentary silence. "Yes, that's a Lirren trick," the white-haired woman said softly. "She must be one of Maara's healers."

"What?"

"Never mind. What do we do now? If Justin's well enough, I think we'd better separate them."

"I can stay with Justin, but, Senneth, I think she's in even worse shape than he is at the moment. Can you—?"

The other woman had a laugh in her voice, though nothing she said sounded funny to Ellynor. "Oh, I think I can. I don't think she'll enjoy it much, though."

"Let's get her into her own room first. Has Tayse calmed our hostess? I give her credit for trying to protect her patients most ferociously."

"I think she sent for her husband. I would guess that very soon Tayse will be pulling out his lions to reassure everyone."

Which, Ellynor thought mistily, made no sense at all. Lions? In a house? Who *were* these people? They knew Justin, though, that much seemed plain. Knew him and cared about him. Some of the burden was to be lifted from her.

Good. She was so tired. She could not carry it all by herself any longer.

The golden-haired woman was leaning over Ellynor now, very gently disentangling her fingers from their clutch on Justin's shirt. "Time to let go, I think," she said in a soothing voice. "You've done a most excellent job, but I'm a healer, too. I can take care of him now. You've kept him alive—let someone else do some of the work. Let go. That's right."

It felt so strange to release him. So odd to take a shallow breath, because she was only breathing for one. Her heart pattered too hard for a moment, not used to the easier task of driving only a single pulse. Her body felt light as one of those discarded quilts.

She might float up from the bed, disembodied as air. She could feel her hair spread out on the pillow, unwinding from the braid she'd made five days ago. It would dangle behind her as she drifted up toward the ceiling—and out the open window—

"*Sen!* Help her!"

Ridiculous. She didn't need help to float away. She tried to say so as the tall woman sat next to her on the bed, gathering Ellynor's hands in one of hers, laying her other hand right over Ellynor's heart. The golden girl moved away, circled around the bed to appear on Justin's other side.

The woman with white-blond hair bent over Ellynor, trying to catch her wandering attention. Her eyes were a strange color, ashy gray, serious. "This might feel uncomfortable," she said, and tightened her hold.

Fire arced through Ellynor's body in great rolling balls. She gasped and tried to scream, but her throat was raw, her voice burned away. Another shock of fire—another. She felt every artery, every hidden estuary of vein, run with an individual flame. The hair on her skin crackled and stood on end; her whole body flushed with heat. She had been languid before, exhausted, sucked clean. Now she was charged with adrenaline, a living conflagration.

"Who are—what did—*stop that!*" she gasped, and both of the women laughed.

"My name's Senneth. That's Kirra. We're friends of Justin's," the white-haired woman said. "Oh, and by the way. We're mystics."

Mystics. *Kirra.* Ellynor remembered that name. Her momentary stab of jealousy was replaced by a sense of profound relief that rolled over her like cooling water, extinguishing Senneth's sprays of flame. "Can you save Justin?" she whispered.

"You've already saved him," said the one called Kirra. Justin had said she was beautiful, but Ellynor hadn't envisioned anyone *quite* so attractive. "You're the one I'm worried about now."

"It doesn't matter about me," Ellynor said. She was feeling remarkably alive after those jolts of power from the mystic's hands, but she was still exhausted. She wanted to sit up, exclaim, check on Justin, get a better look at Kirra's face, but she couldn't. She wanted to close her eyes and sleep for a week.

"Oh, I'm guessing Justin believes it matters very much about you," Senneth said. "Stay here a moment. I'm going to see if I can find the room our hostess has set aside for you."

"I don't want a room," Ellynor said drowsily. "I don't want to leave Justin."

"He'll be here when you wake up," Senneth said. "I can't imagine, after all this, he'd leave *you* behind."

CHAPTER
31

IT was nighttime when Justin woke, opening his eyes to a sudden and complete sense of consciousness.

Nighttime. In a place he did not recognize. And great burning Mother, he felt like fifteen different kinds of hell.

It was instinct to attempt to piece together where he was and what had happened, all the while lying so still no one in the vicinity would realize he was awake. Softness below him—he was in a bed. Shapes arranged like doors and windows against the denser materials of walls—he was in a good-sized room. No shackles on his wrists. He was among friends.

So he was a guest in someone's house, and he must have come to rest here after the battle to end all battles, because he certainly recognized the feel of a sword wound and, holy Mother, there were dozens on his chest and arms.

And just like that, he remembered. The fight in the forest. The Lestra's men. Taking a blade through the ribs just as he lunged to cut the other man's throat. He had fallen to the ground knowing his wounds were most likely fatal, bitterly cursing himself for having failed Ellynor, who would come down this track in five days and find him missing—

That he still lived could only be attributable to magic. He squeezed his eyes shut, trying to remember anything that had happened since that fight in the forest. He had the sense that a good deal of time had passed—days, he hoped, instead of weeks—but he had only the most confused impressions of movement, voices, touch. A hand on his shoulder, a hand over his heart. That much he remembered. Whose hand? Ellynor's? How long had she tended him? Was she still here? Where was he?

Still not moving his head, he sent his gaze around the room. This wasn't his rented place in the boardinghouse, that much he was sure of. And he didn't think it was the interior of the convent, which Tayse had described as far more stark and severe. Had someone found his fallen body on the road and brought him back to safety? Was he in Neft?

Was somebody caring for him?

There was a chair next to the bed. He narrowed his gaze and strained to see. Yes, someone was sitting in the chair. A woman. It was impossible to see her clearly in the darkness, but he could make out a long tumble of hair, a silky sheen where her pale skirts were gathered around her knees.

"Ellynor?" he whispered, not daring to believe. He struggled to sit up—damn, that was painful—and succeeded in pushing himself onto his elbows. "Ellynor?"

The woman stirred and straightened, then leaned forward in her chair. He could tell before she spoke that she wasn't Ellynor, and a great blow of disappointment landed in his stomach.

"You're awake!" the woman exclaimed, and most of his disappointment evaporated.

"Kirra? What are you doing here?"

She bounced out of the chair and perched beside him on the bed, running her cool hands lightly over his face and shoulders. "Long story. Give me a minute. How do you feel? How's your breathing?"

"Hurt all over. Weak. Breathing's fine, though. Why? Did I get a sword through my lung?"

"Nicked the edge of it, from what I can tell. Though, really, you had so many wounds I haven't had time to catalog them all."

"What happened to me?"

She reached over to light a candle on the bedside table, then folded her hands in her lap and looked down at him. The single flame ran a loving glow down her golden hair, painted a saintly expression on her beautiful face. "What do you remember?"

"Fight against some convent guards in the woods. I think I killed them all, but some of them were pretty good. From what I remember of the last couple of blows, I could have died."

"Should have died," she said. "I've never seen anyone live when they had wounds like yours."

He was silent a moment, for that was a strange thing, to be told you had knocked on the door of death. "How did you find me in time?" he said. "I had no idea you were anywhere near Neft."

She was smiling now. So much for the pious expression; this look was pure Kirra. "But I wasn't," she said in a dulcet voice. "I'm not the one who saved your life."

He felt an emotion knock through him—hope or apprehension or something he couldn't identify. "Who did? What happened?"

"We're still piecing it together. And it's not entirely credible. But apparently the young woman you've grown so fond of—"

"Ellynor?" he said sharply. "She's mixed up in this?"

Kirra nodded. "Oh, yes. Apparently she found you on the trail, surrounded by corpses, and as close to death yourself as makes no difference. And she—I don't know what she did—she put a *spell* on you or something, and then came racing into town to find the man who lives here. Faeber? Is that his name?"

That made sense. So he was in Faeber's house. "I'd told her she could trust him if she ever needed help."

"So he got a wagon and drove out to pick you up, and they carried you back here. Where everyone expected you to expire at any minute. But you didn't die. Not from blood loss. Not from infection. Not from anything."

She waited, watching him expectantly. "Why didn't I die?" he asked, since she was obviously waiting for the question.

"I have no idea. Marney—Faeber's wife—says Ellynor wouldn't leave your side. Lay beside you on this bed for five days, her hand always touching you. Like she was feeding you with her own strength. I don't know how else to explain it. When I got here, Ellynor herself was practically a wraith. Like she'd given up every ounce of energy in her body. Given it to *you*."

He felt a sudden surge of fear that made him fight to sit up again. This time he succeeded. "Where is she? Is she all right? I didn't—I wouldn't— if something happens to her because of me—"

"Well, I think it was a pretty near run thing," Kirra admitted. "I think, as close to death as you had been at first, that's how close she was by the end. It was like she traded everything with you. Gave you her health while she took on your weakness. I can't imagine how she did that. I want to learn, though."

Who cared about mystics' tricks? "But is she all right?" he said impatiently. "Where is she? Can I see her?"

She leaned close enough to push him in the chest, and he collapsed back on the pillows. "She's sleeping. Senneth's with her. And you know Senneth can keep anybody alive."

That news made a small bright ball of happiness inside him. "Senneth's here?"

"Oh, we're *all* here. Tayse, Cammon, Donnal—all of us."

"Really? Why? For me? How'd you know I was hurt?"

She watched him a moment, grinning. "I'm just going to let you figure that out on your own."

It wasn't hard. "Cammon."

"Cammon, indeed. Clutches a hand to his heart, shrieks 'Justin!' and falls to the ground most dramatically. Got our attention, I assure you. We were a couple days outside of Ghosenhall, but we altered course and came flying down here so fast I feel like I must have left a hand or a foot behind on the road. At least a couple of pairs of shoes."

"When did you get here?"

"This afternoon."

"So it's been about five full days since I've been hurt. And I've done nothing but lie here this whole time?"

"Lie there and heal," she corrected.

"I need to get up." He lifted a hand and made a fist. No strength in his fingers. How long would it take before he'd be able to heft a sword? "I'm so weak."

"You will be for a while, I'd think," she agreed. "I can help you along a little, but your body will have to do some of the work itself."

He pushed the covers back. He was wearing some kind of long nightshirt, certainly not his own. Faeber's, maybe. Beneath it, his legs looked spindly and wasted. Bright Mother of the burning skies, his whole body flexed with pain when he swung his legs to the side of the bed and paused there, gathering his strength.

Kirra was watching closely. "You might want to wait till Tayse is around. He can help you up."

"Don't need Tayse's help to walk across the room," he said with a grunt.

"Well, if you fall over, *I* can't lift you."

"Guessing Donnal's right outside the room," he said. "But I'm not going to fall over."

She shrugged and stopped arguing; Kirra was never much of one for urging caution. She did come to her feet, though, ready to help him if she could. Justin braced his heels on the floor and then heaved himself up, feeling the shrieking protest of every half-healed wound. But he stood steady, once he got over the initial dizziness. As soon as he had readjusted to the sense of his own weight, he took a few careful steps, hands outstretched to grab at furniture if he needed to. But he felt stronger with each step, more sure of himself. He crossed to the wall and rested a moment before beginning the short journey back.

Just as he reached the bedpost, the door pushed open a few inches and a large black dog nosed in. "He's up," Kirra said to the dog, who came all the way into the room and flowed into the shape of Donnal. The mystic was smiling through his beard.

"Thought I heard voices," Donnal said. "How are you feeling?"

"Lucky."

Donnal nodded. "That seems to be the general opinion."

"And sore as hell." He paced slowly back toward the wall. It did not escape his attention that Donnal remained by the door, Kirra by the bed, both of them close enough to catch him if he fell.

"So tell us about these people whose house we're in," Kirra said. "They've been exceedingly gracious, but I can't think they're delighted to have so much company all at once, and so many of them at death's door."

Justin grinned as he shuffled back toward her. "He's magistrate of the town. Runs the civil guard, settles disputes. He made a point of getting to know me—I think he probably makes a point of getting to know any drifters who start to hang around."

"Did you tell him who you were?" Donnal asked.

He shook his head. "No. But I know he thought I was here for some purpose. And we had a couple of guarded conversations about the Daughters of the Pale Mother that led me to believe he didn't agree with the Lestra's persecution of mystics."

Kirra laughed. "Gods, let's hope not! With four of them in the house." She glanced at Donnal. "Five, I suppose. Including Ellynor."

"I had the feeling I could trust him, but—" He shrugged. "I suppose you don't ever know for certain till you put your trust to the test."

"Cammon likes him," Donnal said, grinning. "So Tayse told him the truth."

"About all of you being mystics?"

"I think he figured that out on his own," Kirra said dryly. "About the two of you being Riders."

Justin had paused with a hand on the bedpost. He was panting a little, but he was far from done with this simple exercise. By the stillness outside, he guessed it had to be an hour or two past midnight. An odd time for either rehabilitation or conversation, but Kirra and Donnal were both perfectly at ease. The shiftlings never seemed to adhere to ordinary rules for behavior.

"And how did Faeber take the news?" he wanted to know.

"Said, 'That explains a lot,'" Donnal replied. "I think he was referring to the five men dead on the road. That seems to be the thing that has impressed him the most. He kept saying, 'I didn't see how that could be possible.'"

"They came at us without a warning," Justin said. Once again, he was headed toward Donnal. "Didn't give us a chance to talk or argue. Jenkins—the man with me—didn't even have a weapon on him. They just slaughtered him. So I didn't hold back. I went for the killing blows. I knew they would cut me down if they got the chance." He touched the wall and glanced over at Donnal. "Any news in town about the dead soldiers? Anyone come looking?"

"Tayse got the story from Faeber, but I haven't heard all the details," Donnal said. "Apparently, convent guards *did* come to the city asking questions, but either there wasn't a house-to-house search or nobody thought to check Faeber's place. There was some talk that the reason your body hadn't been found was that it had been dragged off into the forest and eaten. Apparently predators had gotten a start on the others. And you got lucky again. Rained the day after your fight—a lot of tracks left on the forest trail, but none on the main road into Neft. No one could follow the wagon to this house, even if they suspected a wagon had come for you."

Justin grunted. "More magic from Ellynor's goddess, maybe."

"Who would that goddess be, do you know?" Kirra asked.

"The Dark Watcher. So she says."

He saw Kirra exchange a troubled glance with Donnal, but he didn't know how to read it. All she said was, "So how does she feel about the Pale Mother?"

He hadn't tried to make the trek back toward the bed yet; he just stood against the wall, resting. "She seems fond of the Silver Lady. I don't pretend to understand it. That's the goddess who seems to incite so much hatred, and Ellynor is not good at hate."

"Well, we'll have to ask her more when she's awake," Kirra said.

Justin nodded, took a breath, and headed for the door.

"Where are you going?" Kirra asked, alarmed. She was instantly beside him. Donnal had moved over just enough to block Justin's exit.

"I want to see her."

"I told you, she's sleeping. She's with Senneth. You can see her in the morning."

"I want to see her now. I just want to—I just want to be sure." He turned to give Kirra a look of open entreaty. There wasn't much light in the room, but enough for her to see the expression on his face. "You'd do it. You wouldn't let anyone keep you out of the room."

"Justin, you can hardly stay on your feet!" she exclaimed, but Donnal stepped aside. Justin gave him a nod of thanks and opened the door. The hallway was dark, and he didn't know this house, but he could see a stairway to his right and doors lined up down the hall to his left.

"The room next to yours," Donnal said, following him out and standing just a pace behind.

Justin ran one hand along the rough surface of the wall to help him keep his balance, but made it without trouble to the designated door. A soft knock, just to alert anyone who might be awake, and then he pushed the door open and went in.

A bed—a chair—a single candle—dark shadows of smaller furniture against the walls. Whoever was in the chair quickly stood up as Justin entered, but the shape under the covers on the bed did not move.

Ellynor. Ellynor lying there, her dark patterned hair spread out over the white pillows, her delicate face pale even by insufficient light. Her eyelids closed. Her hands lax on the quilt. Not appearing to move at all.

He had taken three steps toward the bed before he realized it was Senneth who had risen from the chair and intercepted him in the middle of the room. "Justin!" she whispered. "What are you doing up?"

She caught him by both arms and held him in place. He felt the heat from her hands burn through the thin cotton of his nightshirt. She was about as tall as he was and, at the moment, stronger; he could not push past her.

"I wanted to see her," he replied. He craned his neck to see past Senneth's shoulder. The blankets rose and fell in a slight but rhythmic pattern.

A strangled laugh from Senneth, and then she shook him, hard enough to make his head wobble. "I'm so glad you're awake and coherent, but, Justin, you need to lie back down. I'll take care of Ellynor. She'll be fine. You can visit her in the morning."

"Has she woken up yet? Said anything?" Kirra asked from behind him, and he realized she had followed him into the room.

"Twice. Just long enough to eat something and ask after Justin." She smiled at him, and he could see, beneath her concern, a genuine delight that he was recovered enough to be up and strolling around. "I told her he was growing stronger with every passing hour. It calmed her enough to let her go back to sleep."

"She'll be all right, though? She won't—she won't die?"

Senneth's hands tightened on his arms with enough pressure to force his attention back to her face. Her expression was serious; she was clearly willing him to believe. "No. Justin. She won't die. I'm here. I'll take care of her. You have to trust me."

"I do trust you," he said, his voice almost a whisper. "But Senneth— Ellynor. She—she doesn't know you. I don't want her to be afraid."

Senneth put one warm hand up to his cheek and smiled at him tenderly. "She's not afraid, Justin. When she heard you were going to live, I think her last fear disappeared. Now you go on. Go back to bed and sleep. You want to be well enough to come see her in the morning."

"Will she be awake then? Will she be feeling better?"

Senneth smiled. "She'll probably be stronger than you."

"Is that a challenge?" Kirra inquired. "Is that an insult to my magic? Come here, gutter boy! Let me see if I can get you returned to a state of glowing health by morning."

Senneth dropped her hands but gave him a little push toward the door. "Go. Let Kirra do her work. Get some sleep. I'll watch over Ellynor till morning."

CHAPTER 32

THE next day, Justin woke feeling sore, ravenous, and edgy. He threw back the covers and came to his feet before he'd even glanced over to see if Kirra was still in the chair, guarding him. No—it was empty. A good sign, he thought. She didn't think he was weak enough to require constant scrutiny. He balled his hands up and bounced on his feet, feeling exponentially better than he had the night before. She must, indeed, have poured more magic into his veins while he slept. He knew enough about sword wounds to know they did not improve this rapidly on their own.

Still, he was far from whole. His muscles responded slowly when he mimed a quick grab at an imaginary weapon. Even cautious steps across the room woke pain in his chest, his shoulders, his legs. Not unendurable pain, though. He lengthened his stride, punching at the air as he walked. He would not be up to fighting strength for weeks.

Days, maybe, if Kirra continued to heal him.

The door opened quietly and Cammon's head appeared. He smiled broadly when he saw Justin was up and came all the way inside. "You look much better! How do you feel?"

"Not so good now, but like I'll mend pretty well," Justin said. He crossed over to clout Cammon affectionately on the shoulder. "How can you do tricks like that? Feel me get sliced by a sword from a couple hundred miles away? How can anybody do that?"

Cammon shrugged. "I just can. Lucky for *you*."

Justin grinned. "No end of luck this trip out, it seems."

"Are you hungry? I brought you food."

"Starving. Bring it right in."

They sat at a small table and ate from the same platter, though Cammon let Justin consume most of the items on the tray. Justin was only halfway through when other visitors started arriving. Tayse was the first to step through the door, moving silently on his big feet and coming to stand beside them. Even through his slight smile, the Rider's dark face looked deeply serious.

"It would have been a grievous day if we had lost you," Tayse said. "The king and all the Riders would have mourned."

Justin swallowed and pushed aside his tray. He came to his feet with much less effort this time. "I almost managed it," he said. "Five was too many."

"You did manage it," Tayse said. "You survived and they did not."

"Well, he survived because someone helped him," Cammon pointed out.

Tayse turned that sober look on Cammon. "And someone helped him because he has the ability to make friends," Tayse said. "That's a weapon as valuable as any blade."

Justin laughed. "No need to lecture Cammon," he said. "He already has that weapon."

"True." Tayse returned his attention to Justin. "Kirra said you would be much improved this morning. And are you?"

Justin nodded. "Weak, though. I need to get to a training yard and see how heavy my sword has become."

Another faint smile for that. "I think your friend would allow us the use of his barn, perhaps. It doesn't seem wise to parade you in public much."

"So no one knows I've survived?"

"No one except the people in this house."

"What about Delz?" Seeing the question on Tayse's face, Justin added, "The man who owns the stables. Where I worked."

"Oh, he thinks you're dead," Cammon said. "After we found you here, Donnal and I went over there and pretended to be looking for you. We wanted to see if he knew anything about the fight, but he seemed completely at a loss. Worried about you, though."

"I hate to have him thinking I ran off on him. Or really am dead," Justin said.

"Perhaps you can swing by and tell him a little of your story before we leave," Tayse said. "But as I don't particularly want to engage in a pitched battle with every soldier recruited to the Lumanen Convent, especially when my own troops are limited in number, I think we'd better keep your survival a secret for now."

Before we leave . . . "How long before we head out?" Justin asked, trying to sound nonchalant. So much still undone here! How could he head back to Ghosenhall? Ellynor was safely out of the convent, but he was far from certain she was willing to leave behind her family—her entire existence—to follow Justin to the royal city. She still didn't even know who he *was*, not really. There was so much they hadn't discussed.

Secrets on her side as well as his.

Tayse was answering the question. "A few more days, I'd think. You have to be well enough to travel, and I'd like you to be well enough to hold a sword. But that might take longer than we can wait."

"I'll be holding a sword by tomorrow," Justin said. "Whether or not I'll be able to do any damage with it—well, we'll find out then."

"What about Ellynor?" Cammon piped up. "What happens to her?"

Tayse was silent. Justin felt his tension go up a notch. "I don't know," he said to Cammon. "I suppose that depends on what Ellynor wants."

"And if we can give her what she wants," Tayse said.

What did that mean? "I'm going to talk to her this morning," Justin said.

Tayse nodded gravely. "Senneth says she's much stronger today. I'm sure she is most anxious to see you as well."

"You might want a bath first," Cammon suggested. "And different clothes."

Both the Riders laughed at that. "I don't suppose you can fetch my own clothes from the boardinghouse," Justin said ruefully.

"Our host said you could borrow something from one of his sons," Tayse said. "But I don't see why Cammon couldn't collect your belongings. That's a good idea."

Cammon was on his feet. "And I'll tell Marney to send up some water," he said, ducking out the door.

"Who's Marney?" Justin asked. "Faeber's wife?"

"Yes. We'll have to make sure Baryn rewards the two of them most generously for all the assistance they've given you."

"If he's rewarding people, he should give Ellynor a hatful of gold."

Tayse said nothing.

"What's happened?" Justin asked outright. "You don't like her. You haven't said so, but I can tell there's something wrong."

Tayse's face grew even more closed. "I think we all owe her a debt too great to repay. But I find myself thinking you wouldn't even have been attacked if you hadn't gone to the convent to see her. She's the reason you drew attention."

Justin was suddenly furious. "And I'd go back tomorrow to see her if that was the only way," he said instantly.

Tayse nodded. "That's what worries me."

"You can't tell me—you wouldn't tell me—not to see her again."

"I wouldn't," Tayse said. "Save your anger. It is just that if I had to pick one of you to protect, you or Ellynor, I would always choose you. I would rather you fell in love with someone who only put your heart in danger, not your life."

Some of Justin's anger faded. "Well, she's out of the convent now," he said.

Tayse nodded. "I wish I could believe that meant she was entirely safe. For you."

Before Justin could answer that, or even demand to know what it meant, the door opened yet again. This time it was an older woman superintending two young men, who looked enough like Faeber to be his sons. All were laden with large buckets of steaming water. One of them went back out in the hallway and returned with a small metal tub.

"Oh, you do look better," the woman greeted Justin, coming over to inspect him. She was middle-aged and brisk, her face lined with kindness. Just the sort of woman he would picture as Faeber's wife. "I'm Marney, you know. That nice young man said you wanted a bath."

Tayse nodded at Marney and glanced at Justin. "My signal to leave, I believe," he said. "I'll come back later." In a moment, he was gone.

Justin felt some embarrassment at the thought that this woman had probably been the one to strip him out of his own clothes and dress him in this borrowed nightshirt. He didn't have Cammon's easy charm, but he tried a smile and a tone of gratitude. "It seems I have a lot to thank you for," he said. "You can't have expected all the trouble that's come down on your house. Taking care of me—and Ellynor—and now all my friends are here—"

Marney brushed this off as if she was used to turmoil and high drama. "I'm glad she thought to bring you to us. I think my husband was pleased that you actually trusted him enough to come here. He said he could never entirely read you." She tilted her head and surveyed him. "You're much bigger than I would have thought when you were just lying there," she said. "Bulky. I think my oldest son's shirts will fit you, though. Not sure about the trousers."

That made him laugh. "Cammon's going to fetch my things from my rented room. I have a couple of changes of clothes."

"Good. Well, here's a towel and some soap. I don't imagine you'll need any help, but if you slip and fall—should I wait outside the door?"

"No. Thank you. No."

She grinned and headed for the door, shooing her sons before her. "Let me know if there's anything you need. You've had breakfast, I see.

Come downstairs for your next meal. Then we'll see how you're really doing."

Finally. Alone, naked, and stepping into the warm bath. Justin cursed as the heated water burned along every half-open sore. The tub was too small to contain his whole body, so he crouched and splashed as efficiently as possible, working to get loose the dried blood as well as the sweat and grime. A hand across his face made him realize he badly needed a shave. Would Ellynor recognize him with stubble?

But Cammon brought his razor along with his spare clothes. Justin had to tighten his belt a notch to keep his trousers on. Weight loss, muscle loss—it would take him appreciable time to recover from this encounter. A quick shave, a careless comb through the hair, a brief look at himself in the small mirror over the dresser. His face looked paler and rather more angular than usual; the eyes had a certain haunted look. He couldn't imagine how anyone could enjoy a personal inspection in a mirror on a daily basis. Well, maybe someone who looked like Kirra.

"Going to see Ellynor?" Cammon inquired when he was done.

Justin gave him a look of exasperation. "Yes. Go away."

"Want me to get Senneth out of the room first?"

Justin paused at the door. "*Yes.*"

Cammon grinned and brushed by him. "Give me five minutes."

Justin waited for the required time, listening to the sounds down the hallway. Voices drifting up from the first story, clinks and thuds that sounded like someone was rearranging furniture, then the closer noises of Senneth and Cammon talking in the hallway and disappearing down the stairs. Justin took a deep breath, stepped out of his room, down the hall, and into the room next door.

Ellynor was standing at the window, her hand resting on the sill, and she gazed down at the streets of Neft as if fascinated by a pageant of color and motion. Her long hair was unbound down her back and looked half-damp, as if she too had taken the time to bathe this morning, to present herself clean and new to the waiting world. The pale design worked into the hair now started around her shoulders; it must have been some time since she had had it renewed by her cousin's hands.

She looked so small. So frail. How could she have had the strength to snatch him back from the precipice of death?

"Ellynor," he said.

She started and whirled around. He would never forget the expression her face showed him then—purest joy at his presence, at his mere existence. She flew across the room and flung herself into his arms, but she was so light she could not overmatch even his precarious balance, and he took her in a hold hard enough to make her gasp. "Justin, Justin, *Justin*," she recited. "I thought you were *dead*! I thought they had killed you! Oh, Justin, I am so glad to see you!"

He demonstrated his own corresponding gladness with a kiss that left them both light-headed. Maybe it was the exultation, maybe it was the physical weakness, but when he set her down, they were both unsteady on their feet. They clung to each other as they navigated the floor and collapsed in the big chair that Senneth had been using the night before. Plenty of room for two. Justin merely pulled her onto his lap and held her as tightly as he could. Ellynor's arms were around his neck; she kissed his mouth, his cheeks, his hair, his forehead.

"I am so glad you're alive," she whispered.

"Only because of you," he whispered back between kisses. "They told me—you saved me. Nobody believed—I could survive. You must—have magic after all."

That caught her attention. She leaned back, not too far, and gazed down at him. "Justin, your friends are here! The mystics! How did they find you? Senneth is the only one I've really talked to, but she's extraordinary. No wonder the Lestra hates mystics if they're all as powerful as she is."

He grinned. "Well, Senneth's exceptional. But she's the one Coralinda hates most. And they found me because Cammon—have you met Cammon?—he could tell I was in trouble. But I don't want to talk about them. I want to talk about you. They said *you* almost died saving *me*. Are you truly recovered now? Because if you are, I'm going to shake you and tell you never, *never*, do that again. Never risk yourself for someone else—not for me, not for anybody."

She kissed him quickly on the mouth, which he supposed was answer enough. "I've been a healer most of my life, but I never lost so much of myself to someone else," she said seriously. "I didn't expect it to happen that way. But I'd do it again if I thought it would save your life. I was so afraid for you."

An opening not to be missed. "And now you know how I've been feeling this whole time you've been at the convent," he said. "Afraid for you and willing to do anything to save you. Now that you're out—"

"Oh, I'm not going back, if that's what you're about to ask me," she said. "I can't imagine what they think! After I disappeared like that—the same day the soldiers were killed—there would be so many questions.

And you know I wanted to leave anyway. So you don't have to worry about me anymore."

"But I do," he said. "Where will you go next? Tell me your plans."

She was silent a moment. "I'm going to write my family. And I'm going to ask Faeber—who is the kindest man!—if I can stay here till my father or my brothers arrive. They won't be happy that Rosurie has been left behind, but once I explain it to them—well. They'll see I had no choice."

"You do have a choice," he said in a very low voice. "You can come with me to Ghosenhall."

She smiled at him, but he couldn't help feeling the expression was sad. It worried him; something about this conversation was going to break his heart. "Is that where you belong? Ghosenhall?"

"Time for telling secrets," he said. "I'll start. Yes, I belong in the royal city. I'm a King's Rider." The expression on her face didn't change; wherever she lived, it was someplace they had never heard of King's Riders. "I'm part of a specially picked, specially trained guard dedicated to the service of King Baryn. I've been in Neft to spy on the Lumanen Convent—to try and see if the Lestra is plotting against the king."

"And you think she is."

"Pretty sure."

Ellynor nodded. "Now and then she would say things like, 'When Daughters rule the country of Gillengaria, all this will be changed.' I thought she just meant, you know, when the doctrine had spread from the convent to the rest of the kingdom. But I think you're right. She's more ambitious than that."

At the moment, he almost didn't care what plans Coralinda Gisseltess was making. "I have to go back to Ghosenhall with the others," he said. "Will you come with me? I never thought I was the kind of man who would marry, but I—"

She stopped him with a finger on his mouth and that sad smile on her own. For a moment, he thought she might start crying. "I can't," she said. "I can't marry anyone my family does not approve of—and they will never approve of you."

He pulled his head back and her hand fell to her lap. "They will! The king himself will vouch for me! And if it's a dower gift they want, well, I don't have much saved, but I know I can acquire enough gold—"

"Justin. No. Not money. No. It's just—my family—they don't allow—women never marry outside the *sebahta-ris*."

The phrase was vaguely familiar; had Senneth used it once? But he said, "What's that? I don't know that word."

"I come from the Lirrens," she whispered. "The land across the mountains. Maybe you don't know much about our customs—nobody in Gillengaria seems to. But women never marry where the families do not approve. If they try—"

"Their fathers and brothers come and duel with that man to the death," Justin said grimly. "Senneth told that story once. I had no reason to pay attention, but that stuck in my mind. I remember thinking, 'No one would fight me to *my* death. I could win any woman I wanted.'"

She put her hands on his cheeks. Now her tears were overflowing, but she kept talking as if she didn't even notice them. "But you couldn't, Justin, don't you see? I love you. But I could not bear it if you killed Torrin or Hayden or my father. I couldn't bear it. I would give you up before I saw them murdered at your hands."

He shook his head, carefully enough so that he did not dislodge her fingers. "They wouldn't be. Ellynor, I'm good enough *not* to kill someone even if he's trying to kill me. I could disable your father or your brother. I could win the fight and walk away."

"And they would send someone else after you, and someone else! Do you think no desperate lovers have ever thought to try that trick before? Someone I love will end up dead unless I give you up! And I cannot bear that! I cannot have such bloodshed on my conscience!"

"It's not on yours! It should be on theirs!" he returned with heat. "What kind of cruel *family* forces women to make such a choice? Why don't all the Lirren women band together and choose unapproved lovers, one right after the other, until all their brothers are dead or starting to reconsider? I guarantee you that you'd see some old traditions fade fast if enough corpses were piled up."

Almost, she was laughing through her tears. "Maybe, but you don't understand! We have been raised—we have always been—Justin, my family is my heart. My core. Until I came to the convent, I couldn't even guess how I could live any other life. I cannot undo the love I have for my family, unkind and wrongheaded though they may be. And I cannot see you slaughter them, any one of them." She leaned her forehead against his. Her hands were still against his cheeks, and it was as if their faces were behind a screen, as if their words would be uttered in absolute secret. She whispered, "Justin, I have to give you up."

He was silent a moment, trying to work it out. It would be two months, perhaps, before he was back to his normal strength, and then there would be the time spent on the travel itself. Tayse wouldn't like it, of course, but he didn't much care, at this point, what Tayse's opinion might be. He could probably convince Cammon to come with him—he would need someone with extraordinary skills to help him cross unfamiliar territory and guide him through unexpected dangers. "I have to go to Ghosenhall," he said. "There will be reports to make, and maybe another commission to handle for the king. Look for me in the Lirrens in three months' time. You can give me directions to your family's place, or not, as you choose—I will find you one way or another. And then I will negotiate with your father, or face him in battle, whatever he wishes. I am not willing to give you up."

"You can't come to the Lirrens looking for me!"

"Well, I will. I walked through the gate at the Lumanen Convent to see you, and I will cross the Lireth Mountains to find you again."

"Justin," she whispered. *"You will be killed."*

He shrugged. "Then maybe you shouldn't have saved me after all. If I was only going to die for you."

Now she grew a little frantic. She pulled her head away, she dropped her hands to his shoulders and gave him as much of a shake as her strength and his size would allow. "And you don't care that it will break my heart? You don't care that if you die, part of me dies, too? Justin, I love you! I love you enough to never see you again! Please don't make me go through the rest of my life knowing you are dead because of me."

"Please don't make me go through the rest of my life without you," he replied.

Now she did start crying, breaking into tearing sobs and beating her small fists against his chest. She tried to pull away from him, escape from his embrace, but he held her more tightly, refusing to release her. "I love you," he said, over and over, as she shook her head and pushed against his shoulders and begged him to let her go.

Into this scene of panic and despair Senneth came calmly walking. Justin didn't even realize she was in the room until she stood right beside the chair, observing them with her thoughtful gray eyes.

"I see Ellynor has told you her secret," the mystic said.

Justin gathered Ellynor even closer, mostly to stop her struggles enough for him to carry on a conversation. "Senneth! Did you know? She's from the Lirrens!"

Senneth nodded. "I knew as soon as you described her to me, that first time we passed through Neft. Her hair. A Lirren style."

Ellynor managed to turn in Justin's arms, though she could not break his hold. "Senneth," she begged. "Please. You're his friend. Tell him. He will die if he comes to the Lirrens to find me. He must let me end this here."

They were both addressing Senneth. "I won't give her up," he said fiercely. "You can't convince me, and Tayse can't force me."

Senneth settled on the edge of the bed, facing them. Her expression remained tranquil as always. "I think there is another option," she said. "I have talked to Ellynor's father."

CHAPTER
33

At the mystic's words, Ellynor started so hard that she almost broke Justin's grip. Not quite—she knew that would require more strength than she possessed—and the Great Mother knew Ellynor wanted him to hold her forever. But Senneth's pronouncement made her whirl around in Justin's arms and stare at this strange, serene, powerful woman in hope and awe.

"You have talked to my *father?*" she repeated. "When? Why? How did you know—why would you think—I don't understand."

Senneth nodded. "Six or seven weeks ago. Justin mentioned meeting you." The mystic smiled. "Well, he did more than mention you. He was clearly becoming very attached to you. And I was alarmed, because I had guessed you were a woman of the Lirrens. I have lived across the Lireth Mountains. And I knew how badly your story must end if, indeed, he loved you and you loved him in return."

"You lived in the Lirrens?" Ellynor repeated. "With a *sebahta?*"

"I am an adopted daughter of Ammet Persal. I lived with his family for more than a year."

It took Ellynor only a moment to trace the connection. "We are kin," she said.

Senneth nodded again. "We are indeed kin. A fact I made plain to your father and brothers."

Ellynor sat up even straighter. "You met all of them? Were you across the mountains?"

"No, I had gone to Coravann to speak with the marlord, and your family happened to be present. I met your uncle and one of your cousins as well."

This was more and more bewildering. "And you talked about me?"

Senneth laughed. "Well, not at first. We talked about the *sebahta*. We talked about the king. We talked about the war that may be coming very soon to Gillengaria. And then I invited Torrin to a duel."

"You fought with *Torrin*? That was brave!" Ellynor paused to give Senneth a doubtful inspection. "I can't believe he would agree to take up arms against a woman. It's not very honorable."

Senneth was smiling. "I goaded him into it, I'm afraid. Insisting I could beat him."

"Well, you can't," Ellynor said.

"But I did," was the mild reply.

There was a moment's silence while Ellynor absorbed this shocking fact. She could feel Justin shift and lean forward as if he had suddenly become very interested in the conversation. "Torrin's the one, isn't he?" Justin asked from over her shoulder. "The one who'd be most likely to meet me in a fight for Ellynor."

"That's what I guessed," Senneth said.

"Yes," Ellynor said, wonderingly. "But no one ever defeats Torrin. I don't think he's ever lost a fight."

"I told him I had been training with the King's Riders, who are legendary in Gillengaria."

"You told him you had just dueled with *me* and you had lost," Justin said.

Senneth laughed aloud at that. "In fact, that's exactly what I said."

"*That's* why you pushed for a fight that night!" Justin exclaimed. "It was so strange. One minute we were talking about Ellynor, and the next minute you were telling me you thought you could defeat me. You knew then—you were *planning* to challenge one of Ellynor's champions to a fight." He stopped. "But how did you know—I mean, you didn't even know her family name, did you? Why would you think you'd find her relatives in Coravann?"

Senneth sighed and leaned back on the bed. "Last summer. When we were at Coravann Keep. Some of Heffel's Lirren relatives were there and I had a chance to talk to them. They told me about the two daughters of the Lahja *sebahta-ris* who had been sent to the Lumanen Convent. So I knew that Ellynor was in some way related to Heffel, and that any Lirrenfolk who might be in Coravann were likely to be kin to her in some way. It was extreme luck that her father and brothers were the ones who were present."

Ellynor shook her head, still amazed at the tale but unable to see how it changed anything. "So you defeated Torrin in battle. And you told him that somewhere there was a man, a King's Rider, who could defeat *you*, so that Torrin would have no hope of standing against him. That doesn't mean that my brother threw down his weapon and said, 'Fine. I will not fight for the honor of my sister.'"

"Maybe not, but it will make him think hard when I come calling," Justin said, sounding excited. "If, going into a battle, he knows that I will win, perhaps he will choose not to fight."

"You don't know Torrin." She looked at Senneth more closely. "But did you even mention my name? After you dueled with him? You had never met me! What could you possibly say?"

"It was more complicated than that," Senneth said. She pulled over one of the bed pillows and propped it under her ribs as she turned onto her side. "Next, I had Tayse duel with Hayden. Well, Tayse is even better than Justin, so you can guess who won that round. Then we talked at length about the Riders, their strength, their skill, their status throughout the kingdom. You can imagine that by the end of it Torrin was considering crossing the Lireth Mountains to try for a position in the king's guard."

Ellynor could hear the grin in Justin's voice. "I wonder what Tayse thought of all this."

"Oh, he thought I was merely recruiting—as, to some extent, I was. I would like to see the king's army swelled by a few hundred Lirren men, who are fierce and fearless fighters. I didn't talk about Ellynor until I was alone with Torrin, Hayden, and Wynlo."

"Who?"

"My father," Ellynor answered.

"I told them that one of the Lirren girls at the convent—pretending I did not know which one!—had been befriended by a King's Rider after she had been assaulted on the street. I might have embellished the story a little, but I certainly made Justin seem heroic. And honorable. The sort of man any member of the *sebahta* would be proud to call kin."

Ellynor felt her mouth fall open. "You didn't."

"I did. Torrin himself said it. 'I would like to have such a man as cousin.' Those were his very words."

"But not, 'I would like to have such a man marry my sister!'" Ellynor retorted.

"Not quite," Senneth admitted. "But we talked literally through the night. Very delicately. About what might happen if a King's Rider came courting a Lirren girl. What kind of reception he could expect. Whether it would ever be acceptable to permit a Lirren girl to marry such a man."

"I can't believe this," Ellynor said. She was feeling a little faint.

"Your father was, at first, very much against the idea," Senneth continued. "And he called your uncle in to confer. Torrin and Hayden thought it might be acceptable if a family could be found to adopt this Rider. I said—"

"I'm willing to be adopted by anybody," Justin interrupted. "Who do I talk to? What do I have to do?"

"I said I thought the Persals would be willing to adopt him, but your uncle didn't like the idea. He said such a thing would only be acceptable if the woman in question were to become *bahta-lo*."

There was another moment's silence while Ellynor absorbed that news and Justin waited for someone to explain. "What's that?" he asked finally. "What does it mean? Does it involve anyone hurting Ellynor? Because if it does—"

"No," Ellynor said slowly. "It involves—it means, basically, that I'm no longer part of the clan. I'm separate. I can return, I am not ostracized, but I am not part of the rituals. Not part of the daily life. I am outside the *sebahta-ris*."

"And that might be a sacrifice too great for you to make," Senneth said quietly. "But it was a solution that appealed to the men of your family. They all were willing to accept it. Even Torrin said, 'If my sister or my cousin were *bahta-lo*, then I would allow one of these King's Riders to cross the Lireth Mountains and expect no harm from me.' He said that, Ellynor. Those very words."

For a moment she could not breathe; the implications were too vast. Then she realized that Justin's arms had tightened around her waist so much that she simply could not draw in air. "I can't—it's almost too much to take in," she said, and her voice sounded dazed and dizzy. "All this time—I have been thinking—there is no hope. And now there's hope, and I—I can't—the idea is too big. I can be with Justin if I become *bahta-lo*. Two things I have never considered as possibilities before."

Senneth pushed herself upright and then came to her feet. "If you want, I can make Justin leave the room right now, so you can think things through without him nearby." She smiled. "I'm sure he's a powerful distraction."

"I'm not leaving," Justin said immediately. "And you're not big enough to throw me out."

"I'll get Tayse, if you don't behave," she said, gently teasing. "He's certainly big enough. Or Donnal will come in here, shaped like a bear, and drag you from the room." She grew quickly serious. "Give the girl time to think, Justin. Don't pressure her into any decision she will later regret."

"I won't. I just want to talk to her."

Senneth looked at Ellynor, a question in her gray eyes. Ellynor nodded. "Let him stay. But—thank you. Thank you so much. I can't believe—you're a stranger to me—I can't believe that you would go to such trouble to make me happy—"

"I did it for Justin, at the time," Senneth replied softly. "I love him, too. But now that I know you, I can only say I'm glad for your sake as well." She leaned down and, unexpectedly, kissed Ellynor on the cheek. Her mouth left a warm imprint behind. "Be kind to each other," she said, and left the room.

Ellynor and Justin sat in silence for a few moments, though she could feel him forcibly restraining his eager questions. She was still on his lap, still with his arms around her waist, but she sat bolt upright, tense, her mind barraged with darting thoughts. *Bahta-lo!* She had only known two other women with that designation. One had left the Lirrens and gone to live in Gillengaria. The other was a strange, solitary, but peculiarly gifted old woman who had the knack of appearing at whatever house was in most dire need of a healer. If a fever had swept through a whole family, she could be found on the doorstep the next day. If there was a feud between *sebahta*, and the wounded lay dying in the fields, she would suddenly be seen kneeling beside first one fallen body, then another. She was one of Maara's daughters; everyone knew that. It was said she could cure anyone, as long as she arrived before the patient had drawn his last breath.

She is probably a mystic, too, Ellynor realized suddenly. *No doubt all the most gifted healers in the* sebahta *are.*

That was a comforting thought—that if she accepted the role of *bahta-lo,* she would only be answering to the call of magic in her blood. Doing what any mystic might be expected to do.

But to leave the *sebahta-ris* behind—! To follow Justin to Ghosenhall, to live among strangers, to give up the daily and seasonal pleasures of her familiar life and learn new rituals, new feasts, new customs. Her heart grew fragile at the very thought; again, it was hard to catch her breath. They were her family and she missed them so much already. . . .

But you have been glad to be gone from them, a small voice inside her head reminded her. *You have been delighted to walk the streets of Neft unaccompanied. And you have been fascinated by the prayers and songs and routines at the convent. If you had not grown afraid, you would be happy at the convent even now. Happier still in Neft, even if you had never met Justin. You have always longed to see the world across the Lireth Mountains. Now is your chance.*

Your chance to see that world—and your chance to have Justin in your life forever.

He clearly couldn't stand it any longer. He pulled her closer and kissed the underside of her jaw, since her head was still turned away from him. "What are you thinking?" he whispered. "Am I in your thoughts?"

She shifted on his legs, put her arms around his neck, rested her cheek against his. She could still feel the heat of Senneth's kiss, and now it lay between them, like a seal or a brand. "You are always in my thoughts," she whispered back. "Since the day I met you. You have taken up residence at the back of my mind, and you share every day with me, whether I see you or not. I have not believed there was any course that would let me live my life alongside you. I have not been able to see my way clear to happiness. Now a way is opened, and I know I will take it, but you have to give me a little time to prepare myself. To inhale a deep breath as I take that first step through the woods on a path I never expected to find. Maybe through a different forest altogether. I am happy, but I am a little afraid."

"I love you," he said. As if it was the only answer.

Maybe it was. She breathed the words against his skin. "I love you, too."

THEY talked and schemed and whispered until, suddenly, all the strength drained from Ellynor's body. She nearly fainted against Justin's chest. "Are you sick? Should I call someone?" he demanded fearfully, rising and carrying her to the bed.

"No—just tired." So tired. Exhausted by fear and hope and happiness. When she closed her eyes, she felt the room whirl about her, even after Justin had laid her carefully on the mattress.

"I'm getting Senneth," he said.

"Don't worry," was her drowsy response. "I'll be fine."

She didn't even hear him leave the room. She was asleep before the door opened and shut.

When she woke, the square of sunlight admitted by the window had shifted from the floor to the wall. Several hours must have passed; it was late afternoon or almost night. Ellynor stirred on the bed, feeling remarkably well, then opened her eyes and sat up.

It wasn't a surprise to glance over and find someone waiting in the chair beside the bed. The surprise was the person who occupied it. Not Senneth or Justin, but the golden-haired woman called Kirra.

The *beautiful* golden-haired woman.

Ellynor hastily pushed herself to a more upright position and tried to strangle her quick surge of jealousy. Justin was not promising to cross mountains and fight off defenders on *Kirra's* behalf. It was Ellynor he loved, and she believed that absolutely. Still, this woman had come running across half of Gillengaria at the news that Justin was injured. She had sat beside him, finishing the job of healing that Ellynor had only started. She must care about him a little bit. And any man with eyes in his head would certainly feel something for *her*.

Jealousy didn't seem to be on Kirra's mind, though, for her smile was quite friendly. "You're awake!" the other woman exclaimed, bending forward. "How do you feel? Justin came racing downstairs to find me, telling me you'd fainted. I think you must be weaker than you realize."

"I'm exhausted," Ellynor admitted. "Though I feel better now that I've rested."

A faint look of satisfaction crossed the perfect features. "And now that you've had a touch of magic," Kirra replied. "I'm not like Senneth! I can do a little healing without making someone feel like her skin is on fire. Much more subtle, don't you think?"

Ellynor forced a smile. "Indeed. Thank you so much."

"But I have to say I envy *your* power," Kirra went on heedlessly. "When you're stronger, maybe you can explain what you do. I'm only guessing, but it seemed like you were actually entwining yourself with Justin. Making yourselves almost one body. Could I learn to do that?"

Ellynor was at a loss. "I don't know. I don't think—I mean, nobody ever showed me. It was just something I knew how to do." She shrugged.

"Yes, and I didn't realize magic could be taught, either, until Senneth and some of my other tutors came along," Kirra replied. "And Cammon's learning all sorts of tricks from mystics in the city. Think about what you do and then see if you can describe it. I'll bet you can tell me enough to help me figure it out."

That sounded like they were going to be spending lots of time together, sharing secrets, close as sisters. Ellynor couldn't imagine it. "I'll try," she said politely. "Will you be returning to Ghosenhall with everyone else?" She didn't say "with us," because she wasn't sure yet of her own destination. Justin wanted Ellynor to accompany the others back to the royal city. She wanted him to come with her to the Lirrens first. He was willing, but needed to clear his schedule with Tayse first.

Kirra leaned back in the chair, wholly at ease. She seemed like the kind of woman who was never uncomfortable. "I haven't decided yet," she said. "My sister might need me back in Danalustrous—she's planning a wedding—but it's been a few weeks since I've seen the king. Senneth says I should return to Ghosenhall just for courtesy's sake."

Ellynor couldn't think of anything to say in answer to that, so she just offered another polite smile. Kirra tilted her head to one side and studied her, making no attempt to be surreptitious about it.

"You're not at all what I would have expected," Kirra said abruptly. "If I were fashioning a woman designed to appeal to Justin? It never would have been you."

That was so rude that Ellynor merely opened her mouth and stared back.

"Why is it that all the big men always fall for the dainty girls?" the mystic added, sounding aggrieved. "The taller the man, the tinier the woman he wants. Have you ever noticed that?"

"Not really," Ellynor said in a choked voice.

"I just—I would have thought Justin would have chosen someone more like Senneth. Or even more like me."

Ellynor sat up even straighter on the bed. "I'm sorry if you think I've stolen him away from you," she said stiffly. "You might—perhaps—I suppose the two of you were in love at some point. But I—"

"In *love*? With *Justin*?" Kirra exclaimed, her incredulity so genuine that it was impossible to doubt her. "Gods, no. We can't stand each other."

Just like that, Ellynor's heart grew light and joyful. Still. "That can't be true," she said. "You came here on his behalf. You must have a relationship of some sort."

"He's my brother," Kirra replied.

Ellynor merely looked at her.

Kirra smiled and spread her hands. "He's my brother. He takes me for granted. He teases me. He scolds me when he thinks I've done something stupid. But he would kill anyone who tried to hurt me—if I didn't kill that person first," she added scrupulously. "I never had a brother before, and sometimes I don't like it. But now I'm stuck with him and he's stuck with me. If he's anything like the rest of my family, it means he's with me for the rest of my life."

Ellynor was nodding, slowly, finally comprehending, finally believing. "I have two brothers, and you have described it exactly," she said. "I would not want to try to imagine my life without them."

Kirra laughed. "Is that why you don't like me? Because you're jealous?"

"I don't dislike you," Ellynor said quickly.

"Because there are a lot of reasons people dislike me, and some of them are valid, but you can't hate me over Justin," Kirra said. She sounded remarkably cheerful. Ellynor thought she probably always did. "You'll have to find something better than that."

"I'd rather find a reason to be friends," Ellynor said.

"I was joking," Kirra said. "Of course we'll be friends. All of us. You'll never have a peaceful moment again in your life."

CHAPTER
34

THAT night, Ellynor joined Justin's friends and Faeber's family for a lively dinner in the pleasantly appointed dining room on the ground floor. It was odd and a little overwhelming to be among so many strangers at once, and for most of the meal she made herself quiet and small in the safe space between Justin and Senneth. But she listened closely and watched carefully, drawing quick conclusions about the others at the table.

Faeber and his two sons she already knew to some extent, and trusted; she was glad to see that in this setting they still seemed to be thoughtful and likable men. Marney was capable and competent, serving excellent food with a minimum of fuss, and seeming not at all put out to have a houseful of people to care for.

Tayse was rather frightening, a large man with dark hair and a somber expression. He didn't talk much, but when he did, everyone, even the flighty Kirra, listened to what he had to say. It was clear that Justin respected the other Rider above anyone else in the room. Most of his comments, and all of his questions, were directed at Tayse. Ellynor knew only the tiniest bit about their history, which Justin had sketched for her this afternoon. She hoped, for Justin's sake, that the big man was kinder than he looked.

She liked Cammon immediately, but Justin had told her she would. She had the sense that she would be entirely comfortable around the taciturn and unassuming Donnal.

If she were to spend time with these people. If she really were to upend her life and follow Justin back into his.

The dinner talk was mostly about people she didn't know—great lords, local bullies, missing friends. After a while, Ellynor gave up on trying to follow the sense of the words, and instead concentrated on the bonds between individuals. Kirra was the bright light, the laughing jester who had them all smiling. She and Justin argued three separate times before the meal was over, but Donnal watched her the entire time with a look of amusement and adoration. Cammon gave everyone his close attention, his gaze flicking from speaker to speaker in turn, seeming to absorb and ponder everything the others said. Tayse was the one they all looked to when the topic turned to strategy or plotting for the future. But Senneth was the heart of this small group, Ellynor decided, the sun they all revolved around. They might have separate relationships with each other, but she was the one they all loved.

Halfway through the meal, Justin set down his fork as if he'd just remembered something. "Senneth! I never asked! What did the king say when you showed up at Ghosenhall with the marlady?"

Senneth laughed. "Oh, we didn't go to Ghosenhall. I thought it might be a little too inconvenient for Baryn to have to explain why he was giving Sabina sanctuary. So I took her to Brassen Court instead."

Justin looked amused. "So that Kiernan could try to make up an explanation instead?"

"Because I don't care if Kiernan's inconvenienced," she said dryly. "Anyway, I thought she would be safe there."

"She was a strange little thing," Justin commented. "So afraid. But trying so hard to be brave."

"I never liked her much before," Senneth admitted. "But apparently the day she decided to escape from Lumanen Convent was the day a courageous new Sabina Gisseltess was born—and she has a certain fragile charm, I'll admit."

Ellynor glanced between them. "Sabina Gisseltess? The wife of the Lestra's brother?"

Justin nodded. "Yes, she came to Neft one night in secret. Apparently she'd been staying at the convent with her husband and had some fear he was going to kill her, so she managed to escape one afternoon. I don't know how she got past the gates."

"I helped her," Ellynor said, her voice almost a whisper. "Small woman—blond—right? She was just standing there, looking so lost, and I told her she could walk outside with the rest of us—and she did. Then she disappeared into the forest, and there was *such* a commotion at the convent when they realized she was gone! I wondered what happened to her. And then, lately, well—everything else has made it slip my mind."

Kirra was laughing. "So *you* set the marlady free? And Justin kept her safe? You two have a strange sort of magic, don't you? You're connected even when you don't realize you are."

"This seems more like coincidence than magic," Tayse said.

Kirra pointed a finger at him. "You only say that because you don't understand magic."

It wasn't until Marney cut and served four pies for dessert that Ellynor realized Faeber's wife had done all the work of preparing the meal. Surely in a house this size, with a man of Faeber's rank, there were normally servants. As Marney put a wedge of pastry before her, Ellynor glanced up.

"Have you been cooking for all of these people ever since I brought them down on your house?" she asked. "I'm so sorry! I didn't think of the extra work I would be making for you."

Marney laughed. "We normally have a maid, a cook, and a couple of footmen, but I thought all of them should have a holiday while our unconventional houseguests were in residence," she said. "It seemed the fewer witnesses, the better."

"Donnal and I have been helping in the kitchen," Cammon said. "I used to work in a tavern, so I know all about cooking and cleaning."

"And Donnal's just naturally good at any chore that needs to be done," Kirra said.

"Well, I'll help clean up tonight," Ellynor said.

"Certainly not!" Marney exclaimed. "You've been doing the hardest jobs of all—saving a life, and mending your own."

Ellynor smiled. "I'm tired of lying around doing nothing," she said.

Justin had finished his pie in about three bites. "I'll stay with you, if you want," he offered. "I can scrub pans, too."

She gave him a sideways look. "Something tells me you have other plans."

He grinned. "Need to start working out again. Thought Tayse and I might practice a little swordplay."

One of Faeber's sons sat forward. "That I'd like to see," he said. "Two Riders in training."

"Well, *this* Rider won't be much to look at for a few weeks," Justin said ruefully. "But you're welcome to watch." He glanced down at Ellynor. "Unless—"

She was laughing. "No, no. Go fighting. You won't be happy again until you've got a blade in your hand."

"Until I've got a blade in my hand and I can *use* it," Justin added.

Accordingly, once the meal was over, most of the men retired to Faeber's barn. Senneth and Kirra disappeared upstairs, deep in consultation.

Marney, Ellynor, Cammon, and Donnal carried dishes to the kitchen and began to clean.

"What do you want to do with this leftover meat?" Cammon asked as he organized the dishes on a sideboard by the sink.

"Save it. I want to make soup tomorrow and take some to serra Paulina."

Ellynor looked up from scraping a plate into the garbage pail. "Serra Paulina? At the Gisseltess house? What's wrong with her?"

Marney looked surprised. "You know her?"

Ellynor nodded. "I visited her a few times when she was sick. They thought she was going to die but I—but she didn't."

There was a shrewd expression on Marney's face. "Oh, that's what happened, is it? I had talked to Jenetta every day for a week, and every morning I expected to hear that her mother had passed on. Then one day, her mother was well, and no one could understand it." She sighed. "Though I'm not sure such a miracle is possible this time. Jenetta's at Nocklyn Towers for some event, and the housekeeper came by this morning to tell me the old woman has taken a turn for the worse. I'm going over tomorrow to see if there's anything I can do, but—well. She's old and sick and frail. It might be her time."

Ellynor was quiet for a moment, remembering serra Paulina's gruff kindness. The old woman had aided Ellynor in her clandestine romance and seemed to exult in every last minute of life she could wring from her final days. Ellynor clenched her hands a moment, feeling the weakness in her fists. Was she strong enough to heal the old noblewoman a second time? She wasn't sure she was strong enough to make it up the stairs on her own.

Marney was surveying the welter of plates and pans. "Eleven healthy people can certainly go through quite a number of dishes, can't they?" she said.

"Yes, but you don't have to be the one to clean them," Cammon said. He took her arm and urged her toward the door. "You go rest. We know where everything belongs by now. You're exhausted."

"I'm not," Marney claimed.

Donnal looked over at her with a gentle smile. "You are," he said. "Cammon always knows. Leave us to the kitchen. We won't break anything."

Still protesting, Marney finally left Ellynor and the other mystics alone in the kitchen. Cammon made Ellynor sit at a stool before the big center table while she dried stacks of plates and rows of glasses.

"You're tired, too," he said. "But you're happier being up."

She accepted a wet plate from Donnal and slowly wiped it dry. "I don't know very much about mystics," she confessed. "Justin says I am one—"

"Oh, you are," Cammon replied.

"But I don't know what kind of power other mystics have."

"Cammon reads souls," Donnal said in his quiet voice. "He can feel emotions—sometimes from very far away. He usually can tell if someone is lying, and he can always see someone's true form."

That was confusing. "Why would someone have a—an *untrue* form?" she asked.

Donnal grinned. "Shiftling," he said, and turned into a bear right as she was staring at him. She gave a little shriek and dropped the plate she was holding, though fortunately it was an inch from the table and didn't break. Cammon handed him another dirty plate as if he didn't notice. Just like that, Donnal was human again and dunking the dish in a tub of water. "Even when I turn myself into an animal, Cammon still sees *me*. It's a handy skill much of the time—"

"But dangerous when I don't realize that one of my friends is supposed to be in disguise," Cammon said. "So everyone always has to remind me who they're supposed to be if we're on some masquerade."

"How often does that happen?" she asked, bewildered.

They both laughed. "More often than you'd think," Donnal replied.

Cammon glanced over his shoulder at Ellynor. "Some people are harder for me to read," he said. "You, for instance. I can't pick up much about you at all. I didn't even know you were with Justin after he was hurt—I could tell he was still breathing, and that something was keeping him alive, but you were a surprise to me."

"What does that mean?" she asked a little fearfully.

"That you have your own kind of magic," Donnal answered. "Not just your healing ability. Some kind of power of concealment."

"Oh. I do." They both looked interested. She shrugged and tried to explain. "But I never thought of it as magic. It's just—a lot of Lirren folks can do it. Can call on the goddess to keep them hidden if they don't want to be seen. My brothers are especially good at it."

"I think you're better than you realize," Cammon said.

She turned the conversation. "What about the others? What kind of magic do they have? Kirra's a healer, obviously."

Donnal nodded. "And a shiftling, like me. Senneth—"

Cammon laughed. "Senneth can do everything."

"Fire is her greatest strength," Donnal said. "But she's also a healer. And she has been teaching herself other tricks. She can't conceal herself from Cammon, the way you can, but she can make herself invisible to most people. And she can change her features a little—not as much as Kirra and I can—but enough to be unrecognizable." He shook his head. "I've never met anyone as powerful as she is."

"She seems like—I mean, someone who has that kind of power can be dangerous, but she seems—like a good person," Ellynor ended lamely.

Cammon nodded. "She is. There's no evil in her at all. And she can be trusted, always, to do what's right, even if it's the hardest thing you can think of. She's amazing. Any one of us would lay down his life for her." He glanced at Donnal, as if uncertain.

"I would," Donnal said softly. "Though Kirra's likely to be the death of me first." The men both laughed.

"So how long have all of you been friends?" Ellynor wanted to know.

"Forever," Donnal said.

"A year," Cammon said, and they both laughed again. Cammon went on to give a longer explanation. "Kirra and Donnal have known each other, what, for thirteen years?"

"Yes. Almost fourteen."

"And Senneth's known them almost that long. Justin and Tayse have been friends—oh, twelve or thirteen years. A long time. But it wasn't until just about a year ago that all six of us came together. The king had asked Senneth to go around Gillengaria, looking for signs of war. She brought Kirra and Donnal along, and then the king decided she needed to be protected—"

"Although Kirra and Senneth never really need anybody's protection," Donnal interpolated.

"So he sent Justin and Tayse to guard them. And they met me in Dormas." He must have read her blank look, for he added, "It's a little town on the western coast. And we've all been friends ever since."

"Tayse is a little intimidating," she said cautiously. "At least at first."

Both men found this highly amusing. "And even after you've known him awhile," Donnal assured her.

"Well, so's Justin, to most people, and you don't seem afraid of *him*," Cammon said in an encouraging voice.

She couldn't help but smile and duck her head at that. A little embarrassed, a little pleased. "I suppose people might find Justin intimidating to look at," she admitted. "But once you start talking to him, he's very kind."

"That's not everybody's experience," Donnal said dryly.

"He seems like a good man," she said, a little anxiously. What did she know about him, after all? Except that he had risked his life to fall in love with her.

"He is," Cammon assured her and gave her a wide smile. "He'll be an even better man now. Because of you."

"I, for one, am looking forward to seeing what happens to Justin now that he's in love," Donnal said. "It didn't do much to turn Tayse soft."

"Tayse?" Ellynor repeated. In love with someone? His stern face seemed so unlikely to relax into affection.

But Cammon was nodding. "Engaged to be married to Senneth."

"A scandal," Donnal said.

"Because she's a noblewoman and he's just a soldier," Cammon explained to Ellynor. Then he glanced at Donnal and retorted, "No more scandalous than you and Kirra."

Now Ellynor's eyes widened. "Donnal and Kirra?" Sparkling Kirra and this quiet, self-effacing man? Although if Kirra was in love with Donnal, that was another reason she wouldn't be interested in Justin. All to the good.

"Not engaged to be married," Cammon said. "They're just—well, nobody exactly knows what their relationship is. But they're always together."

Donnal grinned and did not amplify.

"I think it's going to take me a while to sort everybody out," Ellynor confessed.

"And we're not together all of the time, so it's even harder," Cammon said. "But we're all going back to Ghosenhall, so if you come with us now—"

"I'm hoping I can go back to the Lirrens first," Ellynor said wistfully. "I want Justin to meet my family. I want to tell them—oh, everything. I miss them all so much. But I *will* come to Ghosenhall. Soon. I promised Justin I would."

"Well, if you come to the palace, you can visit the raelynx," Cammon said. "Then you won't feel so homesick."

She thought she might drop another plate. "The king has a raelynx? They never cross the Lireth Mountains." She remembered the one she had seen just a few days ago, far from the mountains indeed. "Well, almost never."

"Senneth found it last year when we were traveling," Donnal said. "Said she wouldn't turn it loose till we could get it to safety. And then, of course, she used it to threaten Coralinda Gisseltess—"

Now she set the dish down, very carefully, on the table. "That was *you*," she breathed. "All of you. Was it—I knew that the Lestra had captured a Rider last year—was it *Justin* who was locked in the convent for a day? And I didn't know it?"

"Wouldn't that have been interesting?" Cammon said, wholly intrigued. "No, it was Tayse, but—what if it had been Justin? And you had brought him food that morning? How strange would that have been? Almost as if you were destined to meet."

"*Tayse* was the one the guards captured?"

"Hard to believe, isn't it?" Donnal agreed.

She was remembering now, and she looked from one face to the other with unfolding marvel. It had been such a terrifying morning, the phalanx of mystics at the convent gate, all the novices gathered in the courtyard, uncertain and afraid. They had been too far back to hear what was happening or see who exactly had come calling, but that the Lestra was furious had been obvious to them all. The Lestra had stood there, proud and scornful, laughing at the pale-haired woman who rode in the lead and demanded the return of her comrade. But the intruder had possessed a dire weapon—a raelynx, which she had loosed into the courtyard, and the Lestra had been forced to relinquish her prisoner. The mystics had retreated, but not before the white-haired woman had set the convent walls on fire—

"That was Senneth," Ellynor just now realized. "Rescuing Tayse. And *you* were with her? All of you?"

Donnal was grinning. "Even Justin. So maybe you *were* destined to meet."

But Cammon had a delighted expression on his face. "That was you!" he exclaimed. "I could tell someone in the convent was a mystic—but the impression was so faint I couldn't tell who. Were you practicing magic right at that moment? Even though you didn't know it was magic?"

"I was wondering if I should step forward and take control of the raelynx," she said. "I'd never actually done it before, but I thought I could. My brothers both can."

Donnal and Cammon looked at each other and burst out laughing. "The one thing Senneth never expected!" Cammon cried. "That there would be a Lirren girl inside the convent! The raelynx wouldn't have done any damage after all!"

"But Coralinda Gisseltess didn't know that," Donnal said. "And she let Tayse go when she didn't really have to."

"Oh, Senneth will love this," Cammon said. "Ellynor had enough magic to foil *her* magic, but Coralinda Gisseltess didn't know enough about magic to harness the power of the people under her own roof."

"There's a lesson to be learned here, but it's pretty obscure," Donnal said.

Cammon was grinning. "Mystics always win. Even when they're not fighting on the same side."

Donnal handed Ellynor another plate, and she realized they'd gotten so involved in the conversation that they'd been neglecting their primary chores. Donnal said, "Well, we're all on the same side now."

"Yes," said Cammon, "now that Ellynor belongs to us."

An hour later, Ellynor was back in her room, standing at the window and staring out at the dark but busy streets of Neft. It was cold out; she could feel winter pressing against the glass, eager to invade the warmth of the room. The sliver of moon had already set and the stars were invisible under a heavy covering of cloud. There might be snow on the ground by morning.

She was tired. She told herself she should change into the oversized nightshirt Marney had loaned her. She should immediately climb into bed and fall fast asleep.

But she was waiting for noises in the hall. The sound of the rest of the household turning in for the night. Justin's voice as he came back from working out with Tayse.

She was waiting for Justin.

She had plenty to occupy her while she waited, since she was still absorbing everything she had learned in her conversation with Cammon and Donnal. It almost seemed as if she had been fated to meet this particular band of sorcerers and soldiers—as if she had been put in their way repeatedly, until the moment they suddenly realized she belonged with them. Ellynor was very certain the Black Mother was capable of plotting such a strategy, and from what Donnal had told her tonight about the Bright Mother and the Wild Mother, she thought it possible all of the goddesses had put their heads together to come up with this particular scheme. Even the Pale Mother, that fickle and wanton girl, might have had a hand in setting this plan in motion. If Ellynor had needed reassurance that she was right to leave her family, to become *bahta-lo*, to follow Justin back to Ghosenhall, the meddling of the goddesses would have been enough to convince her.

But she had not. Justin himself was all the reason she needed.

Finally, she heard the sounds she had been listening for. Men's voices, the heavy tread of men's boots on the stairs. Then a woman's voice—Senneth's, she thought—and a smothered laugh. "Even better tomorrow," said someone. One of Faeber's sons, perhaps. More voices, more footsteps. Then silence.

A few moments later, a quiet knock on her door. She wanted to call out a welcome, but her breath wouldn't come; she could not speak. Noiselessly, the handle turned, the door was pushed open, and Justin peered in. She saw his eyes go first to the empty bed, then he looked around with quick alarm. Relief shaped his face when he saw her standing by the window.

"Are you all right?" he asked in concern.

She could only nod.

"May I come in?"

She nodded again.

He came inside, closing the door firmly behind him. She couldn't speak, but she could move, and she came across the room to greet him, meeting him in the middle. It was clear he was going to ask again after her health, but she didn't want to talk. She put her hands behind his head and pulled it down, kissing him on the mouth. His arms closed around her hard enough to lift her from the floor as he returned the kiss with enthusiasm. Against his strength, she felt curiously dainty, fragile, cherished. She remembered what it was like to be kissed by Justin when he wasn't slowed by week-old wounds.

He lifted his head and gazed down at her, his face a mixed study of worry and desire. "You need to rest," he said, but he did not sound certain.

She found her voice, or at least a whisper. "Stay with me."

He carried her to the bed and laid her upon it as tenderly as if she were a sleeping child. When he would have backed away, she caught his arm and pulled him down alongside her. She could tell he thought he should resist, but he simply couldn't bring himself to leave her. He lowered himself carefully on the bed, arranged his long legs beside her and draped an arm over her waist before resting his head beside her on the pillow.

"You must be feeling better," he said in a low voice.

It made her giggle. Laughter glanced through her, knocking through her bones and leaving a trail of warm light behind. She felt as if her skin must be glowing. She placed one hand on Justin's exposed cheek and with the other started to unbutton her borrowed clothes.

"What about you?" she whispered back. "How did the swordplay go?"

"Better than I expected. I could probably defend myself if I had to—

and there was only one opponent—and he wasn't very good. What are you doing?"

"Taking off my gown."

He said nothing. She sat up and shrugged out of the top of the dress so that she was left only in a sheer chemise. Justin's breath caught; his eyes roamed the contours of her body.

"You should get undressed, too," she suggested.

He sat up more slowly. "You're not well enough," was all he said, but longing colored his face and turned the words into a question.

She laughed again. "I am if you are. Unless—your wounds are so fresh—are you afraid that—?"

She left the question hanging delicately in the air. For an answer, Justin yanked his shirt over his head with one quick motion. That exposed the half-healed crisscross of sword marks on his chest, not at all disguised by the light covering of curly brown hair. Ellynor paused in her own act of undressing to place her fingertips gently on the ugliest wound.

"This should have killed you," she whispered. "You should be dead."

"I'm not, though," he said.

Just the thought of losing him made her wild. She flung her arms around him, kissed him with a desperate frenzy, drew him back down beside her on the bed. Whatever doubts Justin had had were gone. She felt his body twist as he kicked his trousers free, felt his hands searching around her waist for the rest of the closures on her gown. All the while, she was still kissing him, not helping at all with the last of the undressing chores. He was efficient, though; in a matter of minutes, they were both naked. Ellynor ran her hands over his battered body, feeling the smooth ridges of old scars cutting across the raised welts of the new ones. Thinking that, for the rest of her life, every time she loved this man, he would be bruised and nicked and slightly beaten. Thinking that she would use all the magic in her power to keep him whole.

"I love you," she whispered, and pressed her body against the length of his. "I want to be with you forever."

They made love carefully, mindful of hurts and a bottomless exhaustion. If the moon had still been up, it would have danced outside the window; as it was, the night sky threw veils over this wondrous house, which held such marvels inside. Ellynor heard the rustlings of all the gods, nodding at each other in approval, as she held her lover tightly in her arms before she finally allowed herself to sleep.

CHAPTER
35

JUSTIN woke, as always, completely and cleanly, orienting himself to his surroundings before opening his eyes or moving a muscle. Morning. Faeber's house. In bed with Ellynor.

That caused his eyes to fly open, and he found himself staring at Elly- nor across the pillow. She was wide awake and gazing at him with a little smile, as if she had been watching him for a long time. The expression on her face brought his own smile in response. Lying very still, he lifted a hand and ran a finger down her cheek.

"Good morning," he said. "How long have you been awake?"

"About an hour."

"Why didn't you wake me up?"

"I liked watching you sleep. It must be the only time you're still."

He laughed. "Probably."

"You're very quiet. I could hardly even hear you breathing."

"Soldier's trick. No snoring. It could draw the enemy."

"Everything in your life is about war, isn't it?"

He felt his body tense, but he lay there motionless, hoping she could not tell. "It always has been. Probably always will be. Except for the part with you in it."

Her hand came up and closed over his, and she snuggled his palm against the column of her throat. "Then I'll have to make that a big part," she said, and he relaxed again. She went on, "What's the plan for today? How much longer do you think Tayse will be willing to stay in Neft?"

"I think he wants to leave tomorrow. Kirra told him you and I both probably needed another day before we were really fit to travel."

"He seems like the kind of man who hates to sit around waiting. He must be getting impatient."

Justin laughed. "He's more patient than Senneth. She's been gone from Ghosenhall weeks longer than she planned, and she's getting edgy. But she can wait a day."

"Good," she said. "Then I want to go to the Gisseltess house this morning."

He stared at her and for a moment could not comprehend the words.

"Serra Paulina is sick again. You remember, the old lady I came here to nurse? Marney says she's fallen ill. I want to—"

"You can't go back in that house!" he exclaimed, sitting up to make his words more forceful. "Everybody recognizes you! Jenetta Gisseltess is the Lestra's *cousin!* If Coralinda Gisseltess is looking for you, and you know she is, surely someone at the house will contact the convent—"

"But Jenetta is gone, Marney said. She'll be away for another week or two. I rarely spoke to any of the servants—and if I dress in ordinary clothes instead of my white robes, no one will know who I am. Well, of course, serra Paulina will, but she won't tell anyone."

Justin shook his head. "No. No. It's a terrible idea. I want to get you to someplace safe, not parade you on the streets of Neft, where everybody is looking to murder mystics."

Ellynor sat up, too, her naked body something of a distraction. She was starting to get angry, though, and that focused Justin's attention. "Kirra and Senneth can walk the streets of Neft and survive just fine."

"Kirra and Senneth can take care of themselves. So can Donnal and Cammon. You have a lot of power, but it's not the kind of magic that helps you much when you need to fight."

"Justin. I won't be fighting anybody. I'll dress like a servant and go with Marney. No one will be looking for me. Jenetta Gisseltess is gone. I'll stay a few hours and then I'll be back. Nothing will happen to me."

Justin sat there, looking at her, shaking his head but unable to think of the words that would make her change her mind. He didn't know what to do. Every instinct in his body shouted to keep her safe, hold her tight, lock her in this room so that she couldn't go. He was powerful enough, he knew, to restrain her—now, and anytime in the future when she considered a course of action he did not like. She was not, like Senneth or Kirra, strong enough to resist him; she did not have the kind of magic that would enable her to get her way.

Which made it doubly important that he not impose his will on her. If he used his strength, it must be to defend her, not to coerce her. He was not used to making choices for other people—how could he be sure the choices he *would* make were the right ones? He had made many wrong ones on his own behalf.

"I don't want you to go," he said.

She was watching him closely, seeming to be aware of his inward struggle. "But you won't stop me?"

Numbly, he shook his head. "I won't. But you shouldn't go. Ellynor, please think about this."

She put her hands on his cheeks, leaned in to kiss him. "Serra Paulina sent me out some days just so I could be with you," she whispered against his mouth. "She requested my attendance at her bedside, just so I could be with you. She's the reason I have you at all. I owe her so much. Let me see if I can repay her just a little bit."

How could he respond to that? He kissed her and took her in his arms. But he couldn't help shivering a little. He would have been hard put to determine if the emotion that shook him was love or fear.

JUSTIN and Tayse worked out again in the morning, this time without an audience, since Faeber and his sons were out patrolling the streets. Every muscle in his body was sore, and his wounds ached with a deliberate fire, but Justin ignored the pain. He was getting his rhythm back. He could lift the sword and swing it in time to intercept one of Tayse's lazier thrusts. He didn't have much strength, though. Just an hour of hard exercise wore him out, and he had to sink to a hay bale, gently panting.

"Better," Tayse said. "I think you'd be able to step it up a notch if someone truly attacked you."

"Hope you're there if someone does," Justin retorted, and Tayse smiled.

When they went inside for lunch, Cammon and Donnal served the meal. Justin realized that Marney and Ellynor must have already left for the Gisseltess house; the thought made him glum enough to feel no interest in food.

"Where's Ellynor?" Kirra asked, glancing around the table. "Is she sick again?"

"I didn't check on her this morning," Senneth said, sounding concerned. "She seemed so much better yesterday."

"She's fine," Justin said shortly.

They all turned to look at him and he realized, with a jolt, that it was just the six of them. For the first time in months. Just the six of them sitting together in a room. Normally, that was the very thing that would put him entirely at peace, but not today. Today there was someone missing.

"Marney went to visit a sick woman, and Ellynor went with her," he elaborated.

Kirra's fine eyebrows rose. "Is she well enough to be healing other people?"

"I wouldn't think so," Justin replied. "But this is a woman she knows. And likes." He took a bite of meat. "Serra Paulina Nocklyn."

"She went to the *Gisseltess* house?" Kirra demanded. "And you let her?"

He gave her a fierce look. "She wanted to go. And it's not my place to stop her."

"Well, no, but you could argue her out of it, couldn't you?"

"Apparently not."

Senneth put a hand on Kirra's arm to silence her. "Ellynor has a right to make her own decisions, and Justin has to respect them," she said gravely. "Marney told me this morning that Jenetta's out of town. None of us have seen any convent guards in the streets. Everything should be fine."

Tayse put down his fork, already finished eating. "Another reason to leave Neft as soon as possible," the big man said. "Tomorrow morning? Will everyone be ready by then?"

"I'm ready as soon as Ellynor's back," Justin said.

Cammon gave him a questioning look. "But you're not coming to Ghosenhall, are you?"

Now all eyes were on him again. Justin shot a look at Tayse and tried not to feel defensive. "I don't know. We hadn't decided."

"You'd rather go straight to the Lirrens and join us later," Tayse said.

Justin nodded. "I would. The longer she is away from her family, without their blessing, the harder it is for her to go back and say she wants to marry me. She has agreed to leave them, leave the life she knows, and come with me to the royal city to live. I want to do something to prove that I value the sacrifice."

"Not the best time and place for a solitary man and a woman with no fighting abilities to be traveling," Donnal observed.

"I know," Justin acknowledged. "But Ellynor has some skill at concealment. I think if we're very cautious, we won't draw any attention."

Tayse shared a look with Senneth, then gave a brief nod. "We'll escort you to the mountains," he said.

Justin felt a rush of profound relief. "You will? I think we'll be safe once we cross the border."

"And we'll all feel less worry about you," Senneth said. "When you come back, try to make the crossing up near Kianlever. Or even go through Brassenthwaite and come back down toward Ghosenhall. It's a longer trek, obviously, but you'll be in less danger."

Justin laughed. "Maybe I'll bring her brothers along to protect us. Sign them up for the king's army."

"I'd welcome that," Tayse said.

Senneth sighed and leaned back in her chair. "Oh, but how many more days does that put us on the road before we get back to Ghosenhall? There's so much to tell Baryn. I sent him a message from Brassenthwaite, but so much has happened since then! I'd write a letter but unless I have a courier I can absolutely trust—"

"I can carry a message to Ghosenhall," Donnal offered. "I can take bird shape and fly it there in a day or two."

"Then fly back and meet us at the mountains," Kirra said instantly. Justin grinned; she never liked to be separated from Donnal for long.

Senneth thought it over. "I like that idea," she said. "At least then he'd understand why I've been gone so long. When can you leave?"

"Within the hour, if you want."

"Stay till morning," Tayse said. His voice was so laced with significance that they all quickly looked at him in inquiry and concern.

All except Cammon, whose gaze flicked between Tayse and Senneth, sitting across the table from each other. Then the younger man smiled so broadly he could have been laughing, but he didn't say a word.

Tayse's face wore its usual severe expression. "Justin knows that it's tradition among the Riders to fail to ask their king for permission to wed," he said gravely. "As a rule, they elope, so that when they return as married men or women, the king must accept their unions with some kind of grace."

Now Kirra gave a little squeal and practically began dancing in her seat. Senneth's face was flushed with color, but her smile was almost wicked. Tayse's face and voice both remained utterly serious.

"I have obtained her family's permission to marry Senneth," he went on. "I had not expected to find a time so soon that the six of us were all together, and I had been reluctant to try to schedule a marriage without the four of you as witnesses. But here we all are. Conveniently, in the house of the magistrate of this town. I asked Faeber this morning. He is willing to perform the ceremony tonight."

He stood up and bowed very low in Senneth's direction. "So if, serra Senneth, you are willing to marry a humble soldier in the king's army—"

Senneth jumped up so fast that her chair fell over behind her. "Don't be ridiculous," she said, and darted around the table to throw herself in his arms. The rest of them stood up, clapping and cheering and stomping their feet. Justin thought their voices could probably be heard all the way out to the street. That was the way of joy, he decided; it was always louder than grief.

Kirra was already making plans. "What time is it? Past noon! When do you want to have this ceremony? Senneth, you just leave off kissing him right now. You and I have preparations to make. You can't possibly have anything to wear."

Senneth laughed and pulled free. She was still blushing, but she looked entirely happy. "I'll be married in travel clothes and muddy boots," she said.

"Well, you won't," Kirra said firmly. "Come with me. The rest of you—oh, you all look like the rat-catcher's cousins. Come find me half an hour or so before the ceremony. You, too, Tayse. You don't want to shame your highborn bride."

"No, I don't," he said. "I'll be there."

THAT was a strange day, hard to live through for so many reasons. Cammon and Donnal disappeared into the kitchen to see what Marney had in the way of feast food, and they sent Tayse out to the butcher's on his wedding day. Justin, still in hiding, couldn't help run errands, so he fetched bathwater for Senneth and performed other chores as Kirra directed him. This included rearranging furniture in the small parlor downstairs and gathering as many candles as he could find in other rooms and placing them in strategic spots in the makeshift chapel.

All the while he was worrying about Ellynor, wondering if she had arrived in time to save serra Paulina or at least ease her way. Hoping she would not foolishly use up what little strength she had managed to regain. Missing her.

About an hour before dark, Marney returned alone. Justin met her at the door, closing it quickly to shut out the eager wind. "Where's Ellynor?" he asked.

Marney was rubbing her hands together, trying to generate some heat. "How can it be this cold?" she wondered.

"Where's Ellynor?" he asked again.

"She wanted to stay till morning. It's very clear that the serramarra will not make it through the night, but she *was* alert enough to recognize Ellynor, at least when we arrived. Ellynor couldn't bring herself to leave."

Justin felt something clamp tight on his rib cage. "I wish she had."

"Yes, so do I, but she's rather a strong-willed girl. I could hardly make a fuss by dragging her out behind me, since we were trying to avoid drawing any extra attention. But she was right. No one appeared to recognize her except Paulina herself. And she knows you want to leave in the morning. She told me to tell you she would be ready to go whenever you came by."

"I want to go by *now*," he said grimly. When Marney looked dismayed, he forced his features to relax. "It's just that I'm worried."

"I know."

"And she'll miss the celebration tonight."

"Celebration? What's happening?"

Justin smiled, trying to let go of his anxiety. "You must have left before Tayse talked to your husband. Faeber's going to perform a marriage tonight between Tayse and Senneth. Cammon and Donnal are cooking even as we speak, and I've been decorating your front room. I hope you don't mind."

But she looked quite delighted and came to inspect his work. "Oh, I've got some garlands up in the attic—let me bring those down—and a couple of houseplants in my room. Not too festive, but then again, we didn't have much time! Does she have something to wear?"

Women always focused on the most inconsequential things, Justin thought. "Kirra's taking care of that," he assured her.

"Then I'll see what those young men have done to my kitchen."

A few hours later, everything was ready. Cammon and Donnal slipped upstairs and returned, outfitted in clean trousers and starched white shirts that Kirra had manufactured from their ragged travel clothes. Justin and Tayse presented themselves next, and she dressed both of them all in black. They had dug their Riders' sashes from their luggage, so now they each draped their embroidered golden lions over one shoulder and strapped on their sword belts. Kirra fluttered around Tayse with a small pair of scissors, snipping carefully at the most untameable strands of black hair, but she merely looked at Justin and shook her head.

"Your hair's too long and I don't have time to give you a good cut. Just tie it back and make sure you shave."

"I did shave!"

"Well, you might do it again."

Finally, most of them were assembled in the transformed parlor. Faeber had put on fine clothes of his own and wore them so easily that Justin almost didn't recognize him. He stood before the fireplace; Marney sat at a miniature harpsichord and played a simple tune with a sunny melody. The groom and his attendants ranged themselves on one side of the room, all eyes turned expectantly toward the door. Tayse seemed taller, darker, more silent than ever. His expression was so watchful that he might have been lying in ambush. Justin thought he was merely trying to conceal a leaping emotion, an excitement almost too great to contain.

At least, that's how Justin would have felt in the same situation.

"They're coming," Cammon whispered. Moments later, Kirra swept into the room. She was wearing Danalustrous red in some plush winter fabric. Her ruby pendant hung against her skin just above the deep neckline of the dress, covering the housemark branded into her flesh. Senneth followed, and everybody looked away from Kirra to watch her. She wore a dress that shimmered between blue and silver; her normally untidy hair had been bound with ribbons of a matching color. Justin thought Kirra must have found or produced cosmetics, for there was more color than usual on Senneth's cheeks and eyes and lips. The only jewelry she wore was her grandmother's gold pendant, hanging, like Kirra's, just where her housemark would be. Justin noticed that, for this occasion, she had even taken off her moonstone bracelet. Maybe that, more than anything, accounted for the color in her face. Her magic had been unchained; the heat that always ran in her body was burning just under the skin.

The music stopped. Faeber lifted his hands and spoke more formally than Justin had ever heard him. "You who have chosen to marry should come stand before me and tell me your names and stations."

Tayse caught Senneth's hand in his and they shared a private smile before turning to face the magistrate. "My name is Tayse. I am a King's Rider."

"Senneth Brassenthwaite. Serramarra of the realm."

Justin heard Marney's quick gasp; Faeber looked briefly startled, though he recovered quickly. Clearly they had had no idea how exalted some of their guests were. Probably didn't know Kirra's heritage, either—though, with the way she was dressed tonight, they would likely figure it out.

"What is your purpose in coming here tonight?"

"To marry," they replied in unison.

"Tayse, why would you take Senneth to be your bride?"

Tayse turned to face Senneth and pulled her hand so that it rested against his heart. "Because I love her."

"Senneth, why would you take Tayse to be your husband?"

Justin could see the smile that touched her lips then as she gazed back at the Rider. "Because he knows my secrets. Because he knows my strengths and weaknesses. Because I know his. Because he will hold me if I fall. Because he will turn to me if he is falling. Because my life is not complete if he is not in it. Because I love him."

"Have you brought friends who will act as witnesses to your wedding? Who will counsel you when you quarrel, rejoice when you celebrate, and comfort you when you grieve?"

"We have."

"Let them identify themselves."

Tayse glanced back at Justin, who had to keep scowling in order to control his expression. "I'm Justin," he said.

The others spoke up in turn. "Cammon."

"Donnal."

"Kirra."

Faeber consulted a book open in his hands. "Let all of you be bound together in fellowship in recognition of this compact. For a marriage is a living thing and must be tended. You who bear witness bear also the responsibility for reminding this man and this woman that marriage is not a step undertaken lightly. Remind them to seek reconciliation when they are far apart, to sue for tenderness when they are tempted to be unkind, and to cherish each other no matter what trials or troubles the outside world affords."

"Well, that should be easy enough," Kirra said under her breath, and the rest of them, even Faeber, had to fight to keep from laughing.

The magistrate poured wine into a goblet and offered it to Senneth. "First you drink. Then Tayse. Then pass the cup among your friends."

She drank from it as if tasting nectar for the first time and handed the goblet to Tayse. He turned it so that his lips rested exactly where hers had, and he took a single sip. Impossible to believe, but the goblet seemed to be trembling in Tayse's hand as he held it out to Justin, so Justin took it quickly so nobody else would see. A swallow, then he handed the cup to Cammon. Each of the others drank, and Kirra handed the cup back to Senneth.

"Bound together in friendship," Faeber said, and it was true. Justin felt peculiar, light-headed, as if there had been some additive in the wine—as if, for a moment, he could see and hear the people around him with the same heightened perceptions that guided Cammon. Not Faeber and Marney—only the other five, the Rider, the mystics. He could sense Tayse's heartbeat, steady and strong but a measure too fast, that iron will concealing a rising excitement. Senneth was a blaze of heat, red-gold and ecstatic; Kirra stood quietly, so pleased she was almost purring. From Donnal there emanated a low, silent hum of happiness. From Cammon, deep delight barely held in check. Justin wondered what the others were picking up from him.

"Bound together in marriage," Faeber was saying now. He had laid one hand on Tayse's head, one on Senneth's. "From this day forward, you will be known as husband and wife."

There was a moment's silence, and then Cammon released a whoop of excitement. Marney's hands crashed down on the keyboard in a chord of celebration, and then she was playing some kind of skirling music. Justin supposed people were meant to dance to it. No one did, of course. Kirra had thrown her arms around Senneth and seemed to be crying into the carefully styled hair, while Donnal and then Cammon came up to shake Tayse's hand. Kirra pushed them both aside so she could hug Tayse, whispering something in his ear that made him laugh. Donnal and Cammon moved to stand on either side of Senneth, first one of them kissing her on the cheek, then the other.

Justin shoved Kirra aside so he could take Tayse's hand. They beamed at each other like idiots; no wonder the king didn't want his Riders getting married in Ghosenhall. The whole lot of them would look like sentimental fools.

"A splendid day," Justin said, still smiling broadly as he dropped Tayse's hand.

"The standard by which to measure them all," Tayse replied.

Senneth came up behind him, put an arm around Justin's waist, and kissed him on the jaw. "Next we've got to see to your wedding," she murmured. "But I have a feeling you'll come back to Ghosenhall a married man."

That made him want to blush, but he concentrated and the heat receded from his face. "Oh, but I liked this," he said, pointing his finger around the room. "The binding with all the friends present."

"We're already bound together," Senneth said. "Nothing else could make the circle stronger." She kissed him again and released him. "So go ahead and marry her in front of her family. Just in case you weren't sure what to do when the moment arrived."

CHAPTER
36

THEY ate the wedding feast, they offered an increasingly sillier litany of toasts to the newly wedded couple, they complimented Kirra on her couture and Faeber on his ritual. Despite the availability of the wine, none of them drank much, except the host and hostess. The rest of them planned to leave in the morning. They wanted their wits at their sharpest as they navigated the dangerous lands here in the southern territories.

Eventually Tayse and Senneth left them for the bridal bower, which Justin imagined was just the room they'd been sharing for the past few days with perhaps a few of Marney's potted plants scattered around to add ambiance. Kirra declared she was too excited to sleep, so she found a deck of cards and convinced Cammon and Donnal to play with her.

"I'm hot," Justin said. "I want to take a walk outside."

"Cool you off fast enough," Donnal commented, shuffling and dealing. "It's pretty cold."

"He's been cooped up inside for days," Kirra said. "I'd be going crazy myself."

But Cammon looked up at him quickly and looked away. Cammon knew where he was going.

Donnal was right—it was downright freezing on the deserted streets of Neft. Justin hunched his shoulders inside his coat and went face-first into a driving wind. His muscles didn't respond as quickly or as effortlessly as he would have liked, but they were working. The deepest wound, the one on his chest, cramped in protest, but he ignored it. He'd have Kirra douse him with a little magic tomorrow before they started out, accelerate the healing process even more. He was in better shape than a man would be without sorcery, but he was still weaker than he liked. He hated the sensation of being anything but entirely healthy.

It didn't take too long to find a cross street that he knew—he'd never been to Faeber's house before, but Neft wasn't that big—and then head in the direction he wanted. Two turns, and then up the hill, until he was standing right outside Jenetta Gisseltess's house.

All the rooms that faced the street were dark. The shrubbery shivered in the rattling wind, and even the wrought-iron fence looked cold. Justin wrapped his hands around two of the thin black poles anyway, staring at the house, willing someone to be awake and watching for him. He knew which room was serra Paulina's, and he kept his eyes on the drawn curtains, wanting with all his heart to see them stir and be pulled aside.

The curtain fluttered. A shadow stepped to the window and glanced out.

Justin caught his breath and stood there motionless, afraid to move or otherwise draw attention in case it wasn't Ellynor at the window. But it was. She pushed the curtain back farther so he could see her face; she lifted her hand and flattened her fingers against the glass. He knew she could see him and so he raised his own hand and held it out as if, across the whole courtyard, he was touching his palm to hers. They stood that way for a long time, hands outstretched, Ellynor in the house and Justin at the gate. As if reminding each other that they had closed the distance between them once before. As if promising each other that they could do so again. As if pledging devotion. As if sealing a pact.

Despite the bitter chill, Justin would have remained there all night, hand lifted to his love, but something inside the house caught Ellynor's attention. She turned her head, then dropped her hand and let the curtain fall. Justin waited another fifteen minutes, another thirty, but she did not reappear. Slowly, because he did not want to go, he turned and headed back to his own solitary bed for the night.

I N the morning, he rose late to find everyone else packed and ready to go. Except for Donnal, who had left with the dawn. Marney had made the rest of them breakfast and prepared food that they could take with them on the road. He couldn't thank her because she was nowhere in sight.

"Ellynor's not back yet," Kirra informed him, licking honey off her thumb. She was sitting at the breakfast table, finishing what looked like a pretty substantial meal. "Marney's gone to get her. Ellynor doesn't have any bags to pack, but Marney's put together some odds and ends of her own clothing and Senneth stored them with her things. We can go as soon as she's back and you've eaten."

"Five minutes and I'll be ready," he said. He didn't even bother to sit down to consume his breakfast. He made it a hearty one; when you were traveling, it was impossible to guess when your next meal might arrive.

Senneth, Tayse, and Cammon came in through the kitchen door. "Horses are saddled and ready to go," Tayse said. "All you need to do is throw your saddlebag on the back of yours."

"Didn't know I had a horse," Justin said with a grin. "I think I lost mine somewhere in the woods around the convent."

"Faeber kept him for you all this time," Cammon said.

Justin finished his food and set his plate on the table. "Can't wait to get out of Neft," he said. "I have been here far too long."

Kirra said, "That's how I feel no matter where I've been, if I've stayed longer than three days."

"Yes, but you're a rootless and somewhat shallow girl—" Senneth started, but then Cammon whirled around to face the door. Everyone fell silent. Justin and Tayse drew their knives and dropped their hands to their sword hilts.

But when trouble came through the back door, it came in the shape of Marney. She had run so hard she could barely speak. Her eyes were wide with fright and they instantly searched for Justin.

"They've taken Ellynor," she gasped out. "Three guards from the convent. The steward recognized her and sent for soldiers. She's been gone since early this morning."

Not even aware that he was moving, Justin leapt for the door. But Tayse's hand shot out and hauled him back. "Think. Plan. Don't be stupid," the big man said sharply.

Justin shook him off, but stayed in place, trembling so hard he could barely put a coherent thought together. The others deployed around Marney, purposeful and grim.

"Since early this morning—did you get a more exact time?" Tayse asked her.

Her eyes were wide and frightened, and the expression on Tayse's face was not likely to reassure her. "No—the footman just said early."

"We have to assume it could have been first light," Tayse said. "So, possibly three hours." He glanced at Justin. "She's already nearly at the convent. We can't catch up."

"I have to go get her," Justin said.

Tayse nodded. "We'll come up with a plan." He sounded so cool, so certain. "You've been inside the gates a couple of times. Can you sketch the layout?"

"Yes. But you've seen it yourself."

"Not much more than the interior rooms. I can draw a map of the inside as best as I remember. But I don't know where the barracks are or what anything looks like in the back of the convent."

Kirra was frowning at Cammon. "Why didn't you tell us something was wrong with her?"

Cammon shook his head regretfully. "I told her the other day. I can't get a sense of her at all. I didn't know she was in trouble."

"The Black Mother's magic," Senneth said briefly. "Concealment."

"Do you have reason to believe her life is in danger?" Tayse was asking.

"Yes," Justin said without hesitation. "If they discover she's a mystic—"

"But as far as you know, no one realized that before she left."

"No, but—she's been gone for a week—and she left without a word—"

"And they've sent guards to grab her and force her back," Kirra added. "I think they suspect something."

"We have to get there today," Senneth said quietly.

They all looked at her, and Justin felt his terror ratchet up to all-out dread.

She added, "New moon tonight. It would be the ideal time to punish a mystic."

"I can get there in half an hour," Kirra said. "You follow—tell me a place to meet you on the road. I'll come back and report."

"That still doesn't help us get inside," Tayse said.

Kirra slapped her hands together. "Damnation! I wish Donnal hadn't left! He and I could circle the convent, find a way inside, discover where she's being held. One of us could stay with her and one of us could find the rest of you and make plans."

"I can call him back," Cammon offered. "He could be here in an hour or two."

"We can't wait that long," Justin said.

Tayse glanced at him. "It might be our best solution. Kirra's right—if we send two mystics into the convent, styled as birds or butterflies—"

"Birds," Kirra said with a faint grin. "Faster and more direct."

"Then that gives us several options. So if Cammon tells Donnal to meet us somewhere on the road to the convent—"

"Take me," Justin said. Now they were all staring at him, but he had eyes only for Kirra. "Take me. Turn me into a bird. You've done it before."

A short silence greeted this piece of news, which clearly came as a surprise to both Tayse and Senneth, and then Kirra put a gentle hand on Justin's arm. "Yes, but don't you remember? You were awkward and unsure of your wings. This is not the time to be trying to learn to fly."

"And you've only recently been almost fatally wounded and still are not wholly recovered," Tayse said.

Justin ignored him. He put his hand over Kirra's; he let his face show everything he was feeling. "Take me," he begged. "Please. I have to go to her. I can't let her die."

"I can't let *you* die," Tayse said. "Sending you into that place in an unaccustomed form would almost certainly mean your death. We can wait for Donnal."

"He's right, Justin," came Senneth's soft voice.

Justin didn't even look at them. At this moment, the only one who mattered, the only one with an opinion he cared about, was Kirra. He was crushing her fingers under his. He was allowing the tears to gather in his eyes. He would grovel to her, if that was what was required. If only she would take him with her.

She stared back at him for a long moment, her laughing face utterly serious, her blue eyes dark with calculation. Her hand moved under his, answering his pressure with pressure of her own. He knew she was trying to gauge the limits of his physical strength. Of all times for the reckless Kirra to be cautious! He willed her to trust him, to take the mad chance. He willed her not to care if he died in this desperate adventure.

"All right," she whispered.

The other three cried out at that, and even Cammon sounded alarmed. But there wasn't much they could do to stop Kirra, Justin thought. She was binding her long hair up in a messy knot on the back of her head and glancing around the room as if checking for anything she'd forgotten.

Tayse grabbed Justin's arm again. "This is folly," he said in a rough voice. "I know you love her. I swear to you, we will work to get her back. But you can't throw your life away like this."

Justin merely stepped back far enough to force Tayse to drop his arm. "You'd do it," he said. "If it was Senneth inside."

"Where do you want to meet us?" Kirra asked practically.

"The plan is to travel toward the Lirrens eventually, right?" Senneth said in a subdued voice. "We'll head for the other side of the convent. The eastern road that leads toward Coravann."

"Show me."

Marney—who had stood mute and miserable this whole time—hurried off to find a map, and they all huddled around it briefly until they'd agreed on the coordinates.

"See you there as soon as we can," Kirra said. "Justin—outside. We don't want bird droppings all over Marney's house."

"That's it? You're leaving?" Marney exclaimed. "Oh, good-bye to all of you! Be careful! Will you—will someone let me know what happens to Ellynor?"

Senneth and Cammon were the only ones who bothered to pause and formally thank her. Justin heard Tayse tell their hostess in a rather ominous voice, "We will try to send you word. But assume that Ellynor lives." He didn't predict Justin's own fate, which he obviously expected to be much more dire.

Justin merely followed Kirra out the door.

CHAPTER

37

Ellynor was so cold.

It was close to noon on a gorgeously bright day, and sunshine danced in through the small window as if it could not contain its delight. There was a fire in the grate and a blanket around her shoulders, and Ellynor still shivered so hard that she could not lift a cup of water to her mouth without spilling it.

She knew that she would only be cold until sunset, at which point she would be lashed to a stake and burned to death. Even now, she could hear the faint sounds from the courtyard, wood being chopped, men's voices calling as they considered the best way to ground a single wooden pillar in the soil.

Fire was the preferred way to kill a mystic. Though swords and stones and bare fists would do.

She had known, when she heard the raised voices in the hall, that someone had come for her. Convent guards. That they knew her secret. She had looked around wildly, but there was nowhere to hide in serra Paulina's room that they would not instantly find her. She'd run for the window, tightly shut against the winter chill, and managed to push the glass-paned panels open wide enough to let the cold swoop in. A moment's hesitation—how to make that long drop to the ground?—and that had cost her. Three men burst into the room, noisy and rough, and spotted her before she had time to draw her veils of darkness around her body. She had struggled and cried out against their hold, begging for help from the wide-eyed servants who crowded around the door, but no one had answered, no one had lifted a hand in her defense. The comatose woman lying on the bed did not stir, did not open an eye. If no one thought to close the window, the serramarra would freeze to death an hour before her heart gave out. Ellynor pleaded and wept as they dragged her down the stairs, through the courtyard, out the gate, and threw her into a waiting cart. Her throat and wrists and ankles were burning; it was only later that she realized the ropes they bound her with had been studded with moonstones.

A hellish ride through the countryside, through the murmuring forest, moving so quickly and bouncing so hard over ruts in the road that Ellynor's whole body was bruised from transit. She had stopped sobbing—she was entirely numb—by the time the wagon pulled through the high gates of the convent. She did not speak, did not resist, as they yanked her out and forced her to walk across the great hall. It seemed as if every soul in the convent had gathered there to watch in shocked silence as she was hustled past them, the novices, the proselytes, the dedicants in their white and green and purple robes. They stared but they did not speak. Their horror was thick enough to breathe.

The guards had forced her up the stairs, their hands clutched so tight on her arms that they practically carried her, though her feet slipped and stumbled as she tried to catch herself on every other step. Not until she had been flung inside this small, bare room—not one she had ever seen before—did Ellynor realize that Shavell had followed them and was coolly supervising this final leg of the journey.

"That's right—attach this chain to the ropes that bind her. We don't want to run any risk that the mystic will use her sorcerous tricks to get free."

Mystic. So they knew. How had they discovered the truth? Ellynor had assumed that the Lestra would be furious to learn that she had run away and would exact some painful punishment if Ellynor ever returned, but she had not expected that this most dangerous secret would come to light.

"Shavell—please—what have I done?" Ellynor begged, as one of the guards padlocked a chain around the loop of rope that held her wrists together in front of her. That chore done, he gave her a hard shove, knocking her to the floor. The other two guards laughed, and all of them tramped out of the room.

Shavell remained behind, staring down at her, haughty and full of rage. "Mystic," she repeated, almost hissing the word.

"But I'm not—why do you think—what would make you call me such a thing?" Ellynor cried.

"You have been denounced," the dedicant declared. Her tall, thin body was shaking with righteousness; her bony face shone with malevolence.

"Who denounced me?" Ellynor demanded, manufacturing a tone of outrage. "Who said such a lie about me?"

"Your cousin Rosurie."

Ellynor gasped and almost collapsed onto the floor. "But she—it's not true! Why would she say such a thing? What did she say I've done?"

"You worship a lesser goddess. You only pretend to adore the Pale Mother. Instead, you claim this—this Black Mother gives you powers of strength and healing." Shavell made a noise that sounded as if she had actually spat in the corner. "*Mystic*," she repeated with unutterable loathing.

"What will happen to me?" Ellynor whispered.

Shavell pointed toward the window, which was so high Ellynor could not have seen out it, even if she had been able to stand. "Mystics burn," she said with a certain satisfaction. "We will light the bonfire tonight."

"Please—" Ellynor breathed, but Shavell did not wait to hear any supplication. She swept through the door and locked it with a loud and deliberate turn of the key.

Ellynor stayed huddled where she was, so cold, so lost, so abandoned. This was how she was repaid for accompanying Rosurie to the Lumanen Convent so that she would not be frightened and lonely when she was far from home! This was how Rosurie proved how much she loved the Silver Lady! *Ellynor* was to be her sacrifice to the Pale Mother. *Ellynor* must die so that Rosurie could win her place in the convent.

"Great Mother, sweet Mother, do not let me die by fire," Ellynor prayed. "Come to me as soon as you can. Throw your dark blanket over my face—halt my breathing. Chill my blood in my veins. Let me die before the first spark flies. Do not make me come to you through smoke and flame."

Justin would be crazed, she knew. He would blame himself bitterly for allowing her to go to the Gisseltess house against his better judgment. He would not want to live—that was what worried her most. He would do something rash, desperate, suicidal, when he found she had been taken by Lumanen soldiers. She had a moment of sparkling white fear at the thought he might try to break through the convent gates in a doomed attempt to rescue her, but then she relaxed. His friends would hold him tight. Tayse and Senneth and the others, they would not let him throw away his life on her.

The irony, of course, was that she had known the minute she arrived at the Gisseltess house that there was nothing she could do. Death had come for serra Paulina, was perched on the headboard, calmly waiting. Ellynor had touched the old woman's throat and chest, chasing away the pain, but there was nothing she could do to extend that frail life by even another day.

She had not been able to save serra Paulina and she would not be able to save herself.

She had never been so cold in her life.

Biting back a little moan, she pushed herself up off the floor, just enough to crawl toward the fireplace. There, a tiny flame was darting around a single heavy log, as if seeking, with its flimsy strength, to dislodge the wood. Ellynor knew that fire was not her friend; she knew that in a few hours she would be screaming in agony as a blaze roared around her. But right now she was freezing. She lifted her trembling hands and held them over the grate, as close to the log as she dared.

Her fingers were so cold that they put the fire out.

Whimpering, Ellynor dropped to the icy stone floor, cradled her head in her hands, and wept.

THE first time the door opened, she looked up, stabbed by a sudden unreasonable hope. Which turned immediately to bewilderment as three—four—*five* novices stepped into the room, their hands clasped before them, their eyes cast down. Shavell entered briskly behind them, her violet robe a dark contrast to their vivid white.

"Look upon this wretched woman and know that she is evil," Shavell intoned, and all five novices obediently lifted their eyes and gravely inspected Ellynor. "She is a mystic, a dabbler in the dark arts, a heretic who worships false gods. What is the only fit punishment for a mystic?"

"She must die," the girls replied in unison.

"She must die," Shavell repeated. "Tonight."

Ellynor was still staring at them speechlessly when Shavell herded her charges back out the door and locked it resoundingly behind her once more.

Half an hour later, another set of novices stepped inside—eight of them this time, crowding as close to the door as they could, supervised by Darris. "A mystic," Darris said, repeating the list of crimes, but unable to replicate Shavell's venom. She sounded, instead, sorrowful and a little afraid, and she couldn't bring herself to look directly at Ellynor. "She will die tonight."

The third group to arrive was led by her cousin Rosurie. This time Ellynor was prepared for them. She couldn't find the strength to get up off the floor, but she had pulled herself together somewhat. She was sitting cross-legged before the dead fire, her bound hands folded in her lap, her tears dry on her face, her expression remote. Still, she almost gaped when Rosurie stepped through the door, wearing a proselyte's green robe and supervising a set of much younger girls. There was Lia, crying and turning her head away; there were three novices just arrived at the convent this fall, wide-eyed and uneasy. Ellynor supposed they hadn't expected anything like this when they begged their fathers to send them to live with the Daughters.

"Here sits the woman who has betrayed the goddess," Rosurie said in an utterly calm voice. Her hair had started to grow back a little, but it was only about a half inch long and did little to disguise the hard, distinctive shape of Rosurie's skull. She looked so foreign to Ellynor, so angular and otherworldly. Not kin at all.

"There stands the woman who betrayed me," Ellynor shot back. Lia gasped and one of the other girls covered her mouth with her hand. Clearly they had not expected the miscreant to speak up on her own behalf.

Rosurie ignored her. "She claimed to love the Silver Lady when instead she worshipped a lesser goddess—"

"A goddess *you* have prayed to in your father's house!"

"She used magic inside a consecrated place. She sought to destroy the Lestra and all her work."

"Which is worse, Rosurie?" Ellynor demanded. "Healing a sick child or condemning a member of your family to death? Which is the true crime?"

"What is the only fit punishment for a mystic?" Rosurie asked.

"She must die," the novices murmured, but none of them looked convinced. Lia was sobbing openly now, and she wiped her nose on the sleeve of her white robe.

"She must die," Rosurie repeated with satisfaction. "Tonight."

Ellynor thought that little interlude was as bad as it could get, but she was wrong. A half hour later another small delegation strode into her room: Shavell again, two proselytes, a novice or two—and the Lestra.

Ellynor was so shocked to see Coralinda Gisseltess that at first she did not realize who else had arrived. She just had a blurred impression of many different colors as the other women arranged themselves behind the black-robed Lestra. No doubt Ellynor was supposed to rise, or bow, or clasp her hands and plead, but she could not bring herself to behave as though she thought this woman was splendid and powerful. So she sat there, sullen and silent, staring up at these new trespassers, hating all of them, fearing all of them equally.

"So," the Lestra said in that magnificent, sonorous voice. "This is the woman who has tarnished the face of the Silver Lady."

Ellynor made no reply.

"I grieve so deeply when I realize how much I loved you," the Lestra said, and indeed her voice sounded full of woe and sorrow. "You were my Dark Moon Daughter! You were the one who understood all the deepest secrets of the night! But your secrets were even blacker than I knew. No gentle light, no blazing moon, can illuminate your soul. You are given over to darkness."

"I have done nothing wrong," Ellynor said.

The Lestra appeared astonished. "Nothing wrong! You have cast spells! You have worked magic! You have practiced the evil arts that the Silver Lady most abhors! But her round eye sees everything, including your treachery. She has discovered you and laid bare your soul. You must be cleansed of evil through the crucible of fire. The Pale Mother will gather you up in her arms and make you anew in a brighter, purer image."

"I don't want to die," Ellynor whispered.

The Lestra came a step closer, and for a moment Ellynor actually thought the older woman would lay a hand upon her cheek. "You will be reunited with the goddess," she said in a comforting voice. "It will not be death, it will be glory."

"It will be murder, and it will be by fire," Ellynor retorted.

The Lestra made an equivocal motion with her hands. "The Silver Lady has room in her heart for penitents," she said.

Ellynor felt a cruel, bitter twist of hope. "How could I show you I repent?" she breathed.

"First you must renounce that false goddess you worship so wrongly."

Deny the Great Mother who was so generous with her power, who had shielded Ellynor from danger and lavished her with gifts? Ellynor was not sure she would be able to force the words out. And yet she had a suspicion the Dark Watcher would urge her to take the counterfeit pledge, swear the sham oath. The Black Mother understood when a lie was necessary, when it was best to conceal the truth.

But that was only the first step? "What else would you require?" Ellynor asked through stiff lips.

The Lestra's lovely voice dropped to a soft, inviting pitch. "It is common, I know, for those who hold contrary beliefs to seek each other out. To band together. To whisper their secrets to each other. Only tell me who else among my novices believes as you do. Are there other mystics among us? Girls who question their faith and disobey the convent laws? Tell me their names. Help me to purify this place and keep it sacred for the goddess."

It was at that exact moment that Ellynor realized Astira was part of the delegation. Perhaps the other woman moved—flinched—at the

Lestra's speech. Perhaps the Great Mother chose that moment to put her hand on Ellynor's chin and turn her head in Astira's direction. At any rate, suddenly Ellynor was staring at the rangy blond girl with the elegant features, her face almost as white as her novice's robe.

Astira had confided in her. Told Ellynor about taking the guard Daken as her lover. Not as heinous as practicing magic, but a crime, nonetheless, in the Lestra's eyes. A sin. Something she would want to know about—and destroy. The look on Astira's face showed terror and supplication in equal parts, both overlaid with hopelessness.

Astira would have told, if she was in this position, Ellynor realized. Astira would have supplied any number of names, repeated whispered conversations, careless words she'd overheard in the hall. Astira would have said anything to save herself.

"I know of no one else who has sinned," Ellynor said.

The Lestra frowned. "That cannot be true. Women are weak and easily tempted. There must be one or two among the Daughters who have strayed from the dictates of the Pale Mother."

"That might be so," Ellynor replied, "but they haven't told their stories to me."

The Lestra stepped back with a swirl of black skirts, anger and contempt in every line of her body. "You are lying or you are unlucky," she said with something of a snarl. "There is nothing you can do to redeem yourself."

Ellynor felt cold fear lance through her. "Not even if I say—if I renounce the Black Mother?"

The Lestra appeared to consider. A small motion caught Ellynor's attention and she looked over the Lestra's shoulder to see Astira shaking her head in short, jerky motions. As if to say, *Such a sacrifice will not save you. You are condemned to death even if you repulse your goddess.* Astira's face was still bloodless and strained, but her expression had loosened. She looked dazed with relief.

"And are you willing to give her up?" the Lestra demanded. "Give yourself over to the care of the Silver Lady?"

Ellynor bowed her head. "I love the Pale Mother," she said in a quiet voice. "I love her in her laughing moods and her proud silences. She is girlish and sweet one day, harsh and unforgiving the next. She is changeable and beautiful and curious, and I hope she believes that I have served her well." She lifted her head and met the Lestra's eyes. "But I am bound to the Black Mother, who loves me as much as she loves her own daughter. It is she who has given me magic, and she I will worship till I die."

"Which will be tonight," the Lestra snapped.

Ellynor dropped her head again. She was so tired. She was so cold. She was completely without hope. "Yes," she said very softly. "It will be tonight."

Two more groups of novices came through in the next hour. Ellynor was beginning to think that the Lestra intended every single soul who lived in the convent to parade by and view the condemned mystic. But the sun was sliding down toward late afternoon, she thought tiredly. Surely there would not be enough time for the more than five hundred novices to come by and stare and whisper. Perhaps this honor had been reserved for only the flightiest girls, the ones who could not absolutely be trusted, the ones who would most profit from such a stern lesson.

It would be dark in less than two hours, Ellynor judged. She came somewhat shakily to her feet, not sure if it was the hunger or the fear or the lingering effects of healing Justin that had left her so unsteady. She was still cold, but by now her bones had turned to ice; she was so numb she almost couldn't tell how miserable she was. The sounds of chopping and construction no longer drifted up from the courtyard. The bonfire must be ready by now, she supposed. All that was left to wait for was sunset.

No need to wait for moonrise. This was the night without a moon.

Ellynor wanted to experience the daylight while she could. The window was too high to see out of, but it admitted a patch of sun that was moving slowly up the wall as the hours passed. Right now it was just about at face-height. She closed her eyes and stepped directly into it, absorbing its brightness on her cheekbones, her eyelids, tilting her chin so that the light ran down her neck. Senneth's goddess was the sun, so Justin had told her. Maybe the Bright Mother had dropped in to offer Ellynor what comfort she could.

A chittering, clicking sound, closer to hand than the distant courtyard, caused Ellynor to reluctantly open her eyes. Two birds were perched right outside the window, pecking at the glass as if trying to break through it. The sight was so unexpected that Ellynor actually smiled. They looked to be spring hawks, lighter and smaller than the common variety, built for speed and agility. They were normally northern creatures; she wondered what they were doing so far south.

One, the smaller of the two, ruffled with impatience and pecked at the window again. Or—no—how odd. The hawk rested its sharp beak against the clear pane the way Ellynor might press her nose against a window if there was something inside that she wanted.

With a faint sizzle of mist, the glass simply vanished.

Ellynor stared, dumbstruck, and watched the birds fly inside. The smaller one landed right at her feet; the larger one circled her head as if inspecting her for flaws or damage. Or perhaps it was looking for a place to land. Marveling—but unable, on this day, to summon any more disbelief—she held her bound hands out, and it promptly settled in her cupped palms. It regarded her from its bright yellow eyes and loosed a cackling stream of chatter that sounded so earnest and determined it might have been trying to communicate with her in human patterns of speech.

Bemused, Ellynor glanced down at the hawk on the floor. Which was no longer a hawk—which was a growing, stretching, blurred, and fantastical creature of skin and feathers and golden hair. Now she gasped; now her heart really did squeeze in wonder.

It was only a moment before her gaping turned to galloping, painful hope, because it was only a moment before the transformation was complete. Kirra Danalustrous stood before her.

CHAPTER
38

"I see by your expression you're not used to watching a shiftling change shapes," Kirra said, throwing her arms around Ellynor and causing the other bird to squawk with indignation. "I can't tell you how relieved I am to see you still alive, though by the stake and the pile of wood they've got laid out in the courtyard, I would say the time of your execution is imminent."

It was this long before Ellynor could find her voice. "Kirra! What are you doing here? How did you know what happened to me? Oh, is there anything you can do to get me out of this place?"

"Yes, but we don't have much time," Kirra replied. "We've been here almost two hours, but every time we thought it was safe to come in, someone else came bursting through the door to point fingers and call you dreadful names. I'm guessing that pattern will continue for the rest of the day, wouldn't you think?"

"It seems likely. They seem very eager to have all the novices look on the face of evil."

Kirra nodded. "Then we can't risk just taking you out of the room. Before we crossed the courtyard, someone would be sure to come in looking for you, and if you were missing, the alarm would be raised before we could get out the gate."

The hawk in Ellynor's hands danced on its spindly feet and loosed an urgent stream of incomprehensible sounds in Kirra's direction.

"Oh, hush," the mystic responded.

Ellynor glanced down at the restless body nestled in her hands. "What did he say?"

"I have no idea."

"Is it Donnal?"

"No. Justin."

Ellynor almost dropped him to the floor. "*Justin?* But he—he's not a mystic! Is he?"

"No. I changed him. He insisted on coming." Kirra was watching her with those divine blue eyes. "To save you."

Now Ellynor cradled the hawk in her hands and brought him up to her face, almost crooning to him. "Justin. I can't believe you came for me—well, of course, I can believe it, it's just like you, but you're not strong enough! How could you try something like this when you're so weak yourself—"

"We don't have time to work through the argument again," Kirra said, cutting her off. "Here's what we're going to do. I'm going to use a little magic to make you look different. Look like any other novice. I'm going to shift shapes and change my clothes, and I'm going to look like a novice, too. Then we will stroll out the room, down the steps, and out the front gates. You will use whatever dark sorcery you have to hide us from the guards and anyone who happens to be watching. Or will such magic not work in the daylight?"

"It will," Ellynor said, hoping that was still true. "But what about Justin?"

"We will leave Justin behind, shaped like you."

"No," Ellynor said.

"The next ten groups of novices who come in to chastise mystics will be making their case against Justin instead," Kirra continued as if Ellynor had not spoken. "When I have gotten you to safety, I will return for him. I will change him into a hawk again, and we will fly from here as swiftly as we can."

"No," Ellynor said. "Let him come with us now. The three of us can leave together. Surely my magic is strong enough to conceal us all."

"Ellynor. If someone enters and finds this room empty, the alarm will be raised so fast we will not be able to make it to the gates. Someone knows you're a mystic—they must also know that one of your powers is concealment. They will have ten guards strung across the gate, hands outstretched, waiting to catch you."

"Then change me into a bird, too—we'll all fly out the window together," Ellynor begged. "Don't make Justin stay here."

Kirra shook her head. "Trust me, you wouldn't make it out of the room. It takes time and patience to learn to fly—Justin has had some practice, and even so he was almost dashed out of the sky three times on our way here."

"Please," Ellynor whispered. "Don't leave Justin behind."

Justin was hopping in her palm now, chattering at a furious rate, trying to convey—something. Ellynor thought she could guess what it was. *I love you. I will risk my life for you. You cannot do anything to keep me safe when you are in danger.* But she could not bear to know that she might escape at the cost of his life.

"He insisted on coming," Kirra said softly. "He defied Tayse—for what was surely the first time in his life—because he wanted to save you. The plan will work no other way. We must stop talking about it and put the plan in motion, or it will be too late for either of you."

Before Ellynor could answer, Justin erupted into a furious tirade and launched himself from Ellynor's hands toward the window. Kirra hastily stepped back toward the wall and shrank into proportions so small Ellynor could not see her. Only then did Ellynor hear the rattle at the door and realize another set of novices was being brought in to view her.

She stayed standing near the window, sunlight on her face, no brighter than the defiance that must now be blazing from her eyes. Shavell led the small group inside, repeated the recitation of evil and death, and shot Ellynor one spiteful look before herding the women out of the room again.

Kirra was right. If someone came into this room and it was empty . . .

"We have to work very fast," Kirra said, materializing again from some shape that seemed to possess hairy black arms, which visibly reformed themselves into Kirra's more elegant limbs. A spider, possibly. Justin darted back into the room, landed on Ellynor's shoulder, and proceeded to nibble at her hair. "I can't change as quickly as Donnal can, and I certainly can't change myself *and* Justin rapidly enough to fool someone who bursts in through the door. Are you done arguing?"

"Yes," Ellynor whispered. "But please, please, please make sure you're back for Justin in time."

"I will be." Kirra studied Ellynor a moment, her eyes sweeping down the length of the chain, pausing on the rope encrusted with moonstones. "I can't touch your shackles. We need Justin, after all."

Imperiously, she snapped her fingers and pointed to the floor, and Justin hopped down from Ellynor's shoulder. Kirra knelt before him and put her fingers against his tiny head. Ellynor watched in a fearful fascination as Justin took shape beneath her delicate hands. As soon as he was himself again, he whirled around and snatched Ellynor into a hard embrace.

"Bright Mother, I have been so worried about you," he whispered into her ear. "I was sure you were already dead."

"Oh, Justin, you shouldn't have come here! I won't be able to bear it if something happens to you—in my place—"

"I'm sorry, we don't have time for sweet reunions," Kirra said, actually sounding sorry. "Justin. Can you cut her bonds? And then hide them somewhere? I will manufacture a piece of rope that *looks* like it's covered with moonstones, and we'll tie you up with that. Otherwise, I won't be able to change you when I come back."

Even before she had finished speaking, Justin had pulled a dagger from a side sheath and sliced through the ropes. Then he lifted first one chafed wrist and then the other to his mouth, as if his kiss held a healing magic. Perhaps it did, or perhaps the moonstones had been burning her flesh even more hotly than she realized. In any case, she felt those kisses like a balm; her hands felt light enough to float.

Kirra was yanking a belt from around her own waist, refashioning it into a length of hemp even as Ellynor watched. Quickly enough it was dotted with small, glowing gems that looked enough like moonstones to fool anyone who hadn't been present in the room. She motioned to Justin.

"Come stand by me and prepare for an even stranger transformation than any you've yet undergone."

He grinned and complied. "Never really wondered what it felt like to be a woman," he said. "Guess I'll find out."

"I'm sure the experience will do wonders for your empathy," Kirra replied. "Hold still."

Again the golden-haired mystic put her hands on Justin's face. Clearly, she couldn't effect a transformation unless she was touching the object or the creature she wanted to enchant. Ellynor watched in equal parts wonder and fear as Justin's face smoothed out, his hair darkened, his burly body shrank down, slimmed out, developed curves.

She was staring at an exact likeness of herself.

It was too strange; she put a hand to her mouth and tried to keep back a little cry. For his part, Justin seemed just as nonplussed. He lifted his hands to study them. He glanced down at his chest to investigate his bosom. When he looked up again, he was grinning. The expression did not belong on her own face. It was utterly Justin.

"I have seen some pretty outlandish things since I took up with mystics," he said, and his voice sounded exactly like Ellynor's. "But I don't think anything compares to this."

Kirra had already started binding his wrists before him with the magical rope, slipping it through the loop of the padlock. "Just remember who you're supposed to be, and don't do anything out of character," she advised him. "If someone speaks to you and you can't figure out what you *should* say, don't say anything at all. I'll be back as soon as I can."

"I'll be waiting for you."

Now Kirra turned to Ellynor. "You might feel a tingle. A sort of fluttering of your skin. It shouldn't actually be painful. I'm just going to make you look like some nondescript girl in a clean white robe. So even if your magic slips and someone sees us, they won't see *you*."

Ellynor nodded, not trusting herself to speak. In fact, Kirra's magic brushed lightly over her, pinpricks against her face and along her shoulders, and then faded. She wished she had a mirror; she would like to see a stranger's face looking back at her. Or maybe she wouldn't. Kirra took a half step back, seemed to focus on something inside her body, and underwent her own subtle transformation. The arrestingly beautiful face was now plain, unmemorable, framed by rather lank hair. The body was hidden under perfectly stitched white robes. There was even a moonstone bracelet dangling from one wrist.

"You wouldn't look twice if you passed me in the hall, would you?" Kirra demanded.

Ellynor shook her head. "No. You're nobody I recognize, but you look like you belong."

"You'd better go," Justin said in Ellynor's voice.

Kirra nodded and reached for the door. Ellynor said anxiously, "It's locked."

Kirra just gave her a droll look and didn't answer. But before she could take hold of the handle, Justin hissed, "Someone's coming," and turned to face the door.

For a moment, Ellynor was blank with panic. Someone would find Kirra and Justin here! They would all be discovered, and there would be no escape for any of them! But then Kirra's hand closed around her wrist, and the mystic pulled her back toward the wall.

"Now would be a good time to use your magic," she murmured in Ellynor's ear. "So all they see is Justin."

Of course. Ellynor fought for calm, for Kirra's unwavering self-confidence. Justin was staring at them in deep apprehension, for there was a rattle at the lock and then the door swung open. But Justin's face relaxed before the first of the novices stepped inside, and Ellynor realized she had managed it, had summoned magic under duress and turned both herself and her companion invisible.

Shavell again. She must have requested this particular duty. She certainly seemed to be enjoying the chance to castigate Ellynor before every audience of wide-eyed novices.

"You see this wretched woman?" Shavell demanded. "Do you see the evil in her eyes? Study the features of the mystic so you might recognize the same kind of magic on another woman's face."

Considering that she was ranting about a man who had no sorcerous ability, Ellynor almost wanted to laugh out loud. Of course, she also wanted to stand unmoving, unbreathing, until Shavell was safely out of the room, and so she merely stood pressed against the wall, her wrist still caught in Kirra's hand.

"Why don't you recant your magic, wicked girl?" Shavell demanded now of the Rider in disguise. "Why don't you renounce your false goddess?"

Kirra had told him to keep silent, but Ellynor supposed there had never been any real hope of that. "I'd rather die," Justin said calmly.

Shavell's eyes narrowed. "And so you shall."

"And so will you," he replied in a soft voice that sounded dangerous even given his circumstances. "Sooner than you like to think."

Kirra's hand squeezed on Ellynor's arm as if to say, *Why can't Justin ever behave?* Shavell gasped and launched into a furious tirade, invoking the name of the Lestra and the anger of the Silver Lady. Justin turned his back on her, clearly not interested. Ellynor had to strangle another laugh at the look on Shavell's face.

"You'll be sorry soon enough," Shavell was promising now, her lean cheeks bright with color as she wrenched the door open and almost shoved the flock of novices out. Ellynor was startled when Kirra suddenly tugged her toward the door, until she realized that Kirra wanted them to exit with this small group and mingle with them casually in the hallway. She obediently fell in step behind the white-robed girls, Kirra at her side. No chance to say a last good-bye to Justin! She wondered if he would even know they were leaving, or if he would speak her name once, twice, after Shavell set the lock. She looked back, but she could not see him through the closing door.

They must get to safety as quickly as possible so that Kirra could return for him.

They followed the group of novices along the hallway and down one set of steps. The magic held; no one noticed them. Ellynor and Kirra continued down the stairway when the novices headed toward one of the chapels on the second floor. It was odd, so odd, to glide through these familiar hallways with absolute stealth, keeping to the shadows, moving along the walls, making no sound. Ellynor felt like a ghost, barred from full participation in a familiar world but still driven to revisit former beloved sites.

Kirra kept her hand locked around Ellynor's wrist and followed her so closely they would only have cast a single shadow. If she had spared a moment to think about it, Ellynor might have worried that Kirra would be clumsy in her attempts to creep unnoticed through a defined space, but Kirra was as silent as a lean raelynx on a bitter winter night. Ellynor could only conclude that the mystic had done some hunting in the past.

Finally clear of the stairwell—now crossing the great hall with care, avoiding the novices, the dedicants, the guards, who bustled in ones and twos through the wide space. Out the door right behind a contingent of guards who were arguing about somebody's horse and its ability to run faster than somebody else's horse. Past the stark, thick stake forced into the ground right in the middle of the courtyard, with plenty of room on all sides for an audience to gather and watch. The fuel piled in a circle around it had to be two feet high. Enough to smolder a good long while. Long after anyone tied to the stake had burned to ash and cinder.

Ellynor glanced up at the sky, even now starting to haze over with gathering dusk. How long would the Lestra wait to put the mystic to death? Till midnight, when the ritual chants were over? Or would she forgo the offering of song tonight, since she had a much more spectacular offering to present to the Silver Lady? Would she bring out the bound captive the minute true darkness fell?

It might be only an hour till sunset.

Ellynor was almost running now as she towed Kirra toward the massive gates. She had been wondering if Kirra planned to treat the wrought iron as she had treated the glass, and turn the barrier to something more permeable, but she didn't have to. Even as the two women arrived at the gates, the guards on duty were pulling them back to admit a small party of soldiers on horseback. It was a simple thing to edge to one side, avoid being trampled by unwary hooves, and ease past the convent walls.

Free. Safe. Rescued from the fire.

They couldn't stop there, of course. Ellynor let Kirra take charge now, since she assumed the other woman had a destination, and Kirra led them at a rapid pace about a quarter of a mile into the forest. Then she pulled them both off the road into an overhang of wood and finally dropped Ellynor's hand.

"Are you going back for Justin now?" Ellynor said eagerly and was bitterly disappointed when Kirra shook her head.

"I need to get you to safety first."

"I'm safe! I'm out! Please, Kirra—"

"All this risk will be worth nothing if we don't truly get you away from here," Kirra interrupted. "I'm going to take the shape of a horse now and carry you to the place where Senneth and the others are waiting. Then I'll come back for Justin. The more you argue," she said, raising her voice as Ellynor was about to protest again, "the longer it will be before I can return."

Ellynor shut her mouth with a snap. "I know where I'm going," Kirra added, "so just let me run."

Practically on the words, Kirra began to shift shapes. Ellynor wondered if it ever got mundane, the sight of a mystic undergoing transmogrification. She, at least, had not grown accustomed to the display, and so she stared as Kirra's head puffed up and her arms lengthened so much they seemed to pull her toward the ground. Her hips turned into haunches, her back extended, her flowing hair became the blond mane of a palomino. Kirra was as pretty a mare as she was a human—and she had thoughtfully manufactured for Ellynor a saddle and a set of stirrups. No bridle, though; clearly, there would not be much hope of controlling this particular animal.

Ellynor grabbed the pommel and quickly mounted, and Kirra took off almost before Ellynor was settled in the saddle. It seemed only logical to maintain her own useful magic, concealing both horse and rider from any chance passersby as they ran through the shadowy forest, racing against the oncoming night.

CHAPTER
39

In the next hour, two more groups of novices dropped by to mock the mystic. Neither of them was led by the sour-faced woman who had spewed such hatred the last time, so Justin figured she had been well and truly infuriated by his brazen attitude. *All to the good*, he thought. He refrained from speaking during the next two visits, just contented himself with leveling a cold stare at the white-robed young girls and their chaperones. Neither of the older women seemed much affected by his expression, but the novices were clearly made uncomfortable. None of them could meet his eyes for more than a second or two, and most of them shuffled their feet and looked longingly at the door.

None of them spoke up on Ellynor's behalf, either to claim she was not a mystic or to argue that it didn't matter. That made him angry—weren't some of these women her friends? Wouldn't the Riders defend Justin if he had been accused of some crime?—and he toyed with the idea of denouncing them for their faintheartedness. But Kirra had told him not to create a disturbance, and so he remained silent and relatively tame during both of these visits.

The rest of the time, there wasn't much to do. The room was too small to permit true pacing, even allowing for the fact that Ellynor's steps were so much shorter than his own. The chain didn't afford him freedom to walk the length of the room, anyway. Mostly he just sat, resting his back against the wall and stretching his undersized legs in front of him. He was more tired than he liked to admit; if he thought he'd have an hour of peace, he'd actually try to get some sleep. But he wanted to be alert in case another set of novices came through the door, or Kirra suddenly reappeared at the window.

He couldn't keep himself from constantly trying to imagine where Kirra and Ellynor were. There had been no commotion from the courtyard in the twenty minutes after they left the room, so he assumed they had successfully slipped out of the gates. Were they still in the forest? Just breaking clear of the trees on the eastern border? Had they found Senneth yet? When would Ellynor finally be safe?

He was thirsty, so he got up once to drink from a small jug by the dead fire. Hungry, too, but clearly the Daughters were not going to waste food on a woman condemned to death. Eventually he needed to empty his bladder—and he stood for a moment, staring ruefully down at the chamber pot that he wouldn't be able to use in his accustomed fashion. Damned inconvenient to be a woman, all things considered.

DARKNESS fell with a complete and ominous suddenness.

Justin had rested his head against the wall and closed his eyes, half listening to the sounds from the corridor outside the locked door. He was sitting in a most unladylike pose, legs drawn up and spread apart, an arm resting on one knee, the skirts of his robe hiked up to show his ankles and quite an indecent length of his slim calves. That might shock the next cadre of young girls who were ushered into the room, required to look him over, and asked if he didn't deserve to die. It might be all he would do to make them uneasy; he wasn't sure, the next time, he'd even bother giving them his soulless glare. He was conserving his energy for the next chapter of this adventure, the flight away from the convent.

Just at that minute, the room went dark. His eyes flew open. Not moving from where he sat, he visually checked the high window. There was a gilding of rosy gold along the deep embrasure, but it was fading fast. The sun had obviously just dropped completely out of view behind the horizon.

Some people might call this night.

He no longer felt any inclination to sleep. Adrenaline was coursing through him, making his muscles sing. He wouldn't have said he was afraid, but he recognized that he was quickly skidding into the territory of very real danger. It all depended on whether or not the Lestra believed in the ritualistic power of midnight, or whether all she required to enact her justice was nightfall. There was no moon to wait for, not tonight; would she have any reason at all to set back the hour of his execution?

A clanking in the hall, and Justin turned his head toward the door. Those weren't the footsteps of novices in their sturdy shoes and flowing robes. Those were the tramping feet of soldiers, wearing heavy boots and scraping their scabbards against the wall. Justin listened, trying to gauge numbers. *Four at least,* he thought. Someone cursed and someone laughed, and there was a rattle at the door.

Five men walked in, wearing formal black-and-silver livery. Justin could see the moons embroidered on their sashes, the moonstones set into the occasional ring or pin. They were here on official business.

They were here to escort him down to his funeral pyre.

"Rise to your feet, mystic," snarled the man in the lead, who was gray-haired and iron-faced, the sort of bastard who could run any barracks with dispassionate efficiency. Three of the others also looked seasoned and tough, but the fourth was young, maybe Justin's age, and trying desperately to keep an indifferent look on his face. He wasn't used to participating in murder, Justin thought. He was the weak one, the one Justin would have tried to coerce or win over—if he'd had any time, any room, to make a play for freedom.

But he was bound and unarmed and completely without opportunities. Slowly he rose to his insignificant height, the hems of the white robes settling around his feet. He could feel the loose knot of Ellynor's hair coming undone, just a little. He wondered how exact Kirra's reproduction had been. He wondered if the Lirren clan marks had been painted onto the hair he wore, and if anyone would notice if they hadn't.

"The time has come for you to die," the lead guard said. "Take hold of her arms."

One of the older soldiers grabbed his left arm fairly roughly, and it was all Justin could do not to lash out with a fast kick to the groin. That would only earn him a swift punch in reprisal, and he didn't want to take any extra punishment if he didn't have to. In case he did see a chance to run, in case there was an opportunity that, at the moment, seemed almost impossible to conceive of . . .

The younger man took hold of his right arm more gently, giving Justin a long, meaningful stare. Justin felt his eyes narrow. In his experience, someone who was uncomfortable with the notion of an execution tried to look anywhere *but* at the person condemned to die. This young man, whose well-modeled features marked him as at least partially noble, might be trying to send him a message of some sort. Was he upon friendly terms with Ellynor? She had said the Lestra discouraged fraternizing between novices and guards, but surely relationships developed now and then. Ellynor had not mentioned any guards with whom she was especially close—and this was surely a strange time to feel jealousy!—but perhaps there was some help here. Perhaps there was something Justin could turn to his advantage.

Not immediately, however. The leader of the group unlocked the chain from around the rope, and then he jerked his head for the door. Immediately, the two guards began to haul Justin across the floor. He had to put some effort into matching their pace, since he could not take his usual long stride. He would have to remember this—how fast he usually walked, how hard it must be for Ellynor to keep up.

He would have to keep to a moderate stroll, the next time he was with Ellynor.

If he was ever again with Ellynor.

They dragged him down two sets of stairs and through the great hall that Tayse had described for him. It was deserted, but he soon learned why. Every soul who lived on the convent grounds—the hundreds of novices and maybe half as many guards—appeared to be gathered in the courtyard outside. A couple dozen flambeaux had been scattered around to illuminate this ceremony. By their light Justin could make out the mass of white robes, the occasional spot of green and violet, the black uniforms of the guards. He only got a quick, blurred impression of the faces—some of the women weeping, some of the women turned away, some of the men curious, some elated, some a little afraid.

One tall torch was planted in the ground just a few feet away from the stake and its surrounding piles of fuel, but it cast enough light to throw the whole execution site into stark relief. The smell of fresh-cut cedar sent a sharp spice into the evening air. Justin realized with a start that it was cold out, a deeply bitter midwinter night. The stars stared down, blinking with curiosity or horror. The moon, of course, was nowhere to be seen, hiding her face from the sight of yet another mystic perishing at her command.

It was clear to Justin that he was going to die. His own small detail of guards was escorting him through a double row of soldiers lined up from the convent door to the first bundle of fuel laid in front of the stake. The two guards still had a tight hold on his arms. Could he break free of both of them? And if he could, how far could he run before one of the others caught him? Still, it might be preferable, if he was going to die, to die in a brutal fight, kicking and punching and inflicting a certain satisfying damage. Ellynor's body was not built for violence, and, of course, the rope around his wrists would drastically limit the kinds of blows he could land, but he still possessed Rider instincts and Rider reflexes. He could probably take out at least one or two of the Lestra's soldiers before he was brought down. If they killed him in the scuffle, so much the better. It was not death itself that frightened him. Any Rider would say he was willing to die in service of someone he had sworn to protect, and Justin was glad to sacrifice his life for Ellynor's. But to die by fire . . . almost any other end would be better.

The guard to Justin's left slackened his grip, and Justin reacted instinctively. He yanked his left arm free, slammed his tied hands into the man on his right, and suddenly he was free. Running—curse these skirts and his short legs!—dodging outstretched hands, plowing his head deep into the stomach of a guard who raced up to try and capture him. Someone grabbed him from behind and he snatched the man's wrist, tried to fling the soldier over his shoulder. But this feminine shape wasn't made for such maneuvers—his balance was centered in his hips—he tried to adjust his stance, tried to fend off the clutching hands. Someone clouted him from behind and the world went dizzy. Before he could recover, hands were all over his body, and he was being dragged backward, through the murmuring crowd, toward the implacable, inescapable pillar of wood.

He twisted and bit and kicked and fought, but they slammed his back against the stake and held him in place with six great loops of rope. They left his hands tied before him, clearly unwilling to risk whatever power he might unleash if they slipped off the moonstone bonds even long enough to retie his hands behind his back. That would have made him laugh, if he had been capable of laughing. He was not a mystic, and the gems were not moonstones. Neither of them possessed any power at all.

The brief battle had caused his heart to start pounding; now his breath quickened even more. The ropes bound him tightly to the stake, passing just over and under his breasts, around his waist, his thighs, his ankles. Four of the soldiers stepped back through the laid fuel, out to the circle of onlookers. A fifth one remained, tightening the knots. It was the young one, the soldier who had looked him so wretchedly in the eye.

The young man's hands checked the ropes around Justin's chest, slid down his arm to test the binding around his wrists. To his utter astonishment, Justin felt a cool, slim length of metal insinuate itself between his palms. By the Bright Mother's red eye, the guard had slipped him a dagger. If only he'd had this a minute ago!

"Not even a mystic should have to die by fire," the young man breathed in his ear. "Thrust the blade in your heart when the flames are too high."

Not waiting for Justin to speak a word, he spun on his heel and stepped out of the circle of firewood. Two other guards kicked a few logs back in place so that there was no gap at all. Three soldiers approached from three different directions, each bearing a lit torch. They came to a halt, standing beside the piled wood, waiting for a signal.

Calming his breath, Justin fingered the dagger, which was short but well-honed. He didn't see how this changed the odds any, though as soon as the fire was high enough and no one could see him, he was going to use it to slit the ropes around his wrists. Could he cut through the other bonds in time? Could he leap through the wall of flame, knife in hand, and battle his way to freedom? It was certainly worth a desperate try.

A shape moved up through an alley of novices, and Justin recognized the short, sturdy form of Coralinda Gisseltess. As usual, she was dressed in black robes heavily embroidered in silver; she glittered like a winter sky. She came to a halt a few feet away from him but did not even give him a second glance. Instead, she turned her back, raised her arms above her head, and addressed the crowd.

"Great and benevolent Mother watch over us all, protect us all, keep us safe from harm," she intoned, and her voice was beautiful and almost hypnotic. "Turn away those who would injure us, mystics who would enchant us, enemies who would see us dragged into despair. Keep your bright silver eye upon us always. And those who would offer us harm, send to their deaths."

She made a half turn and over her shoulder addressed the men holding the torches. "Light the fire."

Justin took a hard breath, unable to keep his muscles from tensing against his bonds. The wood was dry and possibly treated; it caught instantly in a flare of yellow and gold. The cold shot back, jumpy as a startled cat. Justin felt the heat on his hands, his exposed face, intolerable already and starting to build. The flames crackled and the logs spit. Cedar and smoke thickened the air to the point that he could hardly breathe it.

He had very little time. If his clothes caught fire, he would be in agony. Working as quickly as he could, he used the little knife to saw at the ropes around his wrists. He didn't have much of an angle—this would take too long. Perhaps, after all, he was better off simply pressing the hilt tightly between his palms and plunging the blade with all the force he could manage straight into his heart.

The heat had made his hands so sweaty it was hard to reposition the knife. He worked his fingers and twisted his palms and somehow managed to get the dagger turned so that he had it in the position he wanted. His thumbs and his forefingers were on either side of the blade; he could hold it steady as he drove it home.

He lifted his hands and rested the knife tip against his chest. A great yellow spark separated itself from the fire, drifted above his head, and landed like a butterfly on his laced knuckles. He waited for the sting of the ember against his skin, but there was no burn. Almost no sensation at all.

The ember danced on his folded hands, spreading its dusty black and gold wings. Not a spark, after all, but no butterfly, either—a moth, drawn like all of its kind to certain death in a gorgeous fire.

The moth shifted its impossibly delicate legs and Justin felt magic skitter across his skin.

By the Wild Mother's woolly head, it was Kirra, come to rescue him from the hot heart of death.

He dropped the knife and shouted her name so that she knew he recognized her. Instantly, he felt the cold tingle of sorcery course along his bones, in direct contrast to the hungry heat pressing in from all directions. He concentrated, holding himself as still as he could, opening his mind, trying to make himself a pure funnel to receive whatever power she poured into him. Would she change him into the same shape she held now, or would she make him some other creature who could more quickly escape this inferno? Something that could fly—that was the most obvious choice. And she knew he understood how to be a bird, whereas he had never been an insect of any sort—

He felt his bones contract, he felt his skin roughen and his mouth purse out and narrow down. The ropes dropped from his hands—they were not hands—he lifted his arms to get a better look and they rose on either side of him in feathered wedges. He could not hold back a triumphant caw of exhilaration as he drove his wings down hard and felt them grab a shaky purchase on the heated, undulating air. He was practically clawing his way above the fire, his balance imperfect and one wing singed by a sudden leap of flame, but he was above the pyre, he was aloft in the cool air, he was flapping his way over the convent walls, too low to the ground to glide.

Disorienting and confusing to fly in the dark through a tangled weave of trees. Where was Kirra? Justin banked and tried to turn around, wondering how well her tiny moth's body could keep up with his bird's wingspan, but then he saw her. Now she was a hawk as well, darting straight toward him through the cluttered mesh of branches. She offered a single cry—welcome or inquiry or instruction to follow—and flew right past him, then aimed upward to break free of the chancy terrain of the forest.

Justin followed, his wings working by instinct, his mind only faintly aware of the shifts his body made to skip from one wind current to the next. Overhead, the frozen stars watched in astonishment or dismay. But the Black Mother smiled, pleased at the outcome of this night's adventure. She exhaled her breath in a tiny puff of air and buoyed Justin through every mile of his flight.

THEY had been aloft maybe thirty minutes, and Justin was so weary he thought he might tumble from the sky, when Kirra dropped sharply toward the ground. His predator's eyes could make out the campsite below—six horses, four humans, one of those humans pointing and waving at the air. Who could spot spring hawks flying silently by night? Who could guess that these were ensorceled creatures returned from hazardous missions? Cammon, of course, Justin decided, as he angled down, wings outstretched to slow his descent, and legs tensed for impact.

He landed awkwardly and felt a moment's blinding pain as the edge of his wing bent backward. A small cry tore from his throat and he hopped for a few paces just to distract himself from the raw sensation. Beside him, Kirra made a flawless landing. The others were instantly on their knees in the grass in a rough circle around them.

"Is that them? Are you sure?" Ellynor asked fearfully, and Justin was so glad to hear her voice that he hopped around another few paces just to get a good look at her. She was disheveled but whole; her face was tight with worry. *I'm fine,* he wanted to say, but all he could produce was a hoarse croak.

"It's them," Cammon said with utter certainty.

"Why are they still birds? Why hasn't she changed them back?"

"I'm guessing she's almost at the limits of her strength," Senneth said quietly. "You have no idea how much energy it takes for her to change a person into something else. And she's done how many transformations in a few short hours? She might not recover for a couple of days."

"So—they'll be like this for another *day?*" Ellynor cried.

"Better a live hawk than a dead Rider," Tayse said.

"So do we stay here tonight or move on?" Senneth asked. "Depending on how spectacular this rescue was, someone might come looking for Ellynor in a matter of hours. We're awfully close to the convent."

"They need sleep," Cammon said.

"We can carry them," Senneth replied.

Tayse glanced up at the sky, gauging the time. "If we can, I'd like to get to someplace that approximates safety," he said. "A town with an inn, if such a thing can be found. It sounds like these two will need to recover, and I'd like that to be inside shelter, if possible."

"Then let's go," Senneth said. She reached out carefully and gathered up Kirra's small, trembling form. "I'll carry this one. Ellynor, I assume—"

"Yes," said Ellynor, her soft hands already under Justin's body. He gave a little cry of pain, and she looked more closely. "I think he snapped his wing," she said. "Does that mean his arm will be broken when he—when he's human again?"

"Probably," Senneth said. "Unless you can fix it."

Ellynor ran one finger delicately down the overlapping feathers. "I've never tried to heal a bird before."

"Then wait till morning. When Kirra changes him back, you can heal him then. Or she can."

"I'll do it now," Ellynor whispered.

"Hurry then," Tayse said. "We don't want soldiers to catch us on the road."

Her hand moved a second time, even more slowly, down the long sweep of his wing. Justin felt the feathered quills straighten and reknit; he felt the pain simply ease away. He bobbed his head up and down and cawed out what thanks he could manage, but he was tired—so tired.

Ellynor scooped him up and cradled him against her throat. "Let's get going," she said in a choked voice.

Justin felt her swing into the saddle, heard Tayse issue orders and Cammon ask a question, but he couldn't sort out the words. Ellynor bunched up the front of her robes to make a nest for him in her lap, and she kept one hand on his back as the horses went into motion. He could not keep his eyes open any longer; he slept away the rest of the journey.

CHAPTER
40

JUSTIN woke suddenly and completely, lying absolutely motionless as he tried to ascertain where he was.

What he was.

Up to a point, he vividly remembered the events of the night before. The fire, the rescue, the flight to safety. Ellynor's hands cupped around his small, feathered body, the sounds and sensations of travel. After that, nothing. He had fallen asleep while they were still on the road. He had no idea when they had arrived wherever they were now or what shape he had been in when they stopped for the night.

Keeping his eyes closed, still feigning sleep in case he had somehow fallen back into enemy hands, he cautiously stretched his extremities. Those were fingers, those were toes. There was a definite and familiar weight to his body. He was human, he was male. His skin was overlaid with cotton and his bones were relatively comfortable. He must be lying on his side between the sheets of a bed, his head resting comfortably on a pillow.

His right arm ached as if it had been recently broken, but there were no ropes on his wrists or ankles. Still among friends.

He opened his eyes and stared straight at Ellynor, whose head rested on the same pillow just a few inches from his. She was awake, and her expression was hopeful. When she saw him conscious, her whole face was transformed with delight.

"Justin!" she squealed, and threw her arms around him.

He was alert enough to participate enthusiastically in the kiss, rolling her over so her back was against the bed and he was practically on top of her. Then he was slammed with protests from half the bones in his body, while at the same time catching a whiff of his own odor—sweat and smoke and some indefinable animal scent—and he groaned and let her go.

"I'm too foul to be kissing anyone," he said, sitting up and stretching his arms high over his head and wincing at every bruise and ache. He hadn't felt this bad since his first weeks training to be a Rider, when every day was a punishment.

For an answer, she pushed herself to her knees, wrapped her arms around his neck and pressed her mouth to his. "I was so afraid you wouldn't live long enough to ever be able to kiss me again," she whispered. "Tell me what happened."

He kissed her cheek and dragged himself out of bed. They must be in an inn of some kind. The room was small and sparsely furnished, but there was a pitcher and basin over in one corner. Justin gulped down half of the water and used the rest to wash his face and upper body. He was stalling for time; he didn't want to tell her how close he'd come to dying.

"First tell me what happened last night," he said through the thin towel that he was using to dry his face. "Last thing I remember is flying down to a camp on the side of the road and Tayse saying we had to move on. How'd we get here—wherever here is—and when did I become human again? Did the magic just wear off?"

Ellynor was watching him with wise eyes. She knew he was trying to distract her. "Kirra stumbled in during the middle of the night and changed you back. Then she left and I think she went to sleep again. I haven't seen her this morning."

"Where are we?"

"I don't know. Some small town on the road to the Lireth Mountains."

He laid aside the towel and came to sit beside her on the bed, his bare feet on the floor. His pants were torn and ripped, and the shirt, which he'd left balled up by the basin, was a dead loss. He hoped someone had brought the rest of his clothes along, or he'd be riding half-naked for the rest of this journey. "Are *you* all right?" he asked gently. "Did they do anything to harm you before we arrived?"

She shook her head. "No. Well, except for what you saw. But what happened? It seemed to take so long before you returned with Kirra."

Before he could answer, the door opened and Cammon stuck his head in. Over his shoulder he called, "I told you he was awake," and then entered without an invitation. He was smiling broadly. His hair and clothes were almost as disheveled as Justin's, and he didn't have the same excuses. "You look terrible," he offered.

"About the way I feel," Justin admitted.

The others filed in one by one—Tayse and Senneth both appearing rested and capable, Kirra still in a nightdress and yawning hugely, Donnal in human form.

"Hey!" Justin greeted this last arrival. "I thought you'd gone on to Ghosenhall."

"I called him back," Cammon said. "I thought Kirra might need him."

Kirra flung herself on the foot of the bed and curled up there. Donnal settled on the floor beside her. "And I do," she said drowsily.

"So the king still doesn't know what's keeping you so long on the road?" Justin asked.

Donnal smiled and shook his head. Senneth groaned and leaned against the wall beside Tayse. "No," she said. "I'm convinced he thinks I've deserted. It might be easier if I did. I'll come with you across the Lireth Mountains and then stay there. Maybe Ammet will take me in for another year."

"So tell us what happened," Tayse said. "Kirra hasn't been coherent enough to recite the tale."

Justin glanced around the room first, feeling a tightness in his chest. There it was again, that lancing light, that strange cord of power that bound the six of them. He always felt stronger when they were all together, his mind clearer, his senses sharper, as if what one of them saw or felt registered in his own sight, his own body. Ellynor sat somewhat apart, disconnected, not bound by the same mystical chain, yet exerting an equal and irresistible pull on his senses. He reached out and took her hand and felt the live spark that seemed to cross from his fingers to hers. She flung her head up and shivered a little, then squeezed his hand between hers. Justin didn't know what that flare of power signified, if it was only a manifestation of his own connection to her or if it represented her binding into the group, but he did not care. Either way, she was linked somehow to him. He tightened his grip.

"I suppose Ellynor told you that they had confined her to a small room," he said. "Bringing in groups of novices all day to look on the face of a mystic and grow faint with fear. Kirra thought it unlikely that she could get Ellynor out the gates before some new group came in, and she didn't want the room to be empty. So she left me behind, shaped like Ellynor."

"I really meant to get back sooner than I did," Kirra said, speaking through another yawn. "I didn't realize how close it was to nightfall."

"A little while after she left Ellynor with us and went back to get you, Cammon just sort of froze in place," Senneth said. "We knew something was wrong."

"Guards came right at sunset to take me down to the bonfire," Justin said, glancing at Ellynor to see how she was taking this. Not very well.

Her dark blue eyes were huge and luminous with fear. "I tried to make a break for freedom, figuring I'd rather die in a fight, but there were too many of them and I had no weapons." He shrugged. "So they tied me to the stake and lit the fire."

Ellynor made a strangled noise and buried her face against his bare shoulder. He patted her hair with his free hand.

"Strange thing was, once I was tied up, one of the guards slipped me a knife," he continued. "Whispered that I should stab myself before I burned to death. I was ready to do just that when Kirra arrived. Turned me into a bird, and we flew away."

Ellynor lifted her head, astonishment replacing horror. "One of the guards gave you a knife?" she repeated. "Why?"

He shook his head. "No idea. He was young, a little shorter than me, dark-haired. Looked like he might be noble, or bastard nobility. I think he might have been the same fellow I saw the last time I was at the convent. Late that night, after I said good-bye to you."

Her face showed even more surprise. "Daken," she said. "But—how strange. I thought—that night, when he came down the path, I was afraid he would see you. I was afraid he reported you to the guards. I thought— Justin, I'm fairly sure he's the one who betrayed you, who sent the soldiers after you the next day. Why would he then decide to save you?"

"Well, he didn't know it was Justin," Cammon pointed out. "He thought it was you."

"Was he in love with you?" Justin asked outright, because he wanted to know. "He looked pretty upset at the thought that you were going to die."

She shook her head. "He was in love with Astira." She paused, thinking that over. "And Astira was grateful that I didn't tell the Lestra she had been meeting Daken in secret. Maybe she's the one who told him to give you the knife, thinking you were me. Maybe that was her way of thanking me."

Justin grunted. "Better way to thank you would have been to try to help you escape."

"I'm sure she thought that would be impossible," Ellynor said quietly.

Tayse spoke up. "So. How visible do you think your transformation was? Did Coralinda Gisseltess and all her novices watch you change into a hawk, or were you obscured by flame? Do they know you didn't die?"

"Don't know what they saw, but I'd bet they realized there was no body," Justin said with a grin. "So unless they think mystics burn to ash and leave nothing behind, they've probably guessed that Ellynor didn't die in the fire."

"Which means they might come looking for her."

Kirra stirred and sat up. "Or it means they're even more afraid of magic than they were before," she said wearily. "Everything we do just makes them decide we're more dangerous than they thought."

Tayse gave her a faint smile. "Well, you are."

"But they might not be in close pursuit," Senneth said. "Still, I don't know that we should be lingering here much longer than we have to. This country is mostly given over to followers of the Pale Mother, and mystics are far from welcome. And we're an odd group by any measure. We arrive last night as a party of four, and this morning there are seven of us, though no friends have joined us in the night. I can see where such inexplicable multiplication might make an innkeeper and his friends uneasy."

"This is how it always happens with us when we travel," Justin murmured to Ellynor. "We ride peacefully into town, looking for a place to spend the night, and by the time we leave, everyone wants to kill us."

"Kirra and I can slip out the door in some other forms," Donnal offered. "And join you later, looking like ourselves."

"I can't," Kirra said through another yawn. "I don't think I'll ever be able to shift shapes again."

Donnal was grinning. "All right. I'll leave three times as a bird, and come back three times as a human. You, myself, and Justin."

Kirra looked interested. "Now, that might work."

"Or we all pack up and exit this morning, not worrying too much about what our hosts think," Tayse said. "Are you two strong enough to travel?"

"I'm well enough to sit a horse," Justin said. "Still not up to full strength, though. Wouldn't want to encounter more than a couple enemies at a time."

"I'm tired, but I can ride," Kirra said.

Tayse looked at Cammon with his eyebrows lifted. Cammon shrugged. "They're both lying," he said.

Tayse nodded. "All right. Then we stay a day." He glanced at Senneth and Ellynor. "Those who have restorative powers might use them to hurry along the recovery of our friends."

"Oh, yes. Of course," Ellynor said so earnestly that Kirra laughed.

"What a ragtag group we are," Kirra said. "The lot of us so bruised and broken that the healers have to cure the healers who were curing them a few days ago!"

"It's strange, though, isn't it?" Cammon said thoughtfully. "How many mystics *are* healers? You three all have such different powers, and yet all of you can lay your hands on someone and save him. And there was that woman Justin rescued on the way to Neft—Lara. She recovered so quickly I have to think she's got that kind of power, too. So many kinds of mystics, so many of them healers. Why would that be?"

"Don't forget that Senneth and I, at least, can kill someone as easily as we can succor him," Kirra answered somewhat grimly.

Senneth was shaking her head. "The gods love life," she said quietly. "That's why they put the power in us to begin with. And that's what we're supposed to use the power for. Making people whole."

"Coralinda Gisseltess doesn't seem to see it that way," Justin said.

Senneth gave him a level look. "Only one of the many things that Coralinda has gotten wrong."

Tayse pushed himself away from the wall. "All right. So we stay a day and then reassess. Donnal, your idea was a good one. If you would reappear a few times styled as your friends, I think we might cause less of a stir. Cammon, you and I should go buy another horse. The rest of you—sleep and mend. We'll convene again at dinnertime and see where we stand."

Donnal and Cammon were the first ones out the door, Cammon chattering and Donnal listening. Kirra stayed where she was, lolling on the bed as if too exhausted to move, and Senneth crossed the room to kneel on the mattress beside her. Justin got up and followed Tayse out the door, shutting it behind them. Cammon and Donnal had already disappeared down a narrow stairway. The inn appeared to be relatively sizable. Justin hoped there were not a large number of other lodgers this particular week, since their party of seven must be taking up a good number of available rooms.

Tayse turned when he realized Justin wanted a private conversation, and waited in silence. Justin took a deep breath. "Are you angry with me?"

Tayse seemed to consider a moment, his face impassive, and then he shook his head. "I knew that day would come sometime."

"The day I disobeyed a direct order?"

"The day something mattered to you more than my opinion."

"No. I will always value what you say. I can't imagine any other situation in which I wouldn't listen to you. But, Tayse—Ellynor—"

Tayse's smile was faintly sad and faintly proud. He clapped a hand on Justin's shoulder. "Ellynor," he repeated. "You had no choice. Although if you had died in that fire, I don't think I would have ever stopped grieving."

"I would have been happy to die," Justin whispered, "to save her."

Tayse nodded. "And that's why you had no choice." He dropped his hand. "But if you countermand me again, I'll have you cut from the Riders." But he was smiling when he said it.

Justin laughed. "Only the king can have a Rider dismissed."

"And you think I have no pull with Baryn? I'll tell him to offer your place to Senneth."

"That would appeal to him," Justin agreed. "I'd better behave."

Tayse jerked his head toward the door. "You'd better get rested. I'd like to leave tomorrow if we can."

Justin paused with his hand on the door. "It's not entirely comfortable, being healed by magic," he said. "As I'm sure you'll learn someday."

"There's very little about magic that I find entirely comfortable," Tayse retorted. "But it has too many uses for me to want to throw it aside. Go on in. Sleep. We'll talk again over dinner."

It was a strange scene to walk into, Justin thought a moment later as he stepped inside and rather doubtfully surveyed the room. The three women were all sitting on the bed, heads together, so that the white-blond hair contrasted vividly with the tangled golden curls and the painted black locks. They were whispering until he came in, and then they glanced over at him and began laughing. Even Senneth, who could generally be counted on not to mock, and Ellynor, who possessed not the slightest trace of malice.

"I think I'll go look for Cammon and Donnal," Justin said, and made as if to step back in the hall.

But Senneth waved him over. "No, no, no, come sit here for a while. We're going to make you well. Don't be afraid, poor frail human boy. The three of us are mystics, but we mean you no harm at all. . . ."

CHAPTER
41

ELLYNOR spent the rest of the day waiting for Justin to wake up. It seemed as if she couldn't think, couldn't act, couldn't really exist unless he was beside her to share her thoughts and experiences.

When had *that* happened? When had she stopped being a complete and self-reliant person and instead become merely a fraction of one, dependent on someone else's breath and heartbeat for her own survival? When she saved Justin's life, she supposed. When she turned her body into the instrument that kept his functioning. But by rights, then, *he* should be the one who needed *her* to live, not the other way around.

He was still far from whole. The desperate flight from the convent had sapped his body of most of its strength, and he had still been suffering from wounds sustained in the battle with the guards. It would be days before he was fully recovered.

"I want to try something," Senneth had said as soon as Justin had fallen asleep again. They had crept back into the room and positioned themselves on either side of the bed, Senneth on the right side of his body, Ellynor on the left. "Your goddess is the Black Mother, mine is the Bright Mother. Night and day. Perhaps we can create a rhythm to our healing that mimics the passing of time. Let me fill him first with sunshine, and you fill him next with starlight. It might not work, but I can't see that it will hurt."

So they alternated their gifts of power, Senneth sending pulses of fire through Justin's veins, Ellynor granting him rest and calm. Again. Again. He stirred and occasionally grunted, but did not wake up while the sorcery sifted down to his bones. It was fascinating and a little frightening to watch his face contract with a twinge of pain at each onslaught of magic, and then smooth out as the healing erased another sore spot, another bruise. His face, which had been entirely too pale, began to take on its usual rosy cast. The set lines around his mouth relaxed.

"I'll be interested to see how he feels when he wakes up," Senneth said at last, folding her hands and resting them on the coverlet.

"Should we try the same thing with Kirra?" Ellynor asked.

Senneth laughed. "Kirra has amazing recuperative powers," she said. "She'll be fine by tomorrow morning with no help from us."

So they left the room, carefully shutting the door behind them, and Senneth went off to find Tayse. Ellynor was left with nothing to do.

She explored the building they were in, which turned out to be a two-story inn with six rooms upstairs and a taproom downstairs. She quickly figured out that her own party had appropriated half the rooms—Justin in one, the women in one, and the other three men sharing the third. Two of the others were occupied by strangers—an older man traveling alone, and a family of four. She hoped none of them were the curious types.

Downstairs, the scent of food made her almost faint with hunger. She could scarcely remember the last time she'd eaten a meal, since she hadn't been served breakfast at the Gisseltess house, the Lestra had not bothered feeding her, and she'd been unable to summon an appetite while she waited on the side of the road for Justin and Kirra to return. How did one buy food in a roadside tavern? She didn't have any money. She didn't even know what anything cost.

Fortunately, Cammon was coming in the front as she stood outside the taproom, wondering what to do. "You look like you're starving," he said.

She nodded. "I am. Is there food here? How can we get it?"

He laughed. "Don't they have taverns in the Lirrens? Come on, I'll eat with you. You can ask me questions about Justin, and I'll tell you everything I know."

This sounded like an agreeable plan, and Cammon was the least alarming of Justin's friends, which made the prospect even more pleasant. They settled around a scarred wooden table in the middle of the taproom, half full with other lodgers and assorted travelers. Cammon helped her order a meal, which turned out to be delicious. He had no trouble doing all the talking while she consumed huge portions of potatoes and chicken, too hungry to bother holding up her end of the conversation. Besides, she had so much to learn. About Justin, about Gillengaria, about everything.

"Well, I've only lived in the country about a year myself, so I'm still figuring some of it out," he told her. "It's almost impossible to keep track of the Houses and who's friends with whom and who hates mystics and who doesn't. But what you need to know for sure is that Coralinda Gisseltess and her brother, Halchon, hate us all."

Ellynor sighed. "I think I learned that on my own."

"But the king likes us, so that almost makes up for it."

The door to the taproom opened, and Justin strode in, the sunlight outside turning his bulky body into a solid silhouette. He looked as healthy and powerful as the day Ellynor had first met him on the streets of Neft. She dropped her fork with a clatter. "*Justin!* What are you doing down here?"

Cammon glanced at Justin, glanced back at Ellynor, and kicked her lightly under the table. "Donnal," he whispered, and then he waved. "Justin! Over here! About time you arrived."

Donnal-as-Justin strode over to their table with all of Justin's self-assurance, pulled out a chair, reversed it, and sat down. He grinned at them both, cocky and amused. "I thought you'd have gotten farther down the road than this," he observed in Justin's voice. "I've been backtracking all morning."

Ellynor could not keep her eyes off of him. He was perfect in every detail, from the color of his eyes to the texture of his skin. If Cammon had not been there to keep her from making a fool of herself, she would have flung herself into his arms. "We needed the rest. It's been a long trip," Cammon said, for the benefit of anyone who might be listening. "Where's Kirra?"

"About a half hour behind me. Has Donnal arrived yet?"

Cammon shook his head. "We're expecting him today, too."

"Travel on in the morning then?"

"That's the plan."

"Well, let me eat something and then I'll go up and sleep. I've been in motion since about midnight."

"I'll give you the key to my room."

Donnal ate quickly and departed, disappearing out the door and, Ellynor supposed, up the stairs. About thirty minutes later, she overheard voices in the hall as Senneth arrived at the door just as Donnal returned in Kirra's form. Senneth, however, was not fooled.

"Serra Kirra," she greeted Donnal in a laughing voice. "So glad you could join us! Let me take you upstairs where I've already got a room."

"I'd appreciate that. When did you arrive? I assume Tayse and Cammon are with you?" Donnal replied, and their voices trailed off as they moved out of earshot.

Ellynor looked at Cammon. "I'm starting to feel dizzy."

He was grinning. "You get used to it after a while."

Tayse shouldered his way into the taproom, spotted them, and came to sit at their table. He took up entirely too much space and caught the attention of every other patron of the bar. Ellynor saw the men eye him as if trying to gauge their chances of besting him in a fight. The women in the room looked just as intrigued, but their speculations appeared to be of an entirely different nature.

"Have all our friends arrived?" Tayse asked.

"Still waiting for Donnal," Cammon replied.

"I'll be glad to be on the move again tomorrow," Tayse said. "Senneth and I just finished buying supplies for the road. We'll be ready to go at daybreak."

"It's been a long trip," Cammon said. "Ghosenhall to Storian to Neft to Coravann Keep to Neft to Brassen Court to Danan Hall to Neft to here. And still not on the way home."

Tayse's grim features arranged themselves into what Ellynor supposed was a smile. "In my experience, every journey with Senneth turns out to be longer than expected."

Cammon laughed. "You're not complaining," he challenged.

Senneth herself came into the taproom at that moment, looked around for them, and approached. Tayse was watching her, and his expression softened. "No," he said. "I wouldn't trade an hour."

Senneth pulled up a chair. "I'm bored," she said. "Who wants to play cards?"

CAMMON helped Ellynor learn the rules to the card game, but even so, she played disastrously and didn't much enjoy the exercise. Donnal arrived in his true form about twenty minutes later and she gladly yielded him her place.

"I think I'll go upstairs for a while," she said, silently adding, *and check on Justin.*

"I'll go out for a walk with you if you want to see the town," Cammon offered. "Not that there's much to see."

Tayse looked up at that. "Perhaps not," he said. "We don't know who might be passing through."

"She's been stuck inside all day," Cammon answered.

"I'm fine," she said hastily, standing up. "I'll get plenty of exercise tomorrow."

Senneth sent her a smile. "Maybe you should get some rest," she said. "I'm sure Kirra wouldn't mind sharing the room with you."

That was a joke, Ellynor realized. All of them knew she was going upstairs to curl on the bed next to Justin. "Thank you, I will," she said, and headed for the door.

"Come back down for dinner!" Cammon called after her, but she was already in the hall.

On the stairs, at the door, silently stepping inside the room where Justin still lay sleeping. She lowered herself carefully on the mattress next to him, put her hand on his chest to check for his heartbeat, and fell asleep.

WHEN she woke, Justin was sitting up and watching her, her hand folded between both of his. "So you *do* sleep," he said instantly. "Usually I'm the one lying here dreaming, and I wake up and there you are, staring at me."

She scrambled upright but didn't free her hand. She could tell her hair was completely loose around her shoulders and she had a suspicion that Justin might have pulled out a few pins while she was slumbering. "How do you feel? You look well."

"I feel superb," he said. He freed one hand to make a hard fist. "I feel better than I have since the last night I spent at the convent, after we'd hauled in supplies. I feel like I could fight ten of the Lestra's guards—and beat them all, too."

"Let's hope you don't have to."

"What did you do? Somebody must have practiced magic on me while I was sleeping."

"Senneth and I together. It's hard to explain."

"Well, it worked, whatever you did." He pulled her over so he could hold her against him, one arm around her shoulder, one hand holding hers, and he kissed the top of her head. "So tomorrow we leave for the Lirrens," he said in a low voice. "How long will it take us to get to your family's place?"

That was just like Justin, she thought. No hesitation, no pausing to mull things over. *I'm healed; now let's go meet your father.* One task completed, the next one faced head-on. "Maybe a week," she said. "Maybe longer, depending on the weather. The terrain's pretty rocky and we have to go slow."

"Do we camp? Stay at inns? Bed down with other clan members along the way?"

"Camping's safest," she said.

He leaned back a little to look down at her. "Safest?"

She picked her words with care. "Until we've made it to my family's house and received their blessing—until I have been formally declared *bahta-lo*—anyone from the *sebahta* who happens to come across us traveling together might feel an obligation to challenge you. You're an outsider, you're not an acceptable escort for a young woman of the Lirrens. It will be better if we keep off the roads and don't interact much with others."

He absorbed this a moment in silence. "Should we bring Tayse and Senneth with us then?" he asked. "All the way to your father's place? I don't want to have a pitched battle with a clan of Lirren men, but if there's going to be a fight on the road, I'd rather have Tayse at my side."

"I can keep us out of danger for the journey," she said. "No one will see us pass by."

He grinned. "That's right. I keep forgetting. I'm going to marry a mystic girl."

The word *marry* hung between them in a sudden silence, heavy and awkward. Ellynor didn't answer, and she felt Justin tense beside her. She didn't have the courage to look up and see his face blurred with confusion or creased with uncertainty. In the chaos of the last few days, he had not had time to think it through; he might only now be realizing what it meant to seriously plan to take a woman to wife.

He was bending down to peer into her face, and when that didn't show him what he wanted to see, he put a finger under her chin and tipped her head up. His own face indeed showed uncertainty, but it was filtered through a layer of anxiety.

"Ellynor?" he said. "Or didn't we settle that? Maybe I didn't come right out and ask you. Maybe I need to work on my proposal. I assumed that when we arrived at your father's house, we would be wed according to your laws. But maybe you're not so sure that's what you want to do."

She curled her hand around his wrist and gazed up at him, searching his eyes. But he didn't seem to be hiding regret or panic. His face was touched by fear, but it was a fear that she would reject him.

"I just want you to be sure," she said quietly. "I don't think you're the sort of man who grew up dreaming of the day he would marry. This changes—so much about your life."

"Well, you have to be sure, too," he said. "And it's pretty clear the changes won't be any easier for you than for me. Maybe you don't want to become—become—*bala-toso* or whatever."

"*Bahta-lo*," she said, smiling.

"Maybe you don't want to leave the Lirrens. And I can't leave

Ghosenhall—not now, not with a war coming. Maybe afterward I could come and live with your family, if that's what you wanted. If they would have me. If *you* would—"

She silenced him with a kiss, and felt his arms close around her, powerful and reassuring. In truth, she couldn't imagine how all the components of their lives would fit together, but those were discussions for another day. She knew the most important detail, the central point: Justin loved her. She would work her way forward from that.

Now she settled against him, her head on his shoulder, her hand once again caught in his. "So tell me how it works," he said, speaking to the top of her head. "We arrive at your family's place and all your brothers come rushing out with their swords upraised—"

She laughed. "Not quite. Though I'm sure most of the family will come running out to greet us. At first they will be terribly formal with you—they will prepare the best foods for you and offer you the finest wine, and they will make only the most polite conversation. When we arrive, I will be whisked off to the kitchens and interrogated because I have *so* much to tell! Not just about you, although that will be a story my sisters and cousins will want to hear in every detail, but about the convent, and the Lestra, and Rosurie." She paused, feeling a wave of sadness so strong that it made her physically ill. "They won't like the news about Rosurie," she said in a softer voice. "And my mother will call in my father and my uncles, and they'll hear the story again, and they won't believe it at first, and I'll have to tell it another time. And maybe they will decide they need to return to the convent and try to retrieve her, and maybe they'll believe me when I say she does not want to come home. That she denounced me and turned her back on the Great Mother."

After a small silence, Justin said, "And all this time I'm left alone out in the hallway with your brothers? Who don't like me?"

She laughed again. "My brothers and my male cousins and a few of my uncles—yes, probably," she said. "But they won't actually *say* they don't like you. They might start to challenge you in subtle ways. Offer you wine and see how well you hold your liquor—"

"Well enough, but not after the fourth or fifth glass."

"And, you know, Torrin and Hayden will stand next to you in conversation and try to gauge if you're taller than they are."

He grinned. "And am I?"

"Yes."

"Is that good or bad?"

"They respect strength, so it's good. If they truly accept you as my husband, they will not engage you in a proper duel, but sometime before the visit is over, *someone* will invite you to a friendly fight."

"And should I win that, if I can?"

"You should always win any fight with a Lirren man, if you can."

"Senneth seems to think my chances are good."

"If Senneth is right, and they have accepted you, then this will be considered our bridal visit. We will need to stay at least seven days, so that outlying members of the *sebahta* have time to travel in to offer us their gifts and blessings. There will be feasts every night—wait till you taste the salt bread—and you will meet more people than you will ever be able to remember. Sometime during those seven days, probably at a dinner, you should publicly offer me your bride gift and explain its significance. The following day—"

"What's that?" he asked, suddenly alert. "This bride gift?"

"Oh—isn't that a custom among the people of Gillengaria? It is something that belonged to your mother that she gave you when you left home, specifically for you to pass on to your wife when . . ." Ellynor's voice trailed off.

Justin's mother had been a whore. She'd died when he was ten. She hadn't been handing him pretty baubles infused with sentimental memories.

"That doesn't matter," she said quickly. "However, before the visit is over—"

Justin straightened his shoulders and sat back against the headboard. She glanced up and saw him frowning. "It matters," he said. "It's part of your family's tradition, or you wouldn't have brought it up."

"Well, it won't be part of our wedding ceremony."

His brows were still drawn in a fiercely serious expression. "Can I buy you something? A necklace or a ring—is it usually jewelry that's handed over as a bride gift?"

"Jewelry, an item of clothing, a kitchen tool, a lace tablecloth—but, Justin, please forget it. I didn't mean to mention it."

"But can I buy it?"

She shook her head helplessly. "It's considered bad luck to give your wife something new. Something—raw. A bride gift that came from your mother's hands is an object that should be well-worn and loved. It is supposed to ease your transition from one family into another—'Look, I am part of the *sebahta*, I have something that has been in my husband's *sebahta* for twenty years.' My father gave my mother a quilt that his

great-aunt had sewn and bestowed upon his mother when he was born."
She took a deep breath. This wasn't helping any, she knew, but he would
only keep asking until she explained it all. "A bride gift is a way for the
people who love you most to say they will love me as well. It signals that
I have been accepted by your family."

"But I don't have a family."

She came to her knees and put her hands on either side of his face,
making him look at her, willing him to believe. "I know," she said. "It
doesn't matter."

Restlessly, he pulled away and stood up, then began pacing the
cramped width of the room. "It *does* matter," he threw over his shoulder.
"If they do accept me, they are already making a huge sacrifice—they are
already tossing out their traditions and contravening some of their own
laws. At some point, I have to give them what they want for you. At *some*
point, I have to show them that I can abide by their customs. I have to
prove that I deserve you."

More slowly, she climbed from the bed and stood there, apprehensive
and miserable, watching him. "If they don't think you deserve me, they
won't let you cross the threshold," she said. "A small thing like a bride gift
is not going to change how they feel about you."

He wheeled around to face her, his expression stormy. "It's not a small
thing or you wouldn't have brought it up," he said.

"I brought it up because it is part of the tradition I know," she said.
"But you must already have realized that I am willing to walk away from
so much that is familiar to me, so I can be with you."

"I don't want you to give up anything you don't have to," he whispered.

"All I want to not give up is you."

In the ensuing and highly charged silence, the knock at the door
sounded especially loud. Neither of them responded; they just continued
to stare at each other, mute and unhappy. The door opened without an
invitation, and Senneth stepped inside.

"Cammon said you were arguing," she said calmly. "And here you
seemed to be so violently in love."

They almost fell on her, both of them raising their voices to explain.
"Senneth, tell her—"
"Senneth, please explain to him—"
"How can I make them break any more conventions?"
"Why can't I make him understand?"
Senneth flung her hands up and they both fell silent, though Justin

looked surly and Ellynor wanted to start screaming. "What is this about?" she said. "Justin, you first."

"The bride gift," he burst out. "It's supposed to be from my family to her, but I don't *have* a family, and she says it's not important—"

"It's *not!*"

"But I know it is," he finished.

Senneth was nodding thoughtfully. "Yes. Ammet's daughter was married while I lived with them, and for a whole month before the groom arrived, all anyone in the household could talk about was what he might bring her for a bride gift. It turned out to be his mother's copper pitcher, which was much more beautiful than I can describe. Ammet was very pleased."

"I don't want a stupid pitcher," Ellynor said, scowling.

"No, but you deserve something," Justin shot back.

Senneth's hands were at the back of her neck, and in a moment she had unfastened a chain and was handing it to Justin. "Take this," she said.

Ellynor felt her heart lurch with hope, but Justin just stood there, shaking his head. "Your grandmother's necklace? You can't give me that!" he exclaimed.

"Oh, but something that goes back a generation is even more prized," Ellynor said.

He gave her a wretched look. "You don't understand. My mother died, but Senneth's father kicked her out of the house. Disowned her for being a mystic. Her grandmother handed her that pendant as she was leaving, and it was the *only* thing anyone in her family gave her. Her grandmother was the only one who loved her." He shook his head again. "I can't take that. I won't."

"No," Ellynor said with a sigh. "You can't."

But Senneth was smiling. She came near enough to take Justin's fist in hers and teased at his closed fingers. "Justin," she said. "My grandmother believed in symbols. She wanted me to know that she loved me, and that the Bright Mother loved me, and that wherever I went, I would not be entirely alone. I was friendless and afraid when I left my father's house, and some days the only reason I did not fall into complete despair was because I had this necklace. Because I knew I had my grandmother's affection."

"Yes, that's why—"

She continued as if he hadn't tried to speak. "And look at me now. Surrounded by friends. Married to the man I love above all others.

Confidante of the king. Time for me to pass this symbol on." She had managed to pry his fist open, and now she laid the gold necklace in his hand, though she still kept her hold on him. Ellynor could see the chain coiling against his palm, could tell that it held a simple circular charm edged with thin filigree. "My grandmother would be pleased," she said. "She always loved *things*. She thought certain objects possessed a power of their own, and she loved to hold the items that she cherished the most. She would be glad to see this necklace passed from my hand to yours to Ellynor's, as long as it was valued."

"I would treasure it my whole life," Ellynor said. "I would always wear it close to my heart."

Now Senneth was folding Justin's fingers over the loops of gold. He was just watching her, his eyes so wide Ellynor thought he might be trying to fight back tears. "I hate my brothers, as you know," she said conversationally, and Justin was surprised into a laugh that sounded suspiciously like a sob. "My only son died in infancy. And I scarcely know my nephews. I have not had much chance to love the men I'm related to by blood, so, Justin, don't consider it an insult when I tell you that I truly think of you as my family. We are kin, as the Lirrenfolk say. You belong to me in ways that can't be explained by any other tie. We are kin. I would be honored if you would take my grandmother's necklace and give it to your bride."

Justin stood absolutely motionless for a moment, while Ellynor held her breath and Senneth waited with her usual serenity. Then he nodded twice, jerkily, and brought his other hand up to crush Senneth's between his. "I am honored that you're willing to give it to me," he said, his voice thick. He smiled with an effort and tried to say something lighthearted. "And sorry that now you will not have a pendant to cover your housemark."

Senneth's answering smile was wicked. "I'll make Tayse buy me something," she said. "I've decided I deserve a bride gift of my own."

THEY left early the next morning, a surprisingly tidy and efficient group, and made good time on the road to the Lireth Mountains. Kirra seemed fully recovered, and Justin claimed he felt perfectly fit, so they pressed on past nightfall to cover an additional ten miles. The air turned bitterly cold once the sun dropped below the horizon, but the night sky was so dizzyingly beautiful that Ellynor, at least, didn't mind. She felt the Black Mother's presence hovering nearby, almost as distinct as another silhouette on horseback, and she silently spoke her prayers of thanks. *Great Mother, you have been so bountiful. I cannot find enough words to express my gratitude for all I have been given. . . .*

They opted to make camp instead of looking for rooms for the night, and it was clear that the other six were used to sharing tasks around a fire. Ellynor was surprised at how much heat the small blaze gave off until Justin laughed and told her it was Senneth's magic that warmed the air around them. After they ate, Justin and Tayse fenced a little while Donnal and Senneth critiqued their swordplay and the other three cleaned up.

"Better than I would have predicted," Tayse judged when they paused to take a break. "You're not at full strength, though."

Justin sheathed his weapon. "But I could defend myself."

Tayse nodded. "Let's hope you don't have to."

They broke camp at dawn and continued eastward. Kirra and Donnal disappeared at the lunch break, leaving Cammon to lead their horses and Tayse to wonder out loud if they'd think to bring back game for the evening meal.

"We'll be at the foot of the mountains by dinnertime," Senneth said.

Tayse glanced at her, glanced at Justin, and nodded. "I know."

He could not have said more plainly he would be sorry to see Justin go. Still, the big man did not dawdle on the trail, did not look for excuses to slow their progress and draw the trip out by another day. When the low, broken peaks of the Lireth range began to hunch up against the eastern horizon, he kept to the course, and he didn't call a halt until the last of the sunlight had disappeared.

"This is as far as the rest of us will go," Ellynor heard him tell Justin. "In the morning, we'll head north toward Coravann."

"Probably best to get an early start," Justin said. "I'd just as soon cross the mountains in two days."

Kirra and Donnal returned, formed like humans but carrying rabbits and squirrels and grouse that they could only have caught in animal shape. The meal was tasty and convivial, though Ellynor noticed that Kirra and Cammon and Senneth did most of the talking. Donnal was always quiet, of course, and Tayse didn't seem like the type who ever indulged much in idle chatter. Ellynor herself was still a little too much in awe of this group to volunteer frequent observations, so she listened and nodded and spoke only when someone addressed her.

Justin was nearly silent, but Ellynor, observing him, did not think he was unhappy. He watched the others with a bright attention, laughed at Cammon, rolled his eyes at Kirra, smiled whenever Senneth spoke. He was absorbing them, she thought, storing them up, like a man taking a long last draught of water before setting out across the desert.

She had done much the same thing the last night she ate at her family's house before leaving with Rosurie for Lumanen Convent. She imagined she would do it again the night before she and Justin left the Lirrenlands and headed back toward Ghosenhall.

He felt her eyes on him and turned to give her a quick smile, utterly guileless, completely free of pain. When he put his hand out, she laced her fingers through his and held on as tightly as she could.

In the morning, the single party broke cleanly into two with a minimum of fuss and farewell. Kirra insisted Justin and Ellynor take the leftover meat—"We'll just hunt every day we're on the road, so we don't need it"—and Tayse asked when Justin thought they might be expected back in the royal city.

"Six weeks, maybe," Justin said, glancing at Ellynor with a question in his eyes. She nodded, thinking most of that time would be taken by travel. "We'll come back through Kianlever."

"I'll let them know when you've crossed the mountains back into Gillengaria," Cammon promised, and everyone laughed.

"No secrets in our little group," Kirra said brightly, and mounted her horse with careless grace. "It's too cold to stand around talking! Travel safely. See you soon."

With that, everyone climbed into the saddle, everyone called out a good-bye, and the two groups of riders went their separate ways.

The brilliant sunshine didn't do much to warm the air, which got colder and thinner the higher they climbed. The trails were either poorly marked or completely nonexistent, and more than once Ellynor thought they had lost the way altogether. She had only crossed the mountains once before, and that was going in the other direction. She had no idea how to pick a route through these slaty slopes and sharp, jumbled boulders. But Justin seemed perfectly at ease in the unfamiliar terrain, watching the paths ahead and confidently guiding his horse across expanses that looked impossible to traverse.

They made camp just below the peak, huddling together for warmth since there was limited fuel for a fire. Sunrise was the most welcome sight Ellynor had ever seen, and they scrambled down the eastern slope of the mountain on foot, holding the reins of their horses. The air warmed considerably with every yard they descended, and they were on level ground more than an hour before sunset.

Oh, and then they were in the Lirrens. Oh, then they were in that wild, beautiful, dangerous, beloved land.

CHAPTER
42

I T took six more days to travel to Ellynor's family's house. Justin watched the miles unfold around them, finding the terrain strikingly different from the lush and mostly fertile land of Gillengaria. The Lirrens were generally rocky, dotted with small stony hills and low, uneven meadows that nurtured only stunted trees and starved weeds. Their route didn't take them past rolling farmland or any cultivated fields that Justin could see, though Ellynor told him most of the homesteads featured small gardens that required unending effort to tend.

"And there are farms near the eastern coast, where the Dalrian *sebahta* grows grains, and they trade with the rest of us," she said. "Except they don't trade with the Cohfens, but the Cohfens buy their grain from the rest of us."

They passed no towns, no roadside taverns, none of the marks of civilization that Justin was used to. Instead, Ellynor pointed out individual homesteads and clan clusters as they passed—usually a collection of low buildings on relatively level land near a natural source of water.

"Not much help for a traveler passing through," Justin commented. "Unless he can count on the kindness of the people who own the houses."

"Well, he can if he's kin," Ellynor said. "But if he's not kin—or if he's from a feuding *sebahta-ris*—then, no. He doesn't ask to stop for the night. He just keeps riding."

He glanced down at her, reckoning. "That's why you need the *sebahta-ris*," he said. "So you have friends everywhere you go. Somewhere to stay when you travel."

"That's *one* of the reasons," she said.

He grunted. "Bet that was the first one, and all the rest of it came later."

She smiled and shook her head.

They talked easily while they rode, since the ground was too rough for them to maintain a fast pace. He was still apprehensive about what to expect when they arrived at Ellynor's home, so he asked for more details about what to say, what not to say, who might be there awaiting them, who might arrive a few days after they did. He made her repeat over and over the names of her closest kin, and within three days he could rattle off her aunts and uncles by blood, as well as their sons and daughters. Pretty soon he could also recite the basic alliances within the Lahja *sebahta-ris*, though he had trouble keeping track of the friendships that developed between individual families of feuding clans.

"It's like learning the names of all the marlords in the Twelve Houses!" he exclaimed. "Kirra can tell you what serramarra married what serramar fifty years ago and how many children they had and where *they* were married off."

"Well, it's easier if you know them," Ellynor said. "If you actually care about them."

"If I actually think it's important," he grumbled, but he could feel himself laughing. "Tell me this," he said. "Do I have to wait for everyone to be present before I give you the bride gift?"

She had told him already that the presentation of the gift should be very public, yet not seem ostentatious or rehearsed. It was supposed to flow naturally from some conversation at a time that would seem per-fectly designed for a declaration of love. Justin was fairly certain that it would be the most awkward moment of his life. He kept asking for details, trying to visualize the setting, trying to prepare.

"No," she said. "Not if the right moment arrives and some of the fam-ily is still on the road. But you don't want to go through the whole visit without presenting it to me! Everyone will know why we're there. They'll think it very peculiar if you never mention you want to marry me."

"But how do I know what the right moment is?" he insisted.

She spread her hands, looking helpless. He realized that, to her, it was such an intuitive thing that it was hard to explain. "Well, this is how my cousin's husband did it. We were talking about chickens, and how to get them to lay more eggs, and what to feed them. And he laughed and told a story about the time his mother lost a ring in the chicken coop and one of the hens ate it, but they didn't know which one. So they started slaughtering chickens, two a day, and poking through the entrails. They were eating chicken every night for a month. He said soon they were beg-ging to be fed venison or grouse or *anything* except chicken. One day, his mother found the ring in the droppings of this mean old hen that was so stringy and tough that no one would have thought to prepare her for the cookpot. And it was her favorite ring, and she was so happy to have it back that she snatched it up and cleaned it off and put it right back on her hand. And then she made a feast dinner for them that very night. And when he was done telling this story, he turned to my cousin and said, 'She loved that ring more than anything, and she gave it to me so that I could give it to my bride.'"

She stopped speaking and looked hopefully over at Justin. He said, "That's it? I talk about chicken dung and entrails? Somehow that doesn't sound like the perfect moment to me."

"No, it's just—I don't know how to explain it. The giving of the bride gift is supposed to seem like a natural extension of the conversation. It's proof that you belong, that you fit in."

"Which I don't."

She reached over and took his hand, giving it a tight squeeze before letting it go again. "Maybe you don't," she said. "But they're willing to accept you. You'll be fine. If you don't find the right moment, then I'll—I'll have my mother ask you a question that makes it obvious this is the time to make the presentation."

"'Justin, shouldn't you be giving my daughter something right about now?'" he said.

She laughed. "I think she can be more subtle than that."

"I don't require subtle. I require knowing what I'm supposed to do. So what other questions are people likely to ask me?"

"They'll want to know about your family," she said a little hesitantly. "It will seem strange to them that you had none. The concept of an abandoned child is not one that they can easily understand."

He glanced at her. He could see that she was trying to speak carefully, not wanting to offend him. He kept his voice gentle as he asked, "What about whores? Is that a concept they understand?"

She looked even more unhappy. "There are women. In most of the *sebahta*. Who do not marry and who do not work in the gardens or help raise the children. They live in the households and they are not cast out, but they—they only play a small part in family rituals. Any man can go to these women, though they have the right to refuse to take a man to bed."

"Not exactly the same thing," he said.

She nodded. "But everyone knows what a whore is," she said sadly. "Enough of our men have traded across the mountains that the word has become commonly known."

"Well, I'm not going to lie about it," he said.

"No, of course you shouldn't lie. But you don't have to tell them more than you want to tell them."

He laughed. "Why do I get the feeling they're going to be very curious about all the details of my life?"

She smiled. "Because you're very wise! They *will* want to know everything." She paused and then said, "And not just about your blood family. They will want to know about your own *sebahta.*"

He was amused. "I don't think I have one of those."

"Your—the people you consider family, with whom you have an unbreakable bond."

Now he was thoughtful. "You mean, like Senneth."

She nodded and gave him a sideways look. "And Kirra."

"*Kirra?*"

She watched him closely and he knew there was something here that would surprise him. He would have to be careful. Ellynor's face was casual, but he had the sense that she was about to say something that mattered to her a great deal. "She said she was your sister."

He felt his eyebrows go up. "She said that?" Ellynor was still watching him and so he did not give a quick, sardonic answer; he considered it. A year ago he had not met the Danalustrous girl. The first three months they had traveled together, he would have said he hated her. They had quarreled half the time they were together last summer—in fact, they were usually quarreling. And yet he had put his life in her hands more than once. He had believed she could save Ellynor and he had known she would come back for him if she could. He trusted her. Wayward and restless and frivolous though she was. She would never betray him. "I suppose she is," he said at last and he saw Ellynor relax, pleased with his answer. He smiled at her. "And I guess that makes Donnal and Cammon my brothers?"

"If you think of them that way."

"They can be my brothers," he decided.

"And Tayse, too?"

That required no cogitation. He said, "Tayse is my father."

THEY arrived at the Alowa homestead in the middle of the afternoon on a sunny but absolutely frigid day. Justin was rapidly taking in details. There were about ten buildings on this roughly defined property, all of them solidly built of wood, some quite large. About half of them sported chimneys that were curling with smoke, so those must be houses where people lived; the others would be barns or sheds. There was a small, well-kept area in the center that appeared to be shared space. It featured two wells, a chopping block, some tools and a cart.

"Which house is yours?" he asked Ellynor, and she pointed at the largest one, two-and-a-half stories high, with brightly painted shutters on the windows. "Do we just go right in?"

"I've brought home a visitor," she said. "I need to announce you."

She slipped from the horse, so he dismounted quickly, and followed her to a hammered gong that hung from a metal frame. "Two strokes means company," she said, picking up a mallet that rested against the frame.

"How many strokes means danger?"

She smiled. "Five. You would think of that."

"You always have to be prepared for trouble."

She gave him a sideways look. "Maybe I should strike the gong five times now."

He grinned. "No. I'm going to be very well-behaved."

She hit the gong twice, and it sent out lovely but urgent notes that Justin guessed could be heard even some distance off the property, especially if you were trained to listen for the sound. The hammered metal hadn't quite stopped quivering on its chains when the first doors opened and figures came streaming out. Justin took a deep breath and planted his feet, bracing himself. But Ellynor dropped the mallet and flung her arms out and ran straight toward one of the women racing from the big house. In seconds, she was enveloped by a shouting, crying, laughing crowd—children, men, women, dogs—and everyone was hugging her and everyone was repeating her name.

This, Justin supposed, was what it was like to belong to a family.

TORRIN had appointed himself Justin's guide and guardian and nemesis; it was clear nothing was going to induce him to leave Justin's side. Hayden and a rotating cast of cousins joined them at various points—for meals, for discussions, for tricky competitive games—but none of them stuck as close as Torrin. Justin was even bedded down in Torrin's room, on a mattress on the floor that was far more comfortable than he would have expected.

Three days after their arrival, no one had offered to kill him, and so Justin thought the visit with the *sebahta* was going fairly well.

"Now here's a game I bet you're good at," Torrin said. Half a dozen of them were lounging in a small open area in the middle of a barn that housed probably twenty cows. They'd spent much of their time there since Justin's arrival. The space was cluttered with tools and broken chairs and partial bales of hay, but the body heat of the cattle kept the place relatively warm. It was a good place to retreat from the interference of women.

Justin looked over, keeping his face impassive. This was yet another test, as all the other games had been. Oh, certainly, they had all been played for the sake of entertainment—or would have been, on any ordinary day—but their real value had been the chance to gauge Justin's reflexes and coordination. So far, he'd managed well enough, even when he couldn't exactly comprehend the rules, because he'd understood the one great overriding rule: Make a show of strength.

It was not, after all, that different from running a gang of thieves on the streets of Ghosenhall and constantly proving you were so tough that no one wanted to challenge you.

"What kind of game?" he said.

One of the cousins—Arrol, Justin thought—was bringing out a wooden case filled with some kind of jangling cargo. He knelt in the middle of the floor and opened it, to reveal a collection of rings of various sizes, all made of metal. Arrol gave Torrin an unsmiling look. He was a strange one, Justin thought—tall, slim, and silent, more standoffish than the rest of the noisy cousins. He often wore an abstracted expression, as though his thoughts were far from this place and these people, and he hadn't bothered participating in most of the contests.

He'd won the ones he did play, though. He was supple and fast, and behind his dreamy eyes was a quick intelligence. Justin thought he was probably more dangerous than Torrin, though Torrin was clearly the one all the other cousins admired most.

"Hoop toss," Arrol said.

"What's that?" Justin asked.

Torrin was pulling the rings out and lobbing them to the other players in the barn, reserving a pile of the smallest ones for himself. "We throw the hoops in the air—you catch them on your sword. The more you catch, the more points you win. The smallest ones are the hardest to capture," he added.

Justin didn't move. "I don't nick up my sword with game pieces," he said. Not that his own weapon was currently hanging at his belt; it had been given over to Torrin's keeping the evening they arrived.

Torrin looked impatient. "No, of course you don't," he said. "We use old ones that have been discarded. There ought to be three of them back here in the barn. You can pick the one that feels best in your hand."

By the Bright Mother's weeping red eye, Justin thought, following

Torrin to a corner of the room. *This man will be competing with me till the day I die.*

The three swords were indeed fairly battered, and two of the blades were bent out of true, but the third one was in reasonably good shape, though lighter weight than the weapon Justin carried on a regular basis. That might be good, he thought, whipping the blade through the air just to get a sense of its reach and heft. If he was going to use it to pluck objects from the air—

"Where do I stand?" he asked.

They pushed him to the center of the open space, then stood around him. It turned out any of them could throw a ring in the air at any time, from any direction, the only stipulation being that it had to rise high enough to afford him a reasonable chance to catch it. They all agreed on the lower edge of the window set in the pointed slope of the barn's upper story. Justin positioned himself, raised his sword, and nodded at Torrin.

Instantly, he was in the middle of a hailstorm of metal rings, and he dashed from side to side, spearing them from the air. One or two hit him on the back or shoulder; more than a few fell with a *thud* to the wooden floor. But he caught a good number, and they rattled against the hilt as he lunged for another one, and another. When all the hoops had been disposed of, he had eleven hanging from his blade. Another twenty or so dotted the floor. He didn't think it was a bad showing for his first attempt to play—then again, he was always going to fare well at any activity that allowed him to have a sword in his hand.

"Good game," he said, tilting his blade down so the hoops slid off in a musical clatter. "Do I do it again or is it someone else's turn?"

No one bothered to tell him if he'd done well or poorly. Torrin held up his hand, and Justin passed him the sword. "Pick up about six rings," Torrin directed. Justin joined the others in gathering the hoops from the floor, then they all made a circle around Torrin.

"Go," the young man said, and the rings went flying.

By the time all motion ceased, Torrin had collected five rings. He looked disgusted, but didn't bother to swear or complain, just handed the sword to his brother.

Hayden only managed to pluck three rings out of the air. Two of the other cousins caught six apiece. Arrol, who went last and therefore was clearly their best player, snagged nine.

Justin began to think that his own performance had been nothing short of spectacular.

"What's the usual score at hoop toss?" he asked when Arrol had emptied his sword.

"Five or six is about average. Better than seven and you're among the best," Hayden said.

Justin arched his eyebrows. No one had complimented him on his own achievement; maybe they all thought he'd just been lucky. "Huh. Wonder how well I'd do on a second try," he said.

Arrol turned smoothly and handed him the sword. "I was wondering the same thing," he said in his smoky voice.

Justin stepped to the center again and waited for them to gather up the rings. "Go," he said, and the air was filled with a flock of flying metal. He stabbed, whirled, stabbed again, convinced that this time the others were releasing all the targets even faster. But when the last ring hit the floor and rolled to the side of the room, Justin had twelve hoops dangling from the blade.

He knew better than to gloat or preen. "Must be my kind of game," was all he said. "I've always been handy with a sword."

"So have I," Arrol replied, "but you must be remarkable."

Justin shrugged and tilted the blade down, watching all the rings pile up on the floor. Ellynor had been right; before this visit was over, someone was going to challenge him to a duel. That it was likely to be a mock battle with all participants still alive at the end didn't mean it wasn't going to be fierce and deadly serious.

"Some people try to be good at a lot of things," he said. "Some people pick one. I picked one, and that's it."

Torrin chucked a ring at him, no force behind the throw, and Justin grabbed it with his hand. "I'm guessing there are one or two other things you're pretty good at," Torrin said.

Justin allowed himself a small smile. "If they have something to do with fighting, probably."

Hayden glanced at Torrin. "My sister says you've been injured recently," the younger man said. "Probably wouldn't want to wrestle."

Now Justin had to smother a laugh. Had she been trying to protect him? Or was she truly worried about his health? "I'm about healed," he said. "I can show you the scars."

That elicited a quick interest from everyone present, so he pulled his shirt up over his head. The silence that followed was profound, and he knew they weren't just cataloging the fresh wounds, still red enough to look angry. They were reading the history of his life carved into his chest and back and shoulders. It was a fairly detailed and mostly ugly tale.

He resettled the shirt and shook his hair back. He should have had Ellynor cut it before they arrived; he was starting to look as shaggy as Cammon. "I could fight if I had to," he said, "but I don't know that I want to wrestle just yet. Just for fun."

"No," Hayden said. "Well—Ellynor told us we couldn't even ask you to."

They all laughed at that. As if women's words carried any weight! Arrol knelt on the floor and began returning the hoops to the wooden case.

"Almost dinner," Torrin said suddenly. "Let's go back to the house."

CHAPTER

43

THE only times Justin had been allowed to see Ellynor in the past three days had been at meals, and so he looked forward to them with more than the usual anticipation. Tonight it was a little hard to find her, since the ranks of family had swelled by another fifteen or twenty—new arrivals who'd come in while he was showing off for the young men, Justin supposed. Tables had been set up in the large dining room that opened into an equally large sitting room, and there was room for about sixty people to sit together in one more or less continuous space. Surely that many were gathered there now, clusters of adults talking with great animation, packs of children running and screaming around the chairs. Chaotic and noisy, but everyone seemed happy. Glad to be together.

And the food smelled wonderful.

Justin spotted Ellynor waving at him from the main table in the primary room, and he worked his way through the crowd, nodding politely. Everyone stared at him, knowing him not only for a stranger, but for the stranger who was the reason they had all convened. The younger girls smiled and ducked their heads. Any man under the age of thirty watched him with a measuring eye. The older women assessed him, too, but for different reasons, he thought. *Will he be kind to Ellynor? Can he be trusted? For what reasons did he win our girl's heart?*

He finally reached Ellynor's side and surreptitiously put his hands on her waist, kissing the top of her head. "Sit," she said, and pushed him into a chair. "I have to help serve."

"Did you cook, too? I don't know what I'm smelling but I can't wait to eat it."

She smiled, pleased. Her face was flushed with heat from the kitchens. She was wearing a simple gown set off with a beautiful collar of black opals. All the women wore similar gems on their hands or around their wrists, Justin had noticed, and a few of the men wore heavy rings set with the same kind of stone. Senneth had once said the folk of the Lirrens wore black opals to honor the Dark Watcher. Ellynor had resumed hers as soon as she stepped back inside this house. "I helped with some of the meal," she admitted. "Sit. I'll be back."

It took a while, but eventually every table was laden with tureens and baskets and serving plates, and every chair was occupied. The dishes were passed around from hand to hand, and there was much talk and laughter among tables and between rooms. Justin filled his plate, ate every scrap on it, and filled it again.

"What's in this *bread*?" he demanded of Ellynor, taking his fourth piece as a basket passed his way again.

"Isn't that good? It's the salt bread I told you about."

"There's more in it than salt," he said emphatically.

She laughed. "It's feast bread. Only made for special occasions."

He watched her as he chewed and swallowed. "Am I a special occasion?"

"Well," she said demurely, "*we* are."

Her attention was briefly claimed by the woman on her right, but she soon turned back to Justin. "So what did you do to amuse yourself while I was working hard in the kitchens?"

He grinned. "What have I done every day? Proved myself to your brothers and your cousins."

She rolled her eyes. "What was it today?"

"Hoop toss. Ever play?"

"No. I've watched it, though. Arrol's usually the best."

Justin nodded. "He was pretty good."

She waited, but finally had to ask. "So? How did you score?"

He grinned. "Better than Arrol."

She looked pleased. "Really? That must have impressed Torrin."

"Oh, I think it did." He glanced away from her to scan the tables. He eventually found Arrol seated deep in the heart of the adjoining room, carrying on what looked like an intense conversation with an older man. "The one who impressed me was Arrol."

Ellynor glanced straight at her cousin as if she had known exactly where he was sitting. In fact, she probably had; she probably could close her eyes right now and recite exactly who had taken what place at every table. She was linked to these family members the way Justin was linked to Senneth and Tayse and his circle of friends. He could almost feel the bonds between them, thick and tangible as woven rope. "He's always been one of my favorites," she said softly. "But he's grown so quiet lately."

Justin tore a fifth piece of bread between his hands. "Why? What happened?"

"Oh, the woman he loved declared herself *bahta-lo* and went to live in Gillengaria. In Ghosenhall, in fact."

Justin shrugged. "He could follow her, maybe. Join the royal army, settle down with her somewhere in the city."

"I don't think so," Ellynor said dryly. "She's married to the king."

Justin almost choked on his bread. He grabbed his glass and gulped down half of his wine. "Arrol is in love with *Queen Valri*? Valri is a *Lirren girl*? Are you sure?"

She looked surprised. "Well, of course I'm sure. Everyone knows it."

"No one *I'm* acquainted with knows it!"

She looked at him helplessly for a moment. "That's right. I keep forgetting. The people of Gillengaria have no understanding of our customs. You probably never even noticed the patterns in her hair—or knew what they meant if you saw them."

He thought rapidly, conjuring up an image of the young, beautiful, and wholly mysterious queen. She had flawless white skin, eerie green eyes, and lustrous—but very short—black hair. "She doesn't have patterns," he said. "Her hair's only down to here." He brushed a finger along Ellynor's jaw.

"She cut her hair off?" Ellynor sounded distressed. "Maybe—I suppose she didn't want anyone to know who she was then. I don't know why."

"Probably because the noble folk of the Twelve Houses would not think so highly of the king marrying a Lirren girl," Justin said. "I'm sure they all think she's from some minor branch of a respectable House."

Ellynor looked affronted. "The Lirrenfolk are respectable!"

He laughed at her. "Perfectly. But the marlords and marladies have strange ideas about class and station." He took another, more meditative sip of his wine. "I wonder if Senneth knows," he said. "About Valri. I don't think she does—she seems as baffled by the queen as everyone else is."

"Then maybe you shouldn't tell her. Or Tayse," Ellynor said. "If Valri doesn't want anyone to know—"

He just looked down at her a moment, trying to decide what to say. "I'm not used to keeping secrets from Tayse," he said at last. "But I'll try."

The woman next to Ellynor tugged on Ellynor's sleeve again, and the man beside Justin began to ask him about travel through Gillengaria, so they lost their opportunity for private conversation. Soon enough, all talk ceased as Ellynor's father stood up and clapped his hands for silence. He was lean and wiry and dark-haired as his daughter. Justin had not spent much time alone with him over these past few days, but he'd judged the man to be an older, somewhat more thoughtful version of Torrin.

"Some of you have traveled far, and all of you have traveled happily to join our family at this time," Wynlo began. "It seems we will be celebrating a wedding! All of you know my daughter, Ellynor, of course, but let me introduce the man she is to marry. Justin, stand up."

He came to his feet, drawing himself up straight and keeping his face entirely solemn. Cammon would call that his intimidating look, but, in truth, he was covering a certain unease. He was never comfortable speaking in front of a crowd. He made a small nod to the assembled group and stood until Wynlo motioned him to resume his seat.

"A man from Gillengaria," Wynlo continued. "But my sons and I have accepted him, and we expect you to do the same."

"What is his station?" someone called out. An older man, maybe one of Wynlo's brothers.

"He is a soldier in service to the king," Wynlo replied. "An honorable position."

"How did he meet Ellynor?" a woman asked.

Wynlo glanced at Ellynor, who answered. "Most of you know my family sent me to the Lumanen Convent to be with my cousin Rosurie." There was a low murmur of anger, outrage, and dismay, heartfelt for all that it was quickly subdued. Everyone here had heard Rosurie's story by now, Justin supposed. Ellynor continued, "I was walking on the streets of Neft, a small town very close to the convent, and a drunken man took me in his arms. Justin came to my rescue."

The crowd's response to that was far more favorable. Wynlo took his seat again. Justin guessed that meant that he and Ellynor would be fielding the rest of the questions.

"Did you think he was handsome?" one of the little girls called, and then dissolved into giggles.

"I did," Ellynor said with a smile. "Don't you think so?"

"How long have you been in service to the king?" a young man asked.

"I have been a King's Rider nearly eight years," Justin replied.

"And it pays well?"

"I am not as rich as the king, but I can support a wife," Justin answered, and that earned a laugh.

"What did you like about Ellynor?" another girl wanted to know.

Justin grinned. "You mean, before she saved my life? Because I liked that a great deal."

That elicited a flurry of questions and exclamations. *She saved your life! What happened? Were you ill? When did this occur?*

"I had gone to visit Ellynor at the convent, but novices were not allowed to meet with men from the outside world," Justin said soberly. He had realized days ago that this story would work in his favor, though he hadn't expected to have such a public chance to recount it. But the Lirren men liked any recitation that had to do with battle and bloodshed. "Some of the convent guards followed me home and attacked me on the road. Ellynor was worried about me, and she came after me, and found me almost dead."

"How many guards?" Predictably, Torrin was the one who wanted to know.

"Five."

There was a moment's silence at that.

"And Ellynor saved you?" her mother asked softly. "For the Great Mother has gifted her with a tremendous healing power."

"She did indeed bring me back from the brink of death." He glanced at Ellynor, who was looking pale. She didn't like to be reminded of his close brush with mortality. "But I had fallen in love with her before that day. For her smile and her kindness and for the way she made me feel." He put a hand to his heart, and there was a sound of sighing approval from the women.

"So you live in Ghosenhall?" someone said.

"Yes."

"Tell us about your family."

This was it. This was the tricky moment; this was the answer that would define him in their eyes. He had considered what to say, but he hadn't rehearsed the words. He spoke slowly, as if remembering it all as he went along.

"I have two families. My mother was a farm girl from the Storian lands, orphaned after some plague. Living with neighbors who didn't care for her much and didn't have much notion of charity. When she was sixteen, she headed to Ghosenhall, thinking she could find work in the royal city. Well, there's not much work suited for a young girl with no skills and no friends. What would you expect? She was pretty enough, and a man offered to pay her to take her to bed. She stayed with him a few months, till he got bored and left, and she found another man. And another."

The silence in the room was absolute. He could not tell if Ellynor's assembled relatives were horrified, repulsed, or saddened. "Eventually she found a house of other women who sold themselves by the day or the hour. A place of filth and stench and rats. She bore four children—a hazard of the job. I was the fourth, and the only boy. My sisters were all gone before they turned fourteen. I haven't seen any of them since. I have no idea if they live and, if they live, what they do. My mother died the year that I was ten."

He thought Ellynor's mother was weeping. Ellynor herself seemed on the verge of tears. She knew the story, but not the details. He was keeping his voice calm because, in reality, he felt no strong emotion, no outrage, no shame, no anger. It had been his life; it had been all he knew. Not until he left it did he find himself marveling that he survived it.

"I left the brothel and lived on the streets," he continued. "Even then I was strong, and I knew how to fight. I made friends, boys just like me, and we patrolled the alleys at night, looking for easy prey. We robbed, we stole, we quarreled. One night I assaulted a rich man and took his wallet and his sword—taught myself how to use it. I'd always been good with a dagger, but I liked the long blade better. There was a crazy old man who lived in the sewers and claimed to have been a fencing master in Arberharst. He gave me lessons that I still remember today.

"I'd been living on the streets three years—a long time for a boy like me to survive—when I picked the wrong man to attack. He was big, but I thought he looked slow, and I didn't see any weapons on him. I tried to rob him, but he pulled a dagger and put up a real fight. He was so good! It wasn't long before I knew he could kill me. And I thought he would. When I slipped and he had me helpless, I waited for his blade to come down. But he sheathed his dagger and pulled me to my feet and told me he wanted to train me for the king's guard."

That caused another murmur in the crowd, this one of interest and approval. Anything to change the bleak tone of the earlier confessions, he thought. He glanced down at Ellynor, who was watching him with a face filled with pain. He smiled. "That was Tayse," he told her, loud enough for everyone else to hear. "He took me back to the palace. He made sure I received the best training available. And when I was good enough, he nominated me to be a King's Rider."

He swept the rest of the tables with a glance. "The King's Riders are the best of the best—the fastest, strongest, and most loyal fighters in the king's army. Baryn chooses each one himself and would trust any one of us with his life. A King's Rider can walk into any room in the palace at any time, night or day, and be admitted into the presence of royalty. If a

Rider makes a statement, the king knows it is true. A Rider has more than skill—he has courage and honor. He would die for his king.

"There are fifty Riders—mostly men, a few women—and they became my second family," Justin went on. "They didn't just teach me more about how to fight. They taught me how to live. They taught me about the sort of strength that does not come from the body. They watched over me, they corrected me when I was wrong, they praised me when I was right, and they made me understand what it meant to belong. I know that, if at any time I were to cry out for help, forty-nine brothers and sisters would come to my aid."

Ellynor had been right, after all, he thought; he knew exactly when he should present his bride gift. He reached into the pocket of his shirt, where he kept Senneth's gold chain, and he pulled it out so that the charm dangled loose for everyone to see. "Two weeks ago, Tayse married a woman named Senneth, who is kin with the Persal family," he said. "In some way I cannot explain, she is also kin to me, though we are not related by blood and we have not formally adopted each other. But she is as close to me as family. Her own tale is as strange as mine, for she left home when she was very young. Her grandmother handed her this pendant as Senneth was walking out the door, a reminder that love still existed, even in a harsh and careless world. Senneth gave the necklace to me, and I give it to Ellynor as my bride gift."

He took Ellynor's hand and folded it over the loops of gold, then lifted her hand and pressed her knuckles to his lips. "My family welcomes you, Ellynor," he whispered. "And they love you as well as I do. I hope that you will very soon be my bride."

IT was a couple of hours before the commotion died down. Justin gauged how well his presentation had gone by the number of women at the tables who were sobbing. Wouldn't Kirra laugh to think any speech of Justin's could reduce young women to tears! As for himself, he felt a little more raw than he had expected to, but he certainly wasn't on the verge of crying. Merely, he was not used to talking so long about such intensely personal feelings. He didn't think he'd want to be returning to the Lirrens all that often if emotions were always going to run so high.

But the speech had signaled the end of dinner and the beginning of a dizzying round of congratulations. Ellynor's relatives—every last one of them, or so it seemed—came pressing up to Justin to take his hand and wish him well. Ellynor had been enveloped in her own crowd of well-wishers, mostly girls, but he watched her dark head as it bobbed in the sea of sisters and cousins and aunts. Several times she turned around to glance at him and always smiled to find half his attention given over to her. Once she laughed and blew him a kiss. He thought the aftermath of the evening would never come to an end.

But slowly the visitors dispersed and sifted out. Hoping that Ellynor was watching him, Justin slipped out the side door and stood in the garden, which was stripped and bare in the dead of winter but still decorated with a few wispy stalks. The moon was a full and perfect circle, though small and high; must be close to midnight. The still, frigid air was a welcome contrast to the heat and chatter inside the house.

In less than a minute, Ellynor found him, coming up from behind and putting her arms around his waist. He turned to take her in a more proper embrace, shielding her from the night air, curious eyes, and any other hazard, small or calamitous, that might trip along to offer her menace.

"That seemed to go well," he said cautiously, in case he'd misread these Lirrenfolk, and it hadn't.

"So *very* well," she murmured into his chest. "And all this time I've been planning how to comfort you when you stumbled through your presentation or didn't manage to find the right words."

He laughed. "Never was much of one for making speeches."

"Well, that's the last one you'll have to make for me."

He kissed her. "So what next? When do we get to marry? When do I get to leave Torrin's room and come to yours?"

She giggled, but even by moonlight, he could tell her face heated up. "Tomorrow, of course. The wedding breakfast is always the day after the groom presents the bride gift."

"Why didn't you tell me that before?" he exclaimed. "I'd have flung the necklace over your head as we were riding up to your parents' house."

"Because this was perfect," she whispered, lifting her mouth once again to be kissed. "And tomorrow we will be married in the morning."

A voice called to her from the kitchen—this was a family that knew better than to give courting couples too much time alone—and Ellynor sighed, kissed him again, and hurried back inside. Justin was too restless to reenter the big house, climb the stairs to the room he shared with Torrin, and lie awake on his mattress, counting the hours till the morrow.

His wedding day.

He strolled out of the garden, through the central open area, and around the barn where the cows were gathered. He felt remarkably good, alive with sensation, excitement buzzing through his veins like the first taste of excellent wine. If there had been another Rider nearby, Justin would have offered him a challenge, a little swordplay by moonlight. As it was, he considered taking off up the road at a run, just to release some of his coiled energy.

A footfall behind him—surely deliberate, because these Lirren men could move without making a sound—and suddenly Torrin was beside him.

"I met this Tayse and this Senneth you spoke of," Torrin said.

Justin nodded. "That's right. In Coravann. Senneth told me."

"She is kin. If he is married to her, that makes him kin as well. They are excellent fighters. They will bring honor to the Lirrenfolk."

Justin had to grin at that, but he answered solemnly. "I think you can be proud to call them family."

"She mentioned that war could be coming to Gillengaria."

Justin nodded. "Some of the noble Houses see an old king on the throne and think they could rule better than his daughter when he dies. We think there are armies being raised in secret and rebels making alliances against the crown."

"The men of the Lirrens have no argument with any of your Houses," Torrin said. "Heffel of Coravann says he will stay neutral if the rest of you fall into a war."

"I wish him luck in that," Justin said a little bitterly. "Sometimes it is harder to stay out of an argument than a man might think."

"Will you be fighting?"

Justin nodded again. "All the Riders will take the king's side. Or his daughter's side, if war only comes once her father is dead."

"When you marry my sister, you will be kin. You will have the right to call on your brothers and cousins to join you in combat. Tayse, too. You could both call on the *sebahta-ris*."

Justin caught his breath. Senneth had not seemed to think it would be so easy. Senneth had also seemed to have grave reservations about embroiling the young men of the Lirrens in a war that could prove desperately bloody. "The King's Riders would be grateful to have their Lirren brothers fighting beside them," he said carefully. "But this isn't your war, and I don't want to be the one to ride back across the mountains to tell your women that you're dead. Anyone who freely chose to fight would be welcome. But I don't want to invoke the bonds of family. Not when so much family could be lost."

"Speaking for myself, I like to fight," Torrin said, and grinned.

Justin laughed silently. "Somehow, I had guessed that."

Torrin's eyes were gleaming with mischief, even by moonlight. "Senneth told me I would not be able to defeat you, if I decided to duel you for my sister's honor."

"Well, *she's* never defeated me," Justin said, drawling the words. "You might have better luck."

"Of course, you were recently injured," Torrin said, as if offering an excuse. "You wouldn't want to duel so soon. Tonight, for instance. If you lost, you might say your wounds made you drop the sword, or wield it in a clumsy manner."

Now Justin had to laugh outright. "I think I'm recovered enough to make a pretty good showing. Who do you think might want to challenge me?"

"Well," Torrin said, grinning broadly, "I would."

"Tell me where my weapon is," Justin said, "and I'll be happy to match swords with you."

Torrin dropped his hands to his waist and began undoing his buckle. Justin realized that he was wearing two belts, two scabbards, two swords. "I brought it with me," Torrin said. "In case you were interested in a duel."

Wordlessly, Justin accepted his belt from Torrin's hands and fastened it around his body, happy to feel the familiar weight at his hips, against his thigh. He drew the blade and held it up for an examination by the watery light of the moon. It didn't seem to have sustained any damage while under Torrin's care.

"Just so I'm clear," Justin said, "this is a friendly fight? No one dies?"

Torrin laughed. He seemed bright with excitement, pleased at the notion of a quick clash by starlight, of measuring himself against someone he was unlikely to defeat. Justin was pretty sure he was better than the Lirren man, but he wasn't going to be stupid; for so many reasons, it was important to win this particular battle. Still, he liked this young man—liked his eagerness and his arrogance and stubbornness. *What a Rider he'd make*, he thought. *We'll have to bring him to Ghosenhall.*

"No one dies," Torrin confirmed. "No one is wounded, either, except maybe for a scratch or two. Insignificant."

Justin nodded. "Then you're on. Raise your weapon."

They swept their hands up at precisely the same moment, and then paused with their swords upright, eying each other past the slim, glittering blades. Justin took a deep breath of the cold air and calmed his mind, steadied his nerves. They were alone out here between the barns and the storage buildings, and yet he could not shake the thought that they had acquired an audience. The night pressed against his back as if someone had laid a cool hand upon his shoulder. The moon peered down through her single round eye. At least two of the goddesses were watching, curious to see how this contest turned out, pleased rather than not to find Lirrenfolk making alliances with Gillengaria men. At least two of the goddesses had tracked Justin farther than he had ever roamed, despite the fact that he had never given any of them a moment's thought, the slightest pledge of honor. One had betrayed him and one had succored him and both of them were jealous for the attention of the women he loved, and so he would have to learn to understand them, to fit them somewhere within the contours of his life.

Where is the god of war? he wondered. *Shouldn't he be here, too, taking an interest in me? Or is he already watching—has he been watching my whole life, caring for me when I did not even realize he was nearby? Maybe all my luck was really some god's intervention. Maybe, like the mystics, I have always drawn my strength from some invisible source.*

"Are you ready?" Torrin asked.

"I'm ready," Justin said. He tightened his hand on his hilt, and he waited.